THE FALL OF THE HOUSE

BOOK 3 OF THE RED ROOM SERIES

BY C. T. PHIPPS & MICHAEL SUTKUSS

It had been one of the first missions I had with Special Agent Ashley Anne Morgan. She was my first partner and one of the strongest psychics the Red Room had ever recruited. Her mother had been one of the finest agents we'd had during WW2 and was now on the Committee.

I knew her nieces and nephew: Anna, Ashley (named for her), and Arthur and sponsored them to the Solomon Academy for future agents. For the elder Ashley, the House was nothing but a prison. Ashley was a short, curvaceous woman with shoulder-length brown hair. She wasn't traditionally beautiful, her gray eyes too large and her frame more muscular than Hollywood said her frame allowed.

In my mind, she was wearing a blue vest, gray overcoat, and white shirt with a knee-length blue dress. I recalled the two of us running down the halls of a two-story Texas mall during one of the biggest supernatural events in the past fifty years.

It was a relatively benign one, all things considered, with the dead in Provost, TX crawling out of their graves to wander to the nearest shopping center. They were, presently, shambling about the place in a mindless state without harming anyone.

The Red Room had cordoned off the building and was using the entirety of its resources to contain the event. Mind-altering charms were being deployed along with cash, intimidation, and agents in the media. It helped, so far, the undead weren't violent. The spirits inhabiting the hundreds of shambling corpses spread throughout the building were revenants, semisentient undead who just wanted to go through the motions of their past lives.

"God, the stench of this place," Ashley muttered, her Southern accent noticeable even in Texas.

PROLOGUE

There are two worlds. The first world is the one you know. It's a place filled with men, women, plants, and animals. It's both exciting and dangerous but most people go out of their way to avoid these two qualities. People like their lives safe, sane, and predictable. They don't want to think about monsters living amongst them. They prefer to turn their back on reality and assume everything is going to be fine.

The House helped make that possible. It's the organization that hides the Truth from humanity. The Truth being that we're not alone on this world and, in fact, at the bottom of the food chain. That it's not just vampires, werewolves, wizards, and demons out there but every conceivable sort of supernatural predator imaginable.

For the longest time, I believed the House was a necessary evil. I thought its lies, manipulations, and murders were justified in the name of the greater good. Specifically, the greater good that regular humans could enjoy carefree lives without having to worry that their loved ones were going to eat them. I've killed hundreds of humans, monsters, and otherwise believing this. Recently, I stopped believing that argument. I saw the House was more interested in maintaining its control over humanity than in protecting it. I was forced to do something unspeakable and it cost me what lingering respect I had for my organization.

I killed my sister.

Rebecca.

Rebecca had perfected a process that never should have been conceived, one which would allow anyone supernatural or human to be mesmerized into following the House's orders.

It was a terrifying technique that would have resulted in the end of free-will as we knew it. The House doesn't know I killed her but the very fact they had her working on it meant they intended to use it.

I can't stop working for the House, though, no matter how much I want to. There is a second world, you see: the Spirit World. Existing on the borderlands between this and the astral plane where thought becomes reality, the Spirit World is a parallel dimension to our own. It is where physics becomes more like suggestions, impossible technology exists, and monsters outnumber humans.

For decades, the Spirit World has remained passive with only an occasional horror and wonder spilling through. A million amazing and terrible things that were kept away from the rest of humanity by virtue of a paper wall we erected to prevent people from seeing them.

There will come a time, though, that the barriers between it and this world will fall. The Truth will come out. Every secret the House has struggled to keep repressed, from the existence of other worlds to the fact they know how to make a car that runs on water, will be exposed.

The world will burn.

I, Derek Hawthorne, former Senior Agent of the Red Room and Committee member of the House am committed to making sure that doesn't happen. Even if it means allying with the kind of people I've spent my life opposing. Too bad I failed. This is how the House collapsed and the supernatural became known to the world.

CHAPTER ONE

It had been one of the first missions I had with Special Agent Ashley Anne Morgan. She was my first partner and one of the strongest psychics the Red Room had ever recruited. Her mother had been one of the finest agents we'd had during WW2 and was now on the Committee. I knew her nieces and nephew: Anna, Ashley (named for her), and Arthur and sponsored them to the Solomon Academy for future agents. For the elder Ashley, the House was nothing but a prison.

Ashley was a short, curvaceous woman with shoulder-length brown hair. She wasn't traditionally beautiful, her gray eyes too large and her frame more muscular than Hollywood said her frame allowed. In my mind, she was wearing a blue vest, gray overcoat, and white shirt with a knee-length blue dress.

I recalled the two of us running down the halls of a two-story Texas mall during one of the biggest supernatural events in the past fifty years. It was a relatively benign one, all things considered, with the dead in Provost, TX crawling out of their graves in order to wander to the nearest shopping center. They were, presently, shambling about the place in a mindless state without harming anyone.

The Red Room had cordoned off the building and was using the entirety of its resources to contain the event. Mind-altering charms were being deployed along with cash, intimidation, and agents in the media. It helped, so far, the undead weren't violent. The spirits inhabiting the hundreds of shambling corpses spread throughout the building were revenants, semi-sentient undead who just wanted to go through the motions of their past lives.

"God, the stench of this place," Ashley muttered, her Southern accent noticeable even in Texas.

I was following behind her, wearing a brown trench coat over a white shirt and gray pants. "That's the embalming fluid. Mixed with years in a box."

The smell, indeed, was overpowering but the whole thing looked rather surreal as the revenants were decayed to the point of looking mummified yet appeared as if they were attending a wedding (or, if you like, a funeral). The mall was empty, thank God, with no stragglers having been found. It was just hundreds of shambling corpses living out their own version of *Dawn of the Dead*.

The zombies, an overarching slang term for mindless undead among House agents, had all crawled out of the surrounding eight cemeteries and shambled their way here. They were unintelligent, at least as far as I could tell, and were mindlessly going through activities from their former life. The mall staff had, thankfully, not yet opened shop except for a few overeager employees and the police had captured most of those. It was a surreal sight but lacking the kind of gore-soaked horror that I'd seen a few times when dealing with draugr (the flesh-eating kind of zombie).

"Well I don't like it," Ashley said, kicking over one of the zombies that moved as if to hug her. "Are you *sure* these things aren't dangerous?"

"They should be fine if you don't antagonize them," I said, watching the other zombie leap at Ashley only to get a bullet in the brain. None of the other revenants reacted and she shot off a few more rounds to take some more down. Apparently, just for stress relief. I turned to her. "Don't waste ammo."

"I'm usually the first person to think monsters are people too but I don't like these things," Ashley said, wrinkling her nose in disgust. "They don't have... souls. Just the echo of them."

"They very much have souls," I said, amused at terminology. "That's what's empowering them."

"You know what I mean," Ashley said. "They lack the quality of people being people. Don't tell me you think these things aren't *wrong*."

I watched an ancient corpse swaying to the bland inoffensive pop music playing over the mall's speakers. The other revenants wandered through the store looking at things as if shopping, living out a parody of their former existence. I even saw a couple of undead teenagers swaying to the generic pop music playing above their heads. Honestly, I thought it was kind of cute. Another sign I'd become a psychopath after years of working for the Red Room.

"Everyone wants a second chance," I said, shaking my head. "I think it's sad more than anything."

"Yeah, well, it's going to get a lot sadder," I muttered, looking for any sign of witchcraft. I meant, you know, aside from the endless hordes of undead wandering around. "Provost is going to wonder who unearthed all their loved ones and spread their corpses around the mall once we kill the necromancers responsible."

"Can you kill them? They might be kids," Ashley pointed out. "A couple of dumb teenagers rather than an insane old witch."

Ashley still hadn't 'blooded' herself in the line of duty. It was unusual since the trainers usually insisted you take a life before they let you out into the field. It was called "The Passage."

I stopped cold. "I hadn't thought of that."

I'd killed a lot of people over the years but had, mostly, managed to avoid doing in any children. I mean, I'd shot some zombie children (the trick was to aim low) and things animated by demons but nothing that was under the age of eighteen and still human. Call me crazy but that meant something versus all the other hundred or so people I'd killed over the years trying to keep the supernatural under wraps.

"I have. I think about that every day," Ashley said, looking at a zombie mime some asshole had buried in his makeup. He was trying to climb an invisible rope. I almost shot that one just for existing.

The information had been sparse but the most likely suspect responsible was either a retired Red Room witch named Melanie Spencer or her grandchildren. Thomas and Steve were a pair of Goths with marginal necromantic skills. People so pathetic the

House had passed them over for recruitment. Together, the two *might* have been able to do this but their reasoning escaped me. About the only detail that stood out from their biography was they'd been seeing the same girl, Sonja Perrin, and she'd been killed in a car accident a few days ago. People did stupid things for love.

"I'm still hoping this is the Network," Ashley muttered. "They're prone to doing stupid shit like this in order to expose the Truth."

The Network was an organization of supernaturals that attempted to resist the major powers of the world. They weren't as extreme as the now-destroyed Emerald Eye but smuggled out mages from the control of the House, helped younger vampires against the Vampire Nation's Council of Ancients, and generally were a pain in the ass. They were our version of Occupy Wallstreet except with more Molotov cocktails—I wasn't a fan.

"Not stupid if it works," I said, avoiding a staggering old lady revenant swinging her purse at me. I causally tripped then stepped over her. "This could result in the collapse of the Great Lie."

"Do you ever wonder what would happen if it all came out?" Ashley asked, checking a shop on the right as I checked one on the left. The source of the outbreak had to be here somewhere.

"The Truth you mean?" I asked, surveying this nightmare and wondering how many people would try it in hopes of seeing some semblance of their loved ones in the dead. Probably millions.

"Yeah," Ashley said.

"The end of the world," I said.

"You don't think humanity could pull through?" Ashley asked, stepping around a twelve-year-old corpse.

"No. I don't think humanity would survive the revelation vampires were real without everyone wanting to become one or locking up their neighbors. I can't imagine what they'd do if they found out all things spooky wer real." The idea of the supernatural out in the public was inconceivable to me. The fact groups like the Vampire Nation were preparing for the eventual revelation of the supernatural disgusted me. Now, if I was a bunch of necromancers performing an evil spell, where would I be in the mall? Upstairs.

"More an X-men than Avengers fan, huh?" Ashley asked. "You don't think the public would embrace the supernatural."

"I love Harry Potter as much as the next man, but the government would nuke Hogwarts the moment they found out about it. Which is why we exist," I said.

"To keep people from knowing the supernatural exists and to shoot monsters who step out of line," Ashley said, with more than a little hint of disgust.

"Yes," I said.

"Even though with modern forensics technology, it's inevitable people will discover the supernatural is real." Ashley rolled her eyes. "It's 2008. You can't keep it secret in a world of cellphone cameras, social media, and a 24-hour news cycle."

"Yes," I said, trying not to be distracted from the walking dead. There were a couple of revenants having a wedding party but none of them seem ready to eat people's brains, specifically ours, and that was a relief. The big danger was the public demanding answers for why their loved ones were out of their graves.

"And we're, essentially, without a plan for when this happens," Ashley muttered.

"Absolutely," I said, finding zilch in a fast clothing shop. Well, there was a catatonic salesgirl hiding behind the counter but that was what memory charms were for. Still no sign of the necromancers responsible for this disaster.

"Our side sucks," Ashley said, knocking down a geriatric looking revenant in a Sunday dress who tried to hit her with a purse.

I agreed with her but didn't answer. Instead, I finished gestured with my head to a set of nearby escalators leading to the second floor. "We need to check the upstairs. Things will get messy if we don't find anything before our backup finishes."

Burn the place to the ground messy. We'd have to wipe the minds of everyone here, including the police helping keep the place cordoned off. Then we'd have to sanitize the area and leave nothing behind. That was assuming there wasn't a permanent rift between this world and the next. The Department of Energy had declared one nuclear plant to be permanently uninhabitable in Washington D.C. because it was a literal portal to hell.

"Gotcha." Ashley found a spot away from the shuffling horrors to close her eyes and concentrate.

I knocked away a couple of revenants that tried to come at her. "Anything?"

"I'm picking up something. Very faint," Ashley said, holding the side of her head. She was clearly sensing something.

"What are my lucky numbers? Will I ever find true love?" I asked.

Ashley stuck out her tongue, my humor distracting us from the horrors around us. Thanks to all the positive reinforcement I'd gotten from her, I'd become a regular jokester.

"Upstairs to the left," Ashley pointed. "I don't think we have much time."

"What do you mean?" I asked.

"I don't know," Ashley muttered.

That wasn't a good sign. Running up the escalator steps, we knocked several corpses out of the way, deftly dodging at least one who lunged at us only to end up falling on his fellows. "Do you think we could get these guys to do the Thriller dance?"

"They're not harmless," Ashley said. "Some of these creatures are angry."

"Oh come on, we've faced much worse," I said, cheerfully. "They're only dangerous if their masters send them after us."

"Great, now you've jinxed it," Ashley said.

"Probably," I said.

As if mocking my claim of harmlessness, a group of six revenants ran at us. They screamed as they moved, making a horrific shriek, and had their arms stretched out as if to strangle us. These revenants were different from the rest of their kind, bleeding from every orifice and looking decidedly 'fresh.' Each was dressed as a mall customer and I guessed them to be individuals killed recently, which meant we weren't just dealing with harmless walking corpses anymore.

"Ghasts!" I shouted, aiming my gun and firing into the closest one's head. I then promptly shot another in the skull, not because headshots were any more effective against revenants but because the recoil knocked them over. If my orichalcum bullets weren't going to destroy them outright, I wanted them knocked back.

Ashley fired as well, using telekinesis to send one that got close to her flying backward into his fellows. The gunplay lasted for less than a minute, involving a lot of missed shots but the orichalcum bullets seemed to do the trick and three rounds into each was enough.

"What the hell are ghasts?" Ashley asked. "I mean, aside from a D&D monster."

"They're like revenants in that they're possessed corpses. It's just whatever's possessing them *really* wants to kill humans," I said, firing an extra round into one that was still twitching.

"So more than ghosts are starting to come through the rift now," Ashley said. "*Demons* are."

"Yeah," I said. "Another reason why people can't know the Truth. If they knew hell was real, you'd have Satan apologists the moment he started buying souls for cash."

"Great," Ashley muttered. "Did I ever tell you how much I love working for the Red Room?"

"Every single day," I said, wondering if we needed backup. Demons were the one thing that scared me. That and ex-girlfriends.

Ashley rolled her eyes. "When we find this rift, how are we supposed to close it? Neither of us is a mage."

That would change in the future for me but, back then, was still true. "Find the anchor and destroy it. Or kill the casters. Either works."

"Assuming it can be closed," Ashley said.

"Yep," I said.

The two of us then saw a large group of revenants congregating outside a specific store. It was a comic book shop with lots of posters in the windows. We didn't have time to do this the safe way. Checking my ammunition, I made sure I had an extra clip then opened fire while Ashley did the same.

The revenants, previously peaceful, turned upon us and moved as one. As a horde, the necromantic energy around them made them faster and stronger. I managed to destroy a half-dozen as they charged but the remaining forty or so were going to be a serious pain in the ass. Ashley put aside her gun, took a deep breath, and then *screamed* at them. A telekinetic wave sent a dozen of them flying.

"Sometimes I forget just how powerful you really are."

Ashley was already moving, running to the comic book store's entrance as I hurried to follow up. The revenants she'd knocked down were already getting up and would tear us a new one if we didn't dispose of the rift soon.

The metal gate was down in front of the shop, blocking the horde from getting in but Ashley causally tore it away, displaying power I envied. She was an M11 on the psychic scale and there were some that believed she might be an M15 who hid her true potential from the rest of the Red Room. Which was scary since the previous record for a human being had been an M12. Really, it was a waste she was working for me.

"Never." Ashley went into the shop.

I followed.

The interior of the comic book shop was a decorated in a Goth style with fake spider webs, posters of Carrie and Jason, plus a lot of other Halloween bric-a-brac. Lacuna Coil played in the background, coming from a private stereo system. In the center of the room was a literal crack, radiating a white-gray flickering light.

In front of the crack was a trio of people in the center of a crudely drawn magical circle, several flaws apparent to even my untrained eyes. Two of them were twenty-something adult men, dead and not rising from the grave, bottles of pills at their sides. Thomas and Steve, I presumed. Sonja standing over them. She was wearing ripped jeans and very much alive. Of a sort. She was a lovely girl, Asiatic in appearance short peek-a-boo bangs and a mesh shirt over a shirt bearing Sister Grimm from *The Runaways*.

"Resurrection spell," I muttered, shaking my head. "Why do people keep trying those?"

"To raise people from the dead?" Ashley said.

I glared at her.

"It didn't work," Sonja said, looking down. "So, they added their own lives. They wanted us all to be together."

I nodded. She was the basis of the anchor. "Yeah."

"Sorry." I lifted my gun to the girl's head.

"I know," Sonja said.

Ashley looked away.

Sonja rejoined her boyfriends.

It was a bad memory.

CHAPTER TWO

It was years later, sometimes it felt like decades, and I was now in a hospital bathroom. Ashley had left the House, smuggled out by my now-vampirized other living(ish) ex-partner Christopher Hang. I'd done my best to keep the fight up and keep the Truth buried. All it had gotten me was a lost hand (replaced by a supernatural prosthetic (and the status of a kinslayer. I'd killed my own sister, Rebecca, because she'd crossed too many lines in the service of the House. The organization I'd devoted myself to had become evil and despite the fact I was part of its ruling Committee—I knew it couldn't be reformed. It was only a matter of time before they had me assassinated and replaced with someone more in tune with their overtly racist anti-supernatural agenda.

I ran the hot water and splashed my face before looking into the mirror. I looked like complete shit and still felt pain in my new artificial hand. It looked identical to my old one since it was covered in a glamour, but I could feel its fakeness. I'd been in a coma since killing Dracula a week ago, yes, that Dracula and only ki manipulation was allowing me to move around after the beating he'd given me.

Shannon, my uncle Talbot, and Christopher were waiting for me to get dressed outside. They'd told me that Ashley was in trouble and that I needed to help her again. I was surprisingly game: it wasn't like I wanted to get back to my wait for the next assassination attempt that was likely to happen. The only reason I'd survived my coma was because my father, Nathan, had watched over me during it. I hated owing that scheming old archwizard.

Getting dressed in a pair of brown pants and a white-button shirt, I opened the bathroom door and stepped out into an all-white private hospital room. My associates were still there. They were an eclectic group of supernaturals, which I wasn't one to talk about, given my parentage included a dragon. Talbot stood well over six feet in height with broad shoulders and over three hundred pounds of muscle. His face was riddled with scars and I knew the rest of his body was just as bad. Talbot was the real-life inspiration for Mary Shelley's *Frankenstein*. He was wearing a large Hawaiian shirt and a pair of baggy beige cargo shorts with flip-flops. A pair of mirror sunglasses rested on his nose. It looked ridiculous but somehow suited him.

Shannon was a woman with shoulder-length straight red hair and blue eyes. I thought her to be one of the most beautiful women in the world, but Shannon didn't exploit her powers to appear supernaturally lovely—despite being able to. She was a Lilin, what laymen called a succubus, and possessed the natural ability to make both men and women want her. Shannon was wearing a plain brown and white suit of the kind House agents were assigned as part of their official wardrobe.

Her aura made her attire look like something off a runway, though she was suppressing it now. My partner and girlfriend's expression was concerned, though I couldn't tell if it was because an old flame of mine was imperiled or it was because the House's security could come in any second to gun down all the supernaturals in my room.

Christopher didn't look a day older than thirty, appearing much as he did when he was dragged off during our battle with the Vampire Nation in New York. He had long shining black hair that trailed down to his shoulders and model good looks. Christopher was dressed smartly, having traded his cheap agent's business suit for a custom-tailored European set of threads one that cost more than my car. It was ballsy for him to come here, to a House hospital, especially since we were currently at war with the Vampire Nation.

"Sorry I took so long," I said, surveying the trio.

"It's okay, Derek." Shannon stood up. "I'm surprised you're able to walk."

"Magic is a hell of a drug." I shook my head. Every second counted. "Christopher, why don't you start from the beginning. We can skip over the part where you explain why you're coming on behalf of my ex-fiancé."

I'd proposed to Ashley despite the enormous warning signs that we weren't going to work out. In the end, my father had told me to put two bullets in the back of her head for her attempts to clue the public into the existence of the House. I hadn't done it, obviously, but he'd been willing to leave it alone. It had destroyed whatever lingering affection I'd still had for the old man, though.

"Ashley is my friend too," Christopher said, his voice low. "Though, if you're suspicious about our relationship being closer than that, you're right."

I wondered when, exactly, he'd had time to hook up with a woman I'd been in love with from the time he'd helped her escape the House and become enslaved to Dracula. I wanted to punch him in the gut, but I didn't have any right to condemn him for it either. Besides, I'd just break my hand and I didn't know how good my prosthetic was.

"Can we talk freely?" Shannon asked, looking at Talbot and Christopher. "I don't know how you guys slipped past, but I don't want to take any chances with Derek."

"I disabled the listening devices while you visited Derek," Talbot said, smiling. "They're hearing a conversation I recorded during the last time you were in the hospital. It's amazing they still haven't gotten the wiring fixed here."

"Still, keep it down," Shannon said. "If we're going to commit treason by helping your ex, I'd like to do it without being tripped up by stupidity."

"Are we committing treason?" I asked, wanting to clarify just what Christopher expected of me here.

"Is there any other way to help Ashley?" Christopher asked. "She is an enemy of the House now after all."

"Point taken," I admitted. "Besides, the House is my enemy now. Fuck those guys."

"Aren't you part of the Committee?" Talbot asked.

I stared at him.

"Right," Talbot said. "That's how you know."

"So repeat the situation," I said. "Please."

"Ashley is missing," Christopher said.

"How long has Ashley been missing?" I asked. "Time is critical in these sorts of things."

"Including time-dilation between dimensions?" Christopher asked. "What happens over the course of a day in the Spirit World can be centuries on Earth and vice versa."

"This isn't my first rodeo, Christopher. Is the Spirit World where you stashed Ashley?"

Christopher nodded. "In a pocket-dimension inhabited by other refugees from the House called New London. The time-dilation isn't bad, about one-and-a-half-years for every year on Earth but it's still noteworthy."

That meant it had been almost a decade since Ashley and I had last seen one another. She might have forgotten me by now. "How long?"

Christopher took a deep breath. "It's been three weeks."

My guts twisted into knots. "Life is pretty unlikely after that absence. Most kidnappers don't bother holding a person for more than a month."

"She's alive," Christopher said. "I know it."

"I'll take your word for it," I said, knowing I'd never stop looking until I had confirmation that she was alive or dead.

Christopher took a cosmetic breath before rubbing the sides of his temples, a human gesture very different from the almost alien movements he'd possessed a few weeks ago while still under Dracula's control. "After we killed Dracula, I was a persona non-grata among the undead to say the least. The fact the Red Room's agents were storming every vampire safe house, nightclub, and blood farm they could made me eager to find some place to hide out. New London was as good a place as any and I wanted to check with the Network."

"The Network?" Talbot asked. "You're associated with them."

"Associate not full-fledged member," Christopher said, flashing some fang. "They don't trust me anymore. Can't imagine why."

"Not their kind of vamp, huh," Shannon said.

Christopher shrugged. "They might take me back in since I killed Dracula."

"*I* killed Dracula," I said.

Christopher smirked.

"No one can figure out who their leader is," Shannon said, "or where they're based."

Christopher grimaced. "Well, I'm about to betray them as the answer is New London and Ashley."

I blinked. "Ashley is the head of the Network?"

Christopher nodded. "The House took everything from her, not the least of which was you."

Shannon looked unhappy with that and why wouldn't she? "What did you find there?"

"I spent a week with Ashley, catching up," Christopher said. "The others distrusted me but many vampires are eager to escape the Vampire Nation and House's purges now. So, the Network and I planned to start smuggling them away too. That was when the stormtroopers attacked."

I paused. "Stormtroopers?"

The Red Room had its own Special Forces Unit, mostly taken from retired members of major world governments, but that didn't sound like them. If they did their job well, you never saw them coming.

"The only way I can describe them," Christopher said, shrugging. "Full suits of plastisteel body armor, laser-based magitech weapons, and Special Forces training. Unlike the ones in the movies, though, they're lethal and cut through the Network's people like wheat. They only took a handful of prisoners, Ashley included."

"What were you doing during this?" I asked, my voice full of accusation. "Since you were apparently there."

"Derek—" Shannon started to say.

"Leave it," Talbot said, warning her.

"I killed six," Christopher said, sighing. "I had to flee in the form of mist, though, after taking too many blasts to the chest. Hurt like hell even though I don't use my organs anymore. When I came back, Ashley was gone, and they'd stripped the bodies of their dead but left their corpses behind."

That said quite a bit by itself. "Any distinguishing features of the dead?"

"Yes," Christopher said. "They were elves."

I blinked. "Excuse me?"

"*Elves* took Ashley," I said, not able to keep the skepticism from my voice.

I'd seen a lot of strange stuff over the years but elves were not on my list of things encountered.

"Elves *with guns*," Shannon said, smirking. "Father Christmas' helpers have gotten hardcore."

"Elves are no laughing matter," Talbot said, somehow not sounding ridiculous. "They're soulless things with human faces."

"You're being a bit harsh, aren't you?" Shannon asked, looking over at Talbot. "They can't have been that bad."

"The High Lord of House Bres once invited me to a feast," Talbot said, a foul look on his face. "The entertainment was mind-controlling a group of children to kill their parents. Then the elves feasted on their remains, sharing them with the kids."

That was horrifying even by supernatural standards. "Uh-huh."

Talbot's expression was like granite. "They thought it was *funny.*"

"Elves are also extinct," I said to Talbot. "You know that better than anyone."

The elves, or sidhe as they liked to call themselves, had decided to side with Hitler during World War 2. The House had taken that personally and exterminated all their remaining members on Earth with the only survivors fleeing to the Astral Plane's depths.

"It's hard to kill an entire race, Derek," Talbot said, looking disgusted with himself. "Children were let go as were those who claimed to be refugees. I couldn't put the trigger on a few of those myself."

I wasn't the kind of guy who blamed the children of Nazis for their parents' actions, so I understood Talbot but I also knew there was a fundamental difference between supernaturals and humans. Vampires drank blood and viewed humans as food. Werewolves were both humans as well as pack animal predators. Those were also races that were still, on some level, human. Many supernaturals had mindsets wholly alien to mankind. That didn't mean they were evil but it also meant they weren't people you could negotiate with either. I didn't know where real elves stood on the Tolkien to Pratchett scale of "pointy eared bastardry."

"Don't feel bad for showing compassion," I walked over and put my hand on his shoulder. "It's better to let a few monsters go than kill innocents on the oft-chance they might be one."

"No race is completely evil and all that rot," Shannon said, looking away. "Not even mine."

"You're a succubus, Shannon," Talbot said, smiling. "Your race is pretty much pure evil."

Shannon smirked, not taking it personally. "Yeah, it kind of is."

"Well, *these* elves took Ashley," Christopher said. "They were also all identical."

"*Cloned* elves?" I asked, staring at him. "Now that's just silly."

"Homunculi, grown from an elvish blood sample," Christopher said. "Though I've never seen someone grow troops en masse, though."

"*Attack of the Elves* by George Lucas!" Talbot said. "Too bad there's never going to be another *Star Wars* trilogy."

I ignored Talbot's barb. "What you're describing is someone with some serious resources. A group that has access to magic, technology, and lots of cash." That narrowed it down to a lot of groups but, ironically, eliminated the House. The House hated fairies and would never create more of them, especially as shock troops.

"I spent days trying to track down leads," Christopher said, sighing. "I learned the people who'd attacked the Network's headquarters were travelers from Earth. Where they moved her was impossible to track but their expensive equipment and cloned nature provided some clues. So, I took an Astral Path here and decided to go to the one person I knew who would help me."

"Talbot?" I asked, wondering why he'd gone to my uncle first.

"I felt getting to one of the Committee without an escort would be difficult," Christopher joked. "Besides, finding Talbot was easier than you."

"I stand out in a crowd," Talbot said, shrugging. "I admit, I almost blew off your vampire friend's head when I first saw him."

I looked between them all. "Well, I'm glad you did. Thank you for bringing me in on all this. By the way, Christopher, how again are you not dead? This is a House hospital. Its security has a shoot vampires on sight policy."

"Magic," Christopher said.

I stared at him then shrugged. "Ask a stupid question, get a stupid answer I guess. So, you all want to help me get Ashley back?"

"Yes," Talbot said.

"I'm the one who brought it to your attention," Christopher said.

"I don't know Ashley but I know how much she means to you," Shannon said, her voice soft. "You love her."

"Loved," I corrected. "I haven't seen her in years."

From the looks on everyone's face, I could tell they weren't buying it. Neither was I. I wondered briefly how she would react to me before I realized it wouldn't be well. I'd been a believer in the House before: now I was a kinslayer. I could still see Rebecca's face, fresh and beautiful, become nothing more than red smear from where I'd struck her down. She'd needed killing, there was no doubt about that, but my sister had never seen it coming. I would never forgive myself for what I'd done, and I deserved to die for it. In my desire to reform the House, I'd become every bit as bad as the rest of it.

"There's more," Christopher added.

I pulled out of my fugue state and shook my head. "There always is."

"Someone followed me from New London," Christopher said. "The group that took Ashley, no doubt. They've tried to make a play for me. To keep me from contacting you, I think."

Talbot gave a short nod. "Someone tried to ambush us. I didn't get a good look at them, but they burned down my house."

"And you didn't think to bring this up until now?"

"People trying to kill me isn't unusual." Talbot shrugged. "I don't know how they're tracking your vampire buddy, but they're determined. I managed to lose the last batch of them in Los Angeles, but it wasn't easy. Lots of bodies were left in the process. They weren't shy about collateral either."

"Still want to be involved?" Christopher looked up at me. His eyes told me he half-expected for me to leave him to whatever forces were coming after him. I was disappointed, I would have thought my former best friend would know me better. If I hadn't abandoned him after his becoming a bloodsucking creature of the night, I wasn't going to leave him because of a few Keebler Nazis trying to kill us.

"Nothing could stop me," I said, simply. "Alight, listen, here's what we're going to do—"

My words were interrupted by the lights going off across the hospital, followed by the emergency lights kicking on.

"That's not good," Shannon said, now covered in red light.

"Really, I hadn't noticed," I said, dryly. "How determined did you say those attackers were, Talbot?"

"Very." Talbot said, looking around.

"Great," I muttered.

Then the emergency lights went out too, plunging the room into darkness. Gunfire echoed from down the hallway. Talbot cursed under his breath and Christopher automatically moved between the door and the girl. I, on the other hand, just stood there.

"I think we need to get some weapons," Talbot said.

Shannon was already pulling out her service pistol. The sound of gunfire then filled the air, someone shooting less than a dozen yards away.

"Yeah, I think you're right."

CHAPTER THREE

Standing there in the darkness with the sounds of gunfire just outside our door, I needed a second to process things.

"It's them," Christopher whispered, his fingernails lengthening into a set of razor-sharp claws. "They've come for me."

"Yeah, that's a pretty safe guess." Shannon's wit was as dry as ever.

Not having a flashlight or lantern, I clasped my hands together and tried to conjure a ball of light around us. Instead, the room illuminated with a kind of weird anti-light. I could see Shannon, Talbot, and Christopher but it was still black as midnight.

I was a hedge magician, a wizard without much real talent, but what little I'd managed to learn of obscuromancy before my battle with Dracula came easily. Magic could be assisted by books and charts but, at the end of the day, it was a product of enforcing your will on reality itself.

And I had plenty of will.

"Wow, I did not know you could do that," Shannon said, shutting the door and locking it. A small act but one that might buy us a few seconds.

"Neither did I." I heard more gunfire, now accompanied by screams. "We need weapons, though. Now."

"*It's a hospital,*" Shannon said, rolling her eyes. "Not like they're on every floor."

"A *House-run* hospital." Talbot walked over to the plaster behind my bed and smashed it in with his fist.

Much to my surprise, I discovered there was a hidden cache

of guns and body armor behind the self. They were placed with holsters, ammo clips, and other things someone might need in the event of sudden attack. Had this stuff been built into the hospital from the beginning? I wasn't sure I wanted to know the answer.

"Will this work?" Talbot asked.

I smiled. "Very much so."

Talbot grabbed Jupiter-92 machine guns and tossed them to both me and Shannon. I would have preferred a pistol but, given I had a new arm, it was better I had the option of rapid automatic fire.

"I really need to sit down and memorize all the House's secrets," I muttered, loading the gun with a clip of orichalcum bullets.

"That'll take a few millennia," Talbot grunted.

"Thank you," Christopher said, taking his pistol. "For all of this."

"Christopher, when this is over we're going to have a long talk about how you told me I could never speak with Ashley again and how it was important to sever all ties in order to make sure the House never found her. You know, right before you went to meet with her again while you were still an agent of the Red Room as well as went to visit her after you were a vampire. This talk will involve me hitting you."

"That's fair," Christopher said. "Will this talk also explain how you've developed demonic magic? Also, how you're regenerating wounds that should have killed you. Albeit, at a progressively slower rate than a full demonically-enhanced human should be?"

"No," I said, thinking of the deal I'd made with Bloody Mary. I'd killed hundreds of people over the years and a demon of war had expressed her love for me. She'd gotten loose into the world because of my actions and was up to who knows what now. One problem at a time, though.

Looking through my weapon's sights, I took a deep breath. "Talbot, Shannon, I'm going to need you both to take point on this. I'm not a hundred percent."

"I've got your back," Shannon said, nodding. "Always."

"Also his front." Talbot grinned.

Shannon rolled her eyes.

Christopher chuckled.

The gunfire had stopped, and I heard movement in the halls beyond. "Everyone knows the drill. I'll take point. Shoot anyone who shoots at us. We need to evac as our top priority. That means the parking lot downstairs."

"Copy," Shannon said.

Christopher took position outside the doors. Talbot just nodded. I'd been in a lot of survival situations before but being assaulted in a hospital was a new one for even me. The possibilities for civilian casualties were tremendous and there were likely dozens from the cutting of the power alone. I tried not to think of the people in surgery, on life-support, or in need of constant supervision.

More gunfire filled the air and I had to wonder if the House had dispatched its security teams to deal with the intruders. The Red Room, the House's operations division, possessed some of the world's greatest soldiers. Unfortunately, guarding a seemingly secure facility in the most well-protected city on Earth wasn't going to draw the House's finest.

Worse, our attackers had come prepared. Talbot was right, whoever these people were, they weren't hesitating to launch an assault in the public eye. Someone who was willing to massacre a bunch of civilians in a hospital wasn't constrained by the usual rules that governed monster behavior. The last people willing to do so were the Emerald Eye—an eso-terrorist organization that had come within inches of destroying the world.

"Do we rush for the stairs?" Shannon asked.

I shook my head. "We need intel."

"They're coming," Christopher said, his voice low. "Many. I can hear their heartbeats."

"Super," I muttered.

Tapping the side of my head, I turned on the magitech scanner in my right eye. I'd lost it just like my hand. Some days I felt like I was becoming a biracial version of Darth Vader. Anyway, it had some benefits as I could see in the dark even without my obscuromancy. There, on the other side of the door,

I saw the outline of a male nurse running down the hall before another set of bullets flew and hit him in the back. The poor man was killed instantly and hit the ground like a slab of meat.

Jogging down the hall towards his corpse were two figures in heavy military gear. I couldn't make anything specific out, but they were carrying assault-rifles and wearing the kind of body armor that soldiers in the United States military wore. They turned to the doorway and one of them turned to open it.

"Aim at the door and fire," I said, doing the same.

The three of us opened fire on the two figures on the other side and they took a dozen rounds each before either had a chance to respond. I made sure to aim at their unprotected faces just to make sure they were both dead. Gesturing with my head, Shannon moved to the door's side, opened it and checked the bodies.

"What's it look like?" I asked.

Shannon gave a half-smile. "I'm sorry, Derek, but Legolas and Arwen are dead."

I glowered at her but headed up behind her to check the bodies. Lying on the ground were two people wearing the attire of soldiers and who looked, to the naked eye, normal. Well, except for the nightvision goggles on their faces.

Without my Ring of Veritas, a standard-issue item for all House personnel, I couldn't see through the illusions I suspected were covering them. Still unsure how far my shadow powers stretched, I stared at them and tried to see under their appearance. What I saw surprised me. Much as Shannon described, they had long-white hair and golden skin. Literally the color of gold, though it was difficult to describe how I knew this since I was seeing through a spectrum that didn't exist in the human eye.

The two dead soldiers were beautiful, bullet wounds aside, albeit in a disconcerting way. Their skin was flawless, their eyes oval-shaped, and ears not so much pointed as knife-edged. The elves had pronounced canines, too, like dogs more than vampires. They looked nothing like Tolkien's creations or even the creatures described in my supernatural biology textbooks back at the Black Room. Beautiful in a purely clinical sense but unnatural enough that they made me sick looking at them as they were just "off" enough to unsettle.

"Hybrids," Talbot said, looking over my shoulder at the bodies. "The product of sidhe biomancy. Looks like the Nazi's research into improving the Master Race didn't die with them. Sidhe hybrids have all the sociopathy of a typical elf but are not dependent on a source of magic to stay alive."

"Great, *mutant* Nazi elves." I rubbed my temples. "As if my life wasn't crazy enough."

"They don't look that bad," Shannon said, looking down the hall for any sign of other attackers. "Are you sure these guys are pure evil?"

"You didn't see the camps where they were produced." Talbot's look was one of pure revulsion. "And what they did when they took over."

I was about to say something about that when both Christopher and Talbot started firing at opposite ends of the hallway. Pulling back, I was about to join them in opening fire when a nightmarish pain filled my right arm. Despite the prosthetic being bonded to me, I'd been warned there'd be an adjustment period. Phantom pains caused me to wince and fall back. It was all I could do just to keep hold of the weapon in my hands.

"Grenade!" Shannon shouted, seeing a pair of them hurled at opposite ends. Neither Talbot, I, or her had time to move away.

Instead, I lifted my hands and tendrils of shadows from them sent the elves spiraling down to the two sides of the hall. Explosions filled both ends, cutting off the shouts of surprise from the elvish soldiers who'd tossed them. I was using more magic than I'd ever used before, which wasn't saying much but the experience was making me feel stronger rather than weaker.

I'll also be with you lover, Bloody Mary's voice echoed in my head. *My power is your power. You must embrace it and the changes it will bring.*

I ignored her words, pretending I'd imagined them. I didn't want to think about being Demon-Touched.

Suit yourself, Bloody Mary whispered. *But you'll need my power again soon.*

Clenching my teeth, I focused on the task at hand. Our quartet moved through the halls of Saint Magnus hospital passing corpse after corpse. The elves weren't taking any prisoners and it seemed they enjoyed killing people who couldn't fight back. Leaning over one of the corpses, I saw a nurse had her cellphone in hand. Lifting it up, I noticed it was on, but the screen was blank. Somehow, the elves had managed to wipe everything on it.

"Check your phones," I said, looking back to Talbot and Shannon.

Both did.

"Dead," Shannon said.

Talbot nodded, keeping his hand over his phone so it didn't reveal any light.

Dammit. "They're going to extreme lengths to keep this contained but they're also going in loud and obvious."

That didn't make sense. What the hell were they up to?

Any chance for further conversation dissolved with another set of elvish soldiers coming around to fire at us. Sliding into one of the rooms beside me for cover, I fired repeatedly. Every single bullet that left my gun felt like a thousand stabbing pains in my right arm. Talbot kept himself in front of the group and we continued forward, exchanging fire and maneuvering ourselves behind the nurses' stations. There were more bodies spread across the ground but also a set of elevators.

The elevator doors had been pried open and there were a set of chords inside next to the cables. The elves had used aerial transport to land on the roof before coming down. It was a strategy based all on offense rather than "in and out" since taking out power meant a quick escape was all but impossible. A quick look at the wall told me we were on the sixth floor of a twelve-floor hospital and egress either way was difficult.

The firefight was intense with Shannon, Talbot, and I holding off a group twice our size. We needed to get to the elevator to escape off this floor. While we managed to pick off another two of the soldiers, more moved to replace them and all we'd succeeded in was giving away our position.

There's six of them on this floor, Christopher said in my mind.

Apparently, telepathy was one of his vampire gifts. *There's another ten in the hospital from the two squadrons they landed on the rooftop. More are coming.*

How the hell do you know—oh right, you're a psychic, I thought back.

I prefer being called a bright. I need to get one of them alone, Christopher said.

We're focusing on helping you! I snapped back at him. *Let me do my job.*

You're a Committee member, you should be leading armies, not fighting in them. You're the only decent one.

That's why they won't let me live, I thought back. *Like Kirk, I never should have gone above Captain.*

Please don't quote Star Trek *at me,* Christopher said. *I have enough trouble keeping up with your Star Wars references.*

I closed my hand into a tight fist, thought about the night vision goggles worn by the elves, and slammed my knuckles down onto the ground. The pain was agonizing but I used it to fuel a makeshift spell, drawing on the darkness around me to send a torrent of invisible tentacles through the air to destroy every single one of their headsets.

"Ahh!

Fuck!

Optics down!" and other near-simultaneous cries filled the air.

That allowed Shannon and Talbot to run forward and start gunning down the now-blinded elves. It was a risky strategy but four of our attackers fell and the remaining two fired blindly. That was when Shannon took refuge behind a janitor's cart before Talbot charged the remaining two elves. What followed was the sound of gunfire, screaming, and the sound of a larger man crushing skulls. It took me a second to realize Talbot had run out of ammunition.

"Talbot, are you okay?" I called over to my uncle. He was laying slumped over the corpses of the final two elves, having crushed their heads in with the butt of his gun.

Talbot didn't answer for a second and I feared the worst. "I took a few rounds but that's one of the benefits of being made of clay and magic as much as flesh."

The others are coming, we need to move, Christopher insisted.

"I know!" I shouted. "Shannon, get some of their grenades and head to the elevators. We're going to take the quick route down. Talbot, are you okay for movement?"

Talbot grunted and got up. "Give me a second. They're using orichalcum bullets. I need to pry these things loose before they poison the enchantments keeping me together."

I reached down, took a knife from a dead elf's side, and tossed it to him. I'd seen Talbot do a lot crazier shit than this on the battlefield.

"Thanks," Talbot said, catching it. He then, without hesitation, started using the knife on his arms and chest.

"You are a very strange group," Christopher observed.

"Tell me about it," I said.

The use of orichalcum bullets by the opposition surprised me. Orichalcum was a metal mentioned by Plato as having once been mined by the bull-worshiping peoples of Atlantis. Orichalcum could kill any supernatural being short of an archwizard or demon. It was strictly controlled as the alchemical process that made it was a well-guarded secret. Its use by the elves meant they had access to House weaponry or had reverse-engineered the process.

Why use them here, though? Regular bullets worked just fine against humans. The only answer I could think of was they knew they'd be up against Shannon and Talbot. Which meant we had another leak.

Great.

Shannon had gotten a set of grenades and rappelling equipment from the fallen soldiers. "I'm ready to go down."

I raised an eyebrow. "Phrasing."

"Oh shut up!" Shannon said.

"You, Talbot?" I asked, watching him pry a sixth bullet from his body. I couldn't see his blood very well, but it was a thick viscous ichor rather than the substance that flowed within the veins of normal human beings.

"I'm ready," Talbot said.

Shannon and Christopher went first. I followed and Talbot came behind me. Above us, I could hear sounds of movement. Our attackers' reinforcements weren't far behind. I regretted the fact I wouldn't be able to deal with these bastards, especially given all the bodies they left behind but I had a priority to getting Christopher out. He was the only one who knew anything about what Ashley had been doing these past few years. It occurred to me there was no way I could help her without exposing myself and losing everything, but I surprised myself by being okay with that. Ashley was worth it.

Grabbing hold of the rappelling cable with a Type-A 'slider' like the kind used by the Red Room, another disturbing coincidence, I started sliding down into the shaft below. I landed beside Shannon, Christopher, with Talbot landing behind me. Talbot walked over to the doors and pried them open with his bare hands, another display of his freakish golem strength. Doctor Franklin Talbot may have been a madman but there was no denying he'd created a superior human being, lifting our guns we headed out into the parking lot below before gunfire followed us.

"These guys don't know when to quit," Shannon muttered under her breath. "What the hell do they want with you? Is it just to keep you off their trail?"

"Their thoughts are difficult to read," Christopher replied. "Too filled with violence and rage. Plus, you keep killing them."

"You suggest we should keep them alive?" I asked, half-joking.

"That's what I'm suggesting, yes." Christopher gave her a sideways glance. "At least until I can find out where they're holding Ashley."

He spoke her name with a bit too much familiarity. Dammit, I wasn't the crazy jealous guy. Hell, I'd been seeing Shannon for a year. That was longer than some marriages. I needed to get my head on straight.

I headed out into the parking lot, fully prepared for whatever lay ahead.

Or so I thought.

CHAPTER FOUR

The first level of the hospital parking lot was filled to the rim with cars. Despite the fact Saint Ignatius' was a building devoted to the care and upkeep of House personnel, it was still a functioning medical care facility. Thousands of people were treated here daily and were caught up in our war. That meant a large amount of potential collateral damage as well as people to convince nothing strange involving Santa's little helpers was going on.

Any further thoughts I might have had on the subject were muted by the squealing of tires and a long black van pulling out in front of us before yet more soldiers started pulling out. I lifted my weapon up and fired while Shannon and Talbot did the same. Christopher, meanwhile, moved supernaturally fast behind a concrete pillar.

Bullets struck against my body armor and I felt like I'd been punched five times by the time the last of the elves fell. Shannon, too, looked like she'd been hit but it didn't seem like any of the soldiers' bullets had penetrated her flesh. Unlike Talbot, it was likely an orichalcum bullet would have killed her outright.

As for the elves, the driver had been hit in the head with a bullet and the rest of them were on the ground, bleeding to death. I was tempted to empty the remainder of my clip into their bodies, but we needed information and taking one of these bastards prisoner would serve our cause.

In the distance, I could hear police sirens and the sounds of ambulances. Someone had been paying attention and was sending help to deal with the humanitarian crisis set off by our attackers. Holding my hands up, I gestured for Shannon to come with me and the two of us advanced on one of the dying elves.

This elf was different from his fellows, his skin like silver as opposed to gold. His eyes were a shade of pink and his face was so pointed it might as well have been carved that way. The man's hair was also the blue and green color of the sea as opposed to the white of the other elves. It was an incongruous image for a man involved in such a despicable attack.

"I'll handle this," Shannon said, crouching down beside the elf.

"Alright," I said, covering her back.

Looking back to make sure no more elves were coming down the elevator behind us, I made a short nod of my hand and Shannon took the elf's hand.

"What's she doing?" Talbot asked.

"Succubus things," I replied.

Talbot went to check the van while Christopher watched us from behind. The rest of the elf's squadron were expiring before our eyes but this one looked like he might pull through.

"Who are you working for?" Shannon asked, her voice soft and melodic.

The elf stared up at us, his hand reaching for his gun only to fall limp to the ground. "The coming storm. You are....so beautiful...but you will burn. The God of the Burning Eye will cleanse this world. The Truth shall be set free. I cannot..."

Shannon looked at him with an expression of deep concentration. "Please, tell us."

Police cars and SWAT support pulled down through the parking lot entrance and began to encircle us.

Talbot pulled out a fake badge and moved to handle the situation, babbling something about Homeland Security despite the fact he was dressed like a Hawaiian beach bum.

"The Sleeper will awaken. The Sleeper will awaken, and the world will be reborn in the fires of his gaze. The children of Bres and Brigid shall rise to the throne of man and the children of Eli will fall. All will...Ahhhhhhrgh!" The elf's insane rambling was cut off by an incoherent scream followed by gurgling, then death.

I looked up and saw Christopher with palm outstretched,

aimed at the now-dead elf's head. It seemed his psychic abilities went far beyond mere telepathy.

"I have what we need," Christopher said, looking at me. "We should go."

"You go," I said, staring. "Just stay close by so we can join back up. I need to look like I'm handling this. Also, I'm going to pretend like I didn't just hear Cthulhu is coming."

"Cthulhu isn't real," Shannon said. "About the only thing that isn't."

"*So far* he's not real," I said. "You never know what spirits are going to assume the form of. I once fought Jason Voorhees in an old abandoned summer camp. Thank God I had a hot camp counselor to distract him. Good luck, Christopher."

Christopher nodded. "See you soon, Derek."

It was pandemonium at Saint Ignatius' Hospital for the next few hours. In a rationale society, I would have been arrested for the fact I had a machine gun in the middle of a hospital parking lot next to a bunch of corpses, but our world was anything but.

The Red Room had dozens of agents spread throughout the Washington D.C. police department and I was, instead, ushered to the side so I looked like a victim. The operatives of the House manipulated the flow of events like masters, sequestering our little group from the rest of the disaster and sending in its soldiers to deal with the last of the elven soldiers. An estimated sixty-three deaths were reported, not including the terrorists, and backup power was restored to Saint Ignatius' while its patients were transferred to other hospitals.

Shannon, Talbot, and I were standing next to an empty ambulance with blankets over our shoulders and Styrofoam coffee cups in our hands. We did our best to look like part of the background as House witches manipulated the memories of those who'd seen us. In time, they'd remember us as bit players in whatever they'd seen. The bodies of the elves would be replaced with more appropriate ones for whatever narrative the House chose to construct, probably young Middle Eastern men, and the whole thing would become political theatre.

Talbot, meanwhile, just sat in the background. It was amazing how a man who was almost seven-feet-tall, covered in scars, and dressed like a character from Magnum P.I. could act inconspicuous but he pulled it off.

I was reading a casualty chart brought to me by my secretary, Ishikawa Sakura, a bleached blonde-haired Japanese woman dressed in an orange sweater and flower-covered skirt, when I heard Christopher's voice in my head. *You're mad at me.*

What an observant little vampire you are, I thought back. *With insights like that, you may someday be scary again and not the object of lust for fourteen-year-old girls.*

Twilight is not the end all of vampire-dom, Christopher said, still sounding upset at my irritation with him. I could feel his anxiety through our telepathic bond.

It is for me, I thought back. *You should just cover yourself in body glitter and give up on ever being taken seriously as a threat again.*

Why are you upset? Christopher asked. *Because I ripped the mind of an elf-hybrid's brain to pieces?*

A little bit. I'm trying to cut down on killing people. Even Mein Alf stormtroopers, I said.

Didn't you attract the attention of a demon who specifically loves you because you've murdered more monsters than anyone in history? Christopher asked.

Yeah, that would be why I'm cutting down, I said, still troubled that I was apparently catnip to demons.

It won't work, Christopher said.

Where are you? I asked, exasperated. *Hopefully outside of the Red Room's range of sight.*

Two blocks away out at a local Starbucks. The Red Room's range of sight is remarkably limited. You, Penny, Ashley, her grandmother, Talbot, me, and Papa Hawthorne are the only agents who were ever worth a damn.

Shannon should be offended, I said.

I'm reserving judgement, Christopher said.

"Is something wrong, sir?" Sakura asked.

"Nothing," I lied, looking at her. "Could you do me a huge favor and get the Professor?"

The Professor, whose real name I knew but never used, was

the head of Division One in the United States and now also the head of global Red Room operations. In a very real way, he was more powerful than me and certainly better qualified to be on the Committee. Unfortunately, the Professor was *not* a member of the Old Blood families that controlled the House and, even worse, was devoid of magic. As limited as my possession of sorcery was, it allowed me to sit at the table that controlled the world. The Professor tried not to hold it against me but, given he was my former boss, it was hard. I needed his help now.

Sakura responded, "He's on the phone with the President, sir."

I sighed. "Afterward, please."

Sakura nodded and got the hint I wanted to be left alone, walking across the minefield of reporters, police, National Guard, and who knows else who'd assembled in the parking lot. Somehow, none of them wanted to speak with us—another benefit of magic.

When Sakura left, Shannon asked, "So, how are you holding up? What with your vampire buddy and ex-girlfriend being kidnapped?"

"Halfway between the Terminator after me and being *Mad Max Beyond Thunderdome*."

"I'll pretend I have any idea what that means," Shannon said. "Can Christopher be trusted?"

"He helped us kill Dracula."

"Which means jack and shit," Shannon said. "He was working for Dracula when he was setting him up."

"I trust him," I said.

"You shouldn't," Shannon said.

I wanted to argue with Shannon. That she should know better. Shannon had been a child when her father had taken her on a world-wide killing spree. The incubus Titus had made it a point to turn children into murderers and was one of the most reprehensible bastards in the entire Red Room's Most Wanted files. Yet, against all odds, somehow Shannon had returned from that horror. She was wrong. Christopher needed understanding, not condemnation.

But there was no way I could argue that and not sound like

a fool given the company I kept. "We'll see."

Talbot surprised me by saying, "It's a truism of spies that you should trust no one. That's wrong, you need to be able to trust the people at your side and at your back. If you can't, then you've already lost."

Shannon said, "Then maybe that's a war we lost long ago."

I was spared having to respond by the arrival of the Professor. The Professor was a tall, balding, African American man in a dark blue suit. He looked like hundreds of bureaucrats who worked in Washington D.C, though he projected a sense of power—something needed for these chaotic proceedings. He was a former CIA operative who'd been "brought in" like the President and served out of a sense of duty, believing it was somehow patriotic to serve a 5,000-year-old global conspiracy. I'd never questioned his rationale until recently and now couldn't help but wonder how many others had such misguided priorities. We'd never gotten along but I respected the Professor, something I couldn't say about most House bigwigs.

"I see you've awoken from your coma," the Professor said, looking unhappy to be here. "A pity, I was getting used to peace and quiet."

Not that the feeling was returned.

"Always glad to make your day a bit better," I said, smiling. "It was too quiet around here."

The Professor narrowed his gaze. "Sixty-three people are dead. This is Washington D.C. This isn't in the middle of nowhere where this sort of thing can just be covered up. There will be inquiries, public outcries—"

I raised my hands in the air as if surrendering. "I'm so sorry the terrorists didn't RSVP their intentions. If they had, we could have booked another venue." I didn't buy the Professor's equivocations one bit. He'd once made an entire destroyed town in Kansas disappear overnight. This was about him wanting to know who the Keebler Elf Death Squad was and what they were doing here. Information I wasn't about to share with him.

"I don't know why I even bother." The Professor sighed.

"Me either," I said.

Talbot came to my defense. "That van had a chemical bomb

in it, a particularly toxic mix capable of taking out a city-block. The elves were going to kill a lot more than sixty-three people here. Probably their way of disguising what they were doing here. Either that or a failsafe if the gun-wielding assassins failed."

I whistled, glad for a distraction. "Impressive."

"Yes, elves," the Professor said the word as if it was distasteful. "These individuals have no respect for the rules of engagement. This could have blown into a much larger disaster."

"Or killed thousands," Shannon said, highlighting the real issue.

"Derek, do you have any reason for why they might be targeting you?" The Professor asked.

The Professor thought I was the target. Good. "No. The most likely explanation if they wanted to take out a vulnerable member of the Committee."

"Then it's lucky you awoke when you did," the Professor said, scrunching his brow. "We're going to get our top people to find out where they came from. Someone had to pay for this assault and when we find out whom, we'll deal with them."

I thought about Christopher and what he'd learned from the fallen elf soldier. "You do that. If you don't mind, I'd like to do my own research on the subject. Talbot has some experience with the elves and their return is cause for worry. I'd also like to keep my whereabouts a secret for the next several days with the circle small about who knows my movements."

"Why does this not surprise me? I think you do less leading and more field work than you did before you joined the Committee," the Professor muttered, looking more tired than angry.

"The benefit of rank," I said.

"You're not an agent anymore, Mister Hawthorne, and you're not recovered from your battle with Dracula. I can't technically advise you to avoid getting into gunfights in the middle of public places when individuals are coming after you—though I will. I don't want to be on the Committee enough to want to see you dead. Remember, Alexander the Great led from the front but he died a very young man."

"Because he was poisoned by his generals." I placed my hand over my heart. "Still, I appreciate the sentiment."

"Don't let it get to your head," the Professor snapped. "I'm glad you're awake."

"Yeah, being a vegetable would have sucked. Take care of yourself and if there's anything I can do…"

"I'll call someone else," the Professor answered.

I smiled. "Thank you, Reggie."

"Don't ever call me that again." The Professor turned around and walked away.

"Wow, that was almost like hugging you," Shannon said. "He must have really missed you."

"Like a root canal," I said, looking down at the ground. "The Committee is going to want answers."

"Can't you put them off?" Talbot asked. "You are a member."

"So I keep reminding them," I said. The truth was it was an organization composed of archwizards, spymasters, billionaires, and demigods. I'd managed to win the seat of their weakest member thanks to epic bluffing skills but after a year of working for them, they'd started to weary of my presence. I was, honestly, surprised they hadn't killed me during my coma. I needed to start thinking about an exit strategy.

Or how to kill them all.

Christopher contacted me again. *I have a name, Derek. That was what I got from the elf soldier's mind. The man responsible for Ashley's kidnapping.*

"A name," I said, repeating his words. "Who?"

"Roland Cassidy." Christopher spoke the name with an expression of emotion that was somewhere between sick to his stomach and hate-filled. It was decidedly uncharacteristic for his usual stoic responses.

I could have been knocked over by a feather. "I see."

"You know him?" Shannon asked.

"You could say that," I said, shaking my head. "He was my brother-in-law."

This day just kept getting better and better.

CHAPTER FIVE

The House was an incestuous organization. Wizards married other wizards who married rich people who married nobility in order to keep all the power concentrated in one tiny group of people. The Cassidys were one of the most powerful families in the House, even if they were relative newcomers. They were far more public than the majority of the House's 'old magic' bloodlines, staying in the spotlight since their immigration from Ireland in the early 19th century.

The Cassidys built their fortune using the House's resources to gain insight into the future while sabotaging their competitors. In exchange, they'd given the House all manner of high-grade military and technological equipment. It had been a very profitable relationship for both sides. It was why my father had married me to their patriarch's eldest daughter, right before she'd gone insane and Shannon had been forced to kill her.

"So I take it he's a relative of your late batshit ex-wife?" Shannon asked.

"Her younger brother, yeah. When Cassandra died, he took over her seat on the board. Roland was the head of Pantheon Corp's R&D division but now spends most of his time promoting the company. You might remember him as the guy who is in all those 'global warming is a myth' commercials."

I didn't know him all that well. Cassandra had been little more than property to her family and the relationship vibe I'd always gotten from them was she was afraid of her male relatives, which was crazy because Cassandra was one of the scariest women I'd ever known. This coming from a man living with a succubus and who was currently sharing his brain with a high-ranking demoness.

"Oh Jesus, Roland's the guy who talks about how the environment is getting better because corporations need a planet to make money?" Shannon asked, disgusted.

"Yeah, that's him."

"Would it be a problem to kill him?" Shannon asked, sounding all too serious.

I glared at her.

"How *the hell* are the Cassidys still in charge of Pantheon Corp?" Talbot piped in. "Cassandra tried to poison the world."

Technically, she'd tried to release a draugr-creating zombie plague to decimate the world but that was splitting hairs. "Digging them out of the House's power structure and the hundreds of places they were involved in the corporate world would have been an economic nightmare."

"You should have insisted on killing them," Shannon said.

In truth, I'd been one of the ones who'd encouraged a diplomatic solution with the Cassidy's. Cassandra had been hideously wronged, and I still regretted our encounter had ended the way it did. It seemed the House was consuming my relatives' sanity at an extremely fast rate. I might not have considered Roland family, but I wasn't eager to blame him for his sister's sins. Too bad the rest of the Committee had taken it yet another sign of my weakness.

"Do you think Roland is involved in the hospital attack?" Shannon asked.

I wasn't sure. "Normally, I'd say no. Many billionaires are more interested in banging supermodels and buying expensive but useless things than financing terrorism. There are exceptions, though. Certain members of the Saudi Royal family, Cassandra—"

"Your father." Shannon said.

"It's not terrorism if it's your side," Talbot said. "Also, show some respect. If not for Nathan, we'd all be speaking Japanese."

"That only goes so far," I said, shaking my head. My uncle had a lot more loyalty to my father than I did. "But yeah, I'll be honest, he does have the resources and magical know-how to pull something like this off. If anyone would be manufacturing Nazi elven clones with magitech, and God do I feel weird for saying that, it'd be Pantheon Corp's R&D division."

"We need to take him down and quickly," Talbot said.

"Yeah, there's just one problem," I said, taking a deep breath.

"What's that?" Talbot asked.

"He's joining the Committee in a week," I said.

The House was rotten to the core. That was one of the things I'd learned recently. Cassandra had used Pantheon Corp's resources to help the Emerald Eye, they'd run a secret plan to try to brainwash supernaturals into being their slaves, and now it seemed Roland was financing terrorism like his cousin. Hell, I was a traitor myself. I was working with a vampire allied with the Network to find its missing leader. If I survived this, I'd have to try to figure out a way to strike off the head of the beast. Reform was impossible.

Shannon reacted to my revelation with appropriate gravitas. "Are you serious? This is a bad joke."

"I fail to see the humor," I said, shrugging. "Adding a thirteenth member of the Committee was justified by the changing nature of the world."

It had been confirmed right before I'd gone off to try to negotiate with the Vampire Nation, which made me wonder if they'd assumed he'd be filling my spot rather than changing the system to break ties.

"He's probably your replacement," Shannon said. "Another reason to kill him."

"Innocent until proven guilty isn't always the case but it is here. Mostly because if he shuts down Pantheon's support then the House won't be able to function." I looked up at the ceiling. "That means we can't just order Roland detained, black bagged, and shipped off to magical Gitmo."

Assuming the rest of the Committee didn't side with him. What was a little magical terrorism between an organization that gave the Illuminati a run for its money? The House blew up space shuttles, sponsored dictators, and lied to everyone every day. Maybe they'd expected me to die fighting Dracula and the hospital attack was a desperation move. If so, Roland wasn't qualified for the Committee. You had to be much more subtle in your moves than that.

"I don't think we can," Shannon said. "You blew up Magical Gitmo."

She was referring to Camp Zero, where I'd executed Rebecca.

"Not funny," I said.

Christopher contacted me again. *If I may interrupt this reminiscing on your various acts of terrorism, it may be that Roland Cassidy's not the mastermind behind these attacks. I say this despite much as I'd like you to torture him to find Ashley's location.*

"Torture doesn't work," I said aloud, glancing over my shoulder. "Unfortunately."

Torture works with a mind-reader on hand, Christopher said. *It's also fun with the right target. Waterboarding, electroshock, or blowtorch—whatever works for you.*

Freed from Dracula's control or not, Christopher was still a vampire. "I'll pass. There are easier ways of finding out the truth. Are you *sure* Roland Cassidy is responsible?"

Christopher was silent for a moment. *Reading someone's mind isn't an exact science. I have a name and it's important to the soldier, but I don't know for certain if it's the person who sent them to attack us.*

"So it's possible he's a *target* rather than their leader?" I asked, hoping this was the case.

It's...possible, Christopher said.

"Good," I said.

"Why?" Shannon asked, responding to my spoken statements. "I, for one, would love to know who the villain is at the start. It'd be a nice change of pace."

"I'd rather not start a blood feud between myself and Cassandra's family. If Roland's a target, we can avoid the repercussions for going after a member of the Committee and still know where they're going to strike next."

Ever since Cassandra's attempted *coup d'etat,* the House had been struggling to regain its footing. This included a meaningless war against the vampire race we were conducting and the business with Camp Zero. The House had lost its confidence and the entire world was suffering. I didn't want to imagine what sort of backlash would occur if I tried to point out a Committee member was a traitor. Or maybe I just didn't want to kill Cassandra's brother.

Either way.

"You're the guy who's always saying we need to see what's there rather than what we want to see," Shannon said. "The Cassidys are corrupt to the last, Derek. If anyone is willing to sell out humanity to ally with a bunch of lembas-eating terrorists, it's them."

He feels guilty for not recognizing his wife was brainwashed for the entirety of their marriage, Christopher said. *As a result, he's overcompensating.*

"Ah, that makes sense," Shannon said, revealing she could hear our conversation.

I closed my eyes, trying not to think about Rebecca, losing my hand, or the mountain of bodies I'd left behind recently. That, unfortunately, left me thinking about Ashley. After two weeks, it was very likely Ashley was dead. Modern magitech techniques could break through even the strongest defenses after just a few days and after that, she would have outlived her usefulness.

I couldn't think like that, though. I needed to believe Christopher's statement that he'd know if Ashley was dead. I also wanted to believe, in some cosmic mystical sense, I'd know as well. Despite the fact I was with Shannon, that Shannon was my best friend, Ashley was the only woman I'd ever loved. Unconditionally. Without reserve.

She is alive, Bloody Mary's voice spoke. *If that makes your situation any more tolerable.*

And I'm supposed to take the word of a demon? I asked.

I will never lie to you, Derek. You are a living work of art.

Because I've killed a lot of people, I said.

Because you've killed a lot of important people, Bloody Mary said. *Anyone can kill a lot of people. It is another thing entirely to kill people who can fight back.*

You're a freaky-deaky demon, Mary, I said.

I'm your demon, Derek, Mary said. *Only yours.*

Oddly, Mary's words were comforting. The demoness was trustworthy in the same way a cobra could be trusted to bite you or a tiger to eat you. She was a creature born in the fires of Hell as an embodiment of war as well as conflict. I wasn't exactly happy to be forced to rely on her for conformation but lying really wasn't in her nature. For all the legends of demons as deceivers, it tended to be the opposite in real life. They broke you by telling you the truth.

Why would I attempt to change you? Mary asked. *You are perfect the way you are.*

You're getting a little stalker-ish here, Bloody Mary.

Call me Mary. I'll back away then, my love. For now.

Yeah, I needed to start considering exorcism rituals. The problem with that was Mary would know about them and take it personally.

You know me so well, Mary said. *I would never let us be parted.*

"Derek?" Shannon said, waving her hand in front of me.

"Hmm?" I said, blinking.

"You zoned out there for a second," Shannon said. "Are you talking to someone else?"

"No, just working on a cunning plan to destroy all my foes," I said, cheerfully. "Putting the Committee off until I can figure out who is behind this and rescue Ashley is going to be a pain in the ass."

"Loss of freedom is a consequence of power," Talbot said, surprising me. "It is why absolute power is the ultimate prison."

"You follow a weird form of Christianity," I said, taking a deep breath. "But yeah, I'm probably not in the best position with my fellow leaders right now."

"You brought down the Vampire Nation," Shannon said, looking straight at me. "That's worthy of a statue. You know, if the Red Room erected statues. Dracula has killed thousands of agents over the years. He's not coming back because of you."

I wasn't sure if the Vampire Nation was destroyed. Dracula was the leader of its Church of Blood and its most famous member but hardly the only vampire of note within it. Hell, he wasn't even the oldest of vampires by a few thousand years.

Indeed, I wouldn't have been surprised if Dracula's death ended up motivating them to strike back harder.

I looked at Talbot, debating speaking freely in front of him before realizing I could trust him. "I also took down their pet mind-control project. If they don't know about it, they suspect and that's punishable by death."

"Or worse," Talbot said. "Still, your father is an ally on the Council. The man I fought with in World War II would never abandon you."

I wasn't so sure about that either. Nathan had a lot of other children to look after and wasn't about to endanger them to protect me. He'd also lost four of my siblings in service to the House without anything more than mild grumbling. He'd also ordered me to kill Rebecca. God, why had I done it?

Because it is your job to make the hard decisions and do the dark deeds that make worse things not happen, Christopher said, continuing to read my mind without my permission. *You're an assassin who just happens to head a massive global conspiracy. It's one of your more charming qualities.*

Could you hear Mary's speech? I asked him.

Christopher didn't respond.

Which was an answer by itself. Mary was blocking me from talking about her and relevant details being heard. Even though Christopher knew about my pact with her. It meant he knew I was powered by hell. That was ominous. Kind of blackmailable. Well, if not for the fact I killed everyone who tried to blackmail me. Kind of a standard operating procedure. Sometimes they had ways of releasing the info but that was easy to find when you were dead and knew necromancers.

"I do have an idea," I said, taking a moment to gather my thoughts. "We can't move against Roland directly but whoever is behind this isn't exactly being subtle about it. He's employing magitech clones and hitting public buildings. If he is responsible, he's not smart enough to realize he's drastically overplaying his hand."

"And this is the guy you're putting on the Committee?" Shannon asked.

"Because I got there on merit and not nepotism," I said, dryly.

"Point taken," Shannon muttered.

"If we can make him overconfident, bring him out into the open, and then reveal we're onto him then he's likely to make a move. Then we've got him," I said, suspecting it wouldn't be that easy.

I'd gotten my position in the Committee by regicide, killing the guy whose seat I currently held, and the others had acted with a collective shrug. The thing about working for the House was they weren't exactly big fans of law and justice.

If I did expose Roland as the man behind all this, they'd probably expect me to handle it. Indeed, the fact I wanted to prove him innocent was another reason I didn't fit in at the mommy and daddy table. I'd known for years the Red Room's bosses were evil, but I'd never quite expected them to be so blatant about it.

I contacted Christopher. *I'm going to need you to lie low for a day or two. I'm going to be going places you can't in order to find more information about Ashley.*

You seem more interested in taking down this Roland man than rescuing Ashley. We can't find out where she's being held if he's dead. Christopher's 'voice', for lack of a better term, sounded almost accusatory.

You'd be surprised what I can get from a ghost. Also, I have alternative methods of finding out her location I'll explore if it comes to that.

If Bloody Mary didn't know where Ashley was being held then she knew a demon who did. The problem with making that kind of deal with the Devil was, well, being a deal with the Devil. I trusted Mary's word, but I also suspected she'd drive a hard bargain for whatever aid she offered. If she didn't, well, that would mean I was doing something epically stupid.

I'll do whatever I have to do to find Ashley, Christopher said. *I was hoping you'd do the same.*

Christopher cut the connection before I could respond.

Dammit.

Shannon "I'm not sure how you think we're going to lure Roland out. If he is plotting something nefarious then he's not going to want to go out in the open where he can be captured and interrogated. Do you remember when we went after Cassandra? She had a *literal* island fortress."

"Don't worry. I have an ingenious plan." I tapped the side of my head. "Shannon, how are you at golf?"

CHAPTER SIX

"This is the dumbest idea you have ever had," Shannon said, standing beside me on the vast green driving range of the Saint George Country Club.

Shannon was dressed in a black shirt and plaid skirt that looked a little too short for the surroundings and was a sign of her rebellion against the atmosphere. I hadn't changed at all, looking out of place in an environment that was frequented by billionaires, Senators, and powerful wizards.

Vast green fields, miniature lakes, and sand traps surrounded us in every direction. Saint George was the most exclusive country club you could join, the property alone costing several hundred million dollars. An expansive mansion served as the club's heart, containing four levels of private rooms and offices.

Saint George's was a Committee-owned resort just south of Boston, existing so members could have conversations in complete safety. The Chairman himself had laid the protective spells down on the place. No living or undead being could harm another while walking Saint George's greens. It was the perfect place to hold a meeting between individuals who might otherwise want to kill you.

"Hey, it worked didn't it? Roland is coming to speak with us in person," I said, swinging my driver and sending the ball far afield of where I'd been aiming. My arm tremors were getting worse and it was difficult for me to get control of them. I needed to dial back on my new arm's usage but that wasn't an option right now.

"It *shouldn't* have worked," Shannon said, watching me tee up another ball. "If he's as guilty as you think, Roland should be paranoid as heck about meeting with the Red Room's second greatest agent. This isn't *Goldfinger*. Real psychopaths are smart enough not to tempt fate."

Clearly, she didn't know the same psychopaths I did. Then I squinted at her. "Wait, second greatest agent?"

"I was being generous," Shannon said.

"Who's the best?" I asked.

Shannon smiled.

"Of course." I knocked a second ball out, this one going so far afield it landed in a nearby lake two holes over.

"Wow, you suck at this game," Shannon said.

"Funny, I kick ass when using the Wii back home," I said, shaking my head. "Video games lied to me."

"I'm still not sure about this plan. If this guy is willing to blow up a hospital to get at me, he's not going to balk at attacking us the moment we go into the parking lot. I already saw a bunch of moving vans outside—they could be filled with an army of elven wizards or something."

"They're setting up for the Chairman's granddaughter's sweet sixteen party. As for my plan, it's simple enough. We get him on the green, chat him up, and find out if there's any holes in his story. Sweat him a bit. He's an alchemist and a businessman—not a trained agent. We should be able to pick up on any tells he might have." I laid down another ball to hit.

"So when's he supposed to arrive?" Shannon asked.

"Any minute now." I primed my swing and pulled it back.

"So, what do you think of Christopher banging your girlfriend?" Shannon asked.

The club went flying out of my hands onto the driving range. I stood there, looking at the sight before grimacing.

"You did that on purpose," Shannon said.

"Yes and no." I shook my artificial wrist in hopes the pain would go away. "Did you seriously just ask that?"

"I'm sorry, did it offend your delicate assassin sensibilities?" Shannon asked, sarcastically. "I know you're still in love with Ashley."

"I'm not," I said, not sure if I was lying or not.

Shannon rolled her eyes. "Spare me. There is no more love

enduring and devoted than to a woman who is either dead or missing."

"That's horrible," I said. "Also, untrue. I've moved on."

"Not to me, I hope," Shannon said, causing me to feel like she'd punched me in the gut. "It's just I think we should have a plan when we find Ashley's dismembered corpse somewhere."

"My, you're a bundle of optimism."

"Do you think we're going to find her alive?"

"Psychics have a way of sensing each other's presence, even more so when they're blood relatives. I wouldn't dismiss it out of hand." I paused. "But yes, I understand our chances of recovering Ashley are low."

"And then what?" Shannon asked.

"I'll mourn." I wanted to believe Ashley was alive but, honestly, years of training said otherwise. "Help Christopher move on."

"You want to have a threesome?" Shannon asked. "I was getting some ex-vibes between you and Christopher too. If so, hot."

I rolled my eyes. "That was one time. Completely meaningless."

Shannon smirked, unsure if I was kidding or not.

I smiled. "I love you."

Shannon didn't respond, instead switching the subject. "He's not coming."

It was almost sundown. There was no sign of Roland or even a messenger saying he wasn't going to attend. I shook my head and picked up my golf bag to start heading over to the first hole. I might as well play a full round if he was going to keep us waiting. It was just another sign of how disrespected I was in the House. If any other member of the Committee called you, you came or died.

Clearly you should have murdered more to establish your dominance, Bloody Mary whispered.

Yeah, I said back telepathically. I was getting too comfortable with a demon in my head. *Probably.*

Good, Mary said. *I have much to teach you about leadership.*

Assuming I want to lead the House, I pointed out.

What other choice is there? Mary asked. *Their reach is across this planet and the Spirit World. You either rule them, kill them, or die.*

I hated she was right. *Yeah.*

"I'm sure he's coming," I lied to Shannon. "You don't stand up a member of the Committee, even if you're trying to kill them."

"Does anyone else know about your meeting?" Shannon asked, more nervous than the situation warranted.

"Roland, Roland's secretary, Sakura, and Nathan," I said, sighing. "I let my father know for insurance."

I loathed bringing my father into this but despite the fact I was a member of the Committee, I wielded only a fraction of his power. I'd loathed him for his cheating, manipulation, and faux sympathy growing up. Unfortunately, against my better judgment, I'd ended up entangled in his schemes and dependent on him anyway. Nathan Hawthorne was just *better* at being a member of the Committee than me.

"Great," Shannon said, sighing. "Can we get out of here and find a place to have steamy hot sex? I need a recharge. Hopefully, somewhere that doesn't reek of white privilege?"

"Says the white-girl to the mixed-race guy."

"Says the poor white-succubus to the mixed-race half-dragon *billionaire.*"

"*Ex*-millionaire. My father's the billionaire. I also used my hundred-million-dollar trust to set up a children's aid foundation."

Shannon blinked. "Wait, *you actually did that*? That wasn't just something you made up to sound cool?"

"Yes. That surprises you?"

Shannon looked appalled. "You at least kept a few million for yourself, right?"

I had because I wasn't crazy but that was beside the point. "Can we go back to the sex thing?"

"Yes, please, let's do!" a male voice called from nearby.

I grimaced as I turned over to see Roland Cassidy and his entourage arriving. An aura projected out from them that made me feel unclean, as if I was in the presence of something corrupt—a curious feeling given Roland Cassidy had the best reputation money could buy.

Roland Cassidy was in the lead of the group, looking like a statue come to life. He was perfect in his physique with well-tanned skin, broad shoulders, brilliant blond hair, and chiseled good looks. He looked like the Platonic ideal of a masculine hero, square-jawed and dashing. His appearance was more surprising since my reports never said Roland Cassidy worked out or underwent plastic surgery. He seemed to have been born fully formed into the world looking like a Greek Adonis.

Roland was wearing a button-down white shirt that had three buttons undone and khaki jeans. He was carrying his golf clubs to his side with one hand despite weighing over a hundred pounds. He didn't look like the corporate shark he was, he looked like a hero, but all positive thoughts went out of my head when I saw his face.

The contempt in his sea-green eyes felt like lasers blasting into my chest and the expression on his face was of a man who'd never had to work a day in his life for anything nor had to live with the consequences of his actions. I'd never gotten to know Roland Cassidy all that well during my marriage to Cassandra but everything I'd read from *People* to *Playboy* bespoke someone who oozed entitlement.

"Glad to see you could finally make it," I said, frowning.

"I just had to take care of a few billion things," Roland said, gesturing for his entourage to join him on the green. "We don't all have ample spare time to go do personal favors for every Tom, Dick, and Harry."

Behind Roland Cassidy were two bodyguards, mystically enslaved Trolls in human form who looked like large bald white men with goatees. They were close to, but not quite, identical. This made them look more like decorations than actual protection. Still, even one Troll was usually enough to kill any number of human attackers. Two was just overkill unless you were under assault by a pack of werewolves or someone with a magic blade—something I lacked at present.

There were also three women dressed in golfing attire even more scandalous than Shannon who I saw were glamour-covered fae women, each more beautiful than was possible without magic and a lifetime of prepping. I couldn't identify what sort of creature they were due to the amount of magic disguising them, but I imagined they served in some other role than just his paid harem.

"Harpies," Shannon whispered. "As enslaved as the Trolls."

Rounding off the nine was a woman who looked nothing like the others. She had a black cowboy's hat pulled down slightly over her face. She had long blonde hair tied down in a long braid falling over her shoulder, a black button-down shirt, blue jeans, and a pair of cowboy boots. A pair of revolvers were at her side, something that other patrons would have been shocked by, even with the protection spells. When the group arrived, she raised the tip of her hat and I saw who she was. Shit.

"Damn," Shannon muttered beside me, recognizing her too.

It was Daelia Thornwood, the so-called Gunmage. The murderous environment and multiple Cold Wars fostered by the Great Lie had created hundreds of independent operators in-between the various powers. If you were willing to work for the monsters as well as the humans, there was no end of work you could find—especially if you were willing to kill.

The Gunmage was one of the worst, having over fifty-confirmed monster kills. And four times that in human deaths. She was also a relative newcomer, having only appeared on the scene in the last couple of years. Roland Cassidy had brought a hitman to our meeting.

"Well," I said, ignoring my discomfort and extending my hand. "I'm glad to see you made it."

"When one of my fellow Committee members invites me to chat, I better come!" Roland said, his voice filled with false cheer and good will. He took my artificial hand and squeezed it. The pain was tremendous, and I knew, in that moment, he could crush the mechanics inside without breathing hard. Roland was just as good at ki manipulation as me, either that or he had some other method of rendering himself supernaturally strong. "Is this the infamous Shannon O'Reilly?"

"Infamous?" Shannon asked, looking at the enslaved fae. Slavery wasn't something the Committee tolerated when it was done to humans—supernaturals were a different story. Indeed, it was only Shannon's willing service and sworn oaths that kept our mages from binding her.

"Yeah," Roland said, making finger guns and pointing them at her. "You killed my cousin."

"Uh," Shannon said, rubbing the back of her head. "Yeah. Sorry about that."

"Liar," Roland said, giving an empty smile.

I mentally flashed back to Cassandra's island base in an old hotel she'd owned. Everything had been falling apart for her, her schemes exposed, most of her soldiers dead, and she'd still tried to kill me. Shannon had put a bullet in her head. It was one of the worst memories of my life. As much chaos and destruction as she'd caused, I didn't hate her. I, instead, saw her as the victim of the mental control of the House and her father, Roland's uncle.

"Great job," Roland said, stretching his smile into painful proportions. "Real bitch, that one."

"Right." Shannon said, as uncomfortable as me.

Roland took a step back and put his hands on his hips. "I will say, not all of the family was pleased with her death. I managed to blunt the worst of their vengeance but watch out for any horrifying death curses or mystical STDs coming your way. Ha-ha."

"Ha-ha," I said, without humor.

My twin sister Penny's spells on me had protected me from over a dozen magical assassination attempts last year. A thirteenth had been deflected by my father, this one having involved human sacrifice. We'd never tracked down the source for half of them.

"No, Cassandra was a horrifying psychopath," Roland said, putting one hand on his side. "It would have fallen to the Cassidys to deal with her if not for you, so I owe you two a favor. You should rejoin the family, Derek. I have sisters, cousins, and even a couple of divorced stepmothers. Take your pick."

"No, thank you," I said, dryly. I could tell Roland hated me. It was good because that was a normal, even sane, response.

"Aww, you sure? They're all lovely and obedient—provided you keep your checkbook open."

Shannon glared at Roland, looking at him like he was something nasty she'd just walked through. I didn't blame her.

My desire to punch Roland in the face grew. "I'm here to discuss business."

"In due time." Roland took a moment to survey the hole we were currently playing. "You know, Cassandra loved golf. She could play at a professional level, ditto tennis. My cousin was a woman of many talents. Businesswoman, politician, scientist. It was her vision to slowly reveal the supernatural to the world and change the world with magitech."

"Too bad her plan involved turning people into zombies," Shannon said. "Oh and cooperating with terrorists."

"They're not terrorists if they're your allies, then they're freedom fighters or partisans," Roland said, smiling. "Pantheon Corp would never sell to terrorists, but we dump more guns onto militant radicals, dictators, and religious extremists than anyone but the United States. If they do their job, it doesn't matter who gets hurt along the way."

"What a lovely philosophy," Shannon said.

"Eventually, of course, we have to kill them too but that just means future markets," Roland said, turning back to us. "Another thing Cassandra knew. Sometimes you need to kill a few elephants to make an ivory piano."

"That's a horrifying metaphor," Shannon said, looking away.

"Only if you like elephants," Roland said, swinging his club wildly. "You know, you really fucked up with that Dracula thing."

"I did?" I asked. "I thought the House hated the Vampire Nation."

"We do," Roland said. "However, he was a nice little voice for the radicals. Without him, the moderates have taken over."

"Vampires have moderates?" Shannon asked.

"Yep," Roland said. "Ones that believe humans and vampires can live together in harmony. Well, at least vampires ruling over humans with their wealth, immortality, and beauty. They've been preparing to reveal themselves for a century. They've started preparing for their reveal with our government contacts. They're offering to bail the US government out in exchange for amnesty."

"Where the hell would they get that kind of money," I asked, stunned. "Vampires are rich but no one is that rich."

"The House is," Roland said, taking a perfect swing with his own club. It was perfect and landed right next to the hole. "A Committee member is helping them with this plan. They hit the House gold reserves where we store all the Knights Templar's treasure and Nazi plunder. The warehouse where we keep UFOs and the Ark of the Covenant too."

"That's real?" Shannon asked.

"Shh," I said. "What's that have to do with me?"

"Honestly, most of us thought it was you," Roland said. "Enough to have you killed."

I was past the point of being suspicious to outright convinced Roland was the enemy in all this. He was baiting me, trying to test my reaction to Cassandra's name and tormenting me with the fact our relationship had been nothing more than politics. Either that or he just was horrible at playing politics. "We didn't come here to discuss elephants or vampires. Are you confessing to trying to have me killed?"

"Confessing? No." Roland went to get a club from his bag. "But I know about your elf problem."

I stared at him, aware of the four-inch difference in our heights. "You know?"

Roland's smile turned dangerous as he gave me a playful slap on the shoulder. "Of course, I know. Follow me."

I gave Shannon a half-confused look. This was either proceeding much better than I expected or about to go horribly wrong. "Alright."

Roland walked to the first hole, his steps long and deliberate as if he didn't have a care in the world. "Do you know what I used to do before they made me President of Pantheon Corp?"

"You worked on drones," I said, remembering the articles on his research in *Newsweek*.

"Pfft," Roland said, picking up his full golf bag with one hand as if lifting a paperclip. "Drones were just the beginning. I worked on *automated warfare*."

Drone warfare was one of the few areas the Red Room lagged behind mundane authorities. We borrowed them on occasion, but it was still something we hadn't fully embraced. For millennium, the Red Room and its predecessor organizations had sent soldiers on the ground to eliminate superhuman threats. The idea of just pushing a button and firing orichalcum bullets or anti-magic rockets into a target took some getting used to. My father, an otherwise modernist sort of fellow, called it 'war with toy airplanes.'

"You don't strike me as the scientist type," Shannon said, keeping her gaze even.

"I don't have to be as long as I have them in my employ. I tell them what I want and they make it happen. It's the way science out to be," Roland said, looking at her as if he wanted to start beating her over the head with the bag in his hands. "Anyway, the United States and House have a never-ending need for expendable soldiers. The little planes I used to make were a stopgap between my real goal—that is to create an autonomous army. What do you think?"

"I think drones save a lot of lives and are an inevitable advance of war. I don't like the laws behind their usage but that's not what you're talking about, is it?" And yes, I understood I was being an enormous hypocrite criticizing drones being used as assassination weapons when I, myself, was an assassin.

"No," Roland said, stopping over his ball. He set down his golf bag and pulled out a nine iron. It was a terrible choice given the shot he needed to make. "Living weapons are the way of the future. Wizards have been creating artificial soldiers since time memorial. Talos the giant statue, the Jewish Golem, and your friend Talbot were just the beginning. My idea is to combine modern technology with what we've learned from the past to create the true electric soldier. A weapon that doesn't fear, hesitate, or die. It'll be the only way to handle the supernatural when they go public. You see, I support a reveal. I support *the* Reveal. One that ends this shitstorm of corporate-controlled democracy, no matter how beneficial to me, and has a return to the wizard kings of old. A world where humanity is so terrified of the supernatural that they abridge all freedoms and turn on their governments."

"So, you're a lunatic," I said, dryly.

Roland smiled. "The funny thing is I'm not the Committee member who is working with the Vampire Nation. I am, however, behind the assassination attempt on you."

"But you just said—" Shannon started to say.

"*Now* I'm confessing. It's all about timing." Roland didn't miss a beat. "Those hybrids are a wonderful product of Pantheon Corp genetics and alchemy. The perfect disposable soldiers. Stronger, faster, and prettier than regular humans but obedient to the end. Best of all, no families to whine and complain when they're dead. The old sidhe magicians knew their stuff, I can tell you."

"The Committee won't stand for this," I said, already having a sneaking suspicion I'd be outplayed there.

Roland turned back to me, a coy grin on his face. He handed his nine-iron back to one of his harpies.

"Oh, Derek." Roland shook his head, amused at my confusion. "It was the Committee who asked me to kill you."

"So this is an ambush," I said, dryly.

Roland nodded. "Pretty much, yeah."

CHAPTER SEVEN

The idea the Committee wanted to have me killed should have surprised me but didn't. After all, I'd been dragging my feet on their decisions, impeding their more batshit insane plans, and working for peace when everyone else wanted war. Given the only way to join the Committee was to kill an existing member and adding a thirteenth diluted their power, it made sense they intended to replace me with Roland. Hell, I couldn't even blame destroying Camp Zero for this, they'd been setting up Roland to replace me before my coma. I'd just been stupid enough to miss the signs. Crap.

Shannon reached over to place her hand on my shoulder. "It'll be alright."

"No, it won't," I whispered.

"You should have seen it coming," Roland said, shaking his head. "No one was exactly happy when you ascended to the throne. You came in with a bunch of swagger, high ideals, and disrespect. You hadn't paid your dues. You could have solidified your place, made the right alliances, and gotten yourself secure. No, instead, you decided to coast on your daddy's wealth and influence. You sought to change things and when push came to shove, they couldn't count on you to side with the humans instead of the monsters."

"Says the man who is creating an army of half-elf slaves," I said, staring at him. "I'm pretty sure most of the Committee thinks our job is to destroy the supernatural, not make more of it."

"Disposable cannon fodder, my friend. The perfect weapons since they're not human and legally have no rights. Made from the remains of the Nazi elves and their children who fled to Pantheon Corp's waiting arms after World War 2. That includes the Cassidys by the way. We were half in Hitler's pocket and half in the House's like good old Henry Ford," Roland said, looking at Shannon. "The hybrids have other benefits too. No one minds if you fuck the monsters, just don't marry them."

"Can I rip his head off, Derek? I really want to."

The Gunmage moved to her weapons as did the Trolls. Even the Harpies seemed ready to go after Shannon, despite the fact their eyes showed approval.

"The spells on this place would prevent that," I said, shaking my head. "I wouldn't go sitting down at the big boy's table just yet, Roland. Other people have tried to take me out before, many of them a lot smarter than you. All of them are dead."

It was quite liberating to know the Committee had marked me for death. I no longer had to work within their rules. I'd hated them for a long time and knowing they were my enemy now, family or not, made things easier. Maybe it was impossible to take down the Committee but I'd sure as hell give it try. I'd start with Roland too.

Good, Bloody Mary purred. *I'll be right there to join you.*

Excuse me? I asked. I hadn't seen Mary since she'd generated a body to physically walk the Earth. She was always in my mind, but I had no idea where she was with an actual form. Mostly because she was a psychotic embodiment of war. I thought she'd be wandering around battlefields somewhere, soaking up the ambiance.

Do not fret, Mary whispered. *I will always be near you.*

"I also refuse to believe the House as a whole would approve of what you've done." Shannon came to my defense. "What Derek has done seems a far cry from blowing up a hospital we keep our operatives in."

Roland gave a shrug, undisturbed. "Everyone wanted it to look like a terrorist attack. You've made yourself annoyingly popular with the rank and file. Killing Dracula and the Wazir has people confused that you're a hero. Better you become a star on the wall giving your life in the service of the Red Room than getting the traitor's death you deserve."

"Why not just pull the plug while I was in a coma?" I asked, noting he hadn't mentioned Ashley. The description of the soldiers who kidnapped her was the same as the appearance of the ones who assaulted the hospital. I wasn't stupid enough to believe there were two armies of half-elf stormtroopers running around. Roland had to be behind both.

"Your father was at your side the entire time," Roland said, taking a step back so I could take my turn. "He objected to his son being killed. I can't imagine why. It's not like he doesn't have a dozen replacements."

I walked over to the tee and placed my ball down, continuing to feign disinterest. "He didn't warn me I was under the threat of death either. So, you accepted this meeting just to, what, gloat? Is there a hit squad in the parking lot?"

"Yes, but not quite," Roland said, watching me send the ball into the air. "Of course, the Committee isn't going to have much of a place soon either."

"What do you mean?" Shannon said, standing protectively behind me. It was telling the Harpies and Trolls weren't anxious to fight her. The Gunmage, though, was smiling in an unwholesome manner.

She *wanted* to fight us.

"I'll get to that," Roland said, shrugging. "I can't say it's not a pleasure watching you squirm like the little half-monster worm you are."

"What do you want, Roland?" He wouldn't be here if he didn't have an angle to play.

"I wanted to see if you might make a deal," Roland said, raising his golf club. "The Committee is as you say, past its prime. You've already killed one member and had enough information on the others to blackmail them into granting you membership. Give it to me and there might be a place for you in the New Order. I could always use a good assassin and my new allies have asked for your pardon."

"You're calling it the *New Order*? Not afraid to stereotype, are we?"

"Why mess with the classics?" Roland asked, smiling. "The seers are all in agreement, a great change is imminent. The

House will fall into chaos, collapsing like dominos, one Division after another. The sole reason Cassandra's coup didn't succeed was your intervention and her inability to control the Wazir."

"And you think you'll be able to do a better job?" I asked, wondering just how crazy Roland is.

"I'm saying that, within the next seven days, the House will cease to exist, and the Truth will come out. Then the world will need new leadership."

"After you make the world terrified of the supernatural," I said.

"Yep," Roland said. "The Committee lacked vision. They should never have covered up the supernatural. They should have been pointing to dead babies and drained white girls on the nightly news every night. Rakshasas teaching schools. Scary brown people throwing lightning, film at eleven. Much better justification for the Military Industrial Complex's continued funding and making sure your votes don't matter."

Roland wasn't just an asshole, he was a fascist. "So, I'm stupid for not making the right friends on the Committee but you're perfectly sane for thinking you can overthrow them? The Chairman will eat you alive."

"You don't know my friends," Roland said, smiling. "Mine are bigger deals than your arm candy."

"You have problems with women, don't you?" Shannon asked, unimpressed. "A sure sign of sexual insecurity."

Roland's glare could have melted steel.

The Gunmage, by contrast, gave a half-smirk.

"What's going to happen in seven days?" I asked, doing my best to appear interested in his offer. "Does this have anything to do with Ashley? Can we negotiate there?"

Apparently, my best wasn't good enough. Roland's eyes darkened and he curled his lip in disgust. "You're humoring me."

"I assume it's something you're used to, what with the fact you believed I'd help you in a plan that seriously involves the idea of world domination. I love comic books as much as the next man but that's just…stupid."

Roland reached up as if to strangle me and I realized he

would have done so, if not for some invisible force keeping him from wrapping his fingers around my neck. This one act confirmed what had been dancing around in the back of my head for a while now, but I only now was confident in believing: Roland *was* a psychopath.

It was almost impossible to run a business as rich and powerful as Pantheon Corp when you were mentally ill, hell any sort of business at all, but the Cassidys were a breed apart. I could see the army of publicists and lawyers covering up his darker deeds. Worse, he had access to the House's resources. I wondered how many people he'd killed over the years and what other sorts of atrocities lied buried in his past.

"It seems Saint George's spells really do keep me protected as much as they keep you from getting a ki strike to the face," I said, watching him fail to strangle me. "Which is good for you, otherwise I would have killed you by now. You're exactly the sort of insane man child with supernatural powers the House was formed to fight."

Roland looked ready to explode, beat me to death, or throw golf clubs—perhaps some combination of the three. The three Harpies looked terrified, shivering while the Trolls looked between each other. I'd never seen an ordinary human have that sort of effect on supernaturals. It was like they'd had all the fight beaten out of them.

As quick as it had begun, Roland was calm. Almost serene. Clasping his hands together, he said, "You're making a mistake. I'm the sole way you're walking off this golf course alive. I've got your ex tied all wrapped up and if you ever want to see her again then you better start negotiating."

Despite knowing it was impossible, I tried to knock his head clean off. My arm couldn't even raise itself to strike. "Ashley is not a commodity to be bought, traded, or passed around. She is a person. Something you seem incapable of understanding."

"Spare me the melodrama. Ashley Morgan's a traitor, a *useful* traitor but a traitor. The only reason she's alive now is because I need her—for reasons you're never going to find out." The haughtiness in his voice was beyond belief.

"You're not an agent, Roland," I said, staring at him. "If you were, you'd have known I've been egging you on this entire time. You'd have made your offer in a way that didn't make you look like a fucking lunatic and you'd have done so from a position of strength. All you've done is let me goad you until you've revealed half your plans."

"I hope you enjoy dying," Roland said, pointing at my chest with another pair of finger guns. It was a childish gesture that made me hate him more. "I'll be doing lines of crystalized vampire blood off a supermodel in Ibiza when I get the news of your execution."

"You shouldn't do that," I said, unimpressed with his posturing. "The stuff impairs your thinking."

Roland grabbed his bag, tossed it to one of the Harpies who caught it and held it in the air despite being twice her size and then started walking off the field. His entourage followed him, the Gunmage staying behind.

The Gunmage just gave us a small salute before resuming her walk behind them. "Nice meeting ya."

"Same," I said, waving.

She walked away.

"That was nice of her," Shannon said. "Too bad we have to kill her."

"Agreed," I said, shaking my head. "How the hell did Roland rise as high as he did?"

Roland wasn't trying to drag me off the golf course, which meant he had another plan on how to deal with me. Something that would plough through the magical defenses of Saint George's Country Club. Either that or just knew we'd eventually have to leave. The entire House was against us now. Hero of the hour or not.

"Yes, because douchebag misogynist frat-boys turned CEOs are so uncommon in the world," Shannon said, watching them depart. "At least we know Ashley is alive."

"For now," I said.

"He wanted her for something other than a bargaining chip. Something there's a limited time frame to. Ashley was the most powerful psychic alive at the time of her disappearance. What could he want her for?"

"Roland said everything would come apart in seven days," Shannon asked, looking at me. "Do you think he's going to be the one to reveal the Truth? Like some big huge act of eso-terrorism?"

"Possibly," I said, staring at her. "If so, he's just derivative of his cousin."

"So what do you want me to do now?" Shannon asked.

I picked up my driver and took another practice swing. "I want to continue following clues to find Ashley and take that sonofabitch down."

"That's going to be difficult if the Red Room starts sending hit squads against us."

"Yes," Shannon said. "You realize we could find the island now and retire there. I can shape-shift and you're a wizard. We can find a way to hide."

I turned to her. "Do you want to spend the rest of your life with me, even if it's on the run?"

Shannon's eyes met me. "Do you remember what your reaction was when you first found out I was a Lilin?"

"I pulled a gun on you. Not the greatest sign of acceptance."

Shannon's lip curled into a smirk. "If you'd accepted someone who just revealed she'd been lying to you and was a part of a race of Satan-worshiping fae responsible for countless deaths over the years, I'd have no respect for you."

Shannon let some of her self-control lapse and I felt a wave of heat rush across my face and body. She was physically unchanged but everything about her just seemed to become magnetic. I wanted to wrap my arms around her and drag her into the bushes for a round of hot, passionate lovemaking and not to stop until we were both exhausted.

"Ever since I turned twelve, Derek, people have wanted to use me or keep me as a pet. You're not the only person I've ever been able to get to think of me as an equal but you're one of the two I've ever loved. I hate admitting it, though, because it's a weakness. I don't know about spending my life with you but I'm considering it."

"Two?" I asked.

"Don't push it." Shannon walked up to me and the two of us

exchanged a passionate kiss, which wiped away all the tension and horror we were feeling. Holding her against me, I felt I could take on the whole world. "I'm willing to stay by you thick and thin. Just don't think that I want to marry you or anything. I'm still as commitment phobic as ever."

"Thank you," I said.

"You're welcome," Shannon said, smiling. It was like the whole world was contained within her mouth. "Now that we're on the same page, how about we go ambush golden boy out in the parking lot, drag him someplace horrible, and smack him around until he talks."

"Torture doesn't—" I started to say.

"Does he know that? Besides, it'll be fun," Shannon said, grinning.

I snorted. "I'm not a sadist."

"I can fake being one. I can find other ways of getting him to talk, though. We also have a psychic."

"Point taken," Shannon said.

I kissed her again. I was starting to think of ways we could pull this off when there was a distinct wheezing noise of machinery and humming in the distance. Pulling back, I turned and closed my left eye before focusing on my right. Like binoculars, I zeroed in on the parking lot and saw a sight that was unusual even by my standards.

There were six of them with more pouring out of the back of the trucks outside. Each stood about ten feet tall with rectangular steel-girder-like legs and a flat-featureless bar-like top on both. The ends of the legs were turned inward, facing one another and I saw the machines weren't walking but floating across the ground. Underneath its top, I saw their bottoms open up to reveal machine guns and miniature rocket-launchers.

These weren't the products of regular science, despite their appearances. Too much was in advance of what was available even to the military. No, they were magitech devices—larger and more dangerous than anything I'd seen attempted. Each had enough firepower, by the looks of it, to give a modern tank a run for its money. The machines might have been operated by remote but I guessed they weren't, instead being autonomous machines with no soul or life to animate them—just as Roland had spoken about working on. Just the sort of devices you'd want if you were going to assassinate someone on a golf course where it was impossible for the living to harm one another. They were impossible devices that violated the Great Lie but perfect for use once the Truth was out.

And they were coming this way.

"What is it?" Shannon asked behind me.

I adjusted my false eye, losing the binoculars function. "It looks like a bunch of robots are coming to kill us."

Shannon blinked then stared at me. "*Robots?*"

The world just got a helluva lot stranger.

CHAPTER EIGHT

I stared at the army of mechanized assassins floating toward us. "We should run now."

"Yeah, to the north-east." Shannon pointed behind her, not taking her eyes off the advancing robot's direction. "There's a lot of hills that way and foliage. It's also where the nearest egress to the roads are."

I nodded and the two of us dropped everything and bolted. I moved in a zigzag pattern, which was a good thing since behind me dirt piles flew up into the air as the creatures started firing from their maximum range. It was a good thing they didn't have a sniper rifle since we would have been killed then and there.

"Do you have any anti-ballistic spells woven into that outfit?!" Shannon called to me as we ran.

"Yeah, but nothing that will stand up to *that!*" I shouted, right before a glancing shot struck my shoulder and eradicated most of my protection, sending me tumbling down a large hill into a sand trap.

"I hate irony." Shannon slid down the hill into the sand trap beside me.

"That's more apropos." I struggled to get up.

"Shut up!" Shannon said, easily picking me up despite her size and putting me in a fireman's carry. The Lilin began running every bit as fast as she'd done before. Faster even, which made me realize she'd been holding back for me.

"This is embarrassing," I said.

"Wonder Woman does it all the time," Shannon said.

"I'm more a Marvel guy. If you'd said Captain Marvel—"

"I will throw you at them!" Shannon shouted.

Pulling out my gun, I struggled to keep my finger tight behind the trigger and my palm around the grip. My hand was shaking like a box with a cat in it, even without Shannon running across uneven terrain beneath me. I didn't know if my pistol was capable of penetrating its armor, orichalcum or not, but I had to try and slow these things down.

When the first of the gigantic robot Space Invaders popped over the end of the hill, lifting its gigantic machine guns in our direction, my doubts became more than severe. They became absolute certainty we were going to die.

Still, I fired.

First, I put two rounds into the robot's miniature rocket launcher and did my best to influence probability with my magic. I'd put on my old wedding ring and, enhanced with a bunch of black magic given to me by a disturbingly helpful demon, it meant the spell went off without a hitch. The rockets inside exploded and the machine went down into the sand trap with a beautiful explosion.

Two more of the monstrous machines moved over the hill we'd fallen under and started aiming their weapons. My next shots went wild, the bullets pinging against their armor as I struggled to get enough magical energy together to aim my shots right.

My artificial arm and eye interfered with my magic, preventing me from summoning my ki perfectly while my most powerful sorcery was related to blood and shadows. Given it was a bright clear day with no handy blood sacrifices, I was out of luck for anything more than parlor tricks.

"We're almost there!" Shannon called out beneath me.

Looking to where Shannon was running, I saw a group of trees forming a small forest and, further beyond, a fence with a road behind it. She was right. We had a chance of making it. We'd have to steal a car, but escape was no longer a ridiculous supposition. Two robots then opened fire at the exact moments.

"TARGET LOCKED ON," the robots spoke in eerie unison. It told me they'd been made in committee because there was no reason for them to speak other than intimidation factor.

Shannon was an amazing runner, an even more spectacular agent, and possessed of superhuman strength but even she couldn't outrun bullets. That required magic to bend the very laws of time and space. The most Shannon could achieve was getting slightly ahead of the rockets before the ground beneath us exploded. Both of us fell and rolled across the grass below.

Above our heads, the sky darkened, and storm clouds blotted out the sun. Shadows covered everything and I felt power run into my fingertips. Combined with the ring, I was far more powerful than I was at the hospital—but it didn't matter because I'd been shot repeatedly in the torso by the robot's high caliber ammunition.

Raindrops started pouring down upon us from above, covering the ground with water to mix with the blood pouring from my chest. I couldn't move because it was taking both hands to keep my guts from falling out of my chest. I didn't feel anything, which was worse than immense agony because I knew it meant I was going into shock. Worse, I knew if I raised my head, it would be blown off by the robot coming in for the kill. I was dying and didn't want to turn my head to see what had happened to Shannon. Roland had us dead to rights. For a man I'd dismissed as a dilettante and a playboy, he'd lured me into the perfect trap. Shannon had to be my priority, though, so I turned my head.

The sight that greeted me made me want to vomit. Shannon's legs were shredded and spread across the ground. She was slowly transforming into her succubus form but not her lower half, orichalcum bullets having been used by the monstrous machine bearing down on us. Shannon might be able to recover from it, the orichalcum bullets having passed straight through, but the amount of energy necessary to heal such wounds would be staggering. Roland had spared no expense in creating his assassins and two Senior agents, no matter how skilled, were no match for a billion dollars' worth of hardware.

That was when I heard a voice in my ear. It was soft, feminine, and familiar. *Do you want to live?*

"Yes," I said, watching the robot come within ten feet of us and aim its machine guns. Time seemed to slow down.

How much? The voice teased. Its tone was relaxed, as if the fact my lover and I were about to die didn't matter.

Enough to do anything, I whispered words that should never be spoken to a supernatural creature. Caveats were good in this sort of situation. *Almost anything, at least.*

Good. The woman's voice. *Take your blade, my love.*

I saw the tip of a sword hilt emerge from the bloody entrails of my guts. The robot stood there, frozen in time, as I saw the raindrops were barely moving. Sticking my right hand into my guts, I felt pain for the first time. Agonizing, horrific, and mind-shattering pain.

Wrapping my fingertips around the blade, I pulled the weapon out of my stomach. It slid out with a sickening noise like a butcher slicing fresh meat. In my hands was a blood-red stained Chinese *jiang*, its hilt decorated with the image of a skeletal cloaked figure on a red horse.

I had the Bloodsword again.

In the Red Room Registry for Mystical Artifacts, the Bloodsword ranked as the sixth most dangerous item in the world. Forged in the fires of Hell by Tiamat-Abaddon, the weapon was presented to Dracula so that he could take peace from the earth, and that men would slay one another. Its keeper, the fury demoness Bloody Mary, had determined I was a better candidate to wield it. She'd helped me against Dracula, proclaiming her adoration for me and that I was the world's greatest assassin. I was never gladder to be helltouched.

Using blood magic, I drew all my spilled blood back into my body. The agony was unlike anything I could conceive but I hardly noticed—the Bloodsword turning that torment into something I could use as a weapon.

The drone unleashed its gunfire upon me and the bullets slowly moved toward me along with a set of rockets. My eyes were crazy with pain and madness, the rage inside my belly from their attack drowning out all reason. Lifting the sword, I drew all the darkness around us and unleashed it outwards like a torrential river.

The ammunition and rockets were swallowed, orichalcum or not, and the top of the robot vanished like it had been eaten.

Obscuromancy did not just control shadows but a primordial stygian *nothingness* that existed between all the substance of the cosmos. The nothingness that compromised the lowest circle of hell.

"Robots!" I shouted, laughing. It was an insane sort of laughter, totally divorced from reality. "I'm not dead yet!"

Had I been in my right mind, I would have immediately gone to Shannon's side and tried to use my power to heal her. The Bloodsword was not a tame artifact, though, allowing its wielder to use it for just anything. The weapon was linked to Bloody Mary, who had fallen in love with me because of my capacity for carnage. When I was at my strongest, I could hold back her influence and use the Bloodsword for good. I wasn't at my strongest.

Four more robots came over the hill, aiming their weapons. I moved like the world was a symphony and I was a note traveling through the air, slashing the first in half with a jump too high for any mortal to make only to slash another in half. as I fell. Gunfire and rockets filled the air before more darkness, each a slithering tentacle of blackness across reality, tearing through them all at once. Exploding pieces of metal, circuits, and wire flew and rolled across the soaked greens around us. There were two more robots, but I had no doubt that they would be little more than an annoyance.

That was when I was shot in my right hand, a rifle round going through it and sending the Bloodsword flying from my grip. The weapon buried itself in the ground several feet away and I felt all the massive power coursing through me leak away into the world around me. Looking up, I saw with my right eye to the tower of the country club mansion. There, lying down, was the Gunmage holding a sniper rifle.

"Crap," I said. "Should have seen that coming."

I fell to the ground as another round zinged over my head. The two robots advanced on me and their weapons re-armed. I had to give Roland credit; I hadn't seen that one coming. Even with me totally outgunned and surrounded, he'd made sure to leave his best agent there to take care of me. Too bad I was *really* pissed off.

Pulling the sword back to my ruined hand and holding it in place with a black tendril of shadow wrapped around the ruined mass, I lifted the weapon to the sky right before a hail of bullets was fired. A bolt of lightning descended into the Bloodsword as I channeled the energy outward, barely feeling it move through my body in two arcs that caused every bullet to scatter before exploding out the backsides of the two robots.

A second bolt of lightning descended where I held it inside the Bloodsword and turned it to the tower of the mansion, unleashing it across the golf course before striking home. The tower became an inferno, fire spreading across the rooftop of the mansion as the hellish energies hungered for the blood of those inside. Somehow, I knew I hadn't killed the Gunmage. But I bet she was feeling a serious headache.

More blood, the voice whispered in my ear. *Feed me.*

You've had your fill, I thought back, struggling to get control of the immense rage coursing through my body. I wanted to go to the mansion and kill every single person inside, guest and server alike. Leave me alone.

Machines don't count, Bloody Mary's voice became clear and distinct. *The blood of living, thinking, feeling beings is all that will satiate me.*

A hissing noise was heard behind me. Something I'd only heard once before in my life, back when I'd been confronting a bunch of draugr with Shannon in the bowels of Division One's underground bunker. Turning around, I felt the agony and exhaustion return to me as the Bloodsword ceased to protect me from their bite. The weapon demanded blood, like a God of Chaos, it wanted it now and didn't care who it came from.

Behind me was Shannon in her true form. Naked, she'd torn apart her clothes reverting to her Lilin self. Her body was impossibly beautiful but terrible and alien as well, a creature from the Spirit World blessed and cursed with the fallen Elohim Lilith's blood. Leather black wings extended from her back while her fingers extended into razor-sharp claws. Fangs jutted out of her mouth while her feet were replaced by hooves. A tail slithered from her backside, red and writhing. As for her other features, they were like an angel's—flawless and lovely.

I'd only seen a single creature in my life more beautiful and that had been a true angel: hell's own ruler.

The look in Shannon's eyes was one of hunger and hatred, the regeneration of her legs having taken away her humanity. She needed to feed every bit as much as the Bloodsword, which is what the cursed relic wanted from me.

The Bloodsword wanted death and had placed someone in front of me to slay in self-defense. Never mind the fact the person it wanted me to kill was the most important one in my life. If I didn't strike down Shannon, though, she'd tear every bit of life-force from my body. Before she knew what she was doing, she'd drain me to death.

Choose, Bloody Mary whispered. *Your life or hers. Show me why you are my champion.*

Shannon leapt for my throat, only to land behind me as I moved the slightest bit of my shoulders to dodge out of the way. Jeet Kune Do, the martial arts style I favored when not using a sword, favored economy of movement. The preservation of energy was vital right now since I didn't have much else.

I could barely keep the Bloodsword in my hands, let alone fight one of the most powerful supernaturals I'd ever encountered. Shannon might not be a god, archwizard, or Lord of the Vampires but she was quick and even in this feral state—probably a better fighter than me.

Shannon was up like a cobra and I ducked under her next strike, pulled back for her second, and felt the third cut light strips off flesh from my abdomen. Bloody Mary was right, I had to choose whether one of us would die. Grabbing Shannon by the wrist, I hurled her over my shoulders into the woods nearby. The incline of the hill caused her to fall across the ground, giving me a few seconds to act.

"I choose...myself," I said.

I lifted the Bloodsword over my head, blade down, before slamming it into my stomach. The end didn't come out the other side but I felt every inch of its dark power enter my body. Summoning the magic, I sent a torrent of ki energy into Shannon so that she might recover. I didn't want her wandering around the Country Club, killing people for their life-force. She deserved better than to have more innocent blood on her hands.

Bloody Mary was speechless.

I collapsed and everything went dark.

CHAPTER NINE

I was familiar with the space between life and death. I'd never been Lazarus-style resurrected from the dead but I'd been close to passing over enough times to know what it's like, at least for individuals aware enough of magic to know when a spirit is about to leave its body or is disassociated from the so-called mortal coil. What magicians called Limbo. Want to know how it feels?

It *sucks*.

It's like being underwater at night without the ability to drown. It's not unpleasant, at least at the start, but I can't recommend the experience. You lie suspended in liquid blackness, the kind I used to fuel my shadow magic, with nothing but your thoughts to keep you company. All you've got is perfect recollection of your memories, which you are forced to relive if you want to have anything to do. This wouldn't be so bad if I could focus on the pleasant memories.

Ashley and I working to heal the trauma of some abused victims of black magic.

Talbot teaching me the basics of Jeet Kune Do.

Christopher and I on that wild mission to Vegas in order to retrieve the future savior of humanity from lusty Kitsune. Penny, Rebecca, Stephen, Nathan, and the rest of the family gathered around the family Christmas tree. No, none of those memories.

It was always the regret and might-have-been memories that bubbled to the surface. I remembered killing Rebecca, my departure with Ashley, losing my partners, Cassandra's dead eyes staring up at me, failing to save Christopher from becoming a vampire, and worse. I tried to focus, instead, on a specific memory. One that was unpleasant but not traumatizing. I could use that to find my way out of Limbo, to either life or the afterlife.

What was going to happen next was nothing more than a remembrance of the past—a memory that I was reliving. I was sitting in the front passenger's side seat of a parked standard-issue black 2007 Cadillac. The sort of vehicle the Red Room liked you to travel in when you were impersonating an FBI agent or other government official. But remember I did. It was like I was there, living out the events of the past, even as I was here in the present.

It's a wizard thing.

It was years ago, and I was still partnering with Ashley. I wasn't a Senior agent yet but was moving my way up the ranks. I hadn't yet killed so many people it'd become common place either. I could still look at myself in the mirror and see a human being with a future.

"Bad dreams?" Ashley asked to my side. She looked so young, or maybe it was just the fact we weren't yet worn down by the compromises and lies yet. It had only been a few months since I'd recruited her from her ill-considered vigilante activities in Boston.

"Yeah," I muttered, blinking. "I dreamt I died on a golf course, stabbing myself, in order to save a succubus."

"You read way too many comic books for an adult man, Derek."

"Oh, like children read comic books anymore. Besides, you're one to talk."

"You're the one who got me addicted." Ashley smiled. "Besides, I prefer the movies anyway."

Ashley was dressed as a government agent, just like me. She was wearing a black suit, tie, and sunglasses just like me. She was a Woman in Black and the look suited her. We were both overly dressed for the investigation but the Red Room's newest paymaster, an annoying prick calling himself the Professor, insisted on a strict dress code. Someone needed to tell him that nothing raised suspicions about government cover-ups than mysterious well-dressed government agents showing up and carting away evidence.

"Remind me again what we're doing here?" I asked, looking past Ashley to a decaying white house with overgrown grass in the middle of nowhere.

"Very funny," Ashley said, looking annoyed. "You know we're here investigating a sluagh."

Recognition dawned in my head as I remembered this case. Sluagh were the spirits of the restless dead taken by members of the Unseelie Court and altered into monsters who possessed the living. Once possessed, a human being transformed into a being that existed to terrify the living and claim young children for their sidhe (elven nobility) masters. With the elves all destroyed, there were no more sidhe to take the children to and a sluagh hadn't been seen in decades. Until now it seemed.

I recalled the reports now. They'd been sketchy but something matching a sluagh's description had been spotted in the area on numerous occasions. The strange thing was while there had been attacks, assaults, no one had been killed yet. The creature wasn't kidnapping children or torturing people to death—it was doing the equivalent of jumping out of bushes before saying boo. I recall finding the event curious but not troubling. After all, there was only one proper solution for non-House aligned supernaturals: destruction.

"Yes," I said, clearing my head. "And we've tracked the sluagh here."

"Are you feeling alright?" Ashley asked. Her voice was like cool rain on a man sunbaked in the desert.

I nodded. "Never better."

"Is this about Gwen and Marcus?" Ashley asked, surprising me.

It was like a gut punch, their names. I suddenly remembered things weren't all that perfect now even then. Gwen and Marcus were my young siblings, born 5th and 6th from my father's mistresses. Both had died not a month before, killed by their insane older brother Stephen. Stephen was possessed by a fallen angel, possessing more power than most archwizards, but the Red Room had chosen not to kill him. Influenced by my father, they'd locked him away in an asylum run by the White Room. Ashley had helped me capture Stephen, one of the many acts I'd never be able to repay her for.

"No," I said, taking a deep breath. "I hadn't been thinking about that at all."

"Liar," Ashley said, unbuckling her seatbelt. "I know you're disappointed with the decision they made regarding Stephen, but this is better. They'll be able to help him. With time, they can drive out the demon and cure his affliction."

I frowned, unbuckling my seatbelt as well. "Stephen didn't get possessed by a demon against his will. No, my brother willingly let the demon in. He was a partner in his own blood's deaths."

Kinslaying was the worst sin a person could do according to the Red Room and all the metaphysical texts I'd read. The gods of every pantheon in the astral plane turned their back on those who spilled the blood of their family. Marcus and Gwen had been good people, loyal servants of the Red Room, and champions of the House. Stephen was a traitor for killing them and turning against the House. I couldn't imagine a viler pair of crimes. I wanted Stephen executed, not helped.

"Are you ready to investigate?" Ashley said, picking up a black flashlight and shaking it in front of me. The house looked abandoned, which was a sure sign it *wasn't* in our line of work.

"Yes, I suppose I am." I said, opening the door and stepping out. The house was a one-story ranch with the grass overgrown and no houses for several blocks. Even before the man had undergone his transformation, he'd decided to live on the outskirts. There was a sense of the 'unclean' in the air, magic unnatural to the human condition.

Fairy magic.

"So what's our method of approach here?" Ashley asked, holding her flashlight tight.

"Find it and shoot it," I said.

Ashley stared at me. "Derek, must you make jokes at a time like this?"

"I wasn't joking," I said.

"No one's died yet." Ashley voice was calm.

"Sluagh aren't protected by any of the treaties we've signed with the other supernatural powers. They're dangerous. Sluagh are designed to derive pleasure from terrifying others and stealing kids. There's not a lot of wiggle room with what to do with them."

"So, if you're tempted to do evil, you should be treated like you've done evil?"

"My experience is humans are very bad at resisting temptation, so yeah."

Ashley stared. "We should try and take him alive. Maybe we can exorcise the spirit within or help him get control somehow."

I chose my next words carefully. "We have a responsibility to the greater good to do lesser evils sometimes. This includes making sure those who hurt other people are prevented from doing so, even if it's not their fault." I was getting tired of Ashley's bleeding-heart tendencies. She should save it for her fellow humans.

"You know I can hear you thinking about that sort of thing, right?" Ashley asked.

"Crap." I grimaced.

"It's alright, Derek," Ashley said, having long since made peace with my lies. "I know you're used to manipulating everyone around you."

"Then why do you stay with me?" I asked.

"Where else am I supposed to go?" Ashley said, shrugging. "Besides, we've done good work."

I remembered Ashley forcing the glowing fallen angel form of my brother Stephen back into his human body, overcoming a being who had help create the stars. "Yeah, I suppose we have."

"Can we try to save this one?" Ashley asked.

I shrugged. "Whatever you want."

I could spin capturing the sluagh and exorcising its host to the Red Room just like I'd done the past seven or eight cases. We hadn't always taken in our opponents alive, even Ashley understood it was sometimes necessary to use lethal force against the monsters, but we'd done it enough times that it was starting to become a pattern. The Red Room didn't much care for patterns, at least if they weren't in its favor, but they were willing to make exceptions for favored operatives.

Like Ashley.

"You can at least try not to think so condescendingly," Ashley said, shaking her head. "My way works."

I shrugged. "Whatever you say."

The two of us walked up onto the porch, the floorboards creaking as we did so. Ashley moved her hand to the door, preparing to knock, before I shot her a glance.

"Remember, we only have to do that when pretending to be the FBI," I said, leaning over. "It doesn't care one way or the other."

"Force of habit," Ashley said, lowering her hand. "I'm used to working with law enforcement rather than ignoring they exist."

"You should get over that. I quite enjoy ignoring they exist."

I reached into my jacket and pulled out my gun before testing the lock. The door was locked but Ashley just closed her eyes and caused it to unlock for us. One of the benefits of being telekinetic.

Saved me from picking it, at least.

Once inside, I saw the damaged and decimated interior of what was once someone's home. There were pieces of furniture scattered across the ground, shredded strips of wallpaper, and shattered picture frames. The place looked like the home of someone at war with themselves and leaning down to pick up a picture, I saw why.

The sluagh had a family. The man in the picture, John Harrison or something (I hadn't paid much attention to what Ashley had found out about him), was an average-looking man in his mid-thirties with ginger hair and a beard. His wife and child were also unexceptional looking—but they seemed happy.

"Sluagh don't often have families. Is there any sign of them in the attack reports?" I asked.

"Shouldn't you have read them?" Ashley retorted.

"I did," I lied, having just skimmed them. "I just wanted to hear your thoughts."

"He's divorced. His wife has full custody," Ashley said.

"Perhaps that's why he can't bring himself to attack

children," I said, shaking my head. "Memories of being a father himself."

Ashley stared at me. "And you think he deserves to die."

"Deserves has nothing to do with it." The supernatural and humanity were competing for their spot on this globe. Only one would survive.

"And a hearty sieg heil to you," Ashley said.

"Please stop reading my mind," I said.

"Please stop projecting racist thoughts. It makes me embarrassed to know you love the same stuff I do."

I rolled my eyes. "Thank you for cluing in our enemy with small talk."

"He's downstairs and can't hear us. He doesn't even know we're here in fact. Daytime is when he sleeps."

I did a double take. "Oh. Never mind then."

Damn psychics.

"I heard that." Ashley frowned.

I shrugged at her words then began checking doors one by one to find the right one. In the end, we found the door to the basement in the kitchen. It led down into complete blackness, all the windows having been sealed up. Checking the light switch to the side, I found it too had been shut off. Sluagh thrived in darkness, which meant this was its lair.

A twinge of fear filled my heart as I kept my gun out and Ashley provided the light with her flashlight. Going into a monster's lair was a last resort, a sign you had no recourse. Sluagh weren't the kind of creature that warranted backup, though—which meant we were on our own.

The stairs were slippery, covered in mud, and the two of us had to walk carefully in order to avoid falling. Once we reached about two-thirds of the way down, the stairs trailed into a large pool of black water. The smell was overpowering, like a swamp. I wondered what sort of horrible things were growing inside, simulating the Spirit World bogs that the sluagh lived in.

Ashley stared forward as if seeing something other than the goo in front of us. "I can see clearly into its mind now. John Harrison doesn't want to hurt people and is repulsed by his actions. It's a constant temptation to go out and do unconscionable things but he resists it. He's considered suicide on numerous occasions but can't bring himself to give up hope."

"An inspiring story," I lied, wondering how we were going to subdue him and drag him back to the Red Room for exorcism. It seemed an awful lot of trouble for a monster.

Ashley shot me a look.

"What did I say about reading my mind?" I snapped back.

"It's hard," Ashley said. "Anyway, it's…oh crap, he's waking up."

I rapidly moved my gun around, seeking some sign of the water's disturbance. I'd managed to survive some pretty hairy ordeals over the years and wasn't about to join the ranks of those many agents who perished in the line of duty. I hadn't yet come to the realization it was the very "shoot first, ask questions later" mentality taught at the Black Room that got so many agents killed.

I didn't have a chance to react before the sluagh emerged from the bottom of the stairs, grabbing me by the shirt with one hand and knocking away my gun with the other. It was a hideous creature that started with a man's body and added on terrifying extra-bits. Naked and hairless, its skin was scaly like a fish while its mouth had enlarged to become four times the size of a normal man's. Mandibles bearing extra-teeth were located on the sides of its gigantic mouth while its hands were more like crab claws.

I screamed while Ashley jolted, watching me get dragged underneath the brackish stinking water, all light going out around me. Reflexes and combat training had me jam my thumbs into the monster's eyes, struggling to hold it from biting a chunk out of my neck like I thought it was trying to do. The creature jolted upwards and we burst out of the water, still on the base of the stairs. That was when three shots rang out, orichalcum bullets striking into the monster in front of me. The sluagh fell backwards, thrashing on the ground.

Turning my head, I saw Ashley was holding her gun with the flashlight on the ground beside her. Her hands were shaking but the gun was held fast. Aiming the gun with both hands at the sluagh's head, Ashley pulled the trigger again and silenced it, no, him, forever.

Wet, beaten, and in need of several shots, I looked to her in gratitude. "Thank you."

"Don't," Ashley said. "This isn't something to be proud of."

I looked to the dead body and shook my head. It was the first time Ashley had ever killed and things would be different between us after that day. She would be more willing to pull the trigger in future engagements but, bizarre as it may sound, I was less likely to. The act of saving my life, even more than helping me capture my wayward brother, led to an understanding between us. A way of knowing that there were things she was willing to do to keep me alive she found reprehensible. All it took was the death of a monster trying to be a man.

It was as the memory ended, I found my way out of Limbo and felt my soul being drawn back to my body. I wasn't dead, for whatever that was worth, and someone was resuscitating me. The touch of the magic was familiar, and I could feel my body's injuries and drained life-force being healed or restored.

Given the fact I couldn't hear hospital machinery or feel CPR, I had to guess it was through magic. This limited the number of people who could be bringing me back. I had a sneaking suspicion as to who might be working their spells on me.

It was time to speak with Bloody Mary.

CHAPTER TEN

I woke up for a second time, this time to reality, with a splitting headache. The first thing I noticed was that I was in the back of a luxurious stretched limousine driving down the road. The next thing I noticed was there was a trio of naked bodies beside me. The second, as you might expect, caught my attention more than the first.

There was a man and a woman on the back of the seat, both beautiful, with the man passed out while the woman was being kissed. Shannon, still in her Lilin form, was atop both with her lips pressed against the woman's. Shannon was taking the woman's life-force. Shannon was feeding, though shallow enough as to not kill her food. Much longer, though, and the woman would die. I reached over, my mind still foggy, knowing Shannon wouldn't want to kill an innocent. Assuming they *were* innocent.

"They aren't," Mary's voice trailed over from the opposite side of the limousine. "However, neither have I allowed your friend to kill. I have bound her Lilin side to feed until it's full or the subject is endangered. I wouldn't worry as both her food sources have an abundance of life-force. Shannon just needed two to feed on as her feral side has been rather...*repressed* of late."

"I encourage her to eat well." I turned around to face my host, faking a smile. "I'd rather her have sex with other people than killing."

Across from me was a woman with dark red hair the color of blood. Mary was beyond gorgeous, forgoing the humility of Shannon but hiding it under heavy makeup and an almost Halloween-ish costume. Indeed, Mary was wearing greasepaint, her red hair in girlish braids, a blood-red corset like my sister favored, and a pair of black leather pants with a Little Red Riding Hood-like cape around her back.

Bloody Mary's eyes were a beautiful shade of blue like Shannon's. There was something both unsettling and reassuring about her, as if she combined a dozen people, I knew into a single entity who looked like all but none of them. I won't lie to you, despite or because of her quirks, I wanted her. Mary pushed every single one of my buttons and I found myself wanting to take both Shannon and her despite how insane the urge was. The Bloodsword fed my desire for carnage and when you suppressed that, the urges had to go somewhere.

"Yet, *you* do not eat as heartily," Mary said, smiling. "Which confuses me."

Mary's voice was silk on velvet, impossibly soft and conjured images to go with the words she spoke. Shameful ones. "If you want to get me into bed, all you had to do was ask."

Of course, Shannon would kill me. We had a strict 'no demons' policy in our relationship. Well, demons who still owed their service to hell.

"Perhaps after we discuss recent events," Mary said.

"Like what?" I asked.

"Look to your right."

I glanced down and saw a bright red and white striped umbrella by my side. It had a handle in the shape of a question mark. "What's that?"

"The Bloodsword," Mary said.

"You're kidding," I said.

"Congratulations, Derek, you've cleansed one of the most powerful artifacts in Hell."

"Whoops," I said, unimpressed. "Didn't mean to get you in trouble. My bad." If you couldn't tell, I was being sarcastic.

"The Lords of Hell are united in their desire to kill you for this affront. Moloch, himself, demanded your head on a pike. All agents of Hell across three dimensions were contacted with orders to take your life."

"And yet I'm here," I said.

"The orders were countermanded," Mary said, taking a bottle of champagne from the limousine's mini-fridge.

"Countermanded?" I asked.

"Yes." Mary said, pulling two glasses out from a rack of them beside the mini fridge. "By the one being who could order it."

"You're saying *the Devil* ordered Hell to stand down," I said, wanting to be very clear about what she was saying. "Lucifer."

"Tiamat-Abaddon, actually," Mary said, pouring us both a glass of champagne. "The difference is academic, though, at least to mortals. The Queen of Hell is what's preventing all of Hell's agents on Earth from descending on you. Curious, isn't it? As far as I know, you are an enemy of evil in all its forms."

"Am I?" I asked, skeptical. "I thought I was a murderer and kinslayer."

"You are also a defender and protector. One of the things I like about humanity is you are full of contradictions that do not exist in the Spirit World. There, everything is pure. Here is so much more...interesting."

I took a glass of champagne from her and took a sip. If Mary had wanted to hurt me, she could have done it while I was unconscious. She didn't need poison. "Anyway, thank you for the assist."

I had no doubt it was Mary who summoned the storm that had allowed me to tap my powers. She was also probably responsible for hiding the Bloodsword in my, well, blood. Mary had been bound to the sword for centuries. Despite her power, she wasn't a fallen angel, just a spirit of violence. Mary claimed she'd been created when Cain slew Abel—ignoring the massive evidence for the existence of evolution.

"You're welcome, my love," Mary said.

"Please don't call me that."

"Why?" Mary took a sip of her champagne. "Do you object to being loved by women other than Shannon or by a demon?"

"I object to someone loving me who tried to get me to kill my other lover." I wasn't about to forget Mary's words on the golf course.

"Sharing is a new experience for me. Though, I suppose,

Shannon has her own appeal." Mary smiled and leaned over to run her finger up my thigh. It was electric, like a jolt of pure concentrated pleasure up my spine into my brain. "I could show you both unimaginable pleasure if you would just let me in—then there is what I could teach you about magic."

"I'm doing fine with magic," I said, deciding to focus on that than the sexual aspect. I'd used sex a hundred or more times on missions, more even, yet I couldn't guarantee my control when dealing with Mary. It was a dangerous situation for an agent, even if I was an agent of nothing now.

"Your battle with Dracula says otherwise." Mary pulled her hand away, looking into my eyes.

"I *did* defeat Dracula," I corrected. "No thanks to—"

Mary raised an eyebrow and interrupted. "Me?"

Mary had been the one to unlock the power of blood magic and obscuromancy, not to mention keep me from dying not once but twice.

"Okay, *a lot* of thanks to you," I admitted. "I—"

"Am afraid of power." Mary shook her head. "It's ridiculous, a member of the Committee not living up to his full potential and a dragon no less."

"*Half*-dragon," I corrected. "I'm all-human despite my parentage."

"Only in body," Mary corrected. "Which I can assure you is the least important part of a person to any spirit."

Her words, I could tell, were directed at Shannon who'd pulled away from the woman. Shannon's 'food' wouldn't die but she'd wake up with one of hell of a headache.

"I think you woke her up," I said, looking at her.

"I'm sorry for interrupting your meal," Mary said, offering her hand. "I'm sure Derek would be willing to offer himself up—as I most certainly am."

"Fuck off, demon." Shannon climbed off the unconscious bodies. She looked embarrassed and searched the limousine for her clothes. They were folded up in a stack nearby, cleaned and pressed. It made me wonder how long I'd been out.

"I like her." Mary smirked. "It's no wonder the Host chose her to be their agent."

"What do you want, Mary?"

"To serve you," Mary replied, picking up her champagne glass again. "I have made arrangements to end my servitude to the Lords of Hell so that I might become your vassal."

"The hell you are," Shannon said, pulling on her underwear. She had reverted to human form now but looked furious.

Due to Shannon's need to feed and political concerns, neither of us was exclusive in our sexual habits, something I wasn't all that enthusiastic about—stereotypes about men aside—but that didn't extend to servants of evil. Bloody Mary was pushing all of Shannon's buttons and I didn't need that right now since I had no idea who was driving the limo or where we were going.

"Shannon, she's just doing her usual buttering me up so I'll lower my—"

Mary clapped her hands across her chest. "I swear by the Primals to obey all of your commands until the end of time."

"—guard." I stared at her like she'd grown three heads. In fact, that would have been less shocking.

The Primals were beings you could swear by if you wanted to make sure a promise could never be broken. If you tried to break them, you not only couldn't but you'd die in the process. This included beings that couldn't die under normal circumstances, up to and including gods. The only caveats were you had to know what you were swearing by and coercion was not possible. People who attempted to force someone into the oaths tended to suffer horrific bad luck. Like, lightning bolts and meteor-strikes levels of bad luck. It was so bad the Red Room didn't bother to make its agents swear by them. The Primals were simply too powerful, too dangerous to swear by causally. By doing so, Bloody Mary had just agreed to make herself my slave forever.

I wasn't having any of that. "I order you to not obey me unless you want to."

"Derek!" Shannon said, staring at me. I suspected it was more to the fact I'd given up an advantage over a demon sitting across from me than any desire to keep her as a slave. Well, unless Shannon wanted me to force Mary to give us insight into Hell's dealings—which, now that I thought about it, would have been a good idea. That way was a very slippery slope, though, and I had no interest in owning a slave.

Mary then stunned me by doing an action I'd never have expected in a million years.

She hugged me.

Kissing me full on the lips, Mary stared into my eyes before settling onto my lap. "You are, without a doubt, a brilliant and impossible man."

"Uh," I said, unsure how to respond to being kissed by a spirit of murder and mayhem. "Please get off my lap."

"Why?" Mary asked, teasing.

Shannon then threw her off, slamming Mary against the seat across from us with enough force I was surprised she didn't smash her through the other side. Shannon was half-dressed now with a white bra and panties on.

I blinked, looking between her and Shannon. "Because I'm pretty sure Shannon can rip your head clean off."

Mary laughed, still delighted from my earlier command. Clapping her hands, she said, "My dear, I have forgotten more about magic than it would take to deal with a stripling Daughter of Lilith like her."

Shannon growled and started growing her claws out again.

I put my hand on her shoulder. "Down girl."

Shannon growled at me.

I pulled my hand away. "Or not."

Reason prevailed, though, and Shannon literally withdrew her claws. Leaning back in her chair, she crossed her arms. "I've dealt with demons before, Derek. They can be very personable and then the knife goes in. I trusted you to do the right thing back when you were first possessed, I hope you'll do the same here."

I looked to Shannon. "If her plan was to swear an unbreakable oath of slavery to me on the oft-chance I'd tell her to be free, then she has really shit planning skills."

"Except if she'd spent days inside your head, learning about your love of freedom and complex regarding fallen women," Mary said, lifting the empty bottle of champagne that had been knocked over. "Such a waste."

"I do not have a complex... " I started to say before looking between the succubus and the demon. Then I thought of Cassandra and Ashley. "You know, screw it, I'm not saying anything."

"A wise choice," Mary said, dropping the bottle. "Tiamat-Abaddon commanded my master to release me from my vows on the condition that I swear allegiance to the one I loved—which is you. Even though I knew what your reaction would be, I can hardly believe it. You have no idea what it is to be a free demon. Unfettered and uninhibited by the commands of a master."

"Why would she do that?" I asked.

"Perhaps she too knew what it was like to love once," Mary said. "Marduk, Dracula, and a handful of others won her love. In the end, they all betrayed her but that is the nature of love."

"Uh huh," I said.

Mary shrugged. "Enjoy life while it lasts. I shall be by your side now, though, until then."

"Yeah, I bet you're just going to be gumdrops and lollipops from now on," Shannon said, sneering. "You can still be sent back to Hell."

"Yes, and I'd return. It is my choice now to serve Derek." Mary tapped the bottle and it re-filled itself as if being fed by an invisible pump. "I am still a spirit of violence and mayhem—which I am sure he will grant in abundance."

"You should take up a hobby," I pointed at Mary. "Roller derby perhaps."

"Perhaps." Bloody Mary gave a look as if considering it. "In any case, we are almost upon our location."

"Where's that?" I asked, not liking the build-up for all this.

"Why? To see my former master," Mary said. "It was his condition that I bring you to him. Your brother Stephen and you need to talk."

For once, I was rendered speechless.

CHAPTER ELEVEN

The mention of visiting Stephen had an immediate effect. Both Shannon and I exchanged a look, before bolting for opposite door handles to escape. They were locked, of course.

Mystically.

"Oh for crying out loud," Mary said, staring between us. "Are you two children?"

I pulled on the door handle again. "You'll forgive me if I'm not at all eager to go see my insane demon-possessed brother."

"Fallen angel, not demon," Mary corrected. "One is born in Heaven, the other in Hell."

Shannon growled at Mary again.

"Shannon, for example," Mary said, gesturing. "Her race is entirely demonic even if it has tried to present itself as a fairy subspecies."

Shannon launched herself at Mary, her claws extended, only for the demon to flick her fingers and send her flying backwards against her seat. The two unconscious bodies beside us bounced around the seats from the force. Shannon struggled but couldn't move. Mary hadn't been lying about their power differences. Negotiation was a better tactic.

"Down girl," Mary said.

"In simple terms," I said, putting my hands together. "I want nothing to do with Stephen."

"I think you'd like Furfur if you got to know him," Mary said.

"Is that what the monster inside him is called?" I asked, glad to finally have a name for the creature who'd helped destroy my family.

"Amongst other names," Mary said, lifting her champagne bottle and taking a drink from it before handing it over. "He has been wandering this Earth since the Great Fire of London signaled his summoning. Furfur chose Stephen to be his first host body since World War 1, however."

The Great Fire of London was in 1666. Cute. "I see."

"No, you don't," Mary said. "I wouldn't be so panicked if I were you. What are you so afraid of?"

"Death and eternal torment," I deadpanned.

Mary shrugged, acknowledging the point. "Fair enough. Your brother told me to tell you one thing to get you to come here."

"Derek, we don't have to listen to this—" Shannon started to say.

Mary's next words silenced her. "He knows who is holding Ashley, where, and why."

"Shit," Shannon said, staring downward. She knew there was no way in hell I was going to leave this alone now.

Even if I didn't. "I haven't agreed yet."

"You will," Mary said, taking another swig of the bottle and handing it over. "If you were afraid of damnation, you wouldn't have killed Rebecca."

My glare became deadly. Mary was one of the most powerful demons in Hell. A Duchess of the Sixth Rank and Patron Anti-Saint of Killing. "You're not helping your case here, Mary."

I was spared from having to respond by the song "Bat Out of Hell" by Meatloaf playing from my front pocket. Reaching in, I pulled out my dried blood-covered cellphone and held it to my ear. It was Penny's ringtone, mostly because she couldn't stand the song and being a twin obligated me to torment her as much as the reverse.

"Hello?" I asked. "Penny, is that you?"

"Who else would it be?" Penny asked, blinking.

"That should be my song," Mary muttered.

"You're *Poison* by Alice Cooper," I said.

Not that I had Bloody Mary's cellphone number. I wasn't even aware she'd survived Camp Zero until her sudden reappearance in my life. Mary seemed pleased by my selection, though, which irritated Shannon further. I suspected it was because Shannon was an ABBA fan.

"I expected it to be you," I said, going back to talking to Penny. "It's just things have been going... downhill."

"You mean like the fact you're officially dead?" Penny said, her voice sounding irritated.

"Excuse me?" I asked, blinking.

"They released a bulletin to the entirety of the Red Room that Derek Hawthorne was killed by a Rakshasa assassin who is now wandering around wearing your skin. Agents have orders to shoot anyone who looks like you on sight. The Professor contacted me and told me he's to make a speech mourning your death."

The Red Room had moved quickly to back up Roland's assassination plan. Unlike most of the Committee, whose identities were unknown to the organization at large, I was famous amongst the lower ranks. I'm not trying to exaggerate my accomplishments, most of them were through a combination of blind luck and enemy stupidity, but they were considerable enough my sanctioning would have drawn fire from certain quarters. Transparent as the idea I was killed and replaced by a Rakshasa was, it wasn't implausible and whoever scored the lucky assault would either be an agent of the Committee or someone who could be told it was a mistake. Probably right before they, too, were eliminated. I'd seen good agents sacrificed for much less important cover-ups. I just hoped my father's influence was strong enough to protect Penny.

"Uh-huh," I said, closing my eyes. "Just make sure they don't play *Dust in the Wind* at my funeral."

"I was going with *Who Wants to Live Forever* by Queen. Though, given you're not dead, I suppose Nancy Sinatra's *You Only Live Twice* is better," Penny said, her jokes not hiding how concerned she was.

Shannon stared at me. "Could you talk less about your music tastes and more about the fact you're an outlaw now?"

"I'm afraid not," I said, dryly. "There is no problem too large that it can't be snarked about."

"I mean, can they track your phone? What about magically?"

Shannon asked. "Do they know your true name."

"I've altered his true name," Mary said, cheerfully.

"I know they can't track my phone. I made a separate deal with a manifestation of Hermes to make sure the signal was bounced across the Earth whenever I made a phone call. Speaking of which, could you take care of my pigeon sacrifices this week?"

"Eww," Penny said, frowning. "That's horrible."

"I remind you the Hebrew god loves lambs," I said, sighing. "The fact of the matter is, Penny, I screwed up. I'm on the run and I don't think I'm going to be able to sort this mess out."

"Jesus," Penny said, realizing what I was saying. This was probably the end of our association. There was no escaping the long arm of the Committee.

Try as though I would.

I continued joking, though. "Jesus likes fish and wine. He can make his own so you might have more luck bringing chips."

Penny wasn't amused. There was too much of the good Anglican girl in her to be. That and we were talking about my imminent demise. "Derek! Be serious."

"*I am serious*," I said, the weight of it all hanging on my shoulders. "Roland Cassidy is going to be taking my seat on the Council and he tried to kill me. He's as dirty as they come and that's saying something in our business. He's the guy behind the elves and their attacks. You need to find some place safe given he's likely to come after you too. I'm going to continue to go after Ashley in the meantime—and maybe try to take out Roland. The last thing the world needs is another psychotic asshole with unlimited funds in charge."

Penny's voice almost broke. "Derek, this could be the last time we talk—"

"It won't be," I said, unsure if I was lying or not. "Is Christopher alright?"

"No idea," Penny sighed, realizing I wasn't going to let this conversation take a darker turn. "Talbot is running down leads on Ashley. I'm trying to find out who is on your side versus the Committee. The numbers aren't great so far."

"Sounds like a lot of fun," I said, sighing. "Know I'm

thinking about you. We may not be seeing each other a lot after this. Okay?"

Penny was silent for several seconds. "Derek... take care. I love you."

"I love you too. You're the most important person in the world to me."

Shannon looked away at that.

"Ditto." Penny gave a half-hearted laugh. "Don't tell Lucy."

"I won't. Goodbye," I said.

"Be seeing you," Penny said,

With that, I hung up my phone and stared at it for a long time. "When the gods made the universe, they split me and Penny in two."

"You're a half-Goth witch?" Shannon asked, trying to lighten the mood. She succeeded.

I snorted, smiling. "Yes, aren't you?"

"Hey, I was a *punk*. Big difference," Shannon said.

"We can solve your problem, Derek," Bloody Mary said, her voice conciliatory. "If it takes a hundred years, I promise you we'll be able to settle it so you're able to meet with your sister again."

"That's a bit long for me," I said.

"Not if you're both immortal and that can be arranged too," Mary said.

"*I don't fear death. It is but a change of scenery,*" I quoted Talbot. "I don't welcome it either but I'm not going to panic at the thought of old age or being killed like so many other junior wizards do."

Mary wrinkled her brow and looked distressed. "Derek—"

"Can we focus on the part about my meeting with Stephen?" I really didn't want to get into any conversation revolving around my death.

"Derek, this is a *horrible* idea." Shannon reached over and put her hand on my shoulder. "The forces of Hell should *never* be allied with. Trust me, I know."

"Stephen killed my family, Shannon. If you think I have a pressing need to meet a fallen angel then you need not worry. I don't. I have even less desire to ever see my traitor of a brother again."

For whatever worth the word traitor had now. I still remembered how terrified I was while hunting Stephen down. How, even with Ashley backing me up, it had been a constant struggle to suppress my fear and anger. Stephen embraced his fiendish powers and destroyed any individual who came after him.

Agents both superior to me in experience as well as power had been crushed like flies by the fallen angel within Stephen. Despite this, I'd managed to counteract my terror of his power with anger. Gwen and Marcus had never been the closest of my siblings, but I'd known them. Loved them. They hadn't deserved to die, let alone at the hands of someone who shared their blood.

Any goodwill I'd had for Stephen, the brother I'd thought most like me, evaporated in the hatred born from his betrayal. In the end, I had done little enough to bring him down, but Ashley's powers overwhelmed him. A fallen angel, manifested as the most beautiful creature in Creation, had been beaten by a human woman not yet thirty. A human woman who needed my help.

"I'll do it," I said, staring at her. "I also promise you that if there's any attempt to break him out of the asylum he's imprisoned in, I'm going to stop it. Even if it requires hunting you. As long as I live, Stephen is never going to be a free man."

Mary placed her hand over her heart. "I promise by you, the thing I hold most sacred, I will do nothing to free your brother."

"I'll hold you to that," I said, not believing her despite her promise.

An itch in the back of my mind kept drawing my attention but I did my best to ignore it. This itch was, of course, the thought that my brother had been imprisoned for the better part of five years in the House's most secure mental health facility. A place that contained the most powerful wards the White Room's wizards could create and a security system designed by the very best of the Red Room's magitech engineers. However, if my brother was carrying around Furfur inside him then how the hell had he gotten a message out to Bloody Mary. It wasn't like she could infiltrate the asylum, human body or not. The only satisfactory answer was he'd found a way around his bindings and was just letting himself be held prisoner.

No. I refused to believe that. Regardless of whether it made sense, I had to believe Stephen was a prisoner and there was no way he could escape without outside help. I preferred to believe Bloody Mary was a liar and this was all some sort of trick than entertain the notion that creature might someday escape. The worst part was I *knew* how irrational this thought was.

Shannon placed her hand on my shoulder. "I'll go with you."

"That may be a bad idea," I said, taking a deep breath.

"What?" Shannon blinked.

"You were recruited by angels to work with the Red Room," I said, remembering Shannon's story about how she was recruited. "The creature inside may sense that and—"

"You're trying to protect me? The guy I had to carry out of a golf course on my back?"

"Okay, that does sound silly," I said, looking down. "Forget I mentioned it."

"Good," I said.

"We're here," Mary said, having finished off the bottle of champagne. The limousine slowed and we passed through a set of wrought-iron gates that opened to a road leading up to the top of a large hill.

As we pulled to a stop at the top, I saw a massive building that was one-part mansion and one-part prison-complex. It was eight stories tall but covered in enough arches, ivy, and wooden shutters to do a passable job at looking like somewhere pleasant to be. The truth was, I could feel the staggering number of spells woven into the mortar from a hundred feet away.

The Red Room was an organization whose agents were in constant danger of insanity. For the most part, this was PTSD and easy to cure. The ethics of scrubbing a person's brain of the exact memories that left them waking up screaming at night were something I left for philosophers to decide but was pretty good at returning agents to the field. Sometimes, though, it didn't work.

The worst cases were those individuals who came to a voluntary choice that it was better to be a monster than a human. Rather than treating this as treason or subversion, the

Red Room had taken a page out of the Soviet Union's handbook. Many of their dissidents had been labeled insane to discredit them. In time, given enough drugs and torture, even the most strong-willed individuals were willing to abandon their beliefs.

Some here were never intended to leave at all, kept sedated for the rest of their lives in a padded room as a lesson to others about speaking against the Committee. Of course, far be it for you to think these were innocent victims, many of the residents here were soldiers for supernaturals that wanted nothing less than the slavery of humanity. The fact, if not for my ties, I would be in there amongst them due to my relationship with Mary didn't change my opinion.

Too much.

"H.P. Lovecraft Memorial Hospital." Shannon stared at the plaque on the side of the wall. "That's a joke in poor taste."

"Poor taste?" I asked.

"Lovecraft's father was institutionalized," Shannon said. "Syphilis."

"I assumed it was a reference to the fact this is a place where rational men who learned the universe's truths and went mad are kept."

Shannon blinked. "Huh."

The doors unlocked. I opened the door to my side and stepped out.

It was time to meet my brother.

CHAPTER TWELVE

"So, will there be a problem with my going in?" I asked, staring at the foreboding building before me. Reaching back into the car, I picked up the umbrella that had once been the Bloodsword. For some reason, I felt more comfortable holding it.

"What do you mean?" Mary asked, stepping out of the car and taking position behind me.

"The Red Room wants to kill me," I said, looking at the facility. "Walking into the maximum-security facility the House stores its lunatics doesn't fill me with a warm fuzzy feeling."

"I can assure you that no one will recognize you," Mary said. "Though, I would have thought you'd have learned such magics yourself."

True, I did. "Sorry, I'm just looking for excuses not to go."

"Derek!" Mary frowned. "That is not the bloodthirsty warrior I know and love."

"Love?" Shannon asked, looking at him.

"I'm catnip to Hell," I said, shrugging.

Shannon rolled her eyes. "Don't worry, I'll protect you."

Shannon started walking to the front door. That was when she stopped in the middle of her step. Blinking, Shannon reached out and moved her hand across the building's front.

"Dammit," Shannon muttered.

"Let me guess, it's warded against Lilin," I said, giving her a sideways glance.

"So it seems," Shannon muttered. "The only way I'm getting in here is with a major abjuration."

"And us without a circle of witches to perform one," I

muttered, looking at Mary. "You can't go in either, can you?"

"No," Mary replied.

"Peachy," I said, walking up onto the porch with no resistance. Turning around, I said, "If I'm not back in half-an-hour, run like hell."

"No," Shannon said, blinking.

"Not a chance," Mary added.

I shook my head. "Redheads."

Waving my right hand over my face and muttering a chant to Anasazi, I made myself an identical replica of my father. Normally, there would be tests against exactly this sort of magic but I also knew bypass codes as a member of the Committee. I just hoped they hadn't been cancelled yet.

Taking a deep breath, I walked into the facility and found myself in an old-time looking front hall with chess-board black-and-white tiles plus a Nurse Ratchet-looking woman at the front desk. There were reinforced steel doors behind her, and the entire place hummed with mystical energy. I saw security cameras, murder-holes in the wall shaped for assault rifles and guessed there was probably explosives underneath the building in case of breakout. A couple of Kevlar-wearing guards with helmets carried expensive-looking rifles with their visors down.

In the end, though, all security systems had one-weakness.

The human element.

I cleared my throat. "Ahem."

"Hello, Mister Hawthorne," the Nurse Ratchet lookalike said. Picking up a lanyard, she handed it over to me. "Here's your clearance pass. Your brother is still on Floor Seven, Room Twelve. Remember not to antagonize the prisoner."

I blinked, taking the lanyard and doing the best to imitate my brother's voice. "Thank you."

Really? They weren't even going to require my clearance codes? The people here should be ashamed. One of the guards opened a steel door for me and I walked through it to a row of elevators to the side of a long hall with a door at the end. Tapping the up button, I headed on up to a featureless white hall with dozens of steel doors monitored by security cameras. Each of them was numbered with just a tiny white window to look in on them. The air was chill and I felt the hairs on the back of my neck stand up as I approached Room Twelve. There was something evil in this place.

And I was going to speak with it.

Heading to the door that marked my objective, I didn't bother to look inside. Instead, I just put my lanyard up against the electronic lock beside it and heard it click open. Walking inside, I saw the entire room was padded. It was like eight mattresses arranged in a cube with the back of the door also covered up. Someone didn't trust my brother not to hurt himself.

There sitting in the white cushioned room in a straitjacket covered in mystic runes was a man with long black hair staring at the ground. His arms were covered in hundreds of sigils that let me know the Red Room had tattooed him with control magic before placing him in the warded straight jacket. Even his feet contained various heretical prayers designed to control demons in the name of the Lord. The figure chuckled and looked up into my eyes. I stared into my own face.

The resemblance between us was uncanny, a product of magic intermixing with the strong genes of mage bloodlines. Despite being my half-brother and two years younger than me, Stephen Hawthorne could have been my identical twin. This made the fact he was a demon-possessed monster more unsettling. Not that I'd tell him that.

Stephen had rampaged across the three continents, murdering and torturing at seeming random. He'd racked up a body count over three-figures twice over before we'd managed to stop him, including more than a dozen Senior agents.

Looking into his eyes, I saw pure evil.

Stephen gave a Cheshire Cat grin before saying, in a voice eerily like my own, "Hello Clarice."

"Oh fuck you!" I snapped back.

"What? I don't get to quip anymore?" Stephen asked, giving a half-smile. "Just because I'm trapped in the nuthouse doesn't mean I've lost my sense of humor."

"You lost that right when you murdered your family."

"I remind you, Gwen and Marcus were trying to kill me at

the time. I'd also like to point out you're not innocent of kin-slaying yourself."

He knew.

"Bloody Mary told you," I whispered, grimacing.

"The rats in the walls told me," Stephen said, rising and leaning against the back of the cell. "Everything on Earth is connected by an invisible web of lies and deceptions. Every time someone lies to someone else or each other, I know. After all, I am the Father of Lies."

"Furfur is no more than the Devil than I am David Bowie because I can sing," I said, keeping my gaze steady. "He's not even one of the ten Archdemons." I knew those names from basic demonology training."

"No, he's much more. Just like you're more than a mere agent."

"I am an agent." An agent of nothing but an agent.

"Says the man who's wielding a Horseman of the Apocalypse's sword and accompanied by an independent demon as well as a Heaven-aligned Succubus," Stephen said, shrugging. "If you're going to judge me, remember I'm not the only person in this room powered by otherworldly forces. You are spoken of in the prophecies of the end of the world but what role, precisely, you play, is anyone's guess."

"I don't believe in the Book of Revelation either." I tried not to think about my dream of the Wazir and Dracula on colored horses. "The Bloodsword is also kind of broken." I shook the umbrella in my hand.

"You're right not to," Stephen said, surprising me. "The Book of Revelations is actually a depiction of the Romans' persecution of early Christians, but its imagery is just too good not to misuse for Hell's purposes. After all, a final battle between Good and Evil has *resonance*. We can use that to bring it about. Sympathetic magic and all that. Think about it. The end of the world. The beginning of a new. Everyone free to do what they want. No more governments. No more death. Ice cream vendors on every corner."

"I'm leaving." I turned around to depart. This was a mistake. There was nothing Stephen could tell me of use.

"Ashley is being held prisoner in a Spirit World gulag known as Fort Happiness. It's where Roland Cassidy is growing his elves and educating them in war and murder. She's hooked up to the Cauldron of Bran the Blessed. They burned out a hundred telepaths and sorcerers trying to find a power source that could make it work but the Celtic deity blood in her veins turned out to be what they needed all along. It's why they're so anxious to get their hands on her daughter."

I looked over my shoulder. "Why would you tell me this?"

"I could give any number of reasons. Roland Cassidy is an asshole. Elves are universally psychopaths—therefore it's impossible to corrupt them to evil. Only the good can fall from grace and are of interest to my patron spirit. Roland Cassidy's master is a pagan god, uninterested in sharing dominion over the cause of wickedness. I owe Bloody Mary a favor and she loves you. Oh, and maybe I'm doing it because I like you—you are, after all, your brother's keeper."

I pulled at my gun and aimed it at his head. "Maybe I'll keep you in a coffin."

"Ouch!" Stephen laughed. "What a terrible pun."

"I'm not laughing." I *wanted* to pull the trigger.

Stephen was unimpressed. "Really, Derek, you're threatening a man possessed by an angel *with a gun*? Be serious."

I put the gun away, realizing either way the weapon wouldn't do any good. Fallen angels broke a lot of the traditional rules of the supernatural. If Stephen had been vulnerable to orichalcum bullets, he wouldn't have been able to tear through the House's agents like wet tissue paper. They'd sent armies after Stephen, only for him to throw them around like toy soldiers. It had required Ashley and my working a distraction to bring him down and I half-thought surprise had played a role there.

"Good boy." Stephen said.

Instead, I lifted my umbrella up by the handle.

Stephen looked confused. "What are you doing?"

I jabbed the metal tip into my stomach, causing him to topple over in pain.

"Oooo," Stephen said, coughing. "That was brilliant! So

filled with love and self-sacrifice! It's torturous! Using that to hurt someone, I mean, bravo!"

I pulled the umbrella away. "Okay, now you're making it weird."

"I killed all those people for a reason, Derek. Those men, women, and children all had a role to play in the apocalypse and because of their deaths, the new future is far more interesting. I can see the future and the disaster would have been much worse without their end. You always liked Gwen too much, too, a subconscious incestuous attraction that probably stems from your abnormally close relationship with Penn—"

I jabbed him with the umbrella.

He laughed this time. "Okay, I made that up. But she would have been the one to kill you had she lived. She'd have hunted you down and murdered you for betraying the Committee as you've done. As for Marcus, the Golden Boy would have ascended to the Committee and instituted mind-control on every airwave and in every jingle. Free-will would have perished!"

"I don't believe you," I said.

"Yes, you do," Stephen said, staring at me. "The House is the enemy and you've always known that. It's why you killed Rebecca. You saw the monster she became."

Stephen wasn't going to convince me he was on the side of angels—no pun intended. "And what about the bus driver you ripped the head off of and played basketball with?"

Stephen paused. "Okay, I admit that was just for fun."

I pulled the umbrella away, letting him talk. "Assume I'm stupid enough to believe the self-proclaimed Father of Lies. What's Roland's end game?"

"He wishes to raise Balor the Evil Eye, the Behemoth of Job, from the dead."

I blinked. "Balor."

"Celtic god of evil. Demon King. Elder God. Chief of the Formorians. Possessed of one eye in the back of his head and another in front that could destroy armies. Inspiration for both the Balrog and Sauron."

"I know who Balor is," I said.

In the ancient days of humanity, before the Norse Ragnarok and several ages of magic had resulted in the dimensions being parted from one another, there had been creatures beyond human understanding: the Elder Gods. Majestic and terrible, the Elder Gods stood a hundred-feet-tall and wielded the power to create or destroy kingdoms at a whim. Ironically, it had been their servitor races that had ultimately slain them: vampires, werewolves, and elves.

Balor had been one of the most powerful of these ancient beings. The god-king of the Fomorians wove races of monsters from nightmares and ruled for an eternity. It had taken his grandson Lugh, High King of the Tuatha, to slay him. Christian mythology said that Balor was an archdemon impersonating a pagan god while pagans claimed that the White God had claimed their god as one of his own. I didn't care either way, Balor was bad news. Worse, Lugh had been turned into a vampire and slain decades ago so there was no chance he was going to help put him down again.

"What you're saying is impossible," I said. "Balor could never return to the physical world. The laws of reality no longer support beings like him."

"The laws of reality can be changed," Stephen said, accenting the word changed. "Appealed, repealed, or amended. Every act of magic is a conscious order for the laws of physics to change—and your dearest Ashley Morgan is the kind of person who can do a lot of ordering."

I couldn't help but think he was telling the truth—which bothered me. "Roland's using Ashley's magic to try and raise Balor from the dead."

"That's what I said, yes. The elves allied with the Nazis planned to bring him back to the dead, only for their books and research into the subject to fall into the hands of Gamen Cassidy, Roland and Cassandra's father, after the war. They've been working on ways to restore Balor for decades but it's only now they have a descendant of the Morrigan they have a chance of succeeding. Magic is a finicky bastard like that."

Against my better judgment, I believed him. "What would the Cassidys want with that kind of monster?"

I already knew. Roland had said as much but I wanted to see if Stephen's story matched it.

"They believe getting a big obviously evil monster thing to rampage up and down the world will help in uniting humanity. Once it's dead, the Truth will be out but humanity will be more concerned about big monsters like it than vampires and Rakshasas. He thinks he'll be able to take over the world in the aftermath."

"So they're stupid," I said.

"Or being controlled by someone smarter who realizes it's a great way to tie up their attention," Stephen said, shrugging. "Balor is unlike anything you have ever faced, Derek. I suggest you prevent its resurrection because you won't be able to kill it. Maybe at half-power it'd be possible but at full power? Balor will be able to rewrite reality like a child playing with crayons."

"How do I find this Fort Happiness?" I lifted the tip of the umbrella again.

Stephen raised an eyebrow in a fashion identical to me. "I thought you disapproved of torture. You're always saying how it doesn't work and it's useless—when what you mean, of course, is to say only a disgusting animal would torture another human being. Even if it was for information."

I pulled the umbrella back and put it over my shoulder. "Torture *doesn't* work." The truth was, though, I could probably bully answers out of him. I just didn't want to. "How do you know all this?"

"Simple," Stephen said. "I'm the one who told Roland the secret of how to resurrect Balor. I directed him to your beautiful Ashley. I knew you'd never kill her, so she was the best option."

I wanted to beat him to death right then and there. "Fuck you."

"Why hold back?" Stephen asked. "You know you want to hurt me. Why not? Ethics and decency?"

"What do *you* know of ethics and decency?" I said, sneering.

"More than you could imagine," Stephen said, giving a

low evil chuckle. "Through my patron's eyes, I have seen the heavens of the Creator and his fellow Elohim and found them wanting. Only by destroying this horrible flawed world can a paradise be made. First must come the Reveal, though. Only when all of humanity knows about magic, vampires, and witches can sorcery enter this world again *en masse*. That is the only way change can occur. Our father believes the same but believes good can triumph over evil. As if there is a difference other than the colors they wear."

"You're never leaving this place," I said, staring at him. "You're going to rot here, for all time if I can arrange it."

"My dear Derek, you've already figured out I've been here of my own volition," Stephen said, the straitjacket falling away from his bare chest. His tattoos changed in an instant. He was now covered in infernal glyphs and tattoos, all designed to increase the amount of hellish energy his body could channel. His eyes shined with an unearthly light and he was upon me before I could move.

Stephen delivered a knee to my stomach before slamming his hands against the side of my head, delivering a brutal ki strike. Holding my head in place, he gave a head butt before throwing me over his shoulders with one hand movement. Stephen grabbed my left arm and then pressed his bare foot against my neck. His strength was immense, dozens of times more powerful than any man.

Stephen could kill me at any time.

"You have no idea how long I have wanted to kill you for bringing me to this place. You and Ms. Morgan defeated me and bound me in those accursed runes. I was forced to stew in my own filth, poked and prodded by the Red Room and water-boarded by holy water amongst other tortures. They offered me wealth and power if I would help them turn Furfur into a weapon for their little organization. Instead, I have turned members of the Committee against one another and guaranteed the Fall of the House. What do you think of that?"

I coughed, struggling to break free as his foot squeezed down harder on my throat. "I should have killed you."

Stephen laughed again. "Yes, you should have."

He gave a twist of my wrist and dislocated my shoulder before slamming his foot down on my face, knocking me out.

The last thing I heard was a series of screams throughout the asylum.

Oh no.

CHAPTER THIRTEEN

I awoke with a splitting headache, the smell of blood in the air. Blinking, I rose to my feet and heard AC/DC's "Highway to Hell" playing in the background. The door to the padded room was wide open and the lights were flickering outside like a strobe light.

Climbing to my feet, I headed out of my brother's cell and saw all the doors inside the hallway were open with the walls covered with bloody letters. Stephen had used some poor unfortunate soul's life fluid as ink.

GOOD LUCK, DEREK.

YOU'RE GONNA NEED IT.

Taking a deep breath, I slowly walked towards the elevator doors and saw they had been pried open. Getting up close, I looked inside to see the cables had been cut and the elevator was at the bottom of the shaft.

There was no chance of getting out that way.

Reaching for my gun, I found it was missing. Shaking my head, I went back to the padded room and picked up the Blood Umbrella. I needed to think of a better name for it. Red Umbrella? Too generic. Crimson Umbrella? Eh, I'd work on it.

Heading down the other side of the hall and through the wide-open door at the end, I found the fourth floor had turned into a charnel house. The administration area was filled with the flayed and decapitated corpses of the hospital staff, some crucified against the ceiling fans that mysteriously held up despite the weight of them. The lights were turned off rather than continuing the strobe light effect of the hall behind me.

The inmates had fared little better than the staff with their blood having been used to write other messages along the wall.

THE LIE IS OVER.

FAMILY IS NOT YOUR FRIEND.

SHANNON WILL LEAVE YOU.

YOU ARE THE DRAGON, NOT YOUR MOTHER.

Oh and my personal favorite: SHAGGY OR FRED FOR DAPHNE?

I snorted, staring at that one. "Shaggy, obviously."

The next words on the wall were I AGREE.

Yeah, that wasn't creepy at all. Not that being in an insane asylum turned abattoir made things any better.

Going through one of the hospital staff desks, I found a flashlight and an extra set of guns and ammunition. This was, after all, a Red Room facility. Packing the gun in my holster, I used the flashlight to navigate around the room.

The doors to the stairwell were easy enough to find but I could hear movement once I pushed it open. There was hooting and hollering along with the sound of gunfire above my head as well as below. Stephen hadn't killed all the inmates and staff it would seem.

Turning the light down before me, I started walking below. As I passed by one of the walls, it started to make a heartbeat noise and black cracks appeared across its surface, slowly spreading through the entire stairwell. Blood oozed from the cracks and I felt a palpable sense of dread wash over me.

"Great, I'm in *Resident Evil*," I muttered, attempting to walk on the now gore-covered steps without slipping.

When I passed by the door to floor three, I heard a man scream followed by another gunshot. I was tempted to head on in to see if I could help but chose, instead, to continue walking. Stephen's escape represented a clear and present danger to the entire world. I was also committed to finding Ashley. Time would tell which of these two agendas proved the more significant. Either way, staying in order to assist any survivors would impede my investigation. I'd done much worse over the years than abandon survivors who might not even exist and had learned to deal with the guilt. I'd learn to deal with the guilt from this too.

In the end, when I reached the final floor, I found the walls were riddled with shifting and horrific images of trapped souls running underneath the skin-like walls. The doorway to the first floor was sealed over with human skin that was marked with an inverted pentagram. It was powerful magic, more powerful than I could dispel on my own. Worse, I knew what was happening to this place.

Stephen, or more precisely the demon inside him, had transformed this into a *Shadow Locus*. Shadow Loci were what happened when the dimensional barriers between a location in the physical world and the Spirit World became so thin that they began to crossover. The problem was that the Spirit World was rarely linked to places like it in physical location but more often those spots that resonated with it on a spiritual level. In short, this place was becoming linked to whatever parts of the Spirit World were like Hell. Getting out of here fast was in my best interests.

Lifting my umbrella, I jabbed into the human skin. It rippled and twisted before screaming like a human being. Closing my eyes, I focused my will for it to open through the umbrella and like a wand or other enhancer, the magic tripled in strength. This caused a tear to rip through its side and reveal the front office on the other side. Jumping through the hole, it sealed up behind me.

The music on the speakers had shifted to "The Devil went down to Georgia" by the Charles Daniel's Band. The interior of the waiting room was trashed, all the guns built into the floor having been ripped to shreds while black demonic-looking roaches crawled out of holes in the walls by the hundreds.

The doorway to the outside was suspiciously open but I could see night had fallen in the meantime. There were stars in the night sky, and they seemed to look down upon the world with an ominous foreboding, but it looked like the sun was about to rise again. It had barely been setting before. How long had I been out? It was at least ten to twelve hours and God knew what Stephen had been up to in the meantime.

Walking forward, I had to cover my mouth and nose as the smell of rotting meat was intense in the room. Despite the door being opened, it smelled like this room had been shut up for days with corpses inside it. It put to rest any thought there might be something human still left in Stephen. Any person willing to do this to his fellow man was undeserving of the title 'person.' As I thought that, I swore I could hear my brother let out a snort of derision.

Stepping on piles of roaches as they scurried across the ground, they crunched beneath my shoes while I approached the door. The hellish resonance of this Shadow Locus was getting worse and I didn't think it would be long until things reached critical mass. Then things would get all *Poltergeist*.

I was almost to the door when I heard a hissing noise behind me, causing me to curse. Turning around, I saw the woman I'd thought of as Nurse Ratchet. She'd been hiding behind the desk. Her skin was putrefying and looking like it was ready to slough off her body while her mouth was inordinately large for her face. It was at least four times the size of a normal human's. Worse, her teeth were all curved and sharp like scimitars.

She was a draugr now.

As I'd told Ashley, draugr were what happened when a human ingested enough vampire blood to kill them but not enough to turn them into a full-fledged member of the undead. They were the lowest form of supernatural, mindlessly hungry and capable of spreading their foul condition like movie zombies. There was one problem. They were *a lot* faster.

While going for my gun, the creature zipped up to my side and grabbed me by the throat. Holding me with both of its reeking hands, the draugr started to grapple me before opening its mouth to rip my throat out. Only my own enhanced reflexes let me grab her by the head and hold her back. It wanted to devour my flesh, blood, and bones.

Draugr was superhumanly strong and I was still feeling weak from having my ass kicked by Stephen. Pressing my fingers into its rotted eyes, the creature didn't seem in the least bit disturbed. Indeed, its mouth got closer and closer to my face. So I threw every bit of strength into my wrists and getting a grip with my thumbs pressed against the inside of its head, I broke the creature's neck.

The draugr fell over, landing on a collection of cockroaches gathered beneath us. Disgusted, I stepped through the door and fell on the porch before getting up and dashing out onto the front of the lawn. The limousine was absent but the couple Shannon had been feeding on were dismembered on the ground along with a man in a chauffer's outfit.

There were a dozen figures in straitjackets shambling around across the front lawn, a couple of which I remembered as individuals working for the White or Blue Rooms during my early years. They looked more drugged than draugr-fied, which surprised me. I looked around for Shannon and Mary, breathing a sigh of relief when I saw the two of them were in the road, backs against one another. They appeared to be asleep, oblivious of the horror which had fallen the asylum.

Cleaning my hands on the nearby grass, I stumbled over towards them, just to hear a cracking noise. Above my heads, storm clouds had gathered and began pouring down rain once more. The cracking noise wasn't thunder, though, and was coming from the asylum. Turning my head, I saw the entire building start to shake before imploding. Rooms collapsed into themselves and floors folded up like paper before the entire thing disappeared down a one-foot-diameter hole in reality.

Vanishing altogether. All that remained of the H.P. Lovecraft Memorial Hospital was the building's empty foundation and some exposed piping mixed with electrical wiring.

"*Poltergeist* was right," I muttered, shaking my head.

Questions filled my head about what the hell had just happened. Why had Stephen spared Mary and Shannon? Why had he spared these other patients? Why kill everyone else? What was he going to do now? Hell, why hadn't he killed me? Was it because he didn't consider me a threat or was it for other reasons? There were no good vampires and my hands still stank of draugr goop. I *hated* those things.

Running to Shannon and Mary's side, I leaned over and saw they were waking up from whatever sort of trance Stephen had put them under. Seeing Bloody Mary like this, I made sure to pull out my gun and hold it tight. I didn't want to do what I was about to do but I needed some answers.

"What the hell just happened?" Shannon asked, blinking like she was waking up with a hangover.

I pointed my gun at Mary's head.

Mary looked at me before blinking several times. "I think I have managed to offend my former master."

Shannon did a double take looking at his gun. "Oh, now, he's showing sense around you?"

"Stephen killed everyone in the asylum and dragged it to hell," I said, gesturing with the side of my head to where the building used to stand.

"Holy shit." Shannon stared.

"I did not intend for this to happen. You must believe me," Mary said, looking... guilty? Regretful? Annoyed Stephen didn't take her with him? I couldn't get a read on her.

"I'm pretty sure I don't have to believe a word which comes out of your mouth," I said, keeping my eyes focused on her. "You led me to Stephen and because of that, I was almost sucked into hell and killed by a draugr."

Mary looked at me. "He didn't kill you, though."

"No," I said. "He didn't. I guess he's saving that for later."

"I wouldn't let him," Mary insisted.

I laughed at that. If Stephen had proven anything, it was there was no stopping him without someone as powerful as Ashley to do it. "You sold me to him, Mary, and I'm not going to forget that. I'm not going to forgive it, either."

"Then pull the trigger," Mary said. "If I do not have my service to you, I have no reason to continue on."

"Oh come on!" Shannon said, getting up. "You're laying it on a little thick."

"I mean this," Mary said. "A spirit serves its concept and I will not lower myself to serve any other warrior than Earth's best."

"You're not buying this bullshit, are you?" Shannon asked me.

"Flattery will get her nowhere," I said, sighing. "I can't trust you, Mary. You led us here and because of that, a lot of people are dead."

"Did you get your information?" Mary asked.

I hesitated. "Yes, yes I did. Assuming any of it is true."

"I am sure it is," Mary replied, smiling as if this fact was all that mattered. "If you have gained the knowledge you require, then it was all worth it."

"I beg to differ," I said.

"What did you find out?" Shannon asked, looking at me.

"Roland Cassidy is working for some ancient evil god which wants to be woken up. He's draining Ashley of magic to give the monster enough magical oomph to manifest. It's classic 'evil wizard out to conquer the world by summoning his demon god' stuff. We need to find Ashley at some place called Fort Happiness in the Spirit World."

"I don't believe it," Shannon said, staring at me. The rain pouring down lightly on us. It was cold but not cold enough to be more than an annoyance.

"Yeah, how stupid do you have to be to destroy the world as part of your deal with a supernatural entity?"

"No," Shannon corrected. "I mean, I literally don't believe it. Roland Cassidy may be a sociopathic asshole who sends assassins after little girls but he's still the CEO of the world's largest corporation. You don't get there, let alone on the Committee, by being as big a moron as your average doomsday cultist."

"You think there's more going on?" I asked, glancing at her.

"When is there *not* more going on?" Shannon asked.

She was right. "This does seem to wrap everything in a neat-little bow."

"Only humans would look at a millennium-old plot to resurrect one of the Elder Gods involving human sacrifice and building an intimate relationship with the organization most likely to stop them and say, that's not complex enough," Mary said, shaking her head.

"Mary, I deal with stuff like that before lunchtime," I said, snorting. "I still can't trust you."

"You have already foresworn my oath of allegiance?" Mary asked.

"Like I said, I may not believe you, but I don't believe in slavery either." I wasn't sure what I needed to do with Mary. At this point, I was leaning on leaving her here.

That was when Mary crossed her arms over her chest and began speaking a shadowy, hissing tongue.

Shannon's eyes widened and she went for my gun. Both of us were bowled back by a wave of force which washed over us before she could fire, though. Falling on the ground, I felt like I'd been hit with a tidal wave.

Shaking my head, I looked up to Bloody Mary and stared at her.

I could *see* her thoughts.

We are now as one, my love.

"What have you done?" I stared at her in shock.

I have made you my familiar. We are now bonded, my love. Forever.

Ah hell.

CHAPTER FOURTEEN

I stared at Mary, shocked beyond belief. She *geased* us together? Bonded us magically? Without my permission! Without asking! More intimate than a marriage. *Forced* upon me. I was *furious.*

Mary blinked, realizing I wasn't as happy with her as she thought I'd be. "I am protecting us both."

The bond between a master and a familiar was a classic one from fiction. A human magician summoned a spirit from the Spirit World into an animal or person's body then bound it to them. They would be able to communicate for the rest of their lives telepathically and know each other's general well-being. If the spirit was a powerful one, like Mary, the wizard would also gain other benefits related to their portfolio. Which, in Mary's case, was bloodshed and murder.

Looking down at my umbrella, I saw it morph back into its Bloodsword form. The weapon took on an evil hue and I felt my entire body seethe with aggression. My hatred for Stephen, the Red Room, and other things I despised grew. Staring daggers at Bloody Mary, I thought about the other aspects of a Familiar Bond. One partner had to be dominant in the relationship because the bond could be used to shape the weaker one's personality. It was why the Familiar Bond was never used by wizard who thought their partner was sentient.

"You... bitch," I hissed, using language I never used.

I clenched my fists.

"With our bond, you do not have to die," Mary said, eyes widening. "My body is immortal and can sustain you. You don't have to go to Hell when you perish."

"Leave," I said, staring at her. "I never want to see you again."

"But—" Mary said, confused.

"Now," I said, my words final. The rage clouded my judgment and I couldn't see anything but my rage over what she'd done to me. What she'd done to us.

Mary stared.

"Derek." Shannon walked over, sensing this wasn't me.

I turned away from her.

Mary looked down at the ground, shook her head, and vanished as if she'd never been there in the first place. I could still feel her though. Her confusion, pain, and regret. I could feel her immense fear for my soul over Rebecca's death. Her worry over whether I'd be alright with the Red Room after me. How terrified she was of my absence from her life. How incarnating as a human-like being on this world had awakened so many alien emotions in her. Things alien to a spirit of bloodshed like fear, envy, jealousy, and love.

I sighed and pushed down those thoughts to the back of my mind. We would be linked from this day forward, there was no way to break the Familiar Bond without killing one of the participants, but I would do my damnedest not to feel.

The rain continued to pour down on my head and I fell to my knees, spent. "I'm sorry, I shouldn't have said that."

Shannon walked over to my side. "Derek, you've killed like four hundred people. I don't think how you talk matters."

"More like two hundred. I dunno, I've lost count." I sighed. "You can still return, you know."

"What? To the Red Room?" Shannon asked.

I nodded. "Just tell them everything you know about me and where I told you I'm going, which won't be true, and they'll take you back."

"Derek…" Shannon started to say.

"God told you to join the Red Room. You do good work in that organization. We need more people like you there than people like—"

"Derek, shut up."

I blinked. "Okay."

"Listen." Shannon took a deep breath. "As of today, we're both fugitives. Even if I managed to come back, there's no way in hell I'm going to be working for a child-killing sonofabitch like Roland. The very fact you'd think I'd abandon you also pisses me off."

"I'm just trying to be noble," I said.

Shannon snorted. "Stop it. You suck at it."

I smiled. "I guess you're right. I need to stick with what I'm good at."

Which was killing people.

I shook my head. "Do you think Stephen was telling the truth?"

"You're asking me if I think your brother, *the Antichrist*, was telling the truth?" Shannon asked.

"Don't say that," I said.

"What? That your brother is the Antichrist?" Shannon asked.

"First of all, the Antichrist is a product of pop-culture. The idea of Satan incarnating like Jesus is a misreading of the text. It'd be better translated as enemies of Christ, as in plural. The Mark of the Beast is about the Roman Emperor Nero who has been dead for—"

"Derek, I don't need a lecture, especially on Christian eschatology. I got enough of that from my Satanist father."

I looked away. "Yeah, sorry."

"Unfortunately, I believe he's telling the truth, or he believes he is. That means we have a lead even if the source is untrustworthy," Shannon said, nodding. "When I was still working for my father, five out of ten missions were to thwart the pagan gods and their ambitions. The servants of Hell want to fight Heaven and its works but they're not too fond of other religions' deities either. If Zeus and company end up back on top, it screws Hell's plans over as much as the Archangel's."

"I think the ship has sailed for Zeus taking over," I said.

"No one expected the tribal god of Egypt's slaves to take over either," Shannon said.

"I have some words on the historical authenticity of the Exodus as well."

Shannon snorted. "All I'm saying is if this Balor guy starts stomping downtown London, I'm sure there will be a lot of converts to his worship."

People liked to think evangelism was handled through developing a genuine love of a faith and its deities. In truth, fear and social pressures had been the best tools for making sure people found Jupiter or Isis. It'd be the same for Balor.

"I still can't believe Roland is involved in this," I said, staring. "He has more power than any man on Earth save other members of the Committee. Why would he put all of that at risk to change the world?"

"More power?" Shannon suggested.

"Men like Roland don't risk power to gain more power. They rig the game so they win no matter what. Believe me, I know, I grew up around a hundred trust-fund kids just like him. The super-rich aren't risk-takers. They're the ultimate conservatives."

Cassandra had been the exception. She'd risked her fortune and position to try and destroy the House but there had been extenuating circumstance: the need to kill us all for revenge. Roland didn't strike as that committed.

"Then someone's controlling him. Either Balor or someone else."

I nodded. "That's my estimation. The problem is the only people in the world powerful enough to control someone like Roland are members of the Committee, gods, and his dead father."

"Or Stephen," Shannon pointed out.

"Or Stephen," I sighed, shaking my head. "Maybe it's Balor. That seems like the simplest and likeliest explanation but—"

"When has it ever been the simplest or likeliest explanation?" Shannon finished. "I mean, in our line of work. Occam's razor applies everywhere except when magic and demons are involved."

"Exactly," I said, wondering if my father was involved. It was an insane idea, especially as I thought he was one of the less repellent members of the Committee. Yet, he'd ordered me to kill my sister. His own child. If a man could do that, he could do anything. Maybe. I mean, I'd pulled the trigger, hadn't I?

"Derek?" Shannon asked, looking at me. "We should leave. It's not going to take them long to notice something is wrong when people start calling and get no answer."

I looked over to the ruins of the asylum. "You're right. We need to figure out a way to get more answers and, perhaps, journey to the Spirit World."

"The Spirit World is a big place. Fort Happiness could be anywhere in a thousand fairy kingdoms and divine realms."

I closed my eyes, deciding my next action. "There's one person who might know."

"I have a feeling I'm going to regret asking my next question. Who?"

"My mother," I said.

"Your mother... " Shannon looked up to me. "The dragon."

"Yes."

Long before Shannon or even Talbot had joined the Red Room, Song had been an ally of our organization. In the centuries before the European branch had rejoined with the Asian, my mother had been a patron of the alchemists, generals, and demon slayers of Imperial China. Many Emperors owed their thrones to her.

Song was old, as in 'let there be light' old. Old enough to remember things that human beings would never learn and more acquainted with the Spirit World than a host of astral explorers. Song wasn't a god, but she was damned close.

I *hated* her for abandoning Penny and me. I'd never put it in those terms before, but it was how I felt. My entire life, I'd lived with the knowledge I was someone my mother could do without and I'd never forgiven her for it. Some abandoned children think up excuses for why their parents did what they did. That there was some reason they were unwanted. I'd settled on my choice a long time ago: that she was garbage as a person.

I supposed that was why I'd always forgiven Nathan, no matter how awful the things he'd done. Despite being a manipulative polygamist megalomaniac, my father had been there for us. I'd been willing to believe him when he claimed he'd never wanted me to kill Ashley, that he still loved Rebecca despite maneuvering me into killing her, and a half-dozen other horrible things all because he'd *been there.*

"Do you even know how to find your mother?" Shannon asked. "What with her having fled reality decades ago?"

I nodded. "I know how."

I didn't. What I did know was a person who'd might be able to narrow things down: Arthur Morgan, Ashley's nephew. He was also someone who was experimenting with magitech in ways that involved strengthening one's psychic consciousness across the Spirit World. He barely knew his aunt, so he couldn't find her despite their blood connection, but he might be able to find my mother. I also knew where Arthur hung out and suspected he wouldn't turn me into the Committee. Even better, if he did, I was pretty sure I could take him down without killing him. Those were all good reasons to go to him rather than other people.

"Great," Shannon said, walking toward the asylum gates. "Let's just hope your mother doesn't eat you then."

We were to the gates of the asylum where a parking lot was just off to the side with a concrete walkway for staff to use. I hadn't seen it on my way in. There were a lot of cars and since I knew where the Red Room stored its tracking devices, there wouldn't be much of a problem boosting one.

I was deciding on which one to choose when my cellphone rang.

"You really need to get rid of that," Shannon said, looking at me. "Untraceable or not."

"Maybe," I said, picking it up. "Hello?"

"Derek?" It was my father, speak of the Devil. A metaphor that was becoming truer every day.

"We can't be heard talking," I said, sighing. "I know what you're going to say—"

"Penny's been attacked," Nathan surprised me.

I felt sick. "*What?*"

"Her house was assaulted by living machines that came from nowhere. Penny destroyed several of them, but they got away. Lucy is injured but alright. If I hadn't been there, both would be dead."

"Oh God." They were after my family now.

"Derek, what have you gotten them into?" Nathan's voice was sharp, almost a hiss.

"Why didn't you warn me?" I asked, deciding to turn the tables on him. I wasn't in the mood for this bullshit.

Nathan paused. "Ah yes, Roland his attempt on your life. Yes, well, you don't need to worry about that."

"What?" I asked.

"Most of the Committee is dead," Nathan said, coldly.

I blinked, needing a second to process that. "Excuse me?"

"Reports started leaking in about an hour ago about a global pandemic of eso-terrorist attacks. Pandemonium is spreading across the globe. A figure bearing a description like Stephen has been seen all over the world but at the homes or businesses of the Committee's councilmen. He's developed the ability to teleport since we last saw him. The Committee were his first targets, but he's hit high-value House facilities globally. This has been a signal to every one of our enemies to move now. The Great Lie is hanging by a thread. It would seem he's escaped from Lovecraft Asylum."

I tried not to wince. "Yeah, that's probably true. How many Committee members are left?"

"I suspect, as of now, you, I, Amanda Morgan, and the Chairmen are the only surviving members of said body. The latter because he's gone into seclusion somewhere even I can't contact him."

"What about Roland?" I asked.

"Roland is an enemy of the House. As the single surviving senior Committee member still in contact with our forces, I'm comfortable saying that. As for warning you, I was going to handle it for you."

Why didn't I believe him? I thought about ways I could help the House maintain its control then shook my head. Fuck it, I was done with this. Was he responsible for Stephen's escape or was Roland? Was he working with the Vampire Nation and other eso-terrorists? I didn't know but something in my gut told me he was. Since Bloody Mary had directed me to Stephen, it seemed hell was involved in this as well.

"Great," I said, taking a deep breath. "Allow me to resign. I would never be part of an organization that would have me as a member."

Nathan wasn't taking me seriously. "You were kicked out so that Groucho Marx quote doesn't work."

"I'm serious. The House and I are done," I said.

"Derek, this goes beyond Stephen having a rampage. Mental health facilities all over the world are reporting riots as the insane and troubled turn violent. Someone has dumped the entirety of our files onto the internet and all attempts to recover or remove them are failing. Storm systems are brewing that threaten to wash away cities. Draugr outbreaks have been confirmed in India, Pakistan, and a dozen other nations. Wars have broken out and governments have fallen. These attacks by our enemies are not small. This full-scale activation of the entirety of their resources. Someone has been planning this for decades."

"It's you, isn't it?" I made my accusation.

Nathan paused. "Pardon?"

"You had me kill Rebecca and take down Camp Zero. You arranged for me to be on the Committee, which required assassinating one of your rivals. You arranged for Roland to come to power despite the fact you must have known he was a lunatic. No way in hell did Roland get a meeting with Stephen without you allowing it. If the Vampire Nation stole the gold reserves they did—"

"Fine," Nathan said, interrupting me. "I'm responsible. I'm containing the terrorist attacks as best I can, but I've killed everyone who could possibly cover them up. Right now, there's damage control or pure chaos but putting the genie back in the bottle is impossible."

Why?" I asked. "You were the one who taught me that the House was the only thing standing between this world and chaos."

"It was bullshit then too," Nathan said. "The world has evolved, and it's become a choice between revelation now or a revelation ten years from now where humanity exterminates the supernatural or supernatural exterminates humanity. A controlled crash was the only option. You know that. You argued that."

"How many innocent people were you willing to kill for this controlled crash?" I asked. "How many of your own family?"

"Less than I've already lost to the House's lies," Nathan said. "I married a dragon when I was still young and believed in a better world. The House had plans to eliminate all supernaturals on Earth with the help of the government over the course of the next decades. They tried before and enough revolted to split the organization in World War 2. There won't be a split this time."

I blinked. "You've unleashed a pair of monsters on the world. Roland and Stephen have their own plans to break the world. Do you think the vampires, rakshasa, and demons are going to behave?"

"I trust you to kill Roland. I'll handle Stephen," Nathan said. "If we both survive, you can kill me. I'm willing to die for my choices. I was when I fought the Imperial Japanese and I am today. You can do it too. That's why they're afraid of you. The House too."

I didn't mention Stephen could have killed me minutes ago but let me live. It was too damn embarrassing. "Yes, alone and without any resources I'm going to take down Roland and his army of Santa's little helpers. Brilliant strategy, dad."

"Derek, I speak to you as one of the smartest men on Earth. If I were the one in charge of this plot against the Committee and House, I would consider all of this justified to take you off the board. You are *that* dangerous."

"You're in charge of this plot," I snapped.

"No. Any alliance you think we have is dead and gone. Roland thought he could take me out too," Nathan said, hanging up. "He sees a world where the supernatural rule from behind the scenes as humanity's bulwark against the monsters. I see a world where humans and supernaturals live together in the same love/hate relationship they do with each other. He believes I've got to go. Funny, he seemed so trustworthy too."

"I'm going to kill you after this," I said, not really meaning it.

"Right," Nathan said. "Be seeing you."

I really hated that phrase. I hung up the phone and threw it on the ground before smashing it with my heel. I wasn't going to be making any other phone calls anytime soon. Penny was also safer away from me, even if she didn't understand what a monster our father had become. He was completely unfettered and willing to do whatever it took to 'save the world.' Yet, it was he who was threatening it now. Bastard.

"Where we headed?" Shannon asked, smashing in the window of a red Porsche.

"A friend's place. Arthur's Arcade, Detroit. As much as I'd like to visit Penny, our need to find Ashley just doubled. Apparently, it's the End of the World."

"And you feel fine?" Shannon asked, quoting R.E.M.

"Not in the slightest," I said.

Shannon reached into the car's broken window, unlocked the door, slid into the driver's seat, and hotwired it.

And we were off.

CHAPTER FIFTEEN

The world was, quite simply, a mess. I had no real idea what was happening and whether it was my father, Stephen's, or Roland's doing but everyone was panicked yet no one really knew what was going on. There were roadblocks on the highways, furious reporting of news on every radio station followed by the emergency broadcast system taking over all of them, and people shutting down all their businesses to go stay home.

The thing was none of the news and broadcasts clarified what was happening. They described a state of emergency, events in foreign countries, attacks on U.S. soil, to stay at home, mobilization of troops, and so on but it was all talking points that described the shape of a thing rather than what it was. Ignorance was everywhere. It got worse on the ground. When we stopped to ask people what crisis was occurring, the answers were confused and disorientated. Officials didn't know much more than the public, only that they were to prepare for *something.*

What surprised me was how calmly everyone was taking it. Humanity was anything but rational in a crisis. People obeyed the orders they heard on the radio, started preparations for a crisis, and assisted each other in the event. Even the massive lines at grocery stores were orderly and polite. It was unnatural.

Stopping the car to talk to some of the people, I got a sense of what people thought was happening. Someone thought we were going to war with Russia. Others thought it was war with China. An idiot thought it was war with the European Union. More imaginative individuals believed it was an invasion by aliens or the Second Coming. One guy believed the government had transformed into a fascist state with the President as the new Hitler. I didn't pay that fellow any more attention than the European Union guy. What was consistent, though, was nearly everyone seemed to think everything was going to work out fine. Which freaked me the hell out.

In the end, Shannon and I just drove. We were professional spies after all. We weren't going to be deterred by the government's hastily erected barricades or by the highways packed with people trying to reach their families. We traveled on the back roads, took shortcuts, and switched cars to a Hummer we stole.

"Do you think we're in the middle of the zombie apocalypse?" Shannon half-seriously suggested. She was in the driver's seat when we'd finally reached Detroit. The roads going into the city were almost empty while the ones going out packed to the gills.

"Zombies don't exist," I said, looking out the window. "Draugr do, but I don't think it's gotten to the point George Romero predicted."

"I heard you talking with Nathan," Shannon said, sighing. "How bad do you think this is going to get?"

"You worried this is going to be the end of the world?" I asked.

"Yes," Shannon said. "The pod people we've passed aren't reassuring me either."

I agreed with her. "I think Cassandra created a biological weapon capable of destroying the world. I think Roland Cassidy is not nearly as intelligent as his cousin and may possibly be under the domination of an Elder God. I think my fallen angel-possessed brother is fully capable of destroying the world by himself if Roland doesn't get there first. I think the collective might of the supernatural nations is enough to destroy humanity by themselves. It's possible we could be seeing the end, yeah."

Shannon was silent for the next minute. "You know, I was actually hoping you'd say I was being alarmist."

"Sorry," I said. "Nathan has well and truly fucked us."

I could already see the House breaking into separate groups post-Reveal. People like Phillip Tzu would take the house's Red

Sky clan ninjas, Amanda Morgan would take the Men in Black wannabes, and the political masterminds would make a kind of Star Chamber. Hell, they'd probably use the names I was thinking of. The Vampire Nation would be the most successful in adapting to the new world because they'd been preparing for this day for a century. But it was going to be an ugly and confusing few years even if Nathan somehow managed to keep everyone from literally killing everyone else.

"This is... world changing," Shannon said, blown away by it. "There's nothing we can do about this either. The cat is out of the bag."

We passed by a few corpses in the road, their bodies not having been picked up from where someone had shot them to death.

"Yep," I said, sighing. "But I'm not really concerned about any of that right now, though."

"What?" Shannon asked.

I sighed. "All I can think of is Ashley, my sister, and you right now. Screw all this craziness."

"I know, Derek." Shannon's tone became all too obviously patronizing. "We're going to get Ashley back. Your sister will be fine."

"Do you believe that?" I asked.

"Do you want me to lie?" Shannon asked.

"Yes," I said.

"Then absolutely." Shannon gave me a sad and embarrassed look, her attempt at humor falling flat. I appreciated the effort, though. "She'll be fine."

"Thank you." I took several long breaths. "I'm giving no thought to tomorrow because it can take care of itself." I loosely paraphrased Matthew 6:34. "We need to focus on something and the thing I'm going to be focusing on is finding Ashley. For that, I need to find Fort Happiness. After that, I don't give a shit what happens. Roland can resurrect Balor and have him rampage down New York's streets for all I care. Let Stephen kill the Committee and burn the world down. Let Nathan rule the likely *Mad Max* world of punks and raiders Earth is going to become. Frankly, Shannon, I don't give a damn."

"You don't mean that," Shannon said.

I wasn't sure I didn't. I'd been considering retirement since before the events of Cassandra's revolt and now I was starting to realize the reasons behind that. I was spent. I'd killed too many people, betrayed too many friends, and told too many lies.

I wanted out. Not just because I didn't want to do the job anymore but because I wasn't sure I physically or mentally *could*. I'd loved the *Lord of the Rings* above all other book series because it provided a sense of good versus evil in a world my father had gone out of his way to paint in shades of gray. Never had it felt more relevant. Defeating Dracula had been my last great hurrah and now I was Frodo on the slopes of Mount Doom, carrying a burden that had worn me to the quick.

"No, I don't," I said, lying much better than Shannon. "I'll do whatever it takes to protect the people of this world, no matter the cost to me or my sanity. There, does that make you happy?"

"Sure." Shannon smiled.

I smiled. Then a random, almost insane thought popped in my head. "Marry me."

Shannon slammed on the brakes as we arrived at an empty intersection. I nearly flew out of my seat, stopped only by my seatbelt.

"That seems an excessive reaction given we've been living together for a year," I said, pulling back.

"I'm sorry, I wasn't aware there was a protocol for end-of-the-world proposals," Shannon said, looking over at me.

"I'm not proposing because it's the end of the world," I said, sucking in my breath. "I'm proposing to you because I love you. We were talking about going on the run together and living in Taiwan somewhere."

"Taiwan, why Taiwan?" I asked.

"Because I like Taiwan. All the China, minus the human rights violations. Please don't change the subject," I said, keeping my eyes focused on her. "If we get through this—"

"*When* we get through this," Shannon said.

"*If* we get through this," I corrected her. "I'd like to know there's a place I can return to with someone I care about. I know we said no formal commitments and all that jazz, but we have a chance to build a life without the Red Room now. I don't want to be with anyone else and I don't think you want to either."

I was shocked by the ease that the words came from my lips. I'd given up on ever getting married again after Cassandra and Ashley running away. I'd closed myself off to the possibility of happiness and did my best to avoid thinking about a future beyond the next mission. In a very real way, I'd resigned myself to death. The reason I hadn't retired wasn't because the possibility of life without violence bored me to tears or even because I was good at it. But I wanted to live now. Live with Shannon. Be...free.

Yeah, I could do that. I could set my guns and somehow get the Bloodsword out of my soul.

Shannon stared at me, a heartbroken look on her face. "Derek...I can't."

Goddammit. Of course life couldn't let me have this. "I see."

"No, you don't," Shannon said.

"You're right, I don't," I said, wondering at her reasoning. Was it because I couldn't sire children? Did she think marriage only mattered if we had kids? Shannon had vowed never to have sons or daughters because the House would try to use them. Also, she hated the Lilin part of her heritage. Was it something else?

Shannon was a Lilin and had a different lifespan than a normal human being. If she kept drinking life-energy, she'd live forever. Did she not want to see me grow old and die? Hell, that wasn't even an issue now since I was immortal while I was linked to Bloody Mary. Maybe that was the problem. Or was it simply she didn't want to be married to me?

It didn't matter, I had my answer. I turned away. "Alright then."

"Derek—" Shannon started to say. "You knew I didn't—"

"We're almost there," I interrupted her. "Let's avoid talking to each other for a while, okay?"

Shannon didn't say anything else. "We don't—"

"Please," I said in response. "You said you loved me."

"That's why I was going to leave," Shannon said. "I wasn't going to tell you that, though."

"Wow, that makes it so much worse," I said, shaking my head.

"Derek—" Shannon started to explain herself.

"Stop," I said. "I don't want to know."

Shannon looked down. "Okay."

We drove about twenty more minutes to find Arthur's Arcade. Downtown Detroit reminded me of a movie set, empty and foreboding, though that was only in the areas that were cordoned off. People weren't dead or missing, they were holed up in their homes or fleeing the city. Either that or had been evicted months before.

Supposedly, the Vampire Nation had been buying up huge chunks of Detroit for the past few years. I'd been so concerned with Dracula and his terrorists that I hadn't followed up on it. However, I saw dozens of signs that indicated many of the buildings had been recently sold. There were also a bunch of vacant lots that were set aside for development. I wondered what the vampires planned and whether it was going to be possible once the Reveal happened. It was a strange place for the Morgan Family to live since they'd left Louisiana, but Amanda Morgan and her grandchildren weren't afraid of vampires. It was also the city where Solomon Academy had been constructed in honor of my only dead-dead ex-partner.

Arthur's Arcade was the cover identity of a House laboratory and research center. An independent White Room lab set up by some whiz kids and teenagers to do their own DIY magitech. The building was about the size of a suburban ranch house with a large sign that proudly proclaimed it was a video game arcade despite it being a decade since they were relevant. The windows were covered up by red plywood and there was a pair of bouncers in front of the door. The parking lot was full, but it was surrounded by buildings in various states of disrepair, limiting the possibility this would be visited by anyone not 'in the know.'

"It looks like a strip club," Shannon said, breaking the silence since she'd refused my proposal.

"It's a nightclub for gamers," I said, staring at the place. "Techno music, alcohol, and video games. I understand Arthur *wanted* it to be a strip club but apparently you have be over twenty-one to run one of those in Michigan. So, he went with this instead. Maybe he'll change it in a few years."

"*How* is that a research center?" Shannon asked, looking at me.

"I have no idea," I said, shaking my head. "I approved it because he was Ashley's nephew. His grandmother on the Committee gave me more shade for it than when I'd refused to make a vampire killing plague."

"And you think he'll have a way to contact your mother?" Shannon asked, parking the car.

"Arthur used a combination of virtual reality interface and astral projection to send Penny to visit our mother," I said, looking at the building. "The equipment should still be there and it's entirely possible he's improved on it since then. Let's go."

I unbuckled my seatbelt and started to the open the door.

"Derek…" Shannon started to say, reaching over. "We need to—"

"Is there anything that I could say that would make you want to stay with me?"

"I'll ruin you," Shannon said. "Someone like Ashley could save you."

"I'm already ruined," I said. "That's why I sent Ashley away. It turns out that karma is a bitch, and this is what it must have felt like to be her. Good one, God."

I opened the car door and left before she could respond. The guards didn't stop me, House facility or not, and I just walked on in. I was greeted, immediately, by the sound of a nightclub for people about a decade younger than me. The pulsing music, the smell of clove cigarettes, and strobe lights effects reminded me of simpler times. Times when I didn't have to pretend to care.

The interior of Arthur's Arcade was more of a nightclub than a video game arcade, but it had elements of both, being a teenage boy's fantasy of what he'd be able to do if he'd had unlimited money or resources. The walls were lined with arcade machines, most of which were little more than home consoles placed in the boxes of their pre-Nineties counterparts.

There was a sunken second level with a balcony overlooking it, showing a mist-covered dance floor in front of an enormous bar. I also saw numerous booths where techno-punks and cyber-goths were chatting away on magitech laptops. Despite the end of the world happening outside, the people here seemed to be having a good time. I envied them.

While it had been a decade and a half since I'd last been a rebellious Goth teenager, there had been a time when my chief concerns had been having a good time and shocking my father's peers. Nathaniel Hawthorne, for his part, was a veteran of World War 2 and required more than black clothing mixed with a bad attitude to offend him. I'd had innumerable girlfriends but kept close friendships with them all, even after the fact. The weirdest thing in my life back then had been how often Penny and I went after the same girls, not monsters ripping out people's throats or House conspiracies.

There had never been a time when I wasn't going to join the Red Room. You didn't have a choice when you were the child of a House member. The organization maintained itself by sending generation after generation of its bloodlines into the meat grinder of the supernatural, but I'd been able to ignore that fact for a time. I wished I could go back to that state of ignorance. I had responsibilities now, though. I needed to find Ashley. That was all that mattered now. Not marriage. Not hope. Not the House. Not the world.

"I'll find you, Ash, I swear it," I said, swearing by the Primals and any other gods that were listening. I didn't care if they struck me down for failing the oath or not.

Leaning up against the balcony overlooking the dance floor, I realized damn near every person in Arthur's Arcade was looking at me. I started to wonder if I'd been put on the FBI's Most Wanted List but suspected these kids didn't often peruse said website.

"They're just surprised to see you," Arthur said behind me. "To younger members of the House, you're a hero."

I turned around, wondering why everyone always got the drop on me. Behind me, accompanied by two teenage Red

Room agent hopefuls I recognized as Alex Timons and Lucien Lyons was Arthur Morgan. The three of them were dressed like rejects from *The Matrix*, Arthur not quite pulling it off since he was a bit on the short and stout side. He was a black-haired kid with the beginnings of a goatee who looked older than he really was and sported a reverse baseball cap that was out of fashion a decade earlier.

Alex Timons was a distant relation of my family and named for one of my half-brothers. Names got recycled a lot in the House since so many of us died so early. Just like Ashley, my Ashley, had a niece named for her that was probably among the crowd here. He was a tall and gawky looking teen who, nevertheless, burned with magical energy greater than anyone I'd known save my father and sister. He had brown hair and was biracial, having the same level of Chinese ancestry as I did (albeit human rather than dragon).

Lucien Lyons was supposedly a dragon himself but not the kind I was descended from. Instead, he was a white-haired half-Japanese kid who could become a size-changing alligator. I suppose being a weregator was less impressive sounding than calling yourself a dragon, but I found it difficult to take him seriously. Like Shannon, he was one of the supernaturals adopted by the House for use against their own kind. Alex's family had adopted him and the two of them were thick as thieves, but I honestly didn't know that much about him. I could tell he was sizing me up, though, which told me that he knew I was a threat. Smart kid.

Hell, they all looked like kids to me and probably were but as soon as they graduated Solomon Academy, they were put to work against all manner of monsters and creatures. There were no ends of casualties every year and we just fucking normalized it. Goddamn, I'd been killing people since I was their age. Maybe father was right, maybe burning it down was the only answer.

"Everyone here is a member of the House?" I asked, shaking his hand.

I was almost immediately overwhelmed by a vision of Arthur, turned into a vampire, and biting into the neck of the Chairman. He was powerful, far more so than his age, and holding the Bloodsword in one hand. I also saw Alex, wearing an FBI tactical vest, and shooting an enchanted gun into the heart of an ancient vampire. Lucien, himself, grew up into being a male model-looking fellow who radiated supernatural power of a very different sort with thousands of fawning sycophants who proclaimed him the 'Messiah of the 99%.' It was an insight into their future and a sign of what was to come.

"You okay?" Arthur asked, pulling back his hand.

I shook my head. "You mean aside from the chaos outside?"

"Yeah, it's an apocalypse party," Lucien said, his voice too deep for a teenager. He'd grow into it, though. "The Reveal is coming and we're all going to have to ease in the public to the idea their neighbor can turn fuzzy three nights a month."

"There's a town called Bright Falls where almost half the population is related to shifters," Alex said. "It's only about thirty minutes away and—"

"Don't care," I interrupted. "I need your help, Arthur."

"You got it," Arthur said. "Is this about finding out where my aunt is?"

I blinked. "You knew she was alive?"

Arthur shrugged. "A lot of us here have been feeding the Network information. Her specifically. We all saw this day coming."

"Apocalypse is accurate actually," Alex said, ignoring that I didn't care. "It means revelation."

"Shut up, Alex," Arthur said.

Alex shrugged.

"You're comfortable telling me about your treason?" I asked, surprised. I wondered if they were very smart or very dumb.

"You're a traitor too, aren't you?" Arthur asked.

He had a point there. Behind me, Shannon came in through the front door and gave the place a once over.

"So this is the infamous Shannon O'Reilly?" Arthur said, turning to her. "If only I was five years older."

Shannon raised an eyebrow. "Then you'd be old enough for me to shoot you down."

"Is it safe to talk here?" I asked, looking out into the nightclub.

"It depends about what you mean by that," Arthur said, nodding. "You're safe here because you're a hero. Also, because I'm clouding everyone's minds of seeing you except for the people I trust. Real *The Shadow* shit."

"You're too young for *The Shadow*," I said.

"Retro is the new, well, new," Arthur said. "But if you've got a plan to save the world, it was too late six hours ago."

"How bad is it?" I asked. "The radios are broadcasting nothing but emergency services and platitudes."

Alex answered. "One and a half million people have died due to a couple of micro-nukes being set off to cover up the draugr plague releases in India and Russia by the Emerald Eye's remnants. Thankfully, neither nation has annihilated any others due to being well-aware of what's really going on. France has a massive student riot going on due to the revelation of the House's activities on the internet. Day-trading is suspended due to the panic over the possibility all this supernatural stuff happening is real. There's a media blackout, including shutting down the internet in most of the world, but it's not working. The Saudi government fell an hour ago. The Chinese branch of the House has temporarily assumed control over the country and is cooperating with Taiwan's Division. I *think* the rakshasas have taken over the part of Pakistan the Taliban was holed up in too. Not sure about the Djinn but they've never been very forthcoming."

I blinked once. "Okay, then."

So much for Taiwan then.

Shannon took a deep breath. "We're out of a job."

"Or are going to be working day and night," Arthur said, smiling. It was the humorless smile of someone who knew how badly we were fucked.

"All these events give me hope for the future, actually," Arthur said, surprising me. "Humanity has the potential to reduce the world to a glowing cinder but hasn't yet. No one is planning to from what I'm getting over the emergency feeds either. The Magicnet is plugged into every wizard's laptop in the world, internet and no internet, and all the divinations say we're going to survive this."

"That's kind of reassuring," I said. "Kinda."

"The question is whether or not casualties will equal a hundred million or more or not," Arthur said.

"That, less so," I said, disgusted.

"I know not with what weapons World War Three will be fought, but World War Four will be fought with sticks and stones." Alex raised his pointer finger into the air. "Misattributed to Albert Einstein."

"I'm not here to save human civilization," I said. "Just a person I love."

Arthur looked at Shannon. "You okay with this?"

Shannon stared.

"And it's none of my business," Arthur said. "I'll help you do it."

"Good," I said. "Lead on, Cyberpunks."

Arthur turned around and walked past his two bodyguards. Waving us to follow, he said, "I can help you, though it's not without its risks."

"I am the king of risk," I said.

"You're not," Arthur said, talking as we walked to an elevator at the back end of the arcade. "You're actually one of the most risk-adverse goal-orientated people I know. It's just the lowest risk for others is the maximum for yourself."

"Yeah, well don't spread it around. I have a reputation to uphold," I said.

Shannon followed behind me, looking as uncomfortable in our surrounding as I was.

"What are the risks?" I asked.

"By supplementing standard astral projection spells with technology, I've been able to enhance them so they can reach any section of the Astral Plane from the highest heavens to the deepest hells. Furthermore, it's possible to track down any soul you have a sympathetic connection to." Arthur reached the elevator and pushed the call button. "The only problem is a lot of the people we send out don't come back. It turns out visiting the highest heavens or the lowest hells can be hazardous to your brain."

"Uh-huh," I said, grimacing. "And what about everywhere else?"

"It turns out that a lot of Spirit World spirits are capable of killing you in your astral form. You die in there, you die outside. I don't think this is going to be the basis for virtual reality anytime soon."

I grimaced. "Right, well, I need to get in touch with my mother."

"Are you sure, we can just get in touch with Ashley Morgan directly," Arthur said, looking forward at the elevator doors. "I know how much you despise Song Hawthorne."

"Call that Plan B. My mother was near-omniscient according to Nathan and I need an outsider's perspective." I paused, weighing what I was going to say next. "Penny described her as a good person. I want to know what she thinks."

"Okay dokey," Arthur said, nodding. "Oh, by the way, you're not the first person to come here today asking about my aunt."

"I'm not?" I asked.

Arthur said, "You can see for yourself."

Shannon looked over at me but I didn't meet her gaze. We waited for the elevator and Arthur headed on in, followed by his entourage. I followed them. Shannon came in last, waiting for the doors to shut in front of us.

The trip down to Arthur's lab took about a minute and a half, highlighting we were far underneath Detroit's surface but not so much as to be ridiculous. When the doors opened, I was surrounded by a long corridor of Pantheon Thought supercomputers and magictech enhancements.

To the side of the long row of identical white wall-like computers, I saw a large black leather chair with a large amount of unidentifiable equipment built into its side. There were medical trays around it as well, one containing defibrillator along various hypodermics. A heart monitor, IV, and other equipment was just to the side.

In the shadows behind the chair, where the lights were conspicuously turned off, I saw the outline of several huge plasma-screen television sets and computer monitors. It looked like a miniaturized version of the control room in *Wargames*. I saw Ashley's nieces, her namesake and Anna Morgan, leaning up to a nearby corner. They were dark-haired pale-skinned new graduates of the Solomon Academy and reminded me sharply of Ashley. Both looked away from me and I could tell neither of them had a high opinion of me—perhaps they were old enough to blame me for their aunt's disappearance.

Much to my surprise, I was also able to see the outline of a figure literally wrapped in the shadows. Had I been anyone else in the House, save possibly Shannon, I wouldn't have been able to see the figure. He'd have been all but invisible. I'd always had a curious ability to pierce these sorts of illusions, however, and I had more experience dealing with their kind than any other agent alive.

"You have a vampire in your lab," I said, nonchalantly.

"Yeah," Ashley (jr.) said. "Not cool, Arthur."

"I'd report this for treason," Anna said. "But I'd rather not get my family killed."

"Thanks," I muttered.

"I know there's a vampire in my lab," Arthur said, walking in. "I think you know him in fact."

I was confused before I saw the shadows part and reveal the figure of my third best friend in the world. Indeed, one of the few people outside of Penny and Shannon that I trusted with my life.

"Christopher," I said, staring at him in a mixture of relief and shock. If there had been ever a time when I needed the comfort of a familiar face, now was it. "Christopher."

Christopher walked over and gave me a hug. "I just wish it could be under better circumstances. No sooner do we destroy Dracula and the Wazir than the Seals of Revelation start being broken."

"Please tell me you're exaggerating," I said.

"Just a figure of speech, Derek," Christopher said.

"I was just saying—" Alex started to speak.

"Shut up, Alex," I said.

"Right," Alex shut up.

I breathed a sigh of relief. "What are you doing here, anyway?"

"I could ask you the same thing," Christopher said.

"I asked first," I said, feeling childish.

"Things have gotten worse," Christopher said.
"How worse?" I asked, wondering what could be done.
"Balor is close to reviving," Christopher said.
Well, shit.

CHAPTER SIXTEEN

"So, it's the end of the world?" I asked, looking at Christopher. "Yes," Christopher said, taking a deep breath. "I had Arthur here give me an astral visit to New London. The entire place is almost deserted. The oracles I know still there are all bleeding from the eyes, babbling prophecy, and talking about the rising of the Sleeping One-Eyed God."

"Sounds like a euphemism for erectile dysfunction," Shannon said.

Everyone looked at her.

"What? Just me?" Shannon said, looking around. "Damn. I thought spies loved double entendres."

"Not during the apocalypse," Arthur said. "I mean, until they make a sexy version of *Mad Max* with harem girls or something."

"That's stupid," I muttered. "I mean, if you got someone like Charlize Theron—"

"I'm going to pass that on to my friends in Hollywood," Arthur said.

"You're like eighteen, you don't have friends in Hollywood," I replied.

"Your dad introduced me to the Wachowski sisters," Arthur said. "I have an idea for a Keanu Reeves crime drama and a fourth *Matrix* movie too."

Christopher coughed. "Derek, as much as I find this kind of discourse amusing, when Balor rises, Ashley is going to die."

Well, that deflated the mood. "I see."

"Her life-force is what is being siphoned off to bring Balor back," Christopher said. "They're doing it slowly, so they don't burn her out, but it's almost done. I can feel her dying."

I stared at him. Vampires sometimes established a psychic connection with their servants, creations, and spouses. "Just how close are you two?"

Christopher looked at him. "You know how devoted I was to my creator. That was a false feeling. I love Ashley."

I blinked. "Good for you."

Christopher looked down. "Listen, there's some other things that you need to know. Reasons why Ashley hasn't just brought down the entire House on them."

"What?" I asked.

Christopher opened his mouth then sucked it back in. "No, I can't. Not yet. It's not my story to tell you. Ashley and I both need to tell you when this is over, though. You deserve to know. I'm sorry I've kept it from you."

"Christopher, I will kick your ass if you continue to jerk me around," I said, simply. "I should note that if you think I'd lose because you're a vampire, I have beaten to death vampires much-much older than you."

Christopher tried to slap me with his superspeed, only for me to catch his hand by the wrist. His eyes widened.

Shannon rolled her eyes. "Girls, you're both pretty."

"Just," Christopher paused and sighed. "Trust me on this, Derek. You don't need this riding on you right now."

I closed my eyes. "You know, I don't care. Just tell me what we need to do."

Christopher stared at him. "There's like sixteen potential Pantheon Corp locations for Ashley to be held at, including one in New London. I couldn't get to check that one out while I was projecting. If you've got a way to narrow things down, then now is the time to do it."

"Derek is going to ask his mother for help," Arthur said, standing beside me. "Which is a lot more badass than it sounds since she's a hundred-foot long fire-breathing scaly thing."

"She actually breathes boiling water," I said, remembering my father's stories. "Which is still pretty dangerous."

"Painful too!" Arthur said, adding. "I think she's like a goddess too or maybe an angel. Some people say she's even a mortal wizard who ascended to become both. I'm not sure what category high dragons fit into."

"There's not much difference in Chinese mythology," I said, still uncomfortable with the whole subject. "She was a powerful diviner with connections to actual gods. I think she can help us." And if nothing else, tell me whether Ashley were alive. I didn't like not knowing whether they were dead or alive.

Oh wait, yes, I did, I'd kill every single member of the Cassidy family and all their followers down to the last man. Then piss on the ashes.

"Will your mother help you?" Christopher asked the question I hadn't been willing to ask myself. "After all, she abandoned you."

Shannon started to say something, but I spoke first. "I'll beg if I have to."

Christopher gave a short nod. "Thank you, Derek. I don't deserve a friend like you."

"Being a blood-sucking abomination against reality, that's probably true," Ashley (jr.) said, keeping my arms crossed. "You better not be mesmerizing my aunt."

"He's not," Arthur said, simply. "Aunt Ashley loves him."

"No accounting for taste," Ashley (jr.) said, glaring at the vampire.

"He's really-really hot," Anna said, simply.

I felt vaguely insulted. "Okay," I said, walking over to the chair. "What do I have to do?"

Arthur walked over to the machine. "Are you sure you want to go now?"

"Every second counts in a kidnapping," I said, trying to keep myself calm. I felt like a pawn in a chess game where I was being maneuvered by both sides. "Especially when it's a sacrifice to bring forth Yog-Sothoth. How long is this going to take?"

Arthur went to a nearby computer console and began booting up several programs. "It'll just take a few moments."

One of Arthur's guards proceeded to attach a set of zip ties to my leg and arms. They also started moving a mouthguard to my face.

"Do I really need something to keep me from biting off my own tongue?" I asked, turning to Arthur.

"Do you want to risk it?" Arthur asked,

"Point taken," I said, biting down on the mouth guard.

What followed was an uncomfortable next few minutes as Arthur got the system booted up. I didn't have time to talk with Christopher about what he'd been up to since the war with the vampires had begun, what he thought of the end of the world, and even how he was getting along as a free vampire.

Despite what had transpired between us, Shannon stood by my side the entire time too. She helped them attach the IV to my arm and helped start the process to put me under. I didn't know what I was in for, but I had a vague idea from Penny's description. I just hoped I'd be able to follow her lead. As I felt my eyes become heavy, Arthur put on AC/DC's "Highway to Hell." I turned my head to one side, wrinkling my brow.

"What?" Arthur asked, shrugging. "Mood music helps in astral projection."

That was the last thing I heard before I went down the rabbit hole, unsure about whether I would come back out again. Astral projection was a technique that was almost unknown in the Modern World. It had hit its heyday in the 19th century with Hermeticism and Theosophist schools of magic, being a common tool of spiritualist-influenced wizards or psychics to visit other dimensions. It wasn't *that* difficult of a technique with many "Near Death" experiences being the mind unconsciously slipping away. Of course, given the nature of the Astral Plane, it was sometimes hard to tell the difference between when you were dreaming and when you are visiting another universe. And whether the two had any real difference. On my end, I fell. I fell a long, long way.

Perhaps it was the influence of Arthur's music choice, but it was down an endless hole that gave rise to a library. The music changed to Golden Earring's version of "Twilight Zone." I passed by a glass coffin containing Cassandra's sleeping (dead?) body in Snow White's dress. A bloody alicorn horn passed by me only for me to grab it from the air and stuff it into my trench coat pocket, piercing the bottom with its lining.

Spinning around in mid-air to see where I was falling, I saw I was coming up to a gigantic football stadium-sized portrait of my extended family with Nathaniel Hawthorne in the center of it. The portrait split in half, revealing an endless darkness beyond.

"That's not good," I said.

In the end, my descent started to slow, and I landed with a gentle bounce on what felt like stone. The darkness was all around me and all-encompassing but not *menacing*, if that made any sense. The air around me was warm and there was a thick humidity, but I didn't get the same fight or flight response I might have in more threatening circumstances. That was when I realized my eyes were closed and I felt like an idiot.

I found myself in an environment I didn't expect: a New Age store that smelled of lavender as well as incense. The walls were covered in books, candles, lotions, and many knickknacks I was surprised all felt of genuine magic. Sitting behind a glass counter was a teenage girl about seventeen or eighteen wearing blue jeans as well as a T-shirt with a DAENERYS WAS RIGHT logo on it. It showed a cartoon version of the Dragon Queen burning down King's Landing on dragon back, which was the dumbest way they could possibly end that book series.

"Where am I?" I asked, wondering where I had astrally projected myself too.

"Walla Walla, Washington," the teenager said, flipping through a magazine. "This is the Tower for all your occult and scented candle needs."

"Song Hawthorne?" I asked, wondering if this was a joke.

"That's one of the names I've gone by," the teenager said, not looking up. "You can also call me... Kim... or Su."

Kim Su was a name the House had on its Most Wanted List as well as more legends than King Arthur, Robin Hood, and the Blue Fairy. She wasn't the strongest mage in the world, more like the top thirty, but she was one of the most influential. Supposedly, the oldest living sorcerer ever, which was still a step down from being an immortal dragon from beyond time. Apparently, Dad had been exaggerating certain elements of her past or Kim Su's history was even more strange than I'd heard. Which was hard to believe. Legitimately, Kim Su is supposed to have been the one to have killed Hitler. The first time he died. Talbot still regrets missing out on that opportunity.

"You look like a teenager," I said.

"When five thousand years you reach, look as good you will not," Kim Su said, smirking.

"You're my mother?" I asked, horrified that she looked barely legal in most states.

Kim Su covered her mouth with one hand and did the Darth Vader voice. "You know it to be true."

I stared at her. "Oh God, the reason everyone in my family talks like they're in a Kevin Smith movie finally makes sense. It's genetic."

Kim Su shrugged. "I'm not related to everyone in your family. Your father is a real horndog."

I felt my face. "Yeah, I suppose he is. Also, even more disgusting now."

"I shape change into a thirty-year-old-woman when we have quickies," Kim Su said, shrugging.

"Because that makes it better," I said, looking away.

"Doesn't it?" Kim Su asked.

"Err, maybe?" I asked, looking away. Weirdly, I found this a lot more troubling than if I had just found her as a huge fire-breathing lizard. "Sorry, this is just weird."

"Your father and I had an on-again, off-again relationship across the past century," Kim Su said. "You're not even our oldest kid."

I stared at him. "Excuse me?"

"Yeah, our oldest kid is Phillip Tzu from the Boxer Rebellion," Kim Su replied.

"Wait, Alex Timon's dad? The one back at the arcade?" I asked, appalled. "His mother tried to set him up in an arranged marriage with Rebecca."

"Yeah, glad Phillip put the kibosh on that," Kim Su said, grimacing. "The House has been trying to get every wizard in the world to work for it for millennia. All it has done is turned you into a bunch of incestuous pseudo-Hapsburg wizards with the regular public gradually losing its magic. There's a book on this."

"I didn't actually come here to talk about this," I muttered.

Kim Su reached under table and pulled out a copy of *Harry Potter and the Half-Blooded Prince*. "You see, all the Pure Blood families are related. It's like a family bush instead of a tree."

"Please stop," I said.

"Mind you, I've ruined him for other women," Kim Su said, going through the book. "That's why he's constantly hooking up with maids, fellow wizards, his secretaries, and Princess Margaret. That was a while ago, though."

I felt my face. "Oh for the love of the gods."

"It's due to the Prophecy of the Suns predicts that one of his descendants will be the one to slay the Elder Gods and bring peace to the world. Thus he's tried to breed the perfect warrior mage so he can control him."

"What?" I asked, doing a double take.

"No, wait, that's my theory about Palpatine creating Anakin Skywalker," Kim Su said, looking down at her book. "But here's the real question: did Luke fulfill the prophecy or did his father? Also, Neville or Harry?"

"I need your help finding my ex-fiancé," I said, taking a deep breath.

"Hire a private detective," Kim Su said.

I glared at her. "She was kidnapped by a bunch of genetically engineered elves as part of a scheme to resurrect an evil god."

"Did Joss Whedon write this script?" Kim Su asked. "Is it for the new *Hellboy*?"

I stared.

"Fine, fine," Kim Su said, crossing my arms. "Why should I help you?"

I kept my gaze level. "Because you abandoned us to be raised by a narcissist megalomaniac and his weird cult."

Kim Su blinked. "Fair enough. To be fair, Derek, I was being hunted by thousands of evil magicians and monsters at the time. I didn't think you wanted to be raised on the run or forced to live in hiding."

"Please don't say it wasn't you, it was your enemies," I said, dryly. "I got sick of that excuse while reading Spider-Man as a child."

"I feel like Spider-Man gets a lot of heat for that when he already has a couple of dead girlfriends," Kim replied. "Mind you, he might have better luck if he didn't constantly taunt the insecure psychopaths he arrests and just killed them."

"Will you help me?" I asked, hoping this wasn't an enormous waste of time.

"Yes," Kim Su said. "However, there's something you need to know about this rescue mission."

"Which is?" I asked, wondering what could possibly be bothering her so much that she was giving me the runaround like this. I thought I was prepared for anything in terms of responses. I was wrong.

Kim Su's face lost all mirth. "Derek, if you continue on this mission to rescue Ashley then you're not coming back. It's a one-way ticket. You'll die at the end of this."

I blinked. "Huh."

CHAPTER SEVENTEEN

I stared at her, blinked, then opened my mouth before closing it. "So, I'm going to die, huh?"

"This is no laughing matter, Derek," Kim Su said.

"Yes, I'm just giddy like the Joker," I replied.

"Cesar Romero or Jack Nicholson?" Kim Su asked.

"I hear that Heath Ledger will be good," I replied, blinking. "How certain are you about this?"

"About as certain as one can be with prophecies," Kim Su replied, looking genuinely concerned. "There's always a little wiggle room but virtually every possible result of you continuing on your quest to save Ashley Morgan results in you dying."

"Dying-dying or becoming a vampire dying?" I asked.

Kim Su drew a finger across her neck and made a cartoon slitting noise. "That kind of dying."

"Well shit," I said, staring at her.

A moment passed between us.

"So—" Kim Su started to say.

"Yeah, tell me where Ashley is," I said, taking a second to collect myself.

Kim Su blinked. "Are you sure?"

"I've been in more combat than Rambo," I replied. "So much so that the Demon of War is actually in love with me. I was maybe too harsh on her for it too. I didn't do that because I thought I was invincible."

"There's the difference between the possibility of death and the certainty of it," Kim Su said.

I closed my eyes. "Yeah, but I also need to be prepared to

give my life. At least this is for something worthwhile. I mean no one lives forever."

"I do," Kim Su said.

I rolled my eyes. "Time is ticking, Puff the Mommy Dragon."

"I could just choose to not help you," Kim Su said.

"Then I'd find another way and hate you forever," I said, dryly. "Not that I'm filled with all manner of warm and fuzzy feelings for the woman who abandoned me."

Kim Su looked down and I could see genuine guilt on her face. Either that or she was an excellent liar like my father. "I am sorry."

"For what?" I asked, wondering if this was a deliberate attempt at distraction.

"For failing you as a mother," Kim Su said, sighing. "When I left your father, I was certain I was doing the right thing and separating from the corruption of the House was the moral choice. I have always acted in the way faith dictated I should. That included the belief my mortal children should be allowed to live normal lives."

"Listen, you don't owe me an explanation—" I started to say.

Kim Su continued speaking. "I saw the effect the House was having on Nathan. How the intrigue, lies, and murder ate at him. How his hatred for the organization and desire to burn it to the ground grew with each passing day. I saw the outrage as you and Penny were turned into weapons to be pointed at beings like myself. Nathan went mad when he discovered his original family was killed on the House's orders."

I blinked. The revelation the House had my father's previous wife and children killed should have stunned me. It didn't. Nothing the House did surprised me anymore.

Kim Su got a faraway look in her eyes. "I longed to reach out as I saw you two become involved in the House's power games. I wanted to help Nathan's other children despite having no blood connection to them. I longed to show you there was another way, one where you wouldn't have to sacrifice yourselves fighting someone else's war. The wars of corrupt men who desire power and wealth. I restrained myself, though. I took comfort in my faith that you were better off with your fellow humans than in my war against Hell and other ruinous powers."

I sighed, not caring about Kim Su's self-justifications. "You're not the first person to abandon their family because they're a religious wacko."

Kim Su burst out laughing. "I am not making any progress here at all am I?"

"If you're trying to tell me the House is evil, no shit. If you're trying to come off as all wise and powerful, I'm not buying what you're selling. I make my own rules, my own morality, and follow my own credo. Now, please get with the scrying, Galadriel. I have a schedule to keep."

"I see." Kim Su looked at me, something new in her eyes. Respect? Wariness? Resignation? I couldn't tell. "Well, let's go find your lover."

Kim Su got up and led me through the back door of her store. There I saw a kiddie pool next to a garden hose sitting on the grass leading into a sickly-looking forest. "Here we go."

"Really?" I asked.

"You expected a mithril bowl and pitcher?" Kim Su asked.

"Yeah, actually, I did," I said.

"Sorry to disappoint," Kim Su said, picking up the garden hose and turning it on. She let the water pour into the kiddie pool.

The pool's contents swirled and churned, becoming a vortex that revealed a new realm beyond. There, much to my surprise, I saw a city unlike any on Earth. It was like something of the imagination of Ridley Scott or William Gibson with massive towers of transparent steel and circuit-board-like interlocking freeways. It was a magitech city where the sciences had been allowed to flourish without interference from the House. Glowing holograms advertised cancer-less cigarettes and baroque pornography while flying cars surged through the air. The sky was black as coal with a thick layer of clouds blotting out all light but what came from the metropolis below.

"Really? This is where Ashley is located?" I asked, stunned.

"It is New London," Kim Su explained, referencing the location mentioned by Christopher. "Ashley unwittingly placed the Network's headquarters within miles of its worst enemy.

It was originally known as Avalon and is one of the Pocket Dimensions claimed by mages after the elves were exterminated and the other fae races driven deeper into the Spirit World. King Arthur's final resting place has become corrupted deeply by the children of men. As centuries have passed in the Spirit World, refugees from the United Kingdom have built their own civilization there on the ashes of Merlin's dream. It is a dark, gritty, and soulless place filled with murderers as well as thieves."

"So I'll fit right in," I said, grinning.

Kim Su narrowed her eyes. "Must you sound so *cheerful* about it?"

"I put the anti in anti-hero," I said.

"Not as much as you'd think, or you wouldn't be pursuing this still." Kim Su sighed. "Keep looking at the vision."

I did. The vision continued to show me New London, eventually circling on an island just off the coast of the urban sprawl. The island's contents looked like Alcatraz with spotlights, large concrete walls, and fortified gunnery positions. In the interior yard, I saw hundreds of human beings and supernaturals, milling about with electrical collars around their neck. Their heads were shaved and eyes vacant. Giant holograms of Roland Cassidy projected onto the wall, taunting the poor bastards within and giving them orders. It was combination of hell and George Orwell's *1984*.

"Jesus," I said, staring at the sight. "What is wrong with that guy?"

"This is Fort Happiness," Kim Su said, frowning. "It is an undocumented project of the House. The people of New London think they are safe from your organization's influence, but they are not. The city's lawless inhabitants pay a security company to deal with their troublemakers, but these are but pawns of the House. Some prisoners are recruited, others killed, and others still drained or experimented on. A substantial number are being brainwashed, albeit very slowly."

"I killed Rebecca to put an end to the House's brainwashing," I said.

Kim Su shook her head. "You only impeded it. It is simply

too useful a skill to abandon and they will not rest until every supernatural being in the world is either dead or enslaved."

"The House is dying," I said.

"A beast is always most dangerous when it's injured and cornered," Kim Su said.

I tried to wrap my head around that before I stopped trying for the sake of my own sanity. "So she's here. Ashley, I mean."

"Yes," Kim Su said, putting down the pitcher. "On the top floor of the interior."

The scrying pool shifted to the image of a black chamber where I saw Ashley for the first time in years. My former partner still had her short black hair and curvaceous frame, though she'd aged and looked to be in her mid-forties now. It was possible Ashley was far older now since powerful psychics and magicians tended to live longer than regular humans even without longevity treatments. I didn't care, though, because just looking at her was like looking into a happy future that might have been.

Ashley was tied to a pair of wooden beams formed into a Saint Andrew's cross by her arms, legs, and waist with rope while dressed in an orange prison jumpsuit. The cross overlooked the top point of a pentagram made of glowing white low-burning fire. Centered in the mystical diagram was a black iron cauldron large enough to fit a full-grown man. An invisible-to-human-eyes-but-not-mage flow of energy was traveling from Ashley's body to the cooking pot.

"Those evil bastards," I said, staring at the chalice. "What are they doing?"

"It is the *Pair Dadeni* or Cauldron of Rebirth," Kim Su explained, staring at the scene. "A talisman created by Welsh giants. It had the power to restore the dead back to life before it was destroyed by Efnisien the Wicked. Its pieces were gathered by ancient wizards of the House and reassembled but they could not repair it. It was not until your father came upon it that he was able to restore its might. Like you and Penny he is a master magician of limitless potential due to the will he possesses."

I got a sick feeling in my stomach. "Nathan is responsible for all of this, isn't he? He's the one who released Stephen and is the guy behind Roland."

Kim Su didn't answer.

I looked at her.

"Yes," Kim Su said, sighing. "Your father has hated the House ever since the Sino-Japanese War when the House had the chance to stop the Imperial Japanese but chose to let them carry out their conquests so the Committee might profit from the aftermath. Nathan's hatred became etched into his soul forever when the Chairman had his first family murdered to increase his antipathy to nonhumans. I tried to ease his troubled soul but failed. Nathan has encouraged the greedy, ambitious, and power-hungry to rise to the top of the House for decades. By feeding their addiction, he knew it would eventually explode and destroy itself. All of this is his *coup de grace* to the sickness that is the Red Room and its sister agencies."

I stared at Ashley's image in the pool. "I don't care."

Kim Su did her second double-take of the evening. *"You don't care?"*

"All you've told me is Nathan is responsible for Ashley's capture. That he put Penny in the hospital. That he let Rebecca become a monster and ordered me to kill her to help destroy the House. He's dead to me."

"I see," Kim Su said. "Fair enough."

"Will Ashley be alright?" I asked, wondering if all of this was for naught.

Kim Su sighed. "No. She's voluntarily allowing her life force to be drained. If they sacrificed her energy all at once, Balor would probably rise but only for a short while. They're going for a slow burn supplemented by many other sacrifices. It means they might be able to restore him to full strength."

"Voluntarily?" I asked. "She could have escaped on her own?"

"Yes," Kim Su said. "They have something of hers that she's willing to die to protect. You know what it is."

I did. There was only one thing that could keep Ashley involved in a plot to resurrect an ancient monster: a child. Christopher had alluded to it and I'd long suspected that may have been a reason why she'd never attempted to contact me again. It was the only way to keep the House's greedy mitts off a child of two powerful magical lineages. Still, I had to be sure. "I see. Is it—"

"Yes," Kim Su said.

I closed my eyes. "I see. All the more reason to save them both."

Kim Su nodded. "So, what are you going to do now?"

I gave a half-hearted shrug. "I'm going to go to New London with Christopher and Shannon then murder the fuck out of everyone there. Then I'm going to get Ashley and her daughter or son as well as die in the process. Hopefully, I can prevent Balor's resurrection in the process."

"And if you can't stop Balor?" Kim Su asked.

"Then it's not really my problem anymore, is it?" I asked.

"No, I suppose it's not," Kim Su said. "Even if you fail, Balor won't destroy the world. Thousands of people may die, even tens of thousands of people, but humanity has gained new weapons that transcend even the enchanted weapons of old. If the stars were right and it was meant to be the true Biblical Armageddon, he might be able to lay waste to the Earth, but that is not this time. Life will go on."

"Wee," I said, not particularly caring about what Balor did. He wasn't the reason I was doing this. "Can I ask you a question?"

"Always," Kim Su said. "Just don't expect an answer if it's the wrong one."

"Is my father a monster?" I asked.

Kim Su stared at me. "I don't know. I think if he knew what Ashley was being blackmailed with then yes. Then again, your father may simply be insane with grief. History will change because of what he's done and people do not make history by being kind of good."

"Tell that to Gandhi," I said.

"You clearly didn't know his wife," Kim Su said. "Man, the things she told me about him."

I gave a half-smile. "Thank you, Kim Su."

"Call me mom."

"No," I said, still smiling.

"You're welcome," Kim Su said, looking regretful. "This conversation didn't go the way I expected it to but that was my fault, not yours. I wish you the blessings of the divine and hope you achieve some measure of peace in the future."

"Peace was never an option," I said, sighing. "And yeah, that was a movie quote."

"I worry about your childhood. Did Nathan raise you on nothing but a steady pile of cartoons and movies?" Kim Su asked.

"No, I raised myself on it," I said, sad that our relationship was going to end on that note. I didn't think I was going to see my mother again. I wasn't sure how I felt about that.

Kim Su sighed and went to open a gateway out of this realm.

CHAPTER EIGHTEEN

A swirling portal opened against the door, looking like a whirlpool built into brick. "This should take you back to your body."

"Thank you," I said, looking at her.

"It was good meeting you," Kim Su said.

"Yeah," I said, walking to the portal.

"No one is beyond redemption, Derek," Kim Su said. "Good and evil are just directions. There's no end to either."

"Do you mean that for me or Nathan?" I asked.

Kim Su didn't answer.

I walked through the portal without saying another word.

Everything became a white blur and my head pounded. I could hear voices around me, but I was sitting, once more, in the chair that Arthur had provided me.

"Waking him up could be very dangerous," Arthur said, his voice chiding. "He could be traveling through the Inferno by jumping from platform to platform."

"Hell is not a video game," Shannon said, appalled then switched her expression to one of confusion. "Probably."

"Well, let's hope he's not braindead,' Arthur said, half-joking by his tone. "If so, I'm not cleaning up after him."

"Don't worry, I won't let the blood go to waste," Christopher said.

"Funny," Shannon said.

"Whose joking?" Christopher asked.

I moaned and shook my head. The white blur was giving away to distinct shapes. "Guys, I can hear you."

"The Dragonborn comes!" Arthur cheered.

"Glad to see you're not a vegetable," Shannon said, becoming the first person my eyes beheld. She had her arms crossed.

"How long was I under?" I asked.

"About ten minutes," Arthur said, walking up to check on me. "Did you get what you came for? The meters went crazy after a couple of minutes."

I didn't know how to tell him my father was responsible for the possible end of the world. So, I decided not to. "Yeah, I found out what I needed to."

"So where to now?" Shannon asked, looking at me strangely. I suspected she wanted to know how my meeting with my mother went.

"I want to speak with Penny. Then we need to go to New London."

"New London?" Christopher asked, surprised. "You mean I missed her?"

"Yes," I said, simply. "Sorry. That's where the pair are being held. I'd also like to see if we can get Talbot's help. This isn't going to be easy."

"Pair?" Shannon asked.

"Never mind that," I said, a little too quickly.

"I can get you there right now," Arthur said, pointing to his machine. "Just give yourself a bit of time to recover."

I shook my head. "We're going to have to physically go there, Arthur. This is a rescue mission. Sorry."

"Damn," Arthur said, frowning. "That means danger. I'm not good with that."

"I am," Christopher said, frowning at me. "I should warn you, though, New London is a dangerous place for the uninitiated."

"I've gotten out of North Korea, Christopher. I think I can get out of a cyberpunk city in the Spirit World."

"That's a rare sentence," Arthur said. "Should I come? I don't like danger but she's family."

Both Ashley and Anna (jr.) nodded in the background.

I shook my head. "Stay alive. Protect yourself. I'm not going to get Ashley's family killed trying to save her."

Arthur shrugged. "I don't know her. Met her like once when I was four. But if you say so."

Ashley (jr.) and Anna frowned, clearly unhappy with my position. My position held firm, though.

I smirked. "We'll get Ashley out and destroy their magical resurrection cup. Then I'm going underground."

"For how long?" Shannon said.

"Awhile," I said, looking at her. "I don't need to solve all of the world's problems."

"Then who else will?" Christopher asked, surprising me.

"It can look after itself," I said.

"The only thing necessary for evil to triumph is blah-blah-blah," Christopher said, looking down. "But I'd be a hypocrite arguing this is your fight."

"Are you going to settle down with Ashley?" Shannon looked at me, blinking.

Christopher cast an annoyed glare at Shannon.

"We need to talk," I said, getting out of the chair. "Both of us, alone. Shannon first."

Shannon looked at me. "Alright."

Arthur frowned. "I always miss the good stuff."

"Come on," Christopher gestured for the others to follow. They departed along with her bodyguards out one of the side doors to another part of the lab.

I looked at Shannon. The feelings I felt when I looked at her were deeper than I'd felt for any other woman I'd known. Ashley was the only one I'd ever felt anything similar for and I believed my love for Shannon dwarfed my love for her. I couldn't lose her and would do everything in my power to convince her to stay. I'd been a fool to try and drive her away.

"You know," I started to say, falling over my words. "I'm not very good at this whole 'feelings' thing."

"That's because you were water-boarded as a child," Shannon said, smiling.

"I was not!" I snapped, wondering how that rumor got started. "I just learned to bottle it all up. You don't live very long in this business if you don't compartmentalize."

"Derek, I'm in the same business you are. Believe me, *I know*. I also know you, better than anyone except maybe Penny. You're one of the most emotional people I know. You just don't show it."

I looked away, uncomfortable. "I show it, sometimes. I try to, at least." Man, no wonder I was better at being an assassin than a regular spy. My empathy skills were shit.

Shannon took a deep breath. "So, I suppose we're going to be talking about the fact I rejected your proposal."

"You don't have to but, yeah, I would like to know why," I said.

"Our relationship is over because of that, right?" Shannon asked.

"I dunno. Maybe?" I looked up at her. "It felt like you were telling me you didn't love me and never could. That you didn't want to be with me anymore. That I was a... convenience, I guess."

Shannon scrunched up her face as if she couldn't believe what she was hearing. "Wow, that's...arrogant and stupid."

I frowned. "Oh, *I'm* the one in the wrong here."

"Derek, how many times have I said I didn't want to get married?" Shannon asked.

"Sixty, seventy?" I said.

"Do you know *why* I don't want to get married?" Shannon asked.

"Not a damned clue," I admitted.

Shannon sighed. "Now you're just being obtuse."

"Because the House would take any of our children away to be turned into killers like us. Because even if a child of yours didn't turn into a succubus, they would be a magic-user and would be turned into a soldier. Because either of us at any time could be called away to do something unspeakable. Because my being a member of the Committee means that there would always be someone ready and willing to jab the knife in my back—which is what happened. I meant why did you not want to get married now? We're free now, after a fashion."

"Ah," Shannon said, looking to one side. "Then you *were* paying attention but not to the part that mattered."

"And which part is that?" I asked, confused. This conversation was not going the way I wanted it too.

I wanted answers. A simple why.

Shannon let her hands drop to one side. "Derek, you make me happy."

I blinked. "And this is a bad thing?"

"Extremely happy. Happier than I deserve." Shannon looked like someone had socked her in the gut.

I started to comprehend. "Ah."

Shannon sighed. "Derek, I can tell you the names of every man, woman, and child I've murdered."

"I can say the same about the people I've killed," I said.

"One of them was a twelve-year-old girl. I ripped her throat out," Shannon said. "I was under the influence of my father, unable to control my hunger for life-force, but that's no excuse."

I looked down at the floor. "I knew who you were before we began our relationship, Shannon. I also know how many lives you've saved. Including little girls."

I admitted, it had changed things between us when I'd seen some of her victims had been kids. I had only a few sets of rules in my belief system. If you hurt children, you deserved to die. I'd once gone off the reservation and sniped a notorious child molester who was too rich to convict. The Committee had given me a reprimand since he'd been an ally. I was willing to forgive the horrors Shannon was a part of, though, because I was in love with her.

I also believed she tortured herself because of what she'd done under her father's influence and would spend the rest of her life trying to make amends.

Shannon looked up at me. "I don't deserve to be happy, Derek. It's as simple as that. God gave me a second chance when he showed me the way to the House and that wasn't so I could spend my life with you. It was to try and save lives. It was wrong of me to take as long as I did to break it off with you. You made me happy, though, and it's time to stop."

I blinked, processing that. "I'm no theologian but that's the most anti-Christian thing I've ever heard in my life."

"Excuse me?" Shannon asked.

"I don't have much faith in the Christian God. I believe in him like gravity or the President. He's a guy, he exists, and he has a vague impact on my life. Very different from the pantheistic sum of everything I believe in. But I know *you* believe in his essential goodness. Penny does too. One thing I learned from her was he's supposed to believe no one is beyond redemption."

I didn't mention my mother who, despite being someone who knew the Divine personally, was a judgmental shrew. Hmm, I guess I hadn't entirely forgiven her.

"Would you forgive Bloody Mary?" Shannon asked. "Come on."

"I would, yeah." I said, sighing. "Eternity is too long to hate anyone."

"Really?" Mary said, appearing behind me. Mary had shorted her hair to just above her shoulders and had taken away most of her make-up, with a light red, almost pink, dress. It was a stark contrast to her usual appearance and so was the expression on her face.

Almost apologetic.

"Fuck!" I said, flying out of my chair and landing on the ground.

"Shit!" Shannon shouted, pulling out her gun and aiming it at Mary.

She also didn't seem to notice, or care, about the gun pointed at her head. Which was to be expected as I doubted orichalcum would do anything to a manifest demon. For that, you'd need unmaking sorcery or cold iron. Just one of the many new facts that was whirling around in my head.

"Were you following us this entire time?" I asked, staring up at her.

"Yes," Mary said, blinking. "I was. One of the advantages of being a demon is intangibility and invisibility when the situation calls for it."

"Jesus Christ," Shannon muttered.

Mary twitched at that name as she was prone to doing. "Please stop saying that."

"Jesus—" Shannon started to chant before I raised my hand.

"Please stop," I said, sighing. "Hi Mary."

"Hello, Derek," Mary said.

I smiled. "Yeah, it is. Mary, I forgive you for being a duplicitous evil demon who released my evil brother onto the world. I have too few friends to care about a little thing like the End of the EverythingTM."

"I understand why you were angry now." Mary frowned at me. "I feel unquiet in my soul and sickness in my stomach rather than joy at the wholesale death that is occurring across the globe."

"It's called a conscience," I said. "It comes with being human."

"Well, I don't like it," Mary said.

I walked over and kissed Mary on the lips. She blinked and stared at me. "Could you wait outside and not stalk me for a bit?"

Mary looked at me, her eyes no longer having their usual murderous gleam. "I don't like leaving you alone. What if something happens like your mother returning to eat you?"

"I don't think Shannon will," I said.

"The jokes write themselves," Shannon muttered.

"Alright," Bloody Mary said, walking to the elevator and disappearing through the closed doors like a ghost.

"You know if this is you trying to get us back together then kissing another woman in front of me isn't the way to do it," Shannon said, blinking.

"I've never minded you kissing other women," I said, smirking.

"Ha-ha," I said.

"I don't know what's going to happen after this." I tried to figure out what to say next. I didn't want to lose Shannon but I could feel her slipping away. I also wanted to change my life, permanently. Yet, I wasn't going to live through this according to my mother.

"No one knows what's going to happen ever, Derek. That's the problem with the future. Even the Fates long ago gave up trying to keep track."

I gave a grim smile to that. "The thing is, I don't want to hurt people anymore."

"But you're so good at it!" Shannon said, sarcastically. "It's like asking Leonardo not to paint."

I gave a pained smile. "Not funny."

"I'm not sure I'm kidding," Shannon said.

I sighed and held my hands together, little sparks of

lightning flying between them. "That doesn't mean my life is going to be normal. I don't know what normal is. I've never had a normal life. I've never gone to high school. My equivalent to college was learning how to forge letters and kill people silently. I did, however, want to spend the rest of my very not-normal life with you."

"And we need to be married to do that?" Shannon asked.

"Is it important to you that we aren't?" I said, clasping my hands together.

Shannon looked down. "Yes."

"Alright then," I said, not understanding in the slightest. "I'd like you to be with me Shannon, by my side, wherever this road takes us for as long as you're willing to travel it with me. I don't think you deserve to suffer any longer for what you've done. No matter how horrendous. You've saved the world, twice, with me and have earned whatever redemption this world has to offer."

Shannon looked to one side, uncomfortable. "I don't believe—"

I didn't let it go. "The thing is, Shannon, I'll love you no matter what. I love you the way you are but I hate you hating yourself. I hate hating *myself*. My offer of marriage wasn't about settling down. It's about saying that we deserve a chance at something good."

"I..." Shannon looked away. "We don't. Neither of us."

"We do," I said.

"I *can't*." Shannon's words caused my heart to break. "I love you, Derek. I'll always love you. I know what you want and it makes me happier than I ever thought possible. It doesn't matter if we're married or not because either way, we will be in your heart. I don't deserve that. I can't be with you anymore, Derek. Not as your wife, not as your girlfriend."

I paused. "Alright."

"Alright?" Shannon asked, surprised.

"I'm not going to argue with you," I said. "We both deserve better than that."

"Okay," Shannon said. "I guess that's it then."

"Yeah," I said, devastated.

"What about Mary?" Shannon said. "Are you taking her

with you? Is she going to be your girl Friday now."

"I'm pretty sure I'm stuck with her."

"Do you love her?"

"I think she loves me."

"And you can't just say go away?"

I *did* say go away. It hadn't stuck. "Love is a trap. When people love you, really love you, they have a way of getting under your skin."

That hadn't saved us, though.

"I'll still help you," Shannon said. "With all this."

"Thanks." I pushed down all the horrible feelings assaulting me and focused, instead on the mission. "I have a few ideas—"

"You don't have to be unhappy," Shannon suddenly said. "I know I said you didn't deserve to be happy either but if you can be, you should seize the opportunity. I know you've been fighting since you were twenty-one. You've earned your rest. Maybe not with me but with someone. You are *more* than a weapon. Don't ever let anyone tell you otherwise."

I looked at my hands. "I'm not so sure."

"I can't stop...but you can."

I changed subjects. "What do you want to do after this? We're free of the House now. Both of us. If God had a task for you, I think it's done now."

"I want to help people. With or without the Red Room. The world is burning, Derek. Someone needs to save it from itself."

"I wish you luck with that," I said, realizing I wouldn't be able to stop killing. Without Shannon, I didn't have anything to tether myself to. "After this, I have to go after Nathan and all the other remnants of the Committee. Otherwise, they'll kill us and everyone else who might oppose them."

"You think Nathan would hunt you down?" Shannon asked, stunned.

"I think a man who kills one child will kill another."

"You killed Rebecca, though." Shannon's expression changed and I realized she regretted saying that.

It was the truth, though. "I don't think you have to worry about what I'm going to do after this."

"Don't be morbid," Shannon said.

I gave a fake smile. "I think I've finally figured out my personality underneath all the lies, half-truths, and deceptions. I am a raging pessimist."

"The Derek Hawthorne I know always managed to pull a few rabbits out of his hat when everything was at its lowest." Shannon's eyes were pleading. "If you want to live a life beyond this darkness, you can."

"Sure," I said, knowing I was doomed. "I can't change the world and events are out of my hands. However, I suppose I can try to change this small part of the world I call my own." It wasn't the truth but was what she wanted to hear.

Shannon pointed at my chest. "God, grant me the serenity to accept the things I cannot change, the courage to change the things I can, and the wisdom to know the difference."

"Don't make this a churchy-churchy thing, please."

Shannon laughed.

It was good to hear that sound again.

I wanted her to be happy.

Too bad she didn't want to be.

CHAPTER NINETEEN

Arthur and Christopher were surprised by the presence of Mary when they came back in but accepted her after a short explanation. So did Arthur's posse, though Ashley (jr.) was especially judgmental about hanging around demons now. Christopher already knew her, but Arthur treated the fact I had a demon accompanying me with a blasé attitude. I was surprised at how accepting people were of Mary, Shannon exempted. I wonder if that spoke well or poor of the House.

"Are you going to be okay through this, Arthur?" I asked, feeling uncomfortable leaving him.

"If the world degenerates into a post-apocalypse Wasteland the answer is no. If things remain at their current level or settle down, I should be fine," Arthur said.

"Do you have a place to go if things do get bad?" I asked, all too serious. It was possible the world wouldn't recover, and things would get worse before they got better. In that case, we'd all have to start making decisions about what sort of lives we wanted to live.

"My friends Tracy and Minji," Arthur said. "I'm seeing them both and they're seeing each other. We can hopefully slide into the chaos of regular humanity away from the House. I mean, I am a trained spy."

I opened my mouth to object then closed it. "Eh, who am I to comment on non-traditional relationships?"

Arthur looked between Christopher, Shannon, and Mary then snorted. "To say the least."

"We're not—" Christopher raised a finger.

I waved my hand to interrupt him then shook my head. "Take care of yourself, I owe you a lot."

"You owe me nothing," Arthur said. "We're all in this together."

What a weird sentiment.

"I did not think events would turn out this way," Mary said, looking pensive. "The destruction that has followed is not to my tastes."

Shannon glared at her. "I thought you were a demon of violence. *The* demon of violence, in fact. Aren't you attracted to Derek because he's the King of Murder?"

"Hey!" I snapped. "I'm a duke at best."

"Well, you are," Shannon said. "You just feel bad about it."

"I always thought I was better at it," Christopher said, crossing his arms. "Not that it's a competition or anything."

"We did a statistical model and Derek's actually like sixth on the list of the World's Best Killers," Arthur said, frowning. "The Gunmage, Talbot, you, and Shannon are above him. Also, a woman named Hilde Brandt in Germany. You haven't heard of her because she has like forty identities. Sunshine and Penny are on the list but don't have quite the experience necessary while Nathan hasn't been active in decades."

"I intend to surpass her," Anna said.

"There's also the vampires Thoth and Lucinda," Alex added. "William and Nancy England too. They're slashers who hunt other slashers."

"They should make a show about those two," Arthur said.

"You actually have a list of the World's Best Killers?" I asked, appalled. "Who the hell keeps score about that sort of thing?"

"Well, obviously, we do," Arthur said, matter of fact. "Duh."

"I'm above Derek?" Shannon asked, sounding a little too irritated. I could tell she was pleased but trying to sound bothered.

"Ahem," Mary said, clearing her throat. "Derek changed my nature. My true name is no longer Discord. It is now something else. I no longer rejoice in unjustified violence. Though, I took a great thrill in watching him stare down his mother and hearing his plans to save the world from Nathan."

Her confession surprised me. The transformation of a true name amongst a spirit was no small deal. It happened once a century at best and altered the fundamental nature of a being in a way akin to a dog becoming a cat.

Mary's true name changing explained a great deal, though, like why she was so desperate to get out of Hell's service and why she wanted to take up service to me. I'd made her my creature before giving her leave to become her own. I wondered if cleansing the Bloodsword was where Mary's transformation occurred or if it had been happening since we were first linked in Nassau.

"What is your nature now?" Christopher asked, as surprised by this revelation as I was.

"I don't know," Mary admitted. "But I am eager to find out. I'm perhaps not even a demon."

"What are you then?" I asked.

"A *goddess*," Mary said, without a hint of irony. "War, bloodshed, and rebirth are still my purview, but I patronize them for my own sake rather than hell's. I may expand beyond that in the future, but humans will offer their enemies lives unto me and I shall reward them with pleasures beyond imagination."

Arthur and Shannon stared at her.

I smirked. "You'll have to talk to the Morrigan and Inanna first about getting in on their business."

"Amateurs," Mary said, sniffing the air. "We shall make an abattoir of our enemies this day and sup from their skulls. Then we shall celebrate until the dawn in ways that shall make the pleasure pits of Dis jealous."

"I like your enthusiasm," I said.

"I don't," Shannon said.

"So, Fort Happiness is in New London?" Christopher said, rapidly changing the subject. "I think I know where it might be then, but It'll take an army to break in."

Everything fell into place in my head. "The Network and what few friends I have in the House left will be happy to provide us an army but only as a distraction. What we need instead is Talbot, Penny, you, me, Shannon, and Mary." I pointed between my associates. "Together, combined with my newfound abilities, we should be able to make a lightning strike in and out once we get a good casing of the joint. We take care of Roland and Stephen afterward."

If that sounded utterly insane, it was because it was. However, Penny was one of the strongest mages in the House and a single mage could make the difference in a battle far more than typical sorcery. New London was in a pocket dimension, which meant its magical rules were going to be different than in the quote-unquote regular world.

If that was the case Mary and I could potentially unleash power that was far in excess of anything but the House's best and brightest—none of which I saw allying with Roland. Maybe I was overconfident and thought I could use the Bloodsword like the Elder Wand, thanks Kim Su for putting that in my head, but I felt we had an advantage here far beyond our numbers. I'd seen that prison from the inside, and it was well-guarded but didn't have an army—probably because Roland hadn't grown one yet.

"That's a shit ton of if's, how's, and maybe's," Shannon said, listening to my plan with an intense look on her face. "However, it's the first actual plan I've heard today."

"Are you sure we need Penny and Talbot?" Christopher said, narrowing his brow. "I can take us to New London now. I know the secret paths to it. Tracking down those two, assuming Penny is in any shape to fight, will take days. Our best bet would be to go in invisibly and pull her out."

"I think this is going to need some more boom. It won't take days to find both and I can help Penny get back on her feet," I said, my mind already filling with the kind of diagrams and spells necessary to restore even a horrifically injured person back to full health. "I'd rather have too much talent on my side than too little."

"I also want to paint the walls with the entrails of our enemies," Mary said, cheerfully.

"Do you have a sister?" Arthur asked.

"You shall be blessed with a life of bloodshed, sex, and corruption put to good purpose," Mary said. "Love on the battlefield will be your reward."

Arthur blinked. "Thanks."

"You're welcome!" Mary said, cheerfully.

"You want to go after Roland and Stephen after this?" Shannon asked.

"Yeah, this should be a rescue mission first," I replied. "We can take care our enemies once Ashley is saved."

I didn't mention I would be dead after this, probably. No reason to plot after that but it would give my friends a direction to go. Truth be told, I hated leaving them with my mess to clean up, but I figured they could handle it.

Death is not always the end, Mary said in my mind.

Shit, you weren't supposed to hear that, I said to Mary telepathically.

I hear all, know all, see all, at least when it comes to killing, Mary said. I do not understand why you would make a blood sacrifice of yourself for others, but it makes your soul all the sweeter to me.

You are a strange chick, you know that? I said.

I am not a baby animal, Mary said, sharply. *I am a warrior goddess.*

My mistake, I said.

Thank you, Mary said.

I gotta ask a question, though, I said, surprised by my desire to know. *Why did Tiamat-Abaddon let you go? I mean, I don't think Hell is in the business of setting free its demons. How did you get free? You said arrangements?*

Oh! Mary said. *I went to Lucifer's prison and got the true names of several Archdemons then ate their souls. I used the remains to bribe others. Daddy always loved me best.*

I blinked. *Ask a stupid question, get a stupid answer.*

I saved some for you, Mary said. *You'll love the taste of fallen angel soul. Like hellish golden apples or ambrosia.*

"What about Nathan?" Shannon asked.

"We'll burn that bridge when we get there," I said, glad I wouldn't have to try to kill him if I died in this mission.

Love and hate are related emotions, Mary said. *You should know that as much as anyone.*

I did too. *Yeah.*

I pledged myself to you with the full intent of developing a hatred to you to occupy me for a few centuries as I came to resent your control, Mary said. *I would eventually revolt and murder you. It is a common thing for demons to fall in love with their infernalist masters and then fall out of it. It's our version of a summer fling. However, you gave me my freedom and now our love is real and eternal.*

I had literally no idea how to respond to that. *I see.*

This is going to be so much fun! Mary said, ecstatic. *I hope we kill at least a hundred elves! Maybe two!*

I felt a sense of calm and balance return as I started taking charge of my situation for the first time since this sorry mess had begun. I was something the House had created like a blacksmith forging a sword, but I oversaw my life. I didn't have to be anything other than what I chose to be. And I chose to make things right. I might fail. Hell, I was supposed to die trying but it wouldn't be because I didn't attempt to use my training for good.

I didn't get a chance to think about things more when there was a buzzing noise coming from Arthur's computers. It wasn't quite an alarm but did sound like some sort of warning.

"Let me guess, something bad?" I asked, frowning.

"Why do you assume that?" Arthur asked, walking over to the computer to check them. His bodyguards were in the back of the room, still silent but exchanging a glance.

"Because I'm a great believer in achieving in the universe's ability to screw people over." I said, sticking my hands in my pocket. "I try to achieve oneness with it. It allows me to mock and put down the world around me at every opportunity."

"You have achieved Jerkvana," Mary said.

I looked at Mary.

"What? I can joke." Mary shrugged.

The screens filled with exterior shots of Arthur's Arcade. A half-dozen black Cadillacs and limousines were gathered around the place. All of them contained black suited men and women with mirror shades with several having already gotten out. Their ears were cropped but their golden skin and identical yellow hair gave them away as elves.

"More of the Keebler patrol?" Shannon said, staring. "How the hell did they track us down?"

"They have magic and access to the world's largest intelligence network?" Christopher suggested.

"No one likes a wise-ass," I said, staring at the screens. "Which screws this group but my point stands."

"Do you have any weapons down here?" Shannon asked, turning to Arthur.

"This is a White Room base with a Red Room adjutant. The question is whether you want something that can level a city or if you want to get serious," Arthur said, smirking. "Amongst those hackers and geeks upstairs are some pretty serious wizards too."

I shook my head. "We're not going to fight them."

"We're not? But I love killing elves!" Arthur said, frowning. "Night, blood, or otherwise!"

"They're just more of Roland's slaves. We can kill them but it's likely guests at your club will be killed in the crossfire. It also won't get us any closer to our goal. We need to get out of here quietly. You should do your best not to antagonize them. If you can take them all out at once, go ahead, but don't endanger yourself on my behalf."

I had no illusions I wouldn't have to kill in the future, but I was going to try and cut down. Besides, I didn't have enough family members left I could start risking them in vendettas.

"We can take them," Shannon said, conjuring a pair of claws in her right hand. She raised it up before grasping it into a fist.

"Yeah and what happens next? They bring in a bunch of robot reinforcements? Roland has an army. We don't." I paused. "Yet."

"Roland has robots?" Arthur asked, blinking. "Awesome!"

Ashley (jr.), Anna, and Alex also looked giddy. Only Lucien looked like fighting robots would be a chore.

Arthur looked guilty. "Well, it's not a *good* thing but it's kind of cool, right?"

"Do you have a secret way out of here?" I asked.

"Yes," Arthur said. "Because I am a supervillain."

I stared at him, not sure if he was sarcastic or not.

Arthur gestured to a nearby wall before Ashley (jr.) walked up to it and opened a passage into what looked like a concrete hall leading through the city's storm sewers.

"Lex Luthor, world's greatest criminal mastermind," Arthur said.

"You guys are insane," Shannon said.

"I prefer differently rational," Alex said.

On the screen, the guards outside were attempting to distract the elves. It wasn't going well and one of the elves pistol-whipped one.

"I hate to leave your friends," I said, looking up at them.

"They'll be fine," Arthur said. "When they get down here, we'll use the poison gas and get rid of the elves."

I stared at him.

"Supervillain," Arthur said, making finger guns at me.

I shook my head and headed out the secret passage. "I'm going to miss you, Arthur."

"We'll see each other again," Arthur said, shrugging.

I didn't respond to that.

CHAPTER TWENTY

We bid our farewells to the Morgan Family and Timons brothers before stealing one of the elves cars. I had no doubt they would die because of Arthur's trapped arcade but didn't think that Roland would have time to take revenge. Mind you, if we failed to screw up his plan then they were probably all dead.

I guessed that Penny would be taken to Saint Ignatius' hospital in Chicago, Illinois because that was the hospital my father had the most influence over after the one in Washington D.C. It was also the closest House facility to where Penny and Lucy had decided to make their home.

Stepping in through the front doors with an obscuromancy glamour over both my face and that of my friends, I was surprised to see it was as full up as it was now. At the nurse's station, I saw they were gathered around a television set that showed an emergency broadcast of the President. They were giving some sort of speech and the ticker at the bottom said reports of Mad Cow Disease had resulted in 'cannibal' attacks. The cover story was unusually flimsy, and I wondered what the Red Room's game was. Were they really trying to cover up the disaster around us or was it just buying time? Probably the latter.

Stretching out my mind, I was surprised to find I could pick up stray thoughts now. The staff was petrified. Most of them were aware of the Red Room, at least on some level, so the thought the world was about to go to shit was at the forefront of their minds. They thought of their families, their friends, and the terrors they'd have to live through if the supernatural came out. A lot of them visualized the apocalypse. I didn't think they were wrong.

Christopher said, "It's the end of an age."

"Are you going to be comfortable here?" Shannon said, making a pair of fangs in front of her mouth.

"Are you?" Christopher asked.

I turned around and saw Mary was dressed in a conservative business suit dress with her hair up and a pair of glasses resting on the bridge of her nose. She'd shut the door behind her and closed the bridge between the hospital and Arthur's club. Her attire was a bit too obvious but amused me, nevertheless. At least she wouldn't draw too much attention, albeit more than any attractive woman would.

And we had Shannon and Christopher also providing the pretty.

"We're not staying long," I said, taking a deep breath. "Just long enough to explain the situation, get Penny, and get going."

"Assuming we can trust your mother's information," Christopher said, crossing his arms. "That's a big if on my end. Dragons are not to be trusted."

"Says the—" I started to say when my cellphone rang. I blinked, wondering how that was possible since I'd destroyed it. Picking it up, I hit send, and put it to my ear. "Yes?"

"Yo, dipshit," Roland said.

"How *the hell* did you find me?" I asked, stunned. A couple of nurses gave me dirty looks and I took position in a nearby corner away from the crowds.

"It's called *magic*, asshole. You'd know that if you'd paid attention in Red Room training."

Shannon and Christopher exchanged a look while Mary chuckled. Apparently, they were more amused at Roland tracking me down than I was. If he could find me here, he might send more robots or drop a cruise missile down on our heads.

"I'm coming for you. I'm going to take back the people you've taken," I said.

"Yeah, yeah, you're the big damn hero who is going to rescue the fair maidens. Except, of course, Ashley is here voluntarily,"

Roland snarled after he spoke. He was overcompensating, showing worried he was.

"Because you have her daughter," I said.

"Details, details," Roland said, confirming it. "In five or six days, I'll be carving up North America with the other supernaturals."

"Awfully confident, aren't we?" I asked, noting his plan had already changed.

"The Red Room's leadership has already been wiped out except for the Chairman, your dear ol' dad, Amanda Morgan, and you. A hundred governments are collapsing now that they don't have anyone to pull their strings. When Balor starts marching through the city streets, people won't *care* about what the President has to say. They'll look to anyone who can provide the answers for what they need to do to survive. We're going to *fix* this world."

"Fix it from you wrecking it." I didn't want to clue him in to the fact I knew where Victoria and Ashley were, but it was hard to keep silent. "You're a pawn in all this, Roland, and you don't even realize that. I'd feel sad for you if you weren't such an asshole."

"I'm nobody's pawn but my own," Roland said, not realizing that was not a very good comeback.

"I know about Nathan," I said. "Stephen too."

Roland was silent.

"You're not going to get away with this," I said. "I'd pity you, Roland, if not for the fact you're a psychopath."

"This world has been propped up by the House for millennia. Once all the dust settles, the monsters are public, and the governments humiliated—they're going to need someone to tell them what's what. That's where I come in. Pantheon Corp will be there to help rebuild the world. Nathan has a vision, Derek, and you're a fool not to be a part of it."

"Yes, because all the supernatural groups in the world will be oh-so-anxious to let you take over. Not to mention all the people with nukes—if you try and force this issue, the planet won't be there for you to rule."

"No risk, no gain. Besides, if the world becomes a burning

cinereous ash, there's always the Spirit World to retreat to."

It took me a second to realize he was serious.

Holy shit.

"You're crazy. You realize that, right?" I said.

"No one conquers who does not fight. In the old days, you conquered a people because they knew they'd murder the shit out of you if they didn't submit. Balor is going to be the big gun that changes the world Derek and if he dies, then I have others. While his eye is laying waste to armies, the world's governments will *beg* us to take over."

I pulled my phone away and stared at the receiver. "I've killed gods before."

"Not like this one," Roland said, once more making a poor comeback.

"Cassandra would never have done this," I said, lying. I didn't know why I was trying to reason with Roland. Perhaps I just wanted him to let something useful drop. Perhaps the stress of having the world falling around down on us was finally getting to me.

"Yeah she would," Roland said. "The last thing she told me before you killed her was that she didn't care about whether her plan worked or not as long as it meant you'd die. She hated you that much for father forcing her to marry you."

I stared at the phone. What did you say to that? I'm sorry I didn't know she was mind-controlled? Instead, I became eerily calm. "Goodbye, Roland. I'm looking forward to killing you."

"The Gunmage is looking forward to her rematch. Naughty-naughty with the fire. Spoiled her pretty looks."

I hung up on him. "I hate that guy."

Christopher looked at me. "So, let me get this straight: Roland is resurrecting an Elder God with Ashley to scare the population with a bunch of other supernatural threats so he can take over the world. He's, however, a pawn of Nathan. Stephen is responsible for a shit ton of other stuff, including assassinating the Committee. Nathan is trying to reveal the Truth and destroy the House. We don't know Stephen's motivations, though, because he's a demon and they're mindlessly evil."

"Are not," Mary said. "We're very mindful evil."

"That's a pretty good summary," I said, shaking my head. "I think the Vampire Nation is getting ready to move when the House collapses too. There's going to be an enormous power vacuum at the end of this and the only thing really up for debate is who fills it."

I didn't know what to think about all this. This was too much for me to process. I'd grown up resenting but loving my father, hating my mother, learning to despise Stephen for killing his family, and thinking the House was a necessary evil. Now I was finding out all of that may have been wrong. No, I still hated Stephen. I just had less room to judge him now that we were both kinslayers. Was this all some crazy attempt by my father to save the world? Roland just seemed like a megalomaniac but if they were trying to do it, then why the hell were they killing so many people to do it? None of it made sense.

I rubbed my temples. "When did my life become all about cluelessly stumbling along from one crisis to the next?"

"Since always?" Christopher suggested.

"Point taken," I said, acknowledging his point. "Okay, let's go talk to Penny."

I wasn't going to tell my twin about Nathan's involvement just yet. Penny idolized Nathan in a way that went well-beyond being Daddy's Little Girl. Even when Nathan ordered me to kill Ashley, she'd assumed he was motivated by a higher calling than just being an enormous asshole to his eldest surviving son. It would break her heart to find out Dad had graduated to full-blown supervillainy, no matter how well-intentioned, and I wasn't about to do that without clear evidence. Even if I had to kill him.

There was also the girl. I didn't know her name, didn't know what she looked like, and couldn't say a single detail about her beyond her sex. Yet, apparently, I had a daughter. Christopher had kept that from me during the Bloodsword affair and had only alluded to it back at Arthur's. I wasn't sure that the child was mine, even though Kim Su had indicated it was. I also wasn't sure how to react to it. Ashley had made a very clear decision to cut me out of the child's life and start a new relationship. Apparently, with my occasionally mind-controlled undead ex-partner. I should have been happy for the both but, I'll be honest, I wasn't and kind of wished horrible death on Christopher for keeping this from me. It was petty and despicable since I was in a relationship with another woman myself or had been in until today. What could I even teach a girl if I was able to become part of her life?

How to kill, maim, destroy, and enslave mates, Mary suggested, reading my mind.

Not helping, Mary, I said.

Then clearly you don't know wisdom when you hear it, Mary said. *I'm not saying you should kill her parents and claim the child as your own. I'm just not-not saying it.*

I think I'll work this out on my own, I suggested.

Suit yourself, Mary said.

I sighed and went to the nurse's station to ask that room my sister was staying in. Before I reached it, I heard a squeal of delight. Lucy wrapped her arms around me, giving me a hug. My sister-in-law was dressed in a plain black sweater and skirt with very little make-up. She looked underdressed with her hair tied back in a ponytail. I gave her a hug and squeezed tight. I often didn't appreciate how much my family did for me, but they were the only reason I got out of bed every morning.

Honestly, I didn't care what happened to the rest of the world. I only cared what happened to my small segment of it. If that made me a monster, so be it but I'd trade the entirety of its safety to know Lucy and Penny were alright.

"Derek, you're alive!" Lucy said, merrily.

"That's up for debate."

"Nathan called us and said it was all worked out," Lucy said, sighing. "I'm so happy."

"What do you mean?" I asked.

"You're no longer an outlaw!" Lucy said. "I mean, they said you were dead and we knew you weren't but they also said someone was impersonating you to shoot but that's all resolved now."

I kept my expression even. Did my father call off my banishment from the House because he wanted to protect me or had he done so because Roland failed and the rest of the Committee was dead? Some combination of the two?

The fact was my father hadn't informed me I was under a death mark and changed it the moment it endangered his relationship with Penny as his other children. If Nathan was playing some grand game of chess with the world, he was doing a shitty job of it. Maybe he just didn't know how to manage a pawn that went in any direction it wanted. I wasn't overly worried either way as the House was on its last legs. Whether they wanted me dead or not wouldn't amount to much in a week or two, even assuming the world was still standing.

"I'm happy too," I said, putting my hands on her shoulders. "How is Penny?"

Lucy looked over to see Shannon, Mary, and Christopher before blinking. Lucy knew Christopher and Shannon but also knew the former was a vampire now. She'd never met Mary but had heard descriptions of her. To her credit, she kept her reaction subdued but her eyes widened. Lucy understood it was probably a bad idea to bring up I'd brought a demon, a Lilin, and a vampire into a hospital run by monster hunters.

Lucy turned back to me, not missing a beat. "Penny's a little banged up but nothing magic and medicine can't fix. How's your new arm?"

I looked at it then back up at her. "I barely notice it's not real. What happened?"

Lucy's expression became grim. "I'm sorry, Derek. We did everything we could. They attacked out of nowhere. I mean, I knew Pantheon Corp was working on drone golems, but I didn't think they'd ever be turned against us. If I wasn't a weak ordinary human, I could have done something."

I gave Lucy a comforting hug. "It's okay. You did everything you could."

"Your father did the lion's share of protecting her," Lucy said.

I grimaced. "Yeah, that's good to hear."

I didn't blame Lucy for failing to protect my sister any more than I was willing to thank my father for saving her. I was more concerned about who had informed Roland of their location.

Had he just tracked them down with magic or was there another force involved? My father was responsible for bringing Penny to the hospital. Was he responsible for that too? Looking at the nearby television, I saw the casualty figures in the United States had reached seven thousand with no cause listed. I doubted all of those were adults. Someone had to pay for this.

Lucy shook her head, pulling away. "I should have—"

"You would have been killed," Mary said, staring at her. "You have no objective combat skills, let alone ones that would affect floating tanks."

Lucy stared at her. "Can I study you? If you really are a manifested demon, I'd love to dissect you."

"No," Mary said.

Lucy's voice remained low. "Pity."

I gestured to where Lucy had come from. "Show me to Penny."

"With pleasure," Lucy said. "She'll be very happy to see you."

CHAPTER TWENTY-ONE

Penny had been given one of the nicest rooms in the hospital. It had ample space, a view of the courtyard outside, and enough magitech medical equipment to treat a mid-sized village. A Chinese mandala designed to suck away evil energy was hung behind her and I could feel a dozen other lesser healing spells working inside the room.

Penny was lying in her bed with a couple of punk magazines in front of her. The television was set to the same emergency broadcasts everyone else was watching. She was wearing a hospital gown and had no makeup on. The right side of her head had been shaved and I wondered if she'd had surgery.

Magic wasn't a panacea for individuals who suffered crippling or life-threatening injuries. There were healing and even resurrection spells, though the latter could be accomplished by archmages necromancers who didn't mind putting the spirits of others through the proverbial blender. Blood magic was the exception but that required a 'tit-for-tat' exchange that often ended up killing more people than it saved.

No, the best normal magic could do was accelerate the natural healing process and lend aid to modern medicine. Sometimes it worked spectacularly well, like with my eye and right arm, but other times it couldn't prevent people from suffering permanent harm. I wondered how badly Penny had been mangled by the situation I'd put her in and how I was going to break her heart by telling her the truth about our father.

Penny looked up from her magazines. "Heya, I guess you're not an enemy of the state."

I tried to smile at her comment. "That remains to be seen."

Her smile left. "I just need a few hours then I'll be ready to help you go after Ashley."

I snorted. "Penny, really—"

"You can't," Lucy said, moving in ahead of me. "It took every bit of sorcery they had here to patch you up after all this. If it hadn't been for Nathan, you would have died. You've still got a couple of weeks healing to do with all that internal bleeding they had to patch."

Christopher, Nathan, and Mary stayed outside. Shannon, by contrast, stood a foot behind me. Putting my arm over Lucy's shoulders, I gave her a kiss on the forehead. "Lucy, do you mind giving me a sec with Penny alone?"

Lucy looked confused. "You never ask for me to leave the room."

I grimaced. "It's just a private matter."

"I have sex with your sister and serve as your doctor," Lucy said, staring.

Lisa giggled in the corner while Penny smirked.

Shannon said, "It's about Nathan."

"Oh," Lucy said, nodding. "One of those conversations. You're right, it's probably best we leave the room."

"I'll give you a heads up on what's been going on," Shannon said. "You know, so you can be prepared."

"Be prepared for what?" Lucy asked, innocently.

Lucy shut the door behind her, leaving Penny and me alone.

Penny looked at me. "So, I see you've managed to pick up your pet vampire and demon."

"I need a pet werewolf and mummy so I can do my own creature feature marathon. I was thinking we could also maybe all move into a mansion together and form our own reality television version of the Munsters."

"I assume you're Marilyn, the Creepy Normal Girl?"

I snorted then paused. "Oh, my god, I am Marilyn!"

"I mean, you're a half-dragon and kinda-sorta a wizard but you're really the token straight."

"Except for that one time in Vegas with Christopher, yes."

Penny stacked her magazines and put them on the nearby breakfast table. "We were assaulted by dozens of those drones.

I did everything I could. So did Lucy. They could have killed us if they wanted to, but they didn't."

"I'm not here about that," I said.

"I heard about the fact the House was going to have you killed then reversed it," Penny said.

"I'm not here about that either," I said.

"The fact the world is coming to an end?" Penny asked.

"Batting zero, sis," I said, shaking my head.

"Then what?" Penny asked, confused.

"I went to see our mother," I said, sticking my hands in my pockets.

Penny blinked. "... I see."

"It was awkward," I said.

"How awkward?" Penny asked.

"She's still alive!" I said, cheerfully. "Though kind of weird. Also, she talks way too much about her sex life."

Penny tried not to laugh and failed. "Seriously, how was it?"

"She's intense," I said, taking a deep breath. "I think she has good intentions for the world but that's not exactly a ringing endorsement. Kim Su wasn't happy with the way my life has gone and I told her it was none of her business since she'd decided not to be a part of it."

"Is that what you told her or what you wanted to tell her?" Penny asked.

I shrugged. "Six of twelve, half a dozen of the other."

Penny sighed. "I'm glad you did it, either way. With all that's happening, I wouldn't want you to not have that opportunity."

"Because you think I'm going to die?" I asked, being very clear.

"Because I don't know what's going to happen in the future. I'd kill the entire world for you, Derek, and I know you'd do the same for me."

I grimaced. "And if I told you she predicts I am going to die on this? That it's fate?"

"Then I'm happy to tell fate to go fuck itself," Penny said, without hesitation.

I had to admire her for having courage I, myself, lacked.

Death would almost be welcome after all the crap I'd gone through. "There's more you need to know."

"What?" Penny asked.

I took a deep breath. "Nathan is taking advantage of this situation to eliminate the Committee and take over."

Penny was silent for a long time. "Good."

I blinked. "Excuse me?"

"Look outside, Derek. It's pandemonium. The supernatural nations have been preparing for centuries for this. Just waiting for us to slip up so they could go on a murder spree."

I wasn't sure that was true. "Sis, don't Anakin Skywalker this. Supernatural beings are people—"

"No," Penny said, shushing me. "Don't even give me that bullshit about them being people too. They're not. Shannon, Christopher, Talbot, Mary (sort of), and Casper the Friendly Ghost are the exceptions to the rule. Most monsters are just that."

I was stunned by Penny's sudden display of racism. Then again, maybe it wasn't sudden. Most people in the House believed there were good monsters, bad monsters, and just plain ol' monster monsters. I was almost unique in believing there were no real monsters at all, just people with fangs and tails.

Penny was in full rant mode now. "And what did the Committee do? They put scumbags like Roland in charge. For the past two years, you've been fighting them tooth and nail to do some good in this world and what has it led to? Nothing."

"You think giving Nathan sole rulership of the House *is a good thing*?"

"Who better?" Penny asked.

This was going to be harder than I thought. I'd always known Penny was loyal to Nathan, but I hadn't realized she was this blind to his faults. "I'm saying he could have probably nipped this in the bud but he's taking advantage of it instead."

"The world won't survive without the House," Penny said. "The supernatural may be public but the House can lead humanity more effectively now that the public knows what it is facing."

Now she sounded like Roland. "Uh-huh."

"You sound skeptical," Penny said. "I thought you believed."

Looking at her, I wondered how I could have blinded myself to just how much Penny believed in the House's values. She was a half-dragon, like myself, and had grown up under the care of Frankenstein's monster. Hell, she was a witch. Yet, here she was, saying an organization devoted to denying the existence of the supernatural and keeping it intimidated into compliance was a good thing. A *necessary* thing.

I walked over to my sister's bedside and sat down on the end. "This reminds me of one of Uncle Ben's stories."

"I don't need to be lectured. If you don't agree with me, that's fine. We'll just agree to disagree," Penny said, raising up her sheets to her neck.

"Just bear with me for a second. Do you remember Talbot's story about his time in Mexico during the Civil War?"

Penny looked suspicious. "Yeah, he was a cowboy married to an Apache woman."

I looked out to the window, remembering the story. "I remember how there was some truly messed up shit in Talbot's stories, stuff inappropriate for kids to listen to. Stuff that gave me nightmares but was helpful in making me aware of just how bad things could get. One of those stories which always stuck with me was the one about the Reverend."

"He's downstairs, you know. Ben came riding to the rescue with Nathan and took down six of those robots himself."

I registered that bit of information for later. "Do you remember?"

"Reverend Seymour Scott. A Red Room agent with a Jesus fetish. He was a scalp hunter," Penny said. "Killed hundreds of people who looked like Grandma Hawthorne for the government. Talbot shot him in a bar and left him to die."

I nodded. "Talbot had been sent to kill him because Scott had gotten too excessive in his genocide and murders. Which, given the United States treatment of Native Americans, is saying something. Talbot made a mistake when confronting him, though. He asked why he did it."

You never asked why someone was a monster. The answer never gave you the answer you wanted.

Penny recited the next part of the story from memory, which surprised me. *"The Reverend looked me dead in the eye and said, over his drink, 'I thought I was doing the Lord's work by killing the heathen savages. I dashed infants against rocks, shot women in the head, and chased children down with my horse. Then, one day, I realized two things. The first was if God wanted the heathens dead, he would have killed them himself. The second was if I was a bandit or a rapist I'd have killed a dozen at most if I was a true monster. Instead, I was worth a hundred bandits or more because I'd been driven by the power of righteousness.'"*

"That always stuck with me," Penny said.

"You're not the man killing innocent people for a righteous cause and neither is Nathan." Penny reached over and put her hand on mine. "I believe in you both."

I gave her hand a squeeze. "Thirty-six."

"Huh?" Penny asked.

"That's how many innocent men I've killed on the House's orders. Not counting collateral damage."

The House had a wonderful way of making sure its operatives continued to believe they were on the side of the angels. Whenever they sent a Red Room agent to kill someone, which was often, they had an entire division of sociopaths who invented reasons for them to die. The targets said to be pedophiles, snuff film enthusiasts, secretly Rakshasa, in the pocket of terrorists, or re-animated corpses with no soul. Upon my ascension to the Committee, I'd learned just how many so-called scumbags I'd killed had just been people the House benefited from dying. A few of them had just attracted the ire of a Committee member. It was nightmarish.

Penny squeezed my hand back. "That's why we have to trust Nathan. The House should only kill for the greater good and under him, that'll be the case. We'll make the House better. All of us. As a family."

"I wish that were true," I said. "Penny he let Stephen loose."

Penny let go of my hand, her eyes widening. "What?"

"He's responsible for Roland's rise to power. He admitted it," I said. "So he either has no control over that evil sonofabitch or he's happy to let him take pot shots at me."

"Derek—"

"He told me to kill Rebecca and I did it," I said, confessing something I had hoped to keep secret for the rest of my life.

Penny just stared. "Goddess."

In that moment, I wondered if I'd lost my twin forever. It was one thing to kill strangers for the House, innocent or not. It was quite another to admit to murdering your own flesh and blood for a cause, no matter how just (or injust). Penny and I hadn't been close to Rebecca, but she was family. Blood was the only tie in the House that meant anything, and I'd violated the one remaining taboo. I'd done it to hopefully break Penny of her loyalty to my father and I suspected I'd succeeded. It had just cost me everything to do so.

That was when the door to my room opened and I saw my friends and family being held at bay by a very heavily armored pair of black-suited guards who were casually carrying around A90 assault rifles. Beside them, entering the room, was the white-suited figure of my father.

Nathan Hawthorne was a fantastically good-looking man for someone approaching ninety, looking like Robert Redford in his heyday. He radiated an aura of powerful magic that had tuned with spirit pacts, enhancers spread all over his body, and decades of training.

There was also the fact he was the product of a lineage that included wizards from a dozen different cultures across the world from Hiawatha to John Dee. In his right hand was a walking stick that was covered in invisible, to normal eyes, mystic runes. I could see the glow through my cybernetic eye and how much power he was putting out in magical watts.

A lot.

"Hello, you two," Nathan said, cheerfully. "Is someone talking about me?"

"Pardon us," I said, to Penny, then turned back to Nathan.

Christopher grabbed the rifle from Nathan's left guard as I launched myself at my father, lifting him up by the shirt and carrying him out by the room across the hall. I left the Bloodsword in its umbrella form by Penny's bedside. The other guard raised his weapon but didn't fire, blocked by my associates.

"Derek!" Penny shouted.

"Just a moment!" I shouted back.

My father and I needed to have a talk. It was only as I dragged him off that I remembered he was one of the most powerful wizards in the world and this was probably going to get me killed.

Don't worry, Derek, Mary said mentally. *I'll help you eat his soul if you want. Then we can take over the Earth with his powers.*

I'll bear that in mind, Mary, I said back.

Just wanted to let you know, Mary said cheerfully.

CHAPTER TWENTY-TWO

Ithrew Nathan into the hospital storage room across the hall and shut the door behind us. We were surrounded by shelves of toiletries, towels, and antiseptics. It was a large room with no window and plenty of space to fight. Albeit, given my father was an archwizard and I was an assassin, would result in my immediate incineration if I didn't kill him in the first blow. Unfortunately, I hesitated and didn't land one so it was probable he would incinerate me with a stray thought.

"Sir, is something wrong?" One of Nathan's guards asked from behind the door.

"Just having a conversation with my son. Pay it no mind," Nathan replied, looking at me with an appraising eye. I could feel his mind brush over mine, trying to read my thoughts, but my shields were the best in the business.

"You son of a bitch," I said, dryly.

"Oh, dear, it's going to be one of those conversations," Nathan muttered.

I swung at his face, only for him to catch it in his palm and immediately force me to the ground.

"Ahhh!" I said, feeling like my entire body was on fire as he drained away my strength.

Are you sure you don't want my help killing him? Mary mentally asked.

Keep on standby, I thought back.

As you wish, Mary said. *Remember you have the Bloodsword. Nathan is, at the end, only human and it is the fang of a goddess.*

I left the Bloodsword behind, I replied.

You can never leave it behind, Mary said, chuckling. *It is a part of you.*

That was surprisingly comforting. *I'll bear that in mind.*

Nathan made a mystical glyph in the air with my fingers, silencing the room from the rest of the hospital. It seemed if he wanted to kill me, he didn't want anyone else to hear. How considerate of him—at least that was screwed since Mary and my souls were linked.

"I know you're upset, Derek, but this is not a good look for you," Nathan said, speaking as if I was a child.

"Millions of people are dying," I said, dryly.

"Billions would be dead if not for the fact this was handled in a controlled manner," Nathan said, sharply.

"You think you *control* this?" I almost snorted in disbelief. The entire world was about to find out their government, media, and religion had been lying to them the entire time. That they were surrounded by predators. That everything they knew regarding science, technology, and philosophy was a lie. You couldn't control something like that.

"I *am* controlling this. The casualty figures are exaggerated, albeit enough to terrify people into losing faith in their leaders. What you are seeing is a controlled panic with all the right people prepared for events."

I gestured to the door and the packed hospital beyond. I was trying to grasp how my father could be so blind. The highways were packed with people fleeing from a danger they didn't even understand existed yet. People knew something terrible was happening, they just didn't know what yet. "This is not controlled!"

Nathan stared. "The option was now or later. I didn't cause Roland's insane plot against the House any more than I did the Committee's work at Camp Zero or Cassandra's alliance with the Emerald Eye. There were a hundred bullets fired at humanity and the only thing I could think to do was choose which ones to hit and where."

I stared at him. "Did you know what would happen to Ashley?"

"And there we have it," Nathan said, dryly. "This isn't about the fact that I started a war to end it quickly, it's the fact you're still mourning a woman I drove away years ago."

I stared at him. "She's the mother of my child."

Nathan kept his gaze level. "And the only reason that your child isn't dead is because I made sure to force Roland into a *geas* that he wouldn't harm her."

"You knew," I said.

"*Of course* I knew," Nathan said. "Who do you think has been making sure the House didn't wipe out her branch of the Network? Funding her and her merry band of revolutionaries. The only way to keep her safe and my grandchild was to make sure she was under control. Unfortunately, events spiraled out of even my considerable ability to maintain order over."

"What happened?" I stared.

"Stephen," Nathan said, dryly. "Stephen whispered how to resurrect Balor and gave Roland a way to strike at the system directly. You didn't help matters by killing Dracula and unbalancing the supernatural political stage. So I decided to play along and help Roland so I could maintain access."

"Stephen is loose and Roland is trying to kill us all," I said.

"Yes," Nathan said. "Our alliance of convenience became inconvenient for him. Stephen's escape is my doing, though. He doesn't realize that I know his demon's true name and implanted the suggestion to kill the Committee."

I shook my head. "We're all just pawns to you, aren't we?"

"Grow up, Derek," Nathan said. "International politics are measured in tens of thousands of lives every day. You needed to learn that lesson the moment that you ascended to the Committee and instead you continued to act like a secret agent. Maybe you can stop Roland, Stephen, and their undead demon god but none of that is going to matter in the end. You aren't losing this game, you weren't even playing."

I stared at my father and realized he was right. I never wanted to be a politician or one of the secret masters of the world. All I ever wanted to be was the good guy and I'd failed that spectacularly.

"Well, you forgot one thing," I said.

"And what's that?" Nathan asked.

I summoned the Bloodsword, the weapon appearing in my hand in an instant. "I'm a really good secret agent."

I stabbed him through the chest in one swift motion before twisting it. This time, my attack cut through his mystical defenses like a hot knife through butter. As powerful as Nathaniel was, he was no match for a sword that was made to kill gods. The sword drained away every ounce of his magic, preventing him from making a counterattack or even attempt to save his life, and he just stared at me in shock. There was, quite simply, nothing else he could do.

"Huh, I didn't think you had it in you," Nathan gurgled out. He fell to the ground, a smile on his face. Withdrawing the sword, I saw a pool of blood grow beneath his corpse. The Bloodsword had drunk deeply of both his blood as well as life-force.

And he was gone.

Strangely, I didn't feel like justice had been served. As bad as my father had been, the destruction of the House was something that had been necessary. You didn't destroy an institution as powerful and broad as it without killing a few innocents along the way. World War 2 was not won by half-measures and taking down my father had been as much about my own personal feelings as anything resembling fitting punishment. Looking down at his corpse on the ground, I wondered what Penny and Talbot would think of me. Hell, I wondered what my mother would since she still loved him after all these years. Nathan Phillip Hawthorne had been one of the greatest magi of human history and I'd taken him down perhaps when the world had needed him most. Eh, no use crying out over spilled milk.

"Do you feel any better?" Mary asked, appearing behind me. Apparently, she could teleport.

I nodded. "Yeah. I guess I do."

"I really don't understand why you beat yourself up the way you do," Mary said. "Life and death are really just two sides of the same coin."

"Says the demon," I said.

"Yes," Mary replied. "We'd know, after all."

"I need to figure out what I'm going to do about his bodyguards," I muttered.

Mary shrugged. "Oh, I already killed them and disposed of the bodies."

I looked to her. "You did what?"

"Well I figured you were going to kill him!" Mary replied. "It's not like I was wrong."

I felt my face. "You're right."

"I am?" Mary asked, surprised.

"Yes," I said, taking a deep breath. "No more half-measures."

"Ah," Mary said, looking down at Nathan's corpse on the ground. "Do you want me to get rid of the—"

"Yes, please," I said, not looking down.

Mary leaned down and picked up Nathan's corpse before vanishing, she reappeared seconds later without it. I didn't want to know what she'd done with it and didn't particularly care. I had bigger things to worry about than the disposition of my father's remains.

"Thank you," I muttered, seeing a stain of blood on the ground before shaking the Bloodsword and turning it back into an umbrella.

"What now?" Mary asked.

I took a deep breath. "We stop Roland. We rescue Ashley. I don't know if there's anything we can do about all this."

"This?" Mary asked, confused.

"The end of the world," I replied.

"It is not the end," Mary said, smiling. "We're not nearly that lucky."

I snorted. "Funny."

"I'm not joking," Mary replied. "No, this probably won't even be as bloody as World War 2. Not that I approve of World War 2. Too much killing of innocents. There's no fun unless people fight back."

"Mary, can I ask you a favor?" I asked.

"Yes, my love?" Mary replied.

"Never say anything like that again," I said, dryly.

Mary shrugged. "Sure, sure. Wait, about World War 2 or other conflicts? I mean, I have some wonderful observations about Vietnam—"

I made a slash gesture across my throat.

"You want me to slash someone's throat?" Mary asked.

I couldn't help myself and burst out laughing. "Oh Mary, never change."

"Well, now I'm just confused," Mary said before changing the subject. "So I take it your relationship with the House is finished for good?"

"It's like smoking. A hard habit to break." I paused. "But I think I got it this time."

"Good," Mary replied. "They were keeping you from reaching your full potential as my consort and a god of murder."

"Are there many of those?" I asked.

"There will soon be one more," Mary said.

Now to break the news to Penny. This next conversation was going to be difficult, Penny loved Nathan. She was Daddy's Little Girl and trusted him implicitly. When he'd ordered Ashley killed, Penny had helped me fake her death but believed our father acted within reasonable limits to protect the House. Discovering he was behind all this would kill her.

Opening the door, I saw two bloodstains against the hallway walls. Shannon and Christopher were looking very upset, perhaps because Mary had just murdered two men in front of them.

"What did you and Nathan talk about?" Penny called from her room.

"We had words. It's resolved now. He's going off to save the world," I said. Lying to my sister felt gross and unnatural but I didn't want to share my shame with her right now. I felt like she would also see right through me. After all, I'd just admitted to killing Rebecca and now I was coming from a closet alone. Hell, she probably already was freaking out because Mary had murdered father's guards.

I teleported them away first, Mary said. *What kind of fool demonling do you take me for?*

"My mistake," I muttered.

Thank you, Mary said. *I don't see why you think your sister can't be trusted with the truth. You have killed your father so therefore you inherit all his possessions—presumably including your siblings.*

I blinked. *Mary, don't take this the wrong way, but shut up.*

Mary shrugged.

"Ah, good!" Penny said, surprising me. "You two need to learn to work together. The world is going to need you both soon."

I looked down. "Yeah."

Shannon looked at me, confused. Christopher knew what I was doing. I couldn't take Penny along with me to her potential death after I'd murdered our father and lied to her. It was stupid, decreased our chance of survival, and was the product of guilt. But I couldn't. I just couldn't. I wondered if I'd ever see my twin again. The thought terrified me. I just wasn't sure which terrified me more.

I shook my head. "I'll see you after all this is done."

"Oh hell no," Penny said.

"Pardon?" I said, surprised.

Seconds later, I saw Penny walk out of her hospital bed, taking several deep breaths as she did so. She was still dressed in her hospital gown but there was a sense of power radiating out from her. She was also holding the Staff of Hiawatha and seemed to draw strength from it. I could feel her ki grow stronger just standing there as she seemed to draw from the ambient magic around us.

"I'm coming with you," Penny said.

I stared at her. "Penny—"

"You're one of the last Committee members left," Penny said. "That means we need to get in touch with the Professor and get an army to hit these elven bastards where they live."

"Uh huh," I said. "Penny—"

"I'll get right on it," Penny said.

I closed my eyes. "Sounds great."

Coward, Mary said. *She deserves the truth.*

On this? Yes, I admitted.

CHAPTER TWENTY-THREE

Walking away from Penny's room after exchanging a few pleasantries, my group followed me in silence.

Once we were out of earshot, Shannon said, "Just so we're clear, did you just kill your father?"

"Yes," I said, pausing. "It was easier than I expected."

I didn't quite believe that Penny accepted my father and I had worked out our differences peacefully. She sure as hell wasn't acting like I'd just killed him, though. I didn't know how to react to it all and my own feelings were impossible to deal with. All I could think of was trying to save Ashley and her daughter. Our daughter.

"Oh," Shannon said, blinking. The news of my patricide clearly shocking her. "If it's any consolation, I want to kill my father too."

"My father was the death of Abel at the hands of Cain," Mary said, looking over her shoulder. "My mother was the tears of Eve for her dead son."

"You realize those people didn't actually exist, right?" I said, shaking my head.

"History has multiple timelines and pasts. The universe is multi-layered and what is true in one's mind is often true elsewhere but false as well," Mary replied.

"Uh-huh," I said.

"It'll make more sense when you're a god too," Mary said. "Immortal, eternity, infinite, and without regret."

"I need my regrets," I said. "They're the only things I have some days."

"Can we talk about our next move?" Christopher asked,

looking nervous. "If you've turned against the House fully then this is a bust."

"The House is decapitated," I said, dryly. "The Chairman is clearly not trying to keep things intact, Roland is rogue, and no one else seems to be at the wheel. I'm as much in charge of this sinking ship as anyone else."

"That's horrifying," Christopher said.

"I agree. We should try and recruit Talbot now," I said.

"Would Talbot side with you after what you did to Nathan?" Shannon took my hand.

That was a good question. My uncle had a serious falling out with my father during my teenage years after taking Penny and I to avenge Nathan's earlier family. We'd killed the wereshark involved in his family's murder not long after completing our training. Nathan had been furious and banished him from our lives. Talbot had, before this, retired from all active duties with the Red Room on moral grounds. Yet, he still loved my father.

I wasn't clear on the entirety of the details but in addition to being partners, they'd been best friends for the better part of a century. Talbot had been the best man at both of my father's weddings and served as the godfather for all his children, including Rebecca. Even during my darkest periods, when I hated my father, Talbot had always insisted Nathan was a good man. I just didn't know if he'd believe me when I said, "No, no he's not. He's bad enough that I killed him and feel only a tiny bit of guilt." I gave Shannon's hand a squeeze. "I'd like to give it a try."

Maybe it was a good thing that I was going to die during this mission.

Do not lose faith just yet, Derek, Mary said, her voice surprising me with its tenderness. *The horrific crimes you have committed are but raindrops in the history of the universe. When you are immortal, the lives of billions are but the flowing of wind. Life and death are the same and no more a concern than the ticking of a clock. Why worry about any murders you commit when the number of deaths at one's hands is as many breaths as you a mortal typically takes? This is the future.*

You are horrible at this reassurance thing, I said.

Sorry, Mary said, embarrassed. *I'm not very good at understanding you. Even if I love you, you are just weird in how you think.*

I practically ran into Talbot, then, missing him stepping out of an elevator in front of me. Stepping back a second, I looked at my uncle. He'd changed out of his ridiculous Hawaiian shirt into a wool flannel lumberjack's shirt, blue jeans, and a pair of thick boots. His terrible scars were barely hidden with make-up, bandages, and a thick set of sunglasses. Even so, he was able to pass himself off as a wounded veteran. Which he was.

I tried to figure out what to say to my uncle as he turned to face me and the others. Looking down at me, he cut such an intimidating figure I almost thought he'd attack me despite the fact he'd been the closest thing to a father I'd ever truly had. Instead, he opened his mouth, closed it, and gave me a hug.

"Uh," I said, feeling him then squeeze. "Oomph."

"Eloquent," Shannon said.

"Thank God you're alright," Talbot said.

Looking at my uncle, I was surprised my first reaction wasn't relief and comfort but anger. I'd trusted Talbot to take care of Penny and yet there was no sign he'd been anywhere near her when she was attacked. I was sure there was an explanation but, right now, I didn't want to hear it.

"Talbot," I said, gritting my teeth.

I was interrupted from what surely would have been an argument by Talbot going for a cloaked weapon I just realized was holstered on the side of his body. "Demon!"

I grabbed his hand, more forcibly than necessary and backed up with ki power. "It's alright, she's with me."

Talbot looked down. "Excuse me?"

"Are you sure? We could totally give her the holy waterboarding treatment," Shannon said, smiling.

"That's blasphemous," Mary said, coldly.

"Like you'd know," Shannon snapped.

"Of course, I would," Mary said, grinning. "It being blasphemous is why we should do it. Torturing me by sacrilege is awesome. Let's get right on it."

Some of the nurses and security staff looked over in our direction. I really didn't want to cause a panic here and hoped Talbot hadn't started one.

Talbot called over. "Just discussing how he'd won a bet with me."

They relaxed, mostly.

"Derek, I've been around the block a few hundred times," Talbot said, lowering his voice. "Demons are never friendly. They're a corrupted, insane, and above all dangerous group of individuals."

"He is correct," Mary said, calmly. "We cannot be trusted. We are the royalty of the universe and masters of Creation. Morality does not bind us. Ahahahhahahahaahahaha."

Everyone looked at her.

"What?" Mary asked, blinking.

I sighed. "Not helping, Mary."

"I like her," Christopher said, laughing. "She reminds me of some of my exes."

Not Ashley. Mary was far from Ashley as (in)humanly possible.

Yes, I am glad not to remind you of other women you've tasted, Mary said.

Oops.

"She's fine, Talbot," I said. "We have bigger issues."

Talbot stared at her. "Okay."

"*Okay?*" Shannon asked incredulously.

Talbot looked at her like she was being the height of hypocrisy, then over to Christopher and shook his head. "We're all monsters here."

"He also freed me from my obligation," Mary said, accenting the word obligation like she was referring to something specific. "I have my freedom because of Derek, golem."

"Don't call him a golem," I said. "I'm pretty sure that's a racial slur."

"It is what he is," Mary said. "Life created by magic to serve mankind."

Talbot's accepting attitude evaporated in a heartbeat. "You gave a *demon* freedom?"

"Yes," I said.

"From both Hell and mortal binding," Mary said. "Hell's queen recognized our love."

Talbot put a hand over his face, looking physically pained. "You... moron."

"Because you've been such a great help during all of this," I said, ready to punch him in the face. It was an utterly irrational response but given I'd just stabbed what I thought was my father back in the medicine closet; I wasn't in a great mood.

Talbot said, "It means she can stay on Earth indefinitely and use her full powers. So, yes, it's very bad. You've unleashed a living god with no treaties to bind her power onto the planet. The only thing similar in recent memory was Stephen's pact with Furfur."

"Uh... Stephen's kind of loose," I said, biting my lip. "He killed the Committee and started this whole kerfuffle."

If you could call the death of millions a kerfuffle.

"Did you do it?" Talbot removed the hand from his face.

"No," I said, offended. "Nathan did. He's responsible for all of this."

Talbot, blinked, staring into my eyes.

I stared right back. "He's dead. I killed him."

Christopher groaned. "Yes, Derek, thank you. That will help our situation. Confess you killed your father, his best friend."

Mary looked over at Christopher. "I'm irritated I'm getting all the flack when you're a vampire and Shannon is the blood of Lilith."

"God above," Talbot muttered.

I walked over to the elevator and pushed the button for the floor below. It, to my surprise, opened immediately with no one inside. "Get in."

The group all headed inside, and I pushed the button for the basement. I hoped we wouldn't be ambushed in the parking garage like before, but I wasn't putting anything past Nathan lately. I told Talbot everything, holding nothing back, not even on details I had kept from the others. Despite my anger at him, no because of it, I wanted him to know just how thoroughly Nathan had betrayed his family.

Betrayed the world.

Finally, the end, when the doors opened to the parking garage, I took a deep breath. "I've been a spy for over a decade, Talbot. I have put up with the Red Room's shit more than you could ever imagine and I know you've served them twenty times longer than me. I've bugged phone-lines, bribed, blackmailed, seduced, lied, cheated, and sacrificed anything resembling a normal life. That's not counting the number of people I killed."

I paused.

Rebecca's face appeared in my mind.

Then a bullet hole in her forehead.

I sighed.

"Including family," I said, slumping my shoulders. "I am spent, going through the motions of it. I don't know if I can stop now or I'll just keep going until I drop over dead in a ditch somewhere but I'm not going to let this stand. I want to know if I can count on you to stop Roland and Stephen. The House itself, even if there's not a damn thing we can do about any of this. To forgive me."

"Not exactly *Henry the Fifth*," Christopher said. "Not even *Richard the Third*."

"I give it a six out of ten," Shannon said.

Mary, however, just nodded.

My stare at them was withering.

Talbot was silent during the entire conversation. "You didn't need to give me a speech, Derek, though I suspect that was more for you than me. We are agents, both of us, individuals who have sacrificed personal happiness and even integrity for the greater good of the world. The House has fallen into ruin and won't survive this but if you're going to state it was always evil, I think we can agree to disagree. For all the horrors it committed in the name of justice and world peace, it also saved countless lives as well as stabilized the planet against dire threats. Nathan chose to put his own feelings over the good of Earth's peoples. There's nothing to forgive. I knew he was lost years before. I lived through him, though, because he was alive and I was dead."

"I think you're overly harsh on your appearance," Shannon said.

"I am an animate corpse," Talbot said, softly. "I love, feel, fear, eat, and breathe. I desire pleasure, women, and acclaim. I am still not human nor ever could be."

"Human is what we choose to be," I said, looking down. "Not what we're born with."

I felt like an enormous hypocrite saying that. After all, I'd chosen repeatedly to be a monster.

Talbot looked forward as the door opened. "What I'm saying is, Derek, you only had to ask. I'll always have your back."

In that moment, he was more my father than Nathan ever was. "Alright, let's go get our people back."

That was when we came to our car and Penny was standing beside it. She was dressed in a black leather skirt, thigh-high boots, and a white blouse with vest, looking Goth but ready to kick ass. "Ready?"

I grimaced then nodded. "Yeah."

CHAPTER TWENTY-FOUR

The trip to the New London portal required us to get across the border to Canada, charter a private plane willing to go across the ocean despite the world being under lockdown, arrive in Wales, and drive to a lesser known stone circle than Stonehenge. Christopher had to sleep in a crate during the daytime, even though he was far in excess of the power a vampire his age should possess. The military had already declared martial law damn near everywhere and it required maneuvering past a lot of roadblocks. Thankfully, we were spies.

As we drove down a deserted back road in the middle of the night, the biggest trouble we ran into was boredom. I admit, in my desire not to think about my father trying to take over the world, the conversation ended up a little... strange.

"Of all the superheroines in the world, you would date Supergirl the most," I said.

"Absolutely," Penny said. "She's a very underrated heroine. Personally, though I think they need to age her up to like her mid-twenties, though, and give her a TV show. Maybe like working for Cat Grant or something."

"Will never happen," I said, glad to have a conversation that was meaningless. "If I was going to date anyone then it would be Oracle."

"Batgirl?" Penny asked.

"No, Oracle," I said. "Much more mature take on the Barbara Gordon character."

"You guys are all nerds," Christopher said. "Now if we were discussing which *Doctor Who* companion to date then the answer is Rose Tyler."

"Rose Tyler isn't even the best David Tennant companion," I said.

Bloody Mary looked out the window, bored out of her skull. "Can we please talk about murder instead?"

"No," I said.

Shannon, who had been listening to this for hours, finally shouted, "For once I'm with the demon. It should be illegal for spies to be nerds. Punishable by death."

"Ooo, execution," Bloody Mary immediately perked up. "Now the conversation is interesting again."

"Well, in any case, we're here," Christopher said, pointing to a sign that read Earthen Ring Park. It was an empty, dark, and foreboding sort of place that still looked reasonably normal. Just one of many tiny little cultural heritage sites that existed along the roads between major metropolitan areas.

"Oh thank God," Shannon muttered. "I was about ready start throwing in for Sarah Jane Smith and that meant forfeiting my sanity."

"Are you sure this is the right place?" I asked, staring at the abandoned picnic tables and overgrown grass. "It seems awfully deserted for an inter-dimensional gateway. I thought the Red Room kept a pretty close eye on all of the Shadow Loci."

"Places like New London provide a safety valve for the supernaturals who want to get away from the Earth's oppression. If they're leaving, I get the impression the Committee was eager to let them go," Christopher said, looking bored.

I frowned. "I doubt that. The Committee, I remind you again, included me."

"Yes, but you did a terrible job of paying attention to anything around you," Christopher said.

He had a point. I decided to move on. Very quickly. "So we just go up to the rocks, place our hands on, and poof?"

"Pretty much," Christopher said. "There's also an incantation we have to read but I know that by heart."

"What's the incantation?" I asked, wondering what it would be and if it would require knowing Latin or Gaelic.

Christopher stepped aside and gestured to the altar. "Put your hand on the altar and say, Klaatu Barada Nikto."

I paused. "You have got to be kidding me."

"No, that's what the gatekeepers chose as the password," Christopher said, looking away. Apparently, they're big *The Day the Earth Stood Still* fans."

"Either that or *Army of Darkness*," Shannon said.

I stared. "That's the most used magical password in history! You might as well have made it Admin!"

"*I* didn't choose it!" Christopher raised his hands in annoyance.

Shannon put her hand on the altar and said the magic words. In an instant, she was gone. There was no puff of smoke, no flash of light, just one moment she was standing there and the next she wasn't.

"I will find my own way," Mary said, looking at the altar.

She then vanished with just as much fanfare.

Leaving just me, Penny, Talbot, and Christopher. It was the mother of all awkward conversations. Christopher and Talbot knew the truth about what I'd done but I was about to head into battle with my sister under false pretenses. She had a right to know the truth and it burned me that I'd kept it from her for half-a-day.

"Penny, there's something you need to know," I said, taking a deep breath.

"Oh for fuck's sake," Christopher muttered. "You couldn't keep a lid on it until you'd rescued your family, could you?"

"Oh, Derek, no good ever comes from telling the truth," Talbot muttered.

I turned away from the stone formation and looked at Penny. "You have a right to know."

"Is this about you killing Dad?" Penny asked.

I stared at her. "... yes?"

"Oh don't worry about that," Penny said. "I'm sure he'll be ticked off when he gets back."

I blinked. "Excuse me?"

"You killed the Wazir like three times before it stuck," Penny said. "I think Dracula is going to stay dead but he's an Old One of his kind so that's iffy. Dad is an archmage. I'm sure he'll be back in time, assuming you killed the real him and not a homunculi."

"That is true," Talbot said. "Nathaniel stole the immortality of a vampire Old One once. It allowed him to regenerate after decapitation."

"I mean, I don't know how to react to Rebecca, but I figure we can resurrect her too," Penny said, clutching the Staff of Hiawatha tightly. "You really open up your mind to new possibilities when you're a reality warping mage."

"I think you're in denial, Penny," I said, wishing I believed it was possible to bring Rebecca back even if she was a psychotic mad scientist. Strange how I didn't have any temptation to do the same for my father.

"Better to be in denial than my brother admitting he killed my sister and our father," Penny replied. "You're not the same as Stephen, Derek. I refuse to believe that. Even if you are a kinslayer and associating with demons."

I opened my mouth then closed it. "Yeah, that is a parallel that I'm less than happy about."

Penny closed her eyes. "The Professor has already got Division One and several other groups remnants, including the U.K's to move in on New London when we give the signal. They're willing to cooperate with the Network just this one time and hopefully will give us the edge we need against Roland's private army. We need to focus on that. We can't start reforming the House until this is taken care of. Then you have to focus on leading us through this time of crisis."

"The House can't be reformed, Penny," I said, dryly.

"Nonsense," Penny said.

"Derek is right," Talbot surprised me by saying.

"What?" Penny asked, doing a double take.

"New London exists because of a deal made between the Knights of the Round Table's remnants and the House decades before either of you were born," Talbot said, dryly. "It would be a refuge for supernaturals and enemies of the House in exchange for them getting the chance to build Fort Happiness."

"What is Fort Happiness?" I asked, staring at Talbot.

"It's a gulag," Talbot said. "Just like Camp Zero and other House blacksites. A place where they disappear people and perform experiments."

"The House commits murders and kidnappings all the time," I said, dryly. "It also has its own science division. It's why we have the Red and White Rooms."

Talbot closed his eyes. "You only know the tip of the iceberg, both of you. As bad as you think the House is, you only saw the part that was justifiable. You don't know about the work on biological weapons, immortality serums, ticking time bombs made from supernatural children, and drawing magical force from the living."

"Talbot—" I started to say.

"Camp Zero," Christopher said. "The House within the House."

"Just one of many locations," Talbot said. "Derek, you thought you got rid of the rot there, but it goes much deeper. The House destroyed the Black Sun and the Nazis' supernatural agents because they were too into mortal ideology. They took many of them back into fold and had them go back to doing the same experiments they were already doing. That's how the Cassidy family came to power."

"Fuck," Penny said, dryly. "You can't make an argument when Nazis are involved."

"Yeah," I said, staring down. "Is this why Nathan did what he did?"

"Yes," Talbot said. "If you can't cure the plague then the only solution is to burn the entire house down."

"So, was he right?" I asked.

"No," Talbot said. "Because he made allies of monsters and monsters are what he's unleashed. I always wondered how Cassandra was able to get away with making something like the Matheson virus. I have to wonder if Nathan was responsible for giving her enough rope to getting away with it."

Penny didn't respond to the accusation our father may have been involved in the deaths of thousands via zombie, possibly millions now. "My country right or wrong. If my country be right, let it stay right, and if wrong let it be put right."

I looked at her. "Penny, I don't know if I'm going to survive this. However, you believe in the House much more than I ever will. So, whatever happens to me, I'm giving you my position on the Committee. Build a better House, one that protects humanity from the supernatural and maybe sometimes the supernatural from humanity."

Penny looked at him. "I'd feel honored if not for the fact you don't give a shit about the organization and just told me it was infested with Nazis. It's like buying me a house only it's built on a graveyard and full of ghost twins."

"And a pet cemetery in the backyard," I added. "Sorry."

"Can you believe this?" Penny asked, looking at Christopher.

"Given I allowed myself to become a vampire rather than continuing to work for the House, yes?" Christopher said, shrugging. "Also, I hate to be the one to point this out but every second we waste discussing existential questions is yet another where Ashley is being tortured as well as her kid."

"Derek's kid," Penny said, highlighting something I'd been happily ignoring.

"Probably," Christopher said.

"Probably?" I asked.

Christopher frowned. "I didn't ask."

"It doesn't matter," I said, dryly.

"It doesn't matter?" Penny asked, incredulous.

"No," I said, simply. "It doesn't matter."

Penny blinked then nodded. "Okay."

"Alright then," I said, walking over to the altar. Placing my hand on the stone doughnut, I said, "Klaatu Barada Nikto."

Physical transportation to another dimension was a different sort of beast than astral projection. Whereas the former was like sending yourself through all of reality, this was more like taking a couple of steps.

Still, on my way through dimensions, I caught a glimpse of New London. It was beautiful, wonderful, and...trashy. Huge glass skyscrapers loomed over enormous slums while the walls were covered in neon graffiti. There was no sign of its past as an Arthurian paradise and it looked more like Hong Kong and Tokyo with a dash of 80s cyberpunk. The sky was like old television static and the place smelled of smog and desperation. Shaking my head, I got my bearings. I found myself with Shannon, Talbot, Penny, and Christopher in a blackened alley between two large buildings I couldn't see the roofs of.

There was powerful magic in the air and I knew why so many supernaturals had fled to pocket dimensions like this one. The old supernatural ley lines were still present and most of humanity's sorcerous energy was not diverted to the House or its minions. Here, the energy flowed freely and even a novice mage like me would be able to use magic repeatedly without blood sacrifices or tiring quickly. J.R.R. Tolkien had talked about the elves fleeing for Arda and while this was nowhere near to the Earthly paradise, it was the same principle. I'd once been on a mission to an alternate reality's Hollow Earth once with Shannon and seen things like dinosaurs as well as Atlantean temples. It saddened me I was going to die here because I really would have liked to explore more of those. It was too bad the place smelled like sulfur and raw eggs.

"What an incredible smell…" I started to quote *Star Wars* but trailed off when I saw my companions were raising their hands in surrender. Two groups were approaching us from both sides of the alley, concealed by glamours until they dropped once there was no place left for us to go.

The Gunmage was at the end of the alleyway, half her face destroyed by fire, with a dozen floating robots armed with what appeared to be magic-tech wands in place of their machine guns. There were also two more squads of cloned elves, their faces staring forward with soulless obedience. The Gunmage had a revolver pointed at my head, fury in her eyes. Apparently, she was taking her facial injury personally.

Dammit.

CHAPTER TWENTY-FIVE

"Hello," I said, raising my hands slowly. "You know, I can recommend a wonderful flesh-sculptor to take care of—"

"Derek, shut up," Shannon said, keeping her hands in the air. "You will make it worse."

The Gunmage stared at me. "I would very much like to kill you, Mister Hawthorne. In fact, I could at any time—"

"YOU ARE ORDERED NOT TO HARM THEM," a shrill, mechanical and screeching voice came from the floating robots beside them. I didn't want to spend my entire remaining life making pop culture references, but the voices really did sound like Daleks. I had to wonder if it was Roland who'd programmed them that way or if he had his own version of Lucy who thought it would be cute.

Shannon tried not to grin. "Well, I guess it's our lucky day."

"Yes, because torture before murder is so much better," Penny muttered.

"Don't be a spoilsport, sis," I said.

"Way not to undermine me, Robot," the Gunmage muttered.

"WE ARE MACHINES. YOU ARE NOT AND NEED CORRECTION," the lead robot said.

"Not got a very good long leash from Roland?" I asked, impressed he'd managed to grant his machines intelligence. Of course, given Roland was a lazy frat boy it was likely he'd just summoned a bunch of elemental spirits to inhabit them. In that respect, they were the metallic cousins to Talbot.

"You're going to die, Hawthorne," the Gunmage said. "If not, then you'll wish for it."

There was something in her voice that surprised me. It wasn't the damage to her face, which was bad enough, but something else.

Call it instinct.

"What has Roland got on you, anyway? You're one of the best killers in the world and he's, frankly, a moron."

"Look at her eyes," Talbot said. "The ears have been surgically altered but you can see it in her."

"She's one of his genetically engineered elves?" Shannon asked.

I looked at the Gunmage again. Her skin was lighter than the others but the right golden color, her features (the unburned ones at least) were a little too perfect, but her eyes were exactly like Cassandra's. They were Cassidy eyes and there were other similarities, almost too minute to pick up, but recognizable to someone who knew what to look for.

"Worse," I said, realizing what it is. "Roland's genetically engineered Santa's Little Helpers are his biological children. She may or may not have been made in a petri dish but she's his daughter."

"You killed my mother," the Gunmage hissed, moving her gun between Shannon and me.

"Your mother?" I asked. Recognition dawned. "Jesus, Buddha, and Santa Clause, *Cassandra*?"

"Who are the Cassidy's? The Lannisters?" Shannon said, looking revolted.

Christopher tried not to laugh, which was good since it looked like the Gunmage was ready to shoot us against orders.

"Cassandra made us," the Gunmage said, clenching her teeth. "Roland provided the human DNA to make us more pliable than our pure elven ancestors, but she wasn't a part of the genetic makeup. Cassandra, however, chose our surrogate mothers and provided our training. We lived in the Spirit World, taught by her agents, and were prepared for the day we would help her rise to power."

"And you're only getting upset about this now?" I asked.

"I thought you were going to die at the golf course," the Gunmage said. "Now I'm pissed."

Okay, it was about her face. "Sorry?"

The elves being Cassandra's rather than Roland's fit with my conception of my ex-wife. She'd been a master of the biological side of magical engineering and constantly campaigned for the House to loosen its structures. Also, as an R&D Executive until recently, there was no way Roland could have pulled off creating an inter-dimensional prison and a race of genetically engineered soldiers. That would have fallen to Cassandra or her minions. Also, possibly, my father. Dammit, how deep did this go?

"You dodged a bullet with her," Penny asked. "Be glad you didn't have kids with her."

"She cursed me to never have kids," I said.

"Then how—" Penny started to say.

I shook my head. "Not now."

"She was a visionary," the Gunmage said.

"I'm sorry to tell you, but Cassandra's ship has sailed," I said, shaking my head. "I seem to recall a lot of her enemies disappearing around the time she made her little coup attempt, though. That was just before you started to make your mark as I recall. Let me guess, you were left high and dry once she ended up shot."

The Gunmage was aiming right at me now.

"I loved Cassandra too," I said, searching for some sign of doubt or emotion I could play on. "The funny thing is, while we were married, the only thing she ever said about Roland was he was an abusive arrogant asshole who coasted by on their father's money."

Actually, Cassandra had never an unkind word regarding her brother. She couldn't because she'd been mind-controlled for most of our marriage (unbeknownst to me). However, I was willing to bet Roland treated his "disposable cannon fodder" less than kindly. Especially the women.

The Gunmage did not flinch, but there was a movement in her eyes that told me I'd hit the mark. "You're not worth it."

Of course I wasn't.

"YOU WILL COME WITH US TO FORT HAPPINESS. YOU WILL DISARM. YOU WILL NOT RESIST."

"You can't harm us," I said, testing the robot's reactions.

Shannon moved an inch, preparing to go for the Gunmage. So did Christopher and Talbot, both moving at once. I chose to stand still, realizing now wasn't the time to make a move but unable to signal my thoughts in time. A series of bright-blue energy bolts flew out, striking Shannon, Talbot, and Christopher simultaneously.

All three of my companions collapsed to the ground, though a quick glance showed me they were all still breathing. They'd been hit with paralysis spells, a relatively harmless attack that would have changed the face of warfare if it had been allowed into the mundane world.

I was surprised the spell flashes were visible, most magic being too fast for the naked eye, until I deduced whoever had constructed the robots had installed tracer effects. After all, if you were going to go to all the trouble of making real-life death machines, then you might as well give them flashy weapons. Roland really needed to talk to his development team.

"Touché," I said, keeping my hands up.

"YOU ARE TO BE KEPT MOBILE IF AT ALL POSSIBLE."

"Give me the Bloodsword," the Gunmage said, holding out her left hand. "Slowly."

I moved down, unsheathing my weapon and handing it over to her. She didn't know I could summon it at will and was not going to tell her. The Gunmage took it and proceeded to place the weapon inside a robot which opened its chest to reveal a rune-covered compartment inside. They were going to prevent me from summoning my blade again, which was smarter than I expected from Roland.

"You realize Roland's being used, right? Just like Roland is using you," I said, trying to undermine her confidence.

"I will serve my purpose," the Gunmage responded, turning around. "You'll carry your companions to the transport one at a time. If you try to resist, we'll paralyze you."

"And spare me carrying them?" I asked.

"You don't want to know what doesn't qualify as harm to a robot," the Gunmage whispered, her voice filled with hate.

"Point taken," I said.

At the end of the alleyway was an armored personnel carrier, not that different from the kind found on Earth with six giant wheels and the Sons of Mars logo stamped on the side in bright white lettering. I found it vaguely annoying I'd travelled to another world and my first encounter was with a bunch of corporate mercenaries from back home. Well, robot mercenaries.

Hefting up Shannon, Christopher, Penny, and Talbot's bodies in turn, I placed them inside the APC before letting the Gunmage place a set of handcuffs on each of us. They severed my connection to my ki centers and I found myself completely blind to magic. For good measure, the Gunmage removed my wedding ring and other focuses too. I still had my tattoos, since they weren't easily removed, but was largely deprived of anything that would allow me to do magic.

Our guns were taken last and the thing she seemed least worried about. After that, I was loaded into the APC's empty back along with several of the floating robots and the doors were shut on me. It seemed our plan wasn't working out very well.

That depends greatly on your perspective I suppose, Mary said, speaking to me telepathically.

Where the hell are you? I asked, feeling the APC start to move.

Inside you, Mary replied. *I admit, I'd prefer the reverse but there will be time enough for that later.*

This is no time for dirty innuendo, I said.

It's always time for dirty innuendo, Mary said. *Roland doesn't know about me and that gives us the advantage.*

Not much of an advantage since we're now prisoners. I was already regretting I'd assumed I could do this with such a small team. With Penny we might have had enough firepower to take down the Gunmage and her collection of tin soldiers.

Keep matters in perspective, Mary said, cheerfully. *They're taking you directly to Fort Happiness.*

I'm surprised they're not shooting us directly, I said, furrowing my brow. *Speaking of which, why aren't they killing us? They didn't hesitate to take me down with maximum force at the country club.*

I imagine that's Nathan's influence, Mary said. *Roland might want you dead, but he still fears your father.*

So I'm only living at Nathan's sufferance, I muttered. *Despite him being dead.*

Death is relative, Mary said, speaking as if she was right beside me. *But don't take that too hard. Sentimentality is a weakness you are very good at exploiting. That is why you were able to elicit the cooperation of your mother. Soon, we will have the powers of a Celestial Dragon at our command and the House. You will be able to assume your rightful place as ruler of Earth.*

Mary... I muttered.

Oh right, Mary said, chagrinned. *I keep forgetting you are not motivated by power.*

Is that so rare? I asked.

Yes, Mary said.

Well, keep your head down. Roland may or may not know of your existence, but Stephen certainly does, and I don't think he'll hesitate to destroy or bind you. It's also certain he's got Fort Happiness warded against spirits since they're a lot more common in the Spirit World than on Earth.

Stephen is here? I asked.

Yes, Mary replied. *It is a pity you're unable to see New London. It is a beautiful monument to near-future dystopianism. Massive glass towers full of light against immense poverty and suffering. You'd love it.*

I'm sure I would, I said, shaking my head. *Maybe when the world isn't ending.*

So, never, then, Mary said.

Yeah, since I'm going to die, I said.

Prophecy is only true if you let it be, Mary said. *Humans have free will. The worst mistake the Creator ever made.*

The trip continued for another half-hour as the paralyzing spell slowly wore off on my companions. There was quite a bit of accusation and ill-feeling about the fact I'd chosen not to participate in their little coup, but I stayed silent during their recriminations. I was too focused on the fact we were almost to our goal.

It was only now, really, I had a chance to ponder what I'd say to Ashley when we met her again. I hadn't lied to Shannon, I'd moved on, at least as much as anyone could from a relationship like ours. I didn't begrudge Christopher having begun a relationship with her, either. Well, much. I was only human after all. Unlike everyone else in my group.

Huh. I never thought about that before, but I'd been destined to go rogue. All my best friends were supernaturals except for Lucy and she was a magitech engineer. There wasn't really much room for a guy who viewed the supernatural as people in an organization devoted to fighting said beings. Ashley would be pleased at least.

"Derek!" Shannon said, snapping her fingers in front of my face.

"Hmm?" I said, blinking.

"Have you been hearing anything I've been saying for the past ten minutes?"

"Clearly not," I said, speaking honestly. "That would require me to be listening."

Penny sniggered.

Shannon glared. "Maybe you should try."

In fact, I'd caught the general gist of it. They'd been yelling at each other but using code in order to communicate. All three of them had been speaking about our options, whether they should try again, or stand down until an opening presented itself. They were all very good agents, but I couldn't help but assume, since the Red Room's contractors had built the robots, they knew exactly what we were saying.

"I have a plan," I said, not using code at all. "Trust me."

"Oh, great," Shannon said. "I hate when you say that."

"It usually works out," I said, shrugging my shoulders.

"No, it really doesn't!" Shannon said.

"Don't worry," Penny said. "Our friends know."

Ah, she'd sent the code to the others. "Let's hope they don't listen to Roland."

Penny grimaced.

The APC came to a stop and the back opened, only to have us covered by many yellow uniformed Son of Mars mercenaries. We were in the center of Fort Happiness' prison yard and it was a combination of Alcatraz, Oceania, and a US Army base. It was a lot larger than my brief vision of the place had suggested, consisting of massive stone walls around numerous fortified buildings with hundreds of guards everywhere.

Three-dimensional film projections showed Roland's face everywhere as he talked in vague slogans like, "EFFICIENCY BRINGS A NEW TOMORROW", "OBEDIENCE AVOIDS PAIN", and most troublingly, "YOU DESERVE THIS."

The guards were a combination of elves and robots, though the former had been surgically altered to look more like humans. The prisoners milled about mindlessly, wearing yellow jumpsuits with bar-codes on their shirts, picking up trash and transporting items around the base. Their shaved heads and mindless eyes spoke of people who had been stripped of all dignity before being brainwashed into slave labor.

It was hard to imagine Roland had managed to assemble an army in the Spirit World without the House detecting it but, I had to keep reminding myself, he hadn't. The only person he had to keep his army secret from was me, given it was clear the Committee had considered me nothing more than a placeholder until Roland took my position.

Bastards.

"I don't think we're going to be able to rouse these people to riot," Shannon said, staring at one of the prisoners as they poked listlessly at a fast food wrapper with a pointed stick.

"No," I said, shaking my head. "But that's what scouting ahead would have been for."

"This plan sucks," Shannon said, playing along as we hoped for reinforcements that might never come.

"YOU WILL ACCOMPANY DAELIA THORNWOOD, DEREK HAWTHORNE," the robot behind me said. I presumed he meant the Gunmage. "THE OTHER PRISONERS WILL ACCOMPANY ME."

"Alright," I said. I was trusting Mary to get us all out of this. Otherwise, I'd lead us all to our deaths.

Shannon and I exchanged one final glance.

"Good luck," she whispered.

CHAPTER TWENTY-SIX

"So, what do you get out of all this?" I said, walking down the empty gray stone circular hallway with a robot in front of me and the Gunmage in front.

"EXPLAIN," the robot said.

"Just saying, if you're an AI, what do you get from serving Roland?" I asked, testing the limits of their devotion.

"WE ARE SERVANTS OF ORDER. ROLAND CASSIDY PROMISES A MORE ORDERED WORLD IN EXCHANGE FOR SERVICE," the machine said, surprising me. Apparently, it was smart enough to have an ideology.

I made a tsk-tsk-tsk noise. "But he's not really making the world more ordered but more chaotic or haven't you looked at Earth recently?"

"Shut up," the Gunmage said. "Both of you."

"WE ARE AWARE OF HIS ATTEMPTS AT MANIPULATION," the robot said, continuing to show how smart they are.

"That doesn't mean it isn't true," I said.

I'd been in several places like Fort Happiness in my years. I'd gone behind the lines to North Korea once to rescue a partner who'd made a hash of a mission. The North Koreans had, justifiably, assumed the random American they found in the middle of their country to be a spy. The funny thing about that mission was I'd seen more human suffering, misery, and despair there than I'd ever seen on any other mission. And it had all been caused by humans. At least Roland had cool sci-fi motifs.

"You know I'm going to try and get out of here," I said, giving the Gunmage a friendly warning.

"Tell me something I don't know," the Gunmage said.

"You're all going to die here," I said.

The Gunmage proceeded to grab me by the lapels of my shirt and physically hurled me through the door next to her. I slammed into the concrete floor and banged my head. It hurt enough I started to wonder if should tone down the backtalk.

Nah.

They might shoot me but they were in all likelihood going to do that anyway. If I was going to die, I was going to be true to myself: a complete jackass.

"YOU WERE ORDERED TO NOT HARM HIM."

"He'll be fine," the Gunmage muttered.

Looking up, I found myself in a dark, cramped, and thoroughly uninviting office. It looked like a World War 2 bunker with a thick oversized wooden desk, a single bare light bulb above, and a cheap metal seat in front of it. Much to my surprise, I saw Roland Cassidy sitting behind said desk. He was cutting cigars and wearing the same clothes I'd seen him in two days ago, looking like he hadn't slept.

"Dial it down, robot," Roland said, waving his hand. "Hello, Mister Hawthorne. Welcome to Fort Happiness. What do you think so far of our little resort?"

"Nice concentration camp," I said, climbing to my feet. "Did you decorate it yourself?"

The Gunmage pistol whipped me in the back of the head, sending me to my knees.

"You are just pathologically incapable of respect, aren't you?" Roland asked.

"I'm not the guy who created this shithole," I said, staying on the ground this time. "It takes a special kind of crazy to look at all of this and describe it as good."

"You're right," Roland said, putting away his cigar cutter.

That surprised me. "I am?"

"Care for one?" Roland offered me one.

"My body is a temple," I said.

Roland snorted, clearly not believing me.

The Gunmage grabbed me by the shoulder with one hand and forced me down into the chair in front of Roland. She kept her other hand on her pistol, which she aimed right at my chest.

I had no doubt she'd shoot me where I stood if given the slightest reason.

I also knew Roland needed me for something.

Which I had to play.

"No thank you," I said, simply.

"I didn't make Fort Happiness because I wanted to. I made this place because I needed to. Stopping the House required an army and resources we couldn't assemble on planet Earth. Creating a prison as the cover for it here in New London was our best solution. The thing is the House has a way of getting into your brain. When I made this place for building up our forces, it was all too easy to end up adding torture and slavery to the list of treatments prisoners endure. It just made things easier."

"You'll forgive me if I assume nobody finds torture and slavery easy but psychopaths," I said.

Roland pulled out a gold lighter from his pocket and lit up his cigar. "The Founding Fathers did. This island is built over miles of tunnels that we've used to house our genetics labs, factories, and more that have had thirty-years to be built up. My father, Gamen Cassidy, started this plan and it's within spitting distance of being realized. A world free from the House and their deals with the supernatural scum of the Earth."

"With you and Nathan in charge," I said, shaking my head. He'd already said he was willing to burn the entire planet in order to see himself put in charge of it. It was a bit late for him to try to convince me he was just a well-intentioned extremist.

"I've been thinking about what you've said," Roland said, taking a few puffs. "It turns out I may have been putting a little too much faith in your father."

"Really? He's such a trustworthy guy too," I said.

"I'd like to make you a counterproposal," Roland said, blowing into the air. "The spell to bring Balor back to life is almost done. You do me a favor and I'll let you go along with all your friends, including the two god psychics. We'll part ways, no harm, no foul."

"Excuse me?" I asked, stunned he'd even consider offering this. "You really think I'm going to buy that?"

"Sir?" The Gunmage said.

"The favor is worth your miserable little ass going free. Contact your mommy dearest and get her to raise Cassandra from the dead," Roland said, puffing on his cigar. "Then we'll take out your father together. So, two favors, technically."

I stared at him, trying not to laugh. "Okay."

"I'm sensing some skepticism," Roland said.

I kept hoping for the sounds of helicopters in the distance or explosions. Unfortunately, I had no sign that we were getting the calvary anytime soon. Had the Professor betrayed us or was it just harder to mobilize an attack against another dimension than I'd anticipated.

"Not at all," I said, lying. "I'm entirely onboard with this plan."

I'd met a lot of delusional, obsessive, and outright unbalanced people in my time as a spy. Roland seemed to be the first one who just flat-out was divorced from reality. I suspected it was the result of having everything delivered to him on a silver platter since birth.

"Don't think I'd ever trust you," Roland said, staring at me. "You have no idea how much I wanted to hunt you down and skull fuck you after I found out about Cassandra's death."

"Your imagery is... vivid."

Roland's eyes focused on me and he looked ready to reach across the table and stab me in the eye with his cigar. I got my first real sense he was a better actor than I'd given him credit for. Psychopath or not, he really did care about his cousin. "I'm going to tell you a story, Derek."

"Must you?" I asked.

"Yes," Roland said, lowering his voice. "I must. Do you know what our father did to Cassandra?"

I did. I didn't like the way this conversation was going since I really didn't want to confront the fact there were damn good reasons why Cassandra had gone insane.

"Your father wanted to secure an alliance between my family and his," I said, divorcing my emotions from the subject. "Cassandra objected to the relationship, so he proceeded to brainwash her into becoming an obedient pliable wife. I never knew. Eventually, she managed to break free of the spell and went insane."

"Insane for wanting to destroy the House?" Roland asked, daring me to say it wasn't the most natural thing in the world to want.

"Insane for wanting to use a *fucking zombie plague* to do it," I said, staring up at him.

Rebecca had perfected brainwashing in the service of the House, but it had existed long beforehand. The problem was, unlike how the movies depicted it, mind-control was the most ineffective and horrific misuse of magic you could employ. If you changed a small element of a person's personality, such as helped them quit smoking, it might be alright but that little seed would have a cascading effect on their entire personality.

In Cassandra's case, making her fall in love with me and become a supportive doting wife was so far removed from her aggressive power-hungry forceful self it had snapped all manner of wires inside her. It had led her to obsess over me and, of course, the plan to take over the House. Given there was an entire military base full of grown elf supersoldiers, robots, and prisoners formed by her family before this I wasn't sure if I was overestimating the event's influence.

Roland looked down on his cigar. "The plan to destroy the House predates both Cassandra and I. For centuries, wizards and supernaturals have wanted to end its reign over the world. The enforced truth, the exile to the Spirit World, and the suppression of knowledge. Dozens, hundreds even, have risen to challenge its monopoly on power but all of them failed in the end. Cassandra didn't hold with those ideals, though, she wanted to just focus on living. She was also in love with someone else."

"What happened?" I asked, surprisingly curious. Also, the longer he talked, the less likely he was to start with the thumbscrews.

"You know what happened." Roland stamped his cigar out in an ashtray on his desk. "Her father tore out her mind, had her lover killed, and then tore her mind apart. He then brainwashed her into being your perfectly obedient little wife.

All to seal the possibility of your family joining his conspiracy. The irony? You still divorced her because, in the end, you found her spectacularly creepy."

It hadn't been entirely like that. I had loved Cassandra but not the woman the magic had turned her into. She broke free in the end and I wish I had been there to help her. Either that or had the sense to leave her alone. "Whatever deal you have with my father, I've never been a part of it."

"That's because I gave my uncle a stroke," Roland said, looking straight at me. "I poisoned him for what he did to my Cassandra and trapped him in a state of living death. It took years, but I eventually found someone who was capable of undoing the spell that turned Cassandra into the Stepford wife you married."

I looked down, guilty. I should have known she was under a spell. She'd always been a little too perfect, too accommodating, too nice. It was part of the reason I'd never truly been happy in our relationship. Little had I known she'd been screaming on the inside the entire time.

"Do you know what she said, the first time she woke up after the spell's influence was removed from her mind?"

"I'm going to kill every last person involved in this?" I asked.

"Huh, you did know her," Roland said, smiling. "After that?"

"I don't know," I said.

"She thought *Derek is going to feel so guilty,*" Roland said, holding his cigar between his hands then breaking it. "My cousin still had feelings for you after the fact she'd been used by you this entire time. The spell had been a part of her so long it had warped her thinking permanently. So, even knowing you'd been a part of her torture for years, she couldn't sort out her feelings to hate you the way she should."

"I didn't know what was happening," I said.

Roland looked ready to come at me. "You *didn't know.*"

I blinked, then shook away my guilt. "Which is no excuse, you're right. That doesn't justify a tenth of the shit you're planning to do. It justifies you killing the Committee, your uncle, me, and maybe even the rest of the House but this is war on the entire planet. Don't think for a second this wins you any sympathy."

Roland smiled. "You're right. The House knew about the brainwashing, at least the Committee did, because they're all about binding the power blocs together. Cassandra is the one who persuaded me to continue her father's dream, to make it her own, and I'm carrying it out now. We will secure her vision."

"I thought it was Nate's vision?" I asked, wondering how much of this he was parroting.

"That was before I found out he was going to cut me out of the New Order."

"And after all you've done for him!" I mocked.

"Please let me cut off his fingers," the Gunmage said, keeping a gun trained on me. "He doesn't need them."

"Laugh all you want, Derek," Roland said, pointing at me. "Your father came to me after Cassandra's death and talked about what a tragedy it was. That she'd been working with him to overthrow the Committee and that we could revive her dream."

"And you believed that?" I asked.

"In retrospect, it seems pretty obvious I was being played. The problem with you Hawthornes is you're such wonderfully good liars. I got control over Pantheon Corp, though, because of his influence and we made excellent progress toward Cassandra's goal. A new world where the Truth is public and science is able to incorporate magic without restriction. It'll be like *Star Trek* only with less disintegration and cloning-based teleportation."

"You don't strike me as much of a utopian," I said.

"I graduated from M.I.T with honors," Roland said. "The party boy persona is just a tool and a good one too since you fell for it hook, line, and sinker."

"Yes, because all the slave girls you cart around are for show," I was ready to get on with the torture now.

Roland shrugged. "Position comes with perks."

I hated this guy so much. "So Nate was manipulating you the whole time. Who could have seen that coming?"

"Says the guy who voted for my inclusion in the Committee

despite the fact he'd murdered my cousin."

"I just thought you were that much of an asshole," I said.

"Your mistake." Roland chuckled. "Nathan has been arresting my people in secret and maneuvering things so I'll be the one taking the blame after Balor's attack," Roland said, frowning. "He needs to be the one to take the blame instead. He won't be able to point fingers if he's dead."

"And how does that relate to my mother resurrecting Cassandra?" I asked.

"It doesn't, but it gives me a reason to want to let you live thereafter. Resurrection magic is restricted to archmages and celestial beings. Your mother should be able to restore Cassandra to life."

"So you two can live happily ever after in the world you've burned to ashes," I said.

"The world's already burning," Roland said. "The question is whether or not you'll be there to see the new one rise."

There was no reason not to agree, even if I fully intended to put a bullet in his head. "Alright, I'll happily do so."

"Splendid," Roland said, chuckling.

I didn't like his confidence.

"Sir, you can't be serious," the Gunmage said, moving her gun away from me.

I was tempted to go for it.

No, Mary whispered in my mind. *Not yet.*

You have a plan? I asked.

You told Shannon you had a plan, Mary said.

My plan is to wait for reinforcements! I said.

Yes. Mary sounded guilty. *I have a plan that's even better.*

Oh no. I'm not going to like it, am I?

No, Mary said.

I sighed. *I trust you.*

Mary chuckled. *Sometimes, Derek, you shouldn't.*

"Remember who you work for, Elf," Roland said, his expression full of contempt. "Cassandra cobbled you together from the D.N.A of a hundred Red Room agents and material taken from dissolved bones. You're a Jurassic Park dinosaur.

You may look like a Cassidy but that's cosmetic. Don't forget that."

That surprised me and I wondered if Roland wasn't aware his family's D.N.A had been used, or whether Cassandra had used her own rather than Roland's.

"I won't forget, sir," the Gunmage muttered, her voice cold and unfeeling. It was unlikely I'd be able to persuade her to side with me after what I'd done to her face, but emotions were funny things. You could manipulate people to do things against their nature as long as the emotional intensity was every bit as strong. Love could become hate, hate could become love, and loyalty turned to loathing with the right incentives. I'd done it many times before with great success. In that respect, I was little different than Rebecca.

"Of course," Roland put his hands together. "I can't trust your word."

"Oh, please, I'm as honest as they come," I said, lifting my hands. "You have me by the balls."

Roland narrowed his gaze. "No, I don't, but I will."

Uh oh.

Roland stared at the Gunmage and gestured to the door. "Take him to Room 101."

CHAPTER TWENTY-SEVEN

"Room 101?" I said, disbelieving. "Man, you're not even try-ing to pretend you're not the bad gu—"

I was promptly struck across the head again, this time the Gunmage's weapon knocking me senseless. I lay on the ground, half-conscious, overhearing her talk to Roland. "I've wanted to do that since I met the man."

"Think how it must feel to be his brother-in-law. I've wanted to kill this guy since before Cassandra's wedding," Roland said.

"Then why don't you?" The Gunmage asked.

"Because Cassandra is *more important*, you stupid tube of vat grown meat. God, I can't even stand to look at you. You look too much like her. Take him to the damn chamber and make sure he gets the works."

"Yes... sir," the Gunmage said.

Man, I had seriously underestimated how much of an asshole Roland was. The only thing I'd misread was that he was doing it out of misogyny. Well, entirely out of misogyny. He wasn't afraid of Nathan, he wanted his cousin back.

I ended up getting dragged by the Gunmage down the hall this time. Being an elf in human disguise, the Gunmage was stronger than a normal human and carried me like a piece of luggage with her arm around my waist. I could have killed her any one of six ways, even with my handcuffs, but the floating robot behind me made that impractical.

On the way to wherever they were taking me, I passed by numerous prison cells that contained those who hadn't been entirely indoctrinated. They were an eclectic bunch, mixing both those who had yet to be processed and those who were in various stages of being broken down to their base component parts.

The unprocessed looked like they'd been grabbed directly off the street. They were like looking at people from another world, which they were in retrospect, with clothing fashions I didn't recognize. People wore their hair in spikes, fluorescent-line covered body wear, sported cosmetic cybernetics, and their body modification went beyond tattoos to full transhumanism.

I saw people with cat-eyes, bear-claws, monkey tails, and ears better belonging to a dog. New London was a strange land and perhaps a vision of what the future might look like. Given all the residents were scared, angry, desperate, or pleading, I hoped not.

The processed ones were easy to separate as they were wearing the uniforms of the prison with newly shaved heads. As I walked further into Fort Happiness, I saw them become more and more depressed before coming across the living zombies I'd seen before. It was a frightening process, especially since it hinted at what I'd find in Room 101. Or what might happen to my loved ones. My heart skipped a beat as I also saw children among the prisoners, some not even into adolescence.

I was dumped in front of a metal door at the end of a side hallway seconds after. The robot hovering over me as the Gunmage stepped back.

The Gunmage smiled. "This is your last stop, Hawthorne. Can't say it happened to a better man."

"You know he'll never appreciate you. To him, you'll always be a tool," I said, looking at her in hopes I might find some sort of kinship.

I found none. "I might be a tool, but I have a purpose in life. So will the rest of humanity when this is all said and done."

The Gunmage sounded like she was trying to convince herself of it.

"Our purpose is what we make of it. Roland has no right to dictate any of that," I said.

"Get up," the Gunmage said. "I'm going to enjoy this."

I picked myself up as the metal door opened to a science-fiction looking room made of reflective mirrors in an octagon set of walls, the door having its own mirrored paneling. In the center of the room was a chair like the kind used by Dentists with all manner of equipment around it I didn't recognize as well as restraints. It was, disturbingly enough, not that dissimilar to the kind I'd been put in with Arthur.

I knew what the device was, because I'd seen it in the Red Room's records, or a variant of it. It was a Dream Chair. To give an idea of what I was feeling, allow me to put said device in context. The Red Room practices assassination, arms trafficking, blackmail, bribery, torture and terrorism. As a member of the Committee, I'd voted against countless actions that involved the deaths of innocents only to be overruled time and time again.

Some of the records I'd read spoke of human trafficking to feed vampire assets, turning over refugees to the governments they were fleeing, and even replacing missing individuals with homunculi so their relatives wouldn't make a stink about their absence. All this being among the things they openly admitted to. Yet, despite this, the Red Room had outlawed the use of Dream Chair on moral grounds.

I proceeded to deliver a stinging blow to the back of the Gunmage's head, spun her around to use as a shield against the robot's stun ray, grabbed her gun, fired it into the machine and watched the magical bullet cause it to explode. Grabbing a pair of keys from the Gunmage's belt, I proceeded to start running down the hall.

The Gunmage reached into her pocket and pulled out a credit card before hurling it at my leg. It sliced into the side like it was a throwing knife and sent me sprawling to the ground. Getting my handcuffs off, I felt my magic return only to catch the next credit card she threw at me, in midair.

I didn't want to kill her, strangely enough, but lifted her gun to put a bullet in her head. That was when I heard the shrill voice of the five robots hovering beside me.

"DISABLE TARGET."

Crap.

A series of paralyzation rays struck me simultaneously, causing me to fall on the ground, bleeding from my leg wound. They didn't hurt but they were a reminder, for all my skills and experience, I was vulnerable to simple numbers. Unable to move, do magic, or even think very hard, I was helpless when the Gunmage came up to my side.

Looking profoundly pissed off, she delivered a series of vicious kicks to my side. Despite being paralyzed, I felt every single one.

"Stupid son of a—" I stated to say.

"YOU WILL NOT CONTINUE. SUBJECT WILL DIE IS SUBJECTED TO MUCH MORE ABUSE," a robot interjected.

The Gunmage delivered another vicious kick to my stomach. "That was a stupid move."

It was.

But the Dream Chair was a nightmare I was willing to die to avoid it. The Dream Chair was conceived in the late Sixties by named Doctor John Winston Jones who looked at Phillip K. Dick's bizarre dreamlike novels and determined to one him up. They allowed a probe to be inserted into the subconscious of a subject and, from there, play with their memories and dreams. Last I heard, Doctor J.W. Jones was heading up a cult on the West Coast called the Ultralogists.

People could achieve time-dilation that allowed them to live potentially months or even years within seconds. It was a perversion of Astral Projection and the applications for torture were tremendous. People were left imprisoned for thousands of years or subjected to horrors that couldn't be replicated in the real world.

You could insert memories of rape.

Killing their own families.

Enjoying killing their own families.

Burning to death repeatedly.

Forgetting their own children.

Remembering children they didn't have.

That was the Dream Chair.

The Gunmage dragged me once more to the chair and strapped me in. I could feel the immense pain from the beating she'd given me. She slapped the power-inhibiting cuffs on me again, but this time did it around my legs. I was bleeding from the cut, dripping my life fluids on the floor, but she paid no attention.

"SUBJECT WILL DIE IF HE DOES NOT RECEIVE MEDICAL TREATMENT," a robot said.

"This won't take long," the Gunmage said. "We have as much time as we need to make him see our point of view from his perspective. We can get him medical attention after he's spent ten thousand years being broken."

I was frightened. "Please don't."

The Gunmage chuckled. That's when she placed a metal circlet around my neck and proceeded to flip a variety of switches on a control panel to my side.

I screamed.

"Enjoy hell, Hawthorne," the Gunmage said.

I fell into darkness.

The memories all jumbled together as I saw the connections in my brain that formed the ones in my spirit. I saw how my pride interacted with my ambition, with my lust, with my wrath, and my insecurities. I saw how childhood fears gave birth to adult neuroses and attempts to make myself better. I saw the pattern that existed in every human soul and how pulling at a single strand could make the whole complicated weave unravel. The Dream Chair was probing my mind and forced itself into those memories that mattered most. The ones at the heart of my consciousness.

I struggled against the machine's attack, forcing it back and drawing on all my willpower. I was not going to submit to the Dream Chair's influence and did everything in my power to stop the invasive force that was pressing itself into my mind. I could resist a hundred mages cooperating, even kill myself, but with my abilities suppressed there was no way to fight with anything but human thought. No human mind could stand against what I faced.

In an instant, I was leaning up against the side of a black van on the side of a hill overlooking a wheat field in Oklahoma. It was two in the morning and I was having a cup of coffee with Ashley. There were numerous crop circles down below, which aside from being the product of clever pranksters, was sometimes the result of fairies playing with humans.

It was busy-work from the Red Room, nothing terribly

important, but we'd managed to make some valuable contacts with the local pooka in the process. We'd use them to shut down a human trafficking ring run by fairies later that year and get some valuable intelligence on sidhe court politics. I remembered this night because it was... peaceful.

"What do you see when you look at the stars?" Ashley said, wearing a thick beige coat and a headband.

I looked up at them. "A million terrible things coming to eat this planet?"

"Really?" Ashley asked.

"No, it just sounded better than stars," I said.

"So you don't see anything else anymore?" Ashley asked.

"I used to see possibilities," I said, taking a sip of my coffee. It was bitter and black. "Now I just see the curtain in front of the windows to a world I'll never see."

"Wow, that's depressing," Ashley said.

"What do you see?" I asked.

"A question," Ashley said. "A question how important we could be if we're one small speck of dust in the space of a single star system in a galaxy that is but one in millions."

"And I'm depressing?" I asked.

"I think it's good to keep perspective that each of us is possibly the only person looking out for ourselves. I thought you'd appreciate that. You're like the least religious person I know."

"I'm actually the most religious person you know," I said.

"... really? Everyone else in the Red Room holds a Bible or prayer beads or copy of the *Necronomicon* like it's a shield," Ashley said. "Well, the ones who aren't all militant atheists who think gods are all aliens coming to eat us."

"Yes, but they know those gods exist. I, however, believe in something I can't see."

"Which I've never seen the point of," Ashley said.

"I believe that everything in this universe is part of something much greater. Something that unites us from top-to-bottom and believing in this one being who is every being, I think it's great enough to be able to know us on an intimate multiple level as much as we can know ourselves if not more so. If a computer can multitask a million times faster than humanity, why not it?"

"Because it probably doesn't exist?" Ashley asked, putting herself in the more traditional atheist category.

I shrugged. "It exists because I thought of it. The question is whether it exists outside of my head. Which, to me, doesn't matter."

"Now you're just screwing with me," Ashley said.

I shrugged. "A lot of people think of religion from the top down. I prefer to see it from the bottom up, a quest for something bigger than one's self."

"I prefer to find my meaning in myself," Ashley said.

"I find it in you and everyone else I love," I said.

Ashley did a double take. "Love?"

"Oh crap," I said, half-joking.

Ashley looked at me. "No, I've known for a long time. One of the advantages of being a telepath. It's just you've never said it aloud before."

"Really?" I said, faking surprise. "You'd think I'd have mentioned it before what with the fact we've been having sex for months."

"I haven't said it either," Ashley said, her voice lowering. "I know you've got a lot of troubled feelings leftover from Cassandra."

"I could never understand her," I said, sighing. "I always sensed she was deeply troubled but every time I tried to reach her, she just retreated deeper into the false persona she'd erected for herself. It was like she was more interested in making me happy than being herself and the more I fell in love with the person she was underneath, the more angry I could tell it was making her yet the more she acted like Polly Perfect."

"That must have been hell," Ashley said. "My family is a bunch of psychics, but we all have each other's backs. We can also be honest with each other because we all know each other's true selves. Well, except for Ashley junior, she's way too eager to please."

"Yeah, Casandra didn't have that," I said.

Despite being an arranged marriage, I'd done my very best to make it work with Cassandra. To learn who she was and support her. It hadn't worked. Now I knew what real love was. "Do you love me back?"

"Do I have to say it?" I asked.

"It'd be nice," Ashley said.

Ashley had her own issues, which she only occasionally alluded to. One of these included a desire to never fall in love. I'd backed her into a corner by my question. "Yes, Derek, I love you. I really do."

She was crying now.

I got down on one knee. "The only way to surprise you is be spontaneous. Will you marry me?"

Ashley stared, closed her eyes, and laughed. "Yes."

She hated the House, hated being stuck inside it, and hated what she was forced to do. But we could survive it.

Together.

Then the Dream Chair removed that memory.

And another.

And another still.

They removed every single decent memory of my life and began replacing them with their own.

Memories of loyalty to Roland.

CHAPTER TWENTY-EIGHT

I was losing myself. That was the only way to describe the Dream Chair's torture. My first memory lost was my proposal to Ashley. My next were Christmases with Penny and the family. I lost the times I managed to help people in my capacity as an agent, despite how much the Red Room stacked the odds against me.

There were times I spent with Shannon, moments with my twin, and even days of joy with Christopher. It was as if my mind was a book and they were tearing out the pages containing every memory of my life, leaving me with only the worst and most terrible moments. Worse, still, were the terrible moments were being modified to become more prominent. The evil becoming as formative as the good.

Gods, immortals, and saints.

I was suddenly back to my time in the Black Room's academy. It was near my graduation and I had one final test before I became an agent.

"Have you ever killed anyone before?" the instructor asked, sitting across from me. He was an older man of Korean descent with a wedding ring, serviceable but inexpensive suit, and several scars around his neck from what I imagined were Rakshasa claws. I didn't know his name but he went by the appellation Mister Black.

The two of us were in cheap metal folding chairs, a card table between us. There was an ashtray in front of us, a pack of expensive cigarettes, a bottle of unopened whiskey, and a card with a brothel's address on it. There was also a gun.

We were in a basement of an old building in Detroit, though

the location was supposed to be secret since we were transported with bags over our heads in vans as well as a fake plane ride that only did circles in the air. Figuring out our location was part of the test. The other part was murder.

"No," I said, leaning back in the chair. I was wearing a pair of sweatpants and shirt with the hoodie down. "That's kind of the point isn't it?"

"The point is really what you make of it, isn't it?" Mister Black said.

"I suppose so," I said, taking a deep breath. "So how does this work?"

"You ask whether or not you want to see the file," Mister Black said. "Then you decide whether or not to do it."

"Why show me the file?" I asked.

"To make you feel better," Mister Black said.

"Wouldn't that just make him, or her, more humanized?" I asked.

"Everyone is different," Mister Black said. "Some people don't want to know who they're killing. They trust the Red Room's judgment and use that to distance themselves from the action. Other people like being able to tell themselves the person they killed deserved to die."

"Does the person deserve to die?" I asked.

"That's why they're here," Mr. Black replied.

I wasn't sure, even then. "Alright, show me the file."

Mister Black nodded and produced a manila envelope from his black leather bag on the floor. I spent about ten minutes looking over it. I still remembered all the details. His name was Winston Parsons and he was a Snatcher. He was a human, not a monster, which was part of the test.

It was Winston's job to take children and substitute Changeling children in their place, which he was paid a great deal for. The Changeling children would grow up in their new human identities and work on behalf of their fairy masters in the Spirit World, undermining the House as well as keeping a steady watch on the progress of humanity. The children taken to the Spirit World were kept as slaves.

Or eaten.

"Does it make a difference?" Mister Black asked, when I finished.

"Yeah," I said.

Mister Black nodded. "Are you going to do it?"

"What happens if I don't?" I asked.

Mister Black shrugged. "You're unfit for agent duty but we'll find something for you to do. You're very good at languages and self-defense. You could teach."

"Experienced agents should do that," I said.

"Perhaps," Mister Black said.

I sighed, knowing I had to do this. "Give me the gun."

Mister Black handed it to me. It was already loaded but I checked to make sure and turned the safety off. My instructor proceeded to lead me to the next room. There, John Parsons was tied to a chair, having shit himself in the meantime, and still whimpering. The smell was overpowering. No one interfered when I raised the gun, aimed it at his head, and hesitated for two seconds. Then pulled the trigger. There was a mess. I ended up taking the whiskey and the card for the brothel. It was the only time I ever paid for sex.

The memory changed so I didn't bother to review the file and didn't hesitate. It was only the first memory they used white-out on and changed the contents thereof. I remembered things that had never happened. Cold-bloodedly murdering people who stood in my way, framing subordinates for my mistakes, and cooperating with Cassandra against the House. They were making me into a monster. Worse, it wasn't so far a stretch. I'd always been close to one. I was then back to my time as an agent with Christopher, a few years after my graduation and failed marriage to Cassandra.

The woman's corpse on the bed was beautiful, which disgusted me and showed how much attention to detail the murderer had taken. In real life, death was messy. People shit themselves, they were torn open, and the looks on faces were horrific. As much as the movies tried to romanticize death, it was always undignified. Death was the end of something great rather than the beginning of something new. I believed that as a religious person. Of course, my opinion was affected by the fact I'd been lovers with the woman.

Tina Redmond.

A woman I'd led to her doom.

Knowingly.

I was in a hotel room with Christopher at my side, a group of Red Room auxiliary moving around the room to remove all trace evidence, enchant it against divination, and dispose of the body. It was like a forensics team in reverse. They were Room Service.

"So, Barnaby finally cottoned to the fact you were screwing his mistress," Christopher said, staring down at the naked redheaded girl. He was wearing a black suit and shades like a member of the secret service. "Is it possible he left her like this as a message?"

"It's absolutely a message," I said, looking down at her. "She's been cleaned up and posed like it's a crime show."

"I always wondered why the victims on those shows were usually women. I never gave much thought to the idea it was just to make it more poignant and artsy. Kind of sick when you think about it," Christopher said.

"Yeah," I said.

"So what was your relationship?" Christopher asked, sticking his hands in his pockets. "You weren't exactly too eager to share details."

"I was told to seduce her," I said, simply. "I took the identity as a Blood Slave of a rival Vampire Captain and played on her feelings of inadequacy and guilt. Barnaby had kept her as a possession since she was twelve years old, feeding on her and later using her as a mistress until she was sixteen. Then he abandoned her for younger prey."

"I take it you were successful. The dossier said she's a blonde," Christopher said.

I closed my eyes. "I think she did that for me."

"Unfortunate," Christopher said. "A vampire is likely to notice such things."

"She thought I was going to get her out. I insinuated my boss would be able to help her become a vampire," I said, taking a deep breath. "The blood I was provided to give to her was pure. We made promises. We would be immortal together."

"Did you ever have an extraction plan?" Christopher said.

I looked down at her, then turned away. I needed some air. "No."

The memories the Dream Chair inserted for that action were horrific in the extreme. Killing women and children. Torture. Terrorism. Enjoying the act of murder. They were juxtaposed against my own, mixing and twisting them. I broke. Just not in the way they expected.

They could make me into anything they wanted. They could make me a murderer, God knows I was one already. They could make me a terrorist, I'd done things close enough to it for government work. They could even make me a traitor. I hated the Red Room and everything it stood for now. They couldn't make me like Roland, though.

Fools, Mary said. *They believe I would give you up so easily. Don't they know your power grows from pain and suffering? They have fed you decades of experience in a few moments.*

Mary, I whispered. *I don't know who I am anymore.*

You are mine, Mary said. *No one else's.*

Like a tidal wave, my memories returned washed into my consciousness through my bond to Bloody Mary. With those memories came power. Demonic power infused my soul and I felt a hatred that allowed me to tap into my damaged soul to access more magic than I had ever felt in my life. I was as much demon as man with Mary having merged fully with me. I welcomed that power.

My eyes opened. I was still inside the room, the Gunmage and a pair of robots standing over me. Less than twenty-minutes had passed. There sounds of explosion in the distance and gunfire, which I heard despite no way of being able to do so. The attack had begun and it was completely unexpected by my captors.

"Stay down, Hawthorne!" the Gunmage said, having only the barest inkling of what had just happened.

She didn't understand she'd taken away my mercy.

I give you my power, Derek, Mary said. *I've been gathering it for weeks now with many sacrifices. Go nuts.*

With pleasure, I thought.

"Put your gun in your mouth and kill yourself," I said, my voice low and forceful. It was filled with pure, hate-filled menace born from living a life without the tiniest bit of peace.

"No," the Gunmage whispered, her hands shaking around her pistol. "I—"

"Do it," I commanded.

The Gunmage started crying then put her gun into her mouth. What followed was messy but final, showing she should have taken my offer of getting her face fixed.

"Such a waste," I muttered.

The robots aimed their weapons at me. Then both exploded without a word from me. Looking down at my restraints, they undid themselves. My leg wound was bad, having covered the floor in blood. I just closed my eyes and healed it over. The pain was exquisite.

Rising, I looked at the world through the eyes of a psychopath. I felt a profound sense of sympathy for Stephen in that moment. I had plenty of memories for him. I remembered how he'd struggled with the tests my father had imposed on us in hopes of awakening our magical powers. Tests we'd failed. It had never been with malice from Nathan, but it had caused Stephen to go deeper and deeper into himself. I understood what it was like to hate yourself so much you wanted nothing more than to wrap yourself in darkness. The world was clearer now. You destroyed that that was in your way. You took what you wanted. Simple. Easy. Right.

"Come forth," I said, gesturing to my shadow. From it came forth a hideous little troll-like thing made of darkness. Another followed. Then more.

The lightbulb above me went out as I slowly sucked out the electricity from the entirety of Fort Happiness. From it, I generated hundreds of shadow-constructs and filled them with spirits from the Stygian Darkness. I could never have summoned, even with the boost I'd gained, if we weren't in the Spirit World where the borders were ephemeral. I created them from my hate, my greed, my anger, and my pain.

I set them on the Fort's inhabitants. Screams occurred

everywhere as the shadow constructs killed, tortured, and murdered everyone they could lay their hands on. I fed on the pain, the suffering, and the bloodshed.

Walking down the halls, whistling "Sympathy for the Devil." Every time I passed a body, I harnessed the freshly spilled blood to summon more constructs or raise the body as a draugr under my control. The armies of elves and robots might have been able to kill them all, but it was hard to destroy an army that grew every time they inflicted casualties. I saw House and Network soldiers several times but they, wisely, ran whenever they saw my monsters.

Good for them.

I only needed the attackers and my army of unnatural minions to provide me long enough of a distraction to reach my goal. It wasn't to rescue Shannon, Talbot, Christopher, Ashley, or Penny. They were like shadows to me, if I remembered them at all, and unimportant. No, now I was going to kill Roland. And I would make him *suffer*.

CHAPTER TWENTY-NINE

I walked through the darkened halls of Fort Happiness, watching my constructs and draugr kill and rend whomever they came across. While I didn't give a shit about them, the prisoners were the lucky ones since neither of my creations was interested in opening their cells to get at them. The ones who were brainwashed into oblivion weren't so lucky but, in a way, they were receiving the only kind of mercy left to them.

It was strange looking at the world through the eyes of an insane archmage. I saw the connections between the dead and the living world around them. The elves who had lived their entire lives in the service of a man who didn't care about them, the maintenance people drawn from lives of poverty in New London, and a few defectors from the Red Room who thought this was their chance to make a difference in the world.

None of their lives mattered.

Even the genetically-engineered soldiers of Roland's conspiracy only cared about his cause in the abstract. The late Gunmage had loved Roland like a father but the others viewed him as a tyrant, leading them to retreat constantly until the majority simply fled.

Sometimes, they decided to attack me in hopes of ending the attack in one swift stroke. Individuals, squadrons, and even rushes of crowds. With the Bloodsword in hand, all of their bullets bounced against an invisible wall before I slaughtered them all. I had no idea how many I'd killed by the time I finally felt Roland's presence.

Dozens? Certainly?

Over a hundred?

Probably.

That triggered a memory in the crisscrossed wreckage that was my demonic magic warped consciousness. Not a pleasant memory, otherwise it would have been erased, but an important one. It caused me to pause over a collection of bloody corpses at my feet. It wasn't that long ago, only a few years, so it was still crisp in my mind.

"Paperwork," I muttered, finding myself in the past. "I hate paperwork."

The giant mass of it was like a dragon guarding a cave, sitting on top of my desk and requiring a brave knight to slay. It was the largest collection I'd seen in years and threatened to spill off the top and onto the floor. My office hadn't been visited in two weeks, the result of a particularly long mission, meaning it had been allowed to accumulate like the horror it was.

"Back foul demon!" I said, making a tiny cross with my fingers.

"Oh for crying out loud, it's not that bad," Sakura said, shaking her head.

"How did it get to be this bad?" I asked staring.

"Your job is like ninety-percent paperwork," Sakura said, staring. "Mission reports, expense reports, weapons discharge reports, equipment requests, casualty reports, and dossier write-ups. Remember, your job is to gather intelligence, *not* shoot people. At least, last time I checked."

"I forget because I usually block it out," I said, frowning. "I'm usually better able to keep ahead of it."

"By which you mean sending it to other departments in hopes they lose it, dumping it on me, and fulfilling the bare minimum of details," Sakura said.

"I'm not that bad," I said.

"Do you really want me to answer that?" Sakura asked.

I shrugged. "Probably not."

I walked over to the chair behind my desk and shook my head, pulling out the rubbish bin. "Then I'll just handle this the usual way: throw away repeating forms, sort by importance, and do the easiest ones first."

"Not the most important?" Sakura asked.

I snorted. "If they sent something actually important to me via paper trail, that's their mistake."

Sakura laughed then turned serious. "A lot of these folders are red binders."

I frowned. Red binders meant I'd killed someone. "Yeah."

"Is it really that violent?" Sakura asked.

"Not for normal agents," I said, sorting those first. "The difference between me and a normal agent is most of them usually only have one violent encounter with the supernatural in their lives. It's usually their last."

I was exaggerating, but not by much. The Red Room preferred to keep its agents from directly confronting the supernatural. When they needed someone eliminated, they sent in overwhelming force and arranged things to be as one-sided as possible. In the business, that was what was considered good tactics. I had a way of surviving encounters that were much more one-sided.

"How many people have you killed?" Sakura asked.

I looked up. "That's in my file. It's not really a question you want to ask someone."

"I know but I've known you since the Black Room. I couldn't do the final test and I have difficulty reconciling the person I know to the numbers I've seen."

I snorted and leaned back in my chair. "Numbers lie. Do you mean the number of people I've put a bullet in directly? Do you mean the number of people I've ordered killed? Do you mean the number of people who died during missions I'm a part of? How about the people who died when I set a building on fire? Are we counting humans, monsters, spirits, or re-animated corpses? How about those people who died because I was stupid?"

Sakura looked at me. "The ones you count."

"All of them," I said, sighing. "But if you want to know, Sakura, I've killed about a person a month on average since I graduated from the Black Room. That doesn't count the times I've been on part of large-scale destruction missions like the incident that lost Christopher. It counts the collateral damage because I bear responsibility for that."

"Ten years of killing," Sakura said, shaking her head. "I

don't know how you can do it."

"Because I'm broken," I said, looking at her. "Kill missions usually take about three-days, the majority being travel time, and represent roughly half of the deaths I'm responsible for. The rest happen because other missions go sideways or someone decides to get clever with me. All in all, I usually take five missions during a month since I prefer to specialize in short-term one-day assignments that clean up other agent's messes. People forget I usually solve them with cash or negotiation. They think I'm an assassin rather than a generalist."

"You're also a workaholic," Sakura said, staring at me. "Other agents take vacations. They have relations. They raise families. They don't just go from one hot spot to the next, minus hospital stays."

"I use magical healing," I said. "Are you asking me out?"

Sakura raised her ring finger. It bore a new engagement ring. "Agent Keaton."

I nodded. "I saw."

Sakura smiled. "I just wanted you to know if you needed someone to talk to, I was there."

"I don't need a therapist, Saki," I said, smiling. "I'm fine. Some people just work better alone."

That had been before Shannon.

Shannon.

Argh!

The memory shattered. It was a good thing it did because no sooner did said memory pass away, then I saw a thick barrel-chested man in a yellow maintenance worker's outfit, swing a sledgehammer at my head.

I caught the head of the hammer with my left hand then jammed the Bloodsword through his heart, drinking of his life-force.

"You killed my... friends," the maintenance worker said, cursing me with his dying breath.

"Yes," I said. "I did."

In the back of my mind, I could feel my true memories trying to push themselves to the surface. They were blocked, however, by the immense mystical knowledge I now possessed.

I knew, subconsciously if not consciously, I could remember the way things were. I could remember being loved, cared for, and appreciating life. But I knew it would come at an immense cost. The cost of the power I now had at my fingertips. I drove those memories to the back of my mind. Better to reign in Hell.

I started walking down an empty corridor, one of the many that had been illuminated by electric torches in order to drive back the terrible darkness consuming their base. Running the tip of the Bloodsword against the concrete, I made a screeching noise, as said, "Roland, come out! It's time to play!"

He was nearby.

I could feel it.

And afraid.

Good.

Roland's response was to send *yet another* team of elven soldiers to kill me. These were armed with what looked to be the electric rifles from the future. Annoyed at Roland's use of comic book weaponry, I telekinetically forced all their weapons up under their chins and caused their fingers to pull down on the triggers. The weapons worked fine, at least, burning a hole through the back of their heads and beyond.

A grenade was then tossed through the door they'd just come through, which annoyed me since that would have been the smart tactic before sending a dozen men to their door. I snapped my fingers and the grenade, coincidentally, turned out to be a dud. This was starting to get boring.

Unfortunate, Mary said. *I'm about to run out of power. All the lives you've taken have helped me but you're cashing checks your body can't cash.*

Top Gun, really? I asked.

See? You're already returning to your normal status, Mary said. *A pity too. You should have saved more for Balor.*

Is he still a threat? I asked, suddenly remembering why I'd come here.

Oh my, yes, Mary said. *The entire place reeks of demonic energy. Good for us, bad for everyone else.*

Walking through the door, I entered a fenced-in courtyard

with a helicopter pad. It was a design that wasn't known on Earth and incorporated all manner of magitech devices that would have made it tear through most military choppers back on Earth. It was starting to spin its blades and Roland was inside the back, visible only through a window.

The helicopter brought around an axial machine gun on its bottom with three barrels, enough to turn a car into confetti. How unfortunately I used the night's shadows to rip the bottom out of the helicopter then crushed the rotors into a thin ball. The pilot jumped out of the side and proceeded to run, abandoning Roland to his fate. Which was good since that took nearly everything I had left. It seemed even archmages had their limits.

"Hawthorne!" The door slid open to reveal Roland, carrying a briefcase and an Uzi. If he'd been combat trained, he'd have realized it was better to ditch the briefcase. Instead, he lifted it up and fired it at me, somehow missing me despite being at point black range.

I ducked behind some of the helicopter's wreckage then telekinetically hurled a tiny piece of jagged metal into his hand. It left me panting for breath but caused Roland to scream and drop his weapon. I'd severed three of his fingers in the process.

Standing up, I kept the Bloodsword drawn in front of me. "Congratulations, Roland, you have successfully pissed me off."

"Fuck you!" Roland snarled. "The House is going to burn. Your family is going to die and I'm going to track down everyone you've ever so much as exchanged pleasant words with and stab them with an icepick."

"Why should I care?" I said, not even sure who he was talking about. I had remembered what I was here for but now I couldn't remember again. Dammit. Stupid demonic magic. You should get more benefit from selling your soul.

Roland realized he couldn't intimidate the psychopath he'd made, his stunned expression leading into a gallows' laugh. "The funny thing is, I was hoping we could be friends after this. I figured I'd give you as a present to Cassandra. You'd suffer like she suffered. She loved you, though, at the end. Just too twisted to—"

I swung my blade around and cut Roland's head clean from

his body, sending it flying from his neck and into a nearby puddle. His body fell over, still clutching his briefcase in a death-grip. It was an anticlimactic way to end the fight, but he'd never been a real threat. No, he'd just been an annoyance. Shaking the blood from my sword, I sheathed it.

That was when I felt the demonic power leave my body and I fell to my knees. I dropped the Bloodsword from my hands and it dissolved back into my body. I felt immense pain and reached to touch my stomach, pulling my hands out to reveal blackish blood. "Oh hell."

"I fear you have taken many injuries," Bloody Mary said, appearing in front of me.

She was wearing a pair of blue jeans, a leather jacket, and had her hair tied in a ponytail. It was the most normal she'd ever looked. In her hands, she was holding a black parosel that was keeping toxic-smelling rain from my face. A storm had begun even as I started to hear the sounds of battle again.

"How bad is it?" I asked.

"You tore through many individuals," Mary said. "However, I fear you took damage in the process."

"Roland didn't miss, did he?" I asked, coughing blood.

"No," Mary said. "He did not."

"I don't suppose you can patch me up?" I asked, realizing that I'd allowed myself to become distracted from what was important here.

"Of course," Mary said. "But you're running on fumes now, my love. We must withdraw if you are going to survive."

"How is the attack going?" I asked.

"Badly," Mary said. "Your distraction gave them an edge, but Fort Happiness was a fallback point for many of the House's worst in addition to the late Roland Cassidy's private army. Unfortunately, that advantage has passed."

"So, I have to keep killing if they're to have a chance," I said.

Mary shrugged. "They're keeping their heavy ordinance back because they sense Balor's resurrection is imminent. You may not be able to achieve anything here. Balor is awake enough to start draining the dead and dying's energy. Ashley's link to it is killing her as well."

I looked at Mary. "Give me enough strength to keep going."

"You won't survive," Mary said, dryly. "You are barely hanging on as is. Your mind isn't well either. You're as likely to kill your friends as your enemies. I tried to heal it after the Dream Chair but—"

"Please," I said.

Mary sighed. "Humans. Kiss me."

"What?" I asked.

"Please," Mary said. "Both to share power and because I want you to treat me not as a demon but as a woman."

I stared at her, then wrapped my arm around her waist, pulled her close, and kissed her.

CHAPTER THIRTY

The kiss was warm, hot, and intense. I couldn't help but let it linger, my hands moving up and down her back. I kissed the side of her neck before pulling away. "I need to get going."

I felt Mary patch up my interior injuries with shadows and blood magic. However, I could feel she'd shared every bit of power she possessed to do so. It couldn't fix me either as the moment she stopped maintaining those patches, would be the moment I'd die. It was in that moment I realized that she was every bit as capable of love as a human woman and I hated the fact I'd treated her the way I had.

"Because of Shannon, Ashley, and the others," Mary said.

"They need us, yes." I nodded then grimaced.

"Because you love them," Mary said, licking her lips.

"Yes," I said, taking a moment to look down at the fallen form of Roland. "This isn't enough."

I stumbled away from him and almost collapsed before Mary caught me.

"You need to be careful, you've channeled more hellish energy than ever before," Mary said, helping me to my feet. "That has its own effects."

"What sort of effects?" I asked.

"If you weren't my familiar, you'd be dead," Mary said. "Or a demon."

I looked at her, realizing for perhaps the first time Mary would never abandon me or turn away from me. "That doesn't sound so bad right now."

Mary's expression was soft and sad. "It is. I was born in the darkness and emptiness of the Abyss. I was created from the violence and anger of humanity's first stories about murder. I was sculpted by Tiamat-Abaddon into a creature that would show the beauty of killing while being repulsive on the inside."

"You're not repulsive." In fact, right now, she was the world's most beautiful woman. The only light I had in this dark place.

"I am," Mary said, leading me through the door and to one of the nearby offices. "I am not human and born of darkness to die in it. My purpose is to lead humans to ruin and misery, only that purpose no longer brings me pleasure."

My shoes were slick with blood and stained the floor as I picked up Roland's Uzi off the ground and conjured a new Bloodsword. The sound of the prison alarm blaring, gunfire, and shouts were distant now. I felt woozy and was sweating profusely now. "Everything is... terrible."

"You're likely to hallucinate soon," Mary said, wiping away the sweat from my brow. "Every man's hell is man-made in the Abyss and you are carrying more darkness in your heart than most."

"Why you love me," I joked, wanting to get up and go look for the others but unable to move my body.

There were few times I'd been more exhausted. Even with all the strength Mary was giving me, I wasn't sure if I'd be able to do much more. I needed to come up with a Hail Mary plan and I wasn't sure that was possible while infused with the power of hell.

"No," Mary said, surprising me. "Your capacity for bloodshed is not why I love you."

"Why then?" I asked.

"Your humanity," Mary said.

I snorted, staring up into her soulful blue eyes. They were more human now than they'd ever been. "I'm a monster."

"Yes," Mary said, nodding in appreciation. "You are a human being. The ultimate masters of every form of horrific vice, terror, and atrocity in the universe. Demons marvel at your species' capacity for evil and I am continually amazed at your, specific, skill at bloodshed."

I let out a gallows' laugh. "Not helping."

Mary joined me in chuckling. "You have done many terrible

things, Derek Hawthorne. You have killed, destroyed, and ravaged your enemies but while that attracted me to you, it was the fact you continued to care that made me realize I loved you. I offered my allegiance to you, freely and unconditionally, but you freed me. You have never wanted me as your slave."

"No." I felt like dying. It would be a welcome release from the Red Room and House's evil.

An end to my suffering but I couldn't die yet. There was too much left to do.

"You never wanted me as your slave." Mary whispered. "But you don't love me."

I looked at her, taking in Mary's face for what might well be the last time. "I love you but I can't love anyone who isn't my equal. You want to either master me or be mastered. I only want a partner."

"Like Shannon or Ashley," Mary said.

I closed my eyes, barely able to stay conscious. "I thought so. It turned out neither of them particularly wanted what I was offering."

"You want a human woman," Mary said.

I shook my head. "I don't know what humanity was. I was raised to be a tool. A weapon of the Red Room."

Mary smiled. "And you are the weapon that helped destroy them, this day."

"Nathan did that," I said.

"Did he?" Mary asked before pressing her hand against my face. "For centuries, millennium, I have done nothing but kill. I have overseen rapes, press-gangs, forced labor, death marches, and mass-executions. I watched villages and kingdoms burn as well as tempted great men to sin. The worst atrocities of men have been my nectar but now? Now, I feel loathing at the idea because you do. What is that?"

"Love," I said. "Through me you have developed empathy."

"Ugh," Mary said, before staring into my eyes with all-too human irises. "Can you love me? Truly?"

I opened my eyes and stared at her. She looked desperate, sad, happy, and longing at once. "Can you be my partner?"

"Yes," Mary said. "Give me a name."

"What?" I asked.

"You are an archmage now, even if you don't know the secrets consciously. I ask you to give me a new name and change my nature. So that I may be with you as your... as your... as your wife."

I stared at her. "You're asking me to define your nature?"

"Yes," Mary said.

I took a deep breath. "I can't make you into my ideal woman."

"Then don't. Make me into a woman. Because I asked you to be. Because it's my choice."

I felt close to death now and I realized I didn't have much time left. The Bloodsword's power had saved me on many occasions before but it was killing me now. "I don't know how... "

"Please," Mary said.

I closed my eyes, delirious now. "Your name is... Mary. Not Bloody Mary. Just Mary. Mary Sanguine."

"So instead of Bloody Mary, I'm Mary the Bloody," Mary said, raising an eyebrow.

"I'm not good at this," I admitted.

Mary laughed. "You are."

Mary stared at me. "Now let me name you."

"What?" I asked.

"Be someone other than Derek Hawthorne," Mary said, whispering in my ear. "Be someone else. For me. Forever."

"Alright," I said. "You are my goddess."

"Dante," Mary said.

"What?" I asked.

"You are the man who ventures through Hell for his love," Mary said, putting her hand on my chest. "You will never die. I promise you."

"I don't even think you can do that," I said.

"Believe in your goddess," Mary said. "Besides, we still have a few tricks left up our sleeves."

"We could use some miracles now," I said. "I don't think I'm going to be much help in my current form."

"Miracles are not always welcome," Mary said, pointing across the sky.

My attention followed where she was pointing, and I saw the storm clouds in the sky swirl as a dark and hideous creature made of shadow began to form out of the concrete buildings across from it. The form it started to take reminded me of Chernabog from Disney's *Fantasia*, an enormous hundred-foot-tall stone demon that stretched out wings like some sort of living gargoyle the size of Godzilla.

"Well, shit," I said, staring at him. Did this mean Ashley was dead?

Much to my surprise, I saw a second fifty-foot-long draconic form descend from the sky and spread out its own wings, blasting the monster with flame that illuminated the night like a second sun.

"Mom?" I asked, stunned at the sight. I had no idea why she'd showed up given she'd shown no interest in helping me in my quest until now. Yet, her presence meant a great deal and potentially meant this would not result in a rampaging demon destroying an entire city before moving onto the Earth.

"Unless she dies," Mary said. "Which would be a shame given she's managed to survive for so many centuries."

"Can she win?" I asked.

"Let's see," Mary said, smiling.

I glared at her.

Balor opened a single red eye and shot forth a ray of death that Kim Su deftly maneuvered before swinging her tail and shattering it with a single blow, causing the Elder God to scream in agony. Its body cracked and it started to fall apart, the monstrous being looking less and less intact with each passing second.

"What's going on?" I asked, watching the battle of the titans look less like a conflict of gods and more like David vs. Goliath.

"Balor's tie to this world Roland," Mary replied. "You severed it before his summoning was complete. Perhaps Shannon and the others may have damaged the ritual or freed Ashley as well. We are, after all, not the only people trying to disrupt their efforts. It's also possible that Nathan's agents sabotaged it before it was done, or Roland simply wasn't capable of pulling it off to begin with."

"That's anticlimactic," I muttered, staring at the door back into the now-ruined prison. Did I dare go back inside to find out what had happened to my loved ones? Did I dare not?

"I said it was possible," Mary said. "Not that it would happen."

To my horror, I saw Balor retaliate. The Elder God brought down a dozen bolts of lightning from the storm above its head. I could see the dragon summon a shield to throw away the bolts, but this didn't protect her from it striking her with a massive concrete fist that sent her flying backward, smashing into a gas station outside Fort Happiness' walls.

"We have to help her!" I called, walking forward.

"We can do nothing," Mary said, dryly. "You need to rescue your friends, if any of them are still alive."

I stared at her. "Are any of them?"

"Your daughter is," Mary said. "So is your sister. I can sense both through our blood connection."

"Our blood?" I asked.

Mary stared like I'd missed something vital. Like, oh, that she was a goddess of blood.

"Right," I muttered. "What happens if we encounter Stephen down there?"

"We die," Mary said.

"Fair enough," I said, heading through the door back into the prison. "I don't suppose you can point me their way."

"Of course," Mary said. "I just don't want you to get yourself killed."

"Too late," I said, feeling the magic already slipping around my injuries.

Mary didn't respond. "Just follow your instincts."

"I will," I said, walking with a limp.

The lights had gone out in the prison as even the emergency power had been cut. The doors had opened to all the cells and there were bodies lying across the ground, either from prisoners rushing the guards or cut down by the many horrible things I'd unleashed. Bits of ceiling lied scattered every few feet as the fortress was no longer stable.

I'd lost control over the draugr and shadowspawn I'd

created. They feasted on the corpses and some of the still-living people spread around. They, thankfully, ignored me as I passed them. Sometimes I took pot shots at them, gunning them down in hopes of trying to carve an egress for anyone I found. I had it in my head that maybe, just maybe, I could try to find a little bit of redemption in all this by rescuing some of Fort Happiness' prisoners.

"The ones that aren't dead because you unleashed hell on Spirit World?" Mary asked, reading my thoughts.

"You're not helping Mary," I said.

"I am explicitly helping a great deal," Mary asked, reaching over and touching a draugr that was ripping out a man's intestines and feasting on them. The draugr choked, spasmed, and then fell over before crumbling to dust.

Mary looked a little brighter and the magic keeping me alive felt a little more solid. There was no way to reclaim all the magic I'd used to tear up the interior of Fort Happiness, but every little bit helped. I tried to concentrate on my instincts like Mary said and felt a small trace of something tugging me down specific hallways and passages.

There were more signs of the terrible battle that took place here and I saw dozens of elves lying on the ground with shattered nonfunctioning robots. There were a few bodies of Network and House soldiers next to them or even prisoners but most of them seemed to have just lied down to die. I wondered if that was because of Roland dying or whether Balor rising had taken all their life above. It didn't really matter, though, but just added to the whole hellish feel of the place.

"It's not remotely like hell, Derek," Mary said.

"Really, what's hell like?" I asked, perhaps making a statement that I never should have.

"Exactly like Earth," Mary said. "Except as how humans want it to be."

"That doesn't sound very hellish at all," I asked, confused.

"You underestimate your race," Mary said. "Hell was originally an empty place, divorced from the Creator and the other gods. Desolate and dark. It was human's desire to be punished that filled it with nightmares of flesh-rending tortures, endless battlefields, and gaudy impossible cities so full of empty pleasures that they become their own form of torture. There's even the universe's largest shopping mall."

"Huh," I said.

"We should take it over," Mary said. "Unless you want to take over this dimension first."

"Never change, Mary," I said.

"I won't," Mary said. "You might, though."

Gunning down a group of draugr that were feasting on prisoners, I heard some more gunfire down the hall and felt a slight tugging of my soul. Heading down, I entered Fort Happiness' cafeteria and saw a skylight open to the storming night sky. Tables were overturned and benches were shattered in half with hundreds of dead elves, robots, draugr, and burning shadowstuff. Standing in the center of the room were a few dozen prisoners and House agents carrying rifles or wands. I'd expected to see Penny, Christopher, and Talbot among them. Instead, I was surprised to see Arthur, Lucien, Alex, Anna, and Ashley (jr.) among the agents.

"What the fuck are you doing here?" I asked, looking at them. "This is suicide!"

"No shit!" Arthur said, looking like he'd survived the *Night of the Living Dead.* "Your mom recruited us, though. Also, it's my aunt and niece."

"Your aunt and niece?" I asked, doing a double take.

That was when the crowd parted and I saw an orange jumpsuit-wearing Ashley stumble out, holding the hand of a young white-haired girl of Eurasian descent. She was sickly looking, rail thin, and her hair looked stringy on her head. Her eyes were sunken but there was a trace of the beautiful vibrant woman that I'd fallen in love with. The girl, the girl leading her forward, was my daughter.

Holy shit.

"Hi, Derek," Ashley said. "Long time no see."

CHAPTER THIRTY-ONE

Looking at Ashley was like something out of a dream. As terrible as she looked, health wise, and I was surely looking equally rough—I found myself remembering when my own life still had a bit of hope in it. When I believed the House was a necessary evil or could be reformed. When I loved my father. When I believed that I wasn't going to end up dead on the floor of a wrecked gulag that currently had two gods fighting it out fifty yards away.

Speaking of which, there was the sound of helicopters flying overheard and launching rockets into the side of Balor's concrete body. Balor made a noise that I would have described as the wailing of the damned turned up to the eleven if not for the fact that it sounded much worse.

How is it going? I asked, walking up to Ashley.

Not well, Mary said. *Balor is growing stronger rather than weaker.*

How is that possible? I asked.

I think we can deduce that the ritual wasn't complete when we attacked, Mary asked. *Balor awakened half-formed but he's drawing from the power of his worshipers to restore himself to full power.*

So Roland wasn't his tether, I said.

No, Ashley is, Mary said. *I don't think Balor is going to kill her, though. In fact, he might start sharing power with her to keep her alive soon.*

That's good, I thought.

No, it really isn't, Mary said. *At least if you care about any of the people here. There's ten million humans living in this pocket dimension. Enough for Balor to feast enough to restore himself to full power. Really, after that happens, our best hope is that he decides to invade hell and challenge Tiamat-Abaddon for rulership. Either that or create his own dimension to rule. At least if you don't want him taking over the British Isles.*

We have nukes, I said.

Oh right, well, then that's an option too, Mary said. *We should get them blessed first, though.*

"You know I can hear you, Derek," Ashley said, taking my hands. "Psychic, remember?"

"That's not my name anymore," I said, staring at her. "I am Gandalf the White. Last of the Red Hot Swamis."

"You're mixing your books there," Ashley said, staring at him. "But it's nice to meet you, Gandalf."

"Dante," Mary said. "Dante the Maimed."

"Really?" I looked over at her.

"You've sacrificed your eye, hand, and parts of your soul for the greater good," Mary said. "It is a worthy epithet."

"Yeah," I said, grimacing. "Super."

"I think it sounds cool!" the girl clinging to Ashley's leg.

I looked down at the girl. "Who is she?"

Ashley smiled. "Her name is Victory."

"Ah," I said. "Good name. You know, if you want to honor the Queen who created an oppressive empire over half the world."

"Victory, not Victoria," Victory said, looking up and sticking out her tongue.

I smiled. "How?"

"I don't know," Ashley said, looking at me. "But yes, she is. I—"

"You don't have to explain yourself," I said, looking at her softly. "I was in the House and that place is a cesspool that eats everything good in a person."

Ashley lowered her gaze. "If that were the case then you wouldn't have come here to save everyone."

"Not everyone," I said, looking over at the carnage around us. "Just you. I'm sorry for what's happened."

"So am I," Ashley said, looking around. "I need you to sever my bond to Balor."

I didn't know what she was saying until I did. If she was tied to Balor and he wasn't fully manifested then severing it, by killing her, would probably cut off its ability to manifest in this world and any other. Balor would be returned to the death-like sleep that true immortals like it had been reduced to during the great was before recorded history.

"Are you fucking serious?" Mary surprised me by saying. "Do you know what he has gone through in order to get here?"

"No, mommy, please!" Victory said, looking up. "Don't!"

I couldn't approximate her age really since she looked slightly older than she should be if she was my daughter. Time moved differently in pocket dimensions like New London.

Ashley looked down. "This is for the greater good."

"Everyone keeps saying that," I muttered, staring forward blankly. "However, it always seems to be right before something horrible is done."

"This is my fault," Ashley said, looking at me. "My blood, my power, and my lineage is what brought back that thing."

"I love how she's completely ignoring us," Arthur said in the background.

"Well she does barely know us," Ashley (jr.) said. "Mind you, it does feel like this entire thing was pointless."

"There's two dozen kids here and other civilians," Alex said, dryly. "That, alone, justifies all this."

"I find it justified because it was fucking awesome fighting our way here," Lucien said. "Seriously, it was like a live action video game."

Everyone looked at him.

"What?" Lucien asked.

"Hell, even I wouldn't say that," Arthur said, staring at him. "Think it? Yes. Say it out loud? No."

There was a scattering of cans and raising of guns as a second group entered into the cafeteria. Much to my surprise, I saw it was the rest of my group. Christopher, Penny, Shannon, Talbot, and a collection of other survivors.

"Christopher!" Ashley said, stunned at his appearance.

He ran across the cafeteria at a speed that rivaled Neo and embraced her. I knew, in that moment, she'd moved on and was surprisingly happy for her.

Liar, Mary said to me, telepathically.

Yeah, I said. *I am.*

Mary reached over and took my hand, squeezing it.

To my surprise, I saw a handful of elves and guards among the Network as well as House soldiers. Apparently, at least some of Roland's forces had broken faith with him and survived Balor's resurrection. That was assuming he wasn't going to start draining our energy soon as well.

He won't, Mary said to me, mentally.

Why? I asked.

He's about ready to triumph over Kim Su, Mary said, *Then he will have an entire city to destroy.*

Goddammit, I said.

Yes, literally so, Mary said. *We do not have much time if you want to save any of them.*

What happens if I take Ashley from here without severing the bond? I asked.

Balor will no longer need her and everyone here will die. Are you prepared to sacrifice them all? Mary asked. *I do not judge, merely enquire. Dying is what humans are best at, Dante.*

Penny, Shannon and Talbot reached my side. The three added a sense of comfort where there might not otherwise be any. My relationship with Shannon hadn't worked out, she couldn't allow herself to be happy, but I wanted her to be. Talbot had stood by me throughout the worst of a life that had been rich in wealth and poor in emotion. He was my real father and the only reason I hadn't become the kind of sociopath Roland had been. Penny? Penny, I wish I'd never brought here because she was proof that the House could create someone good and pure. Well, maybe not so much pure as I'd seen her torch a bunch of people over the years but pretty good.

"You look like hell, Derek," Shannon said, oh so gently.

"He does not look like hell," Mary snapped then turned to me. "Okay, maybe some sections of it. He also has a new name."

"Our forces have fallen back," Talbot said, having shifted to full tactical mode. "Balor is almost at full strength and he's damn near unstoppable. As far as I can tell, we may be the only survivors left in Fort Happiness."

"Sit-rep: screwed," Penny said, looking down at the girl by Ashley. "Oh wow."

"There's a way out we managed to scout," Arthur replied. "Well, at least in the context of the fact there's a lot fewer halls to navigate when they're collapsing all around you. It leads to the motorpool and we can use it to evacuate. We need some people to handle the remains of Derek's George Romero-ing the place, though."

Some of the prisoners stared at me with hatred and I wondered if they'd lost friends and loved ones to my rampage. In the end, there was no point to thinking about that. I'd made my choices and had to deal with the consequences.

Christopher looked at Ashley and the two of them exchanged a silent glance before turning to me. "Penny, you need to lead the others away. Take Victory with you as well. Derek, Ashley, and I need to do something."

"I don't take orders from you, vampire," Penny said, glaring.

"Please, Penny," I whispered. "Do this for me."

Penny looked at me, opened her mouth, and then closed it. It was clear she understood what exactly I was contemplating even though she didn't know why. "Derek—"

"I'll be fine," I lied.

Penny knew it was a lie.

"Save my daughter," Ashley said.

"Mom, I—" Victory started to speak before Christopher looked down into her eyes and waved his hand.

"Sleep," Christopher said.

Victory collapsed and Penny picked her up, handing her to Talbot.

"We can still escape," Penny said, looking directly at me. "All of us."

"Look after her, Penny," I said, turning to Talbot. "You too, dad."

Talbot gave a half-smile. "See you on the other side."

"Eventually," I said.

Shannon just hugged me tightly and buried her face into my chest.

"Forgive yourself," I whispered. "No one deserves happiness, which is why everyone should seize as much of it as possible."

Shannon looked like she was going to argue but then simply exchanged one last kiss with me before turning away.

I don't understand why humans try to make death seem so romantic, Mary said, sniffing. *There is nothing noble about sacrifice. Everyone mortal dies eventually.*

You look like you're tearing up, I said.

It's the rain and cold, Mary said.

Sure, I said.

Penny ordered everyone into orderly groups and started following Arthur's lead down the hallways. I heard a crashing helicopter and knew Balor was nearby. The conflict here had been a series of sudden reversals and bad intelligence. If we'd had time to plan better, maybe it wouldn't have been a complete disaster. In the end, though, it was just the four of us: Ashley, Christopher, myself, and Mary. Penny didn't even have the strength to give me one last look as she departed.

"I can't do this," I said, holding the sheathe of the Bloodsword.

"You're the only one who can," Christopher said. "I'm not a wizard. Even if I killed her, she'd just be resurrected by Balor's magic."

"He's right," Mary said.

"Not helping, Mary," I said.

"I can't let my daughter live in a world like this," Ashley said, gesturing to the skylight where the outline of the monster could now be seen.

"Alright," I said, holding up the weapon. "I'll be a monster one last time."

"Not a monster," Ashley said. "Never."

Christopher stepped in front of Ashley. "Please, do us both."

"Christopher, no!" Ashley started to say.

The cracked and monstrous eye of Balor glowed a brilliant red above us as it turned its gaze our way. We'd run out of time.

"Too late," I said, not sure if I was speaking to myself or Balor.

I took a single step and stabbed both Christopher and Ashley through the chest with the Bloodsword. The weapon instantly severed the complicated web of spells, enchantments, and incantations filling my ex-partner. It also extinguished Christopher's undead form, causing him to dissolve into a rotting corpse before my eyes.

Mary teleported away moments later. With her, I felt all the magic keeping me alive vanish and agonizing pain that I couldn't keep away with my mastery of ki manipulation. I collapsed on the ground and started to bleed out. My last sight was of Balor's eye unleashing hellish fury on us both as he started to crumble back into his base concrete parts.

I managed to flip him off with my last breath.

EPILOGUE

I looked at Penny and Lucy playing with Victory in Lafayette Central Park in New Detroit. They were sitting on a bench while Victory was operating a magitech drone that she was flying around. Apparently, the young girl was a super-genius like so many others made of lineages cultivated by the House. The sun was shining in the air and there was a sense of brightness and optimism to the world that was as much a delusion as it had always been. Shannon was standing a dozen feet away, wearing a trench coat and sunglasses as if trying to disguise herself in the most conspicuous way possible. She'd appointed herself the child's bodyguard and had already threatened to break one soccer mom's wrist for getting too close.

"They can't see us, can they?" I asked, standing there beside Mary.

"No," Mary said. "I can make it so they can see us, though."

"No," I said, sighing. "I'm still getting a hang of this demon thing."

"God, not demon, Dante," Mary replied.

"How about we split the difference and I call myself a spirit?" I asked.

Mary rolled her eyes. "You're never going to develop a cult of fanatical worshipers with that attitude."

"I don't *want* a cult of fanatical worshipers," I replied.

Mary shook her head. "I will never understand you, truly. Thankfully, I don't have to understand you, I just have to love you."

It had been a couple of years since I'd died, and I'd spent that time slowly going through my memories and building myself back up from the transformation. I could try to explain what dying was like but as Spock would say, it's impossible to discuss without a common frame of reference.

I was linked to Bloody Mary, though, and the Bloodsword. Both had allowed me to undergo a transformation post-mortem that meant I was slightly more tied to the Prime Material Plane than most. I was pretty sure that was a good thing since going to hell wasn't something high on my list and on the oft chance heaven would take me, they wouldn't have accepted Mary.

"They look like they're okay," I said, watching the quartet.

"They are," Mary said. "At least as mortals reckon things. Shannon has started a relationship with Talbot."

I frowned. "I'm not sure how I feel about that."

"The curse of being immortal," Mary replied. "All of the people you knew as children are bound to eventually grow up to be beautiful as well as fu—"

"Stop," I interrupted. "Please don't finish that sentence."

Mary shrugged. "She still mourns you, though, and always will. It amuses me to take pleasure from her pain."

I rolled my eyes. "What about Victory?"

"Traumatized," Mary said. "But her aunts are people who will raise her with love and affection."

"Good," I said, taking a deep breath. "Do you know where Christopher and Ashley... went?"

"No," Mary said.

I looked down. "I suppose I should just let that go, then."

"Yes," Mary said.

I'd spent the last month trying to re-acquaint myself with the world since I'd managed to finally manifest myself. The world had changed a great deal since the Reveal and, yet, was now starting to look exactly like it used to be. People knew about vampires, mages, werewolves, the spirit world, and more. However, they still went to work, had families, spent way too much time watching television.

In the United States, Europe, Mexico, and Canada at least, vampires were now citizens with legal rights. The Vampire Nations had rebuilt Detroit in a staggeringly short amount of time and the place was starting to look more like Dubai than

Motor City. They even had a Las Vegas-esque strip where the first of what was bound to be millions of tourists had started to arrive in order to experience a year-round Halloween. Penny had decided to move here because, unfairly or not, witches were lumped in with less savory supernaturals.

"I notice she didn't try to reform the House," I said, looking at her sideways.

"Yes," Mary replied. "She was smart enough to realize that some things deserved to die. Also, the organizations the governments are cobbling together are corrupt race-driven groups that seek to oppress as well as control."

"So, exactly like the House," I replied,

"In miniature," Mary replied. "Mind you, I suspect part of it is the fact that Chairman Hawthorne is handling much of this behind-the-scenes."

"Ah yes," I said, making a sour face. "Turns out Penny was right on that."

It had been to my considerable disgust that my father had, in fact, managed to cheat death and become the self-styled savior of humanity in the aftermath of the Reveal. He'd won dual Nobel prizes for both Peace as well as Economics by helping integrate the supernatural into regular society.

Nathan created the Dracula Accords, as they'd been nicknamed, that had become the basis for citizenship rights for almost all citizens. It hadn't always worked out well, shifters had something called "Varmint" laws in most states where anyone could kill them as long as they felt threatened, but he'd done a pretty good job overall. Not enough to make up for the millions who'd died but people were already pretending that didn't happen. Old news.

"What was the *Firefly* quote?" I asked, turning to Mary. "It's my estimation that every man ever got a statue made of him was one kind of sumbitch or another?"

"I have no idea what you're saying," Mary said, smiling. "However, yes, that's a fairly accurate summation."

It helped that my father was now absurdly rich. With the death of Roland and the collapse of the House, he'd taken over as Chairman of Pantheon Corp and increased that organization's power a dozen fold. There were already new megacorporations popping up in the aftermath of his new corporate empire's establishment.

The key to peace between humans and supernaturals hadn't turned out to be strong laws or understanding but cold hard cash. You could buy vampire blood skin cream, watch shifters on reality shows, and learn how to conjure a candle-sized globe of light if you ordered the right books on the internet. Ironically, that had done more to keep the names of demons and other horrors from the general public than anyone else. Pantheon Corp had copyrights and algorithms to make sure anything truly dangerous remained in their hands alone.

"Yeah, well, fuck him," I said. "He's not my problem to deal with."

"No," Mary said. "Neither is Balor or any of the other evils left in the world. Yours is to gain power and conquer the Earth!"

"Down Rita Repulsa," I said.

"Who?" Mary asked.

"We need to get you to watch some cheesy television," I said, smiling.

"We don't," Mary said, leaning her head on mine.

"What happened to Balor anyway?" I asked, not quite sure but curious since, well, he'd killed me.

"He returned to the death-like slumber of his kind," Mary replied. "Your mother limped away so she's fine. I understand she's even tried to contact Penny and her grandson Alex."

I nodded. "Good for her."

"Balor still gained from this," Mary replied. "He was all but forgotten before due to his slaying at the hands of mortals during the revolt. Now humans have spread his name. He is on plush dolls, slippers, television shows, and in cheesy novels. People even invoke his name as Balor-Cthulhu so that their spells to their racist author prophet will work."

I snorted. "Wait, that's not going to end the world, is it?"

"No," Mary said. "It does mean he'll probably regenerate fully in a few centuries. He's half-awake you could say now with the alarm clock blaring beside him but not quite able to get up."

"Ah," I said. "Well, as you say, not my problem."

"That's a long time to gather new strength," Mary replied. "New friends and new allies."

"How are the House kids?" I asked.

"Arthur is a vampire now," Mary said. "He willingly chose it. Alex Timons and Lucien Lyons are hunting vampires together. Ashley wishes to live a normal life but has somehow managed to start dressing up as a superhero. Anna? Well, I fear she will follow the path of the New House."

I nodded. "And my other half-siblings?"

"All but Penny have decided to follow your father," Mary replied.

No surprise there. "Great. Wait, does that include Stephen?"

"No," Mary said. "He's here."

A sense of cold, terrifying dread filled me as I searched the landscape for some sign of my insane brother. "Why? What? How?"

"It is something I've arranged," Mary said, confidently.

I stared at her in horror. "For the love of God, why?"

"For the love of the only god I worship," Mary said, smiling. "Follow me."

The two of us headed into a tiny patch of forest that had grown in the past few months due to a dryad taking up root in Lafayette Park. There were no children or tourists in this section of it and sunlight didn't peak through the tight tree branches above us. There, standing among them was the deranged-looking figure of my half-brother Stephen. He was dressed in a disgustingly dirty trench coat caked in blood, a filthy white button-down shirt, and pants smeared in viscera. He was thin and Coyote-like in his eyes, the demon having gained almost full control of himself.

"Hello, Derek," Stephen said, chuckling.

"Hi Stephen," I said, unhappy he could see me. "You've looked better."

"Says the ghost," Stephen said. "You know, I thought I was going to be the harbinger of the apocalypse, but it turns out humans can't even get the end of the world right."

I shrugged. "People want to live. Who can blame them?"

"I can," Stephen said.

"I'll leave you two alone," Mary said, vanishing.

"So," I said, taking a deep breath that I didn't need. "What have you been up to?"

"Killing, murdering, torturing," Stephen said, frowning. "The irony being that I couldn't even do as much as a small war. There's parts of the world where being a psychotic evil scumbag is just standard operating procedure."

"There always were," I replied. "You'll never do as much damage with deliberate malice as the rest of humanity will do with apathy."

Stephen stared at me. "Why did you do it?"

"Which part?" I asked.

"Sacrifice yourself, *for them*," Stephen said, his voice low and full of hatred.

I shrugged. "It seemed like a good idea at the time."

Stephen looked at his clawed hands. "It took me two years to track the Chairman. I planned all manner of horrible things to do to him, ranging from anal penetration with a chainsaw to forcing him to watch the worst children's programs back to back. He was already dead, though, his throat torn out by vampires."

"Yeah, those guys will getcha," I said. "Turns out Dracula is more useful as a martyr than he ever was a leader in the Vampire Nation."

"I'm going to trigger a war between humans and supernaturals," Stephen said, his voice low and threatening. "Something that will bring about the end. You're going to help."

I raised an eyebrow. "Excuse me? Why the hell would I do that?"

"Dead or alive, you have something to lose," Stephen said, pointing at me. "This United States of Monsters you and father have created cannot last. It will end in fire and death just like all of humanity's other civilizations. I will kill—"

"Stop," I said.

"What?" Stephen asked.

"Is this what you want to do with the rest of your eternity?" I asked, staring at him. "Chase ghosts, threaten people, and plot the end of the world? Can't you be *more*?"

Stephen looked confused. "More?"

"Have someone worth dying for rather than killing for," I said, pitying my brother in that moment.

Stephen narrowed his gaze. "No."

"I'm sorry to hear that," I said, genuinely sad he'd come to this. Death really changed your perspective on things.

"I think I'll kill Lucy fir—" Stephen started to speak before the Bloodsword's tip shot out his front and then went forward until the entirety of the blade was visible.

I looked over Stephen's shoulder and saw Mary standing beside Arthur. He'd lost a hundred pounds or so and looked a lot better, though the pale skin and glowing eyes were a bit distracting. He still dressed like a Goth rocker, though.

Stephen blinked, confused as the demon inside him perished first. I reached out to him, only for him to spit blood on my face before the light left his eyes too. Arthur pulled out the sword from Stephen's back and took a step backward.

"Happy deathday!" Mary said, throwing her hands in the air. "I thought you'd like this present!"

Arthur held up the sword. "She gave me the Bloodsword. I hope you don't mind."

I stared down at Stephen's corpse then looked up at Arthur, glad he could see me too. "Yeah, sure."

"You want to go possess someone and get some fries or something?" Arthur asked. "I'm like immune to sunlight as long as I have this sword?"

"Ooo, I like fries," Mary said. "But can we eat a slaughtered animal with it, too?"

"Yeah, I suppose a burger would be nice too," Arthur said.

I looked between them then laughed. "Yeah, well I don't want to spend my days stalking my family. Sounds good."

"We'll eventually get your cult to make you a new body," Mary said. "It may be a century or two but such is the way of gods."

So this was my eternity, huh?

Eh, I could have had worse.

ADDENDUM

Hey everyone,

I wanted to thank you all for reading the entirety of the Red Room series. Hopefully, you've enjoyed the adventures of Derek Hawthorne and Shannon as they come to their conclusion. If you feel so inclined, please drop a review for one or more of the books at Amazon, Goodreads, or Bookbub. Every review counts and indie publishers like Crossroad Press depend on the positive buzz generated by fans.

Those who have read my other books are likely to have noticed a lot of references in this book that reveal this series was a prequel to my United States of Monsters series. Yes, while Derek and Shannon aren't doing any more adventures, the world transformed by the Reveal continues in other series.

If you want to continue reading about magicians, shifters, and vampires then I suggest checking them out too:

* The Bright Falls Mysteries (w/ Michael Suttkus): Set ten years after the Reveal in the town of Bright Falls, Michigan. The city is full of shifters and has a hundred secrets behind every corner but amateur detective Jane Doe is ready to root them all.

* Straight Outta Fangton: Set ten years after the Reveal in New Detroit, the city has become a vampire mecca funded by the tourist dollars of those begging to be fed upon. Peter Stone, convenience store clerk, gets none of that. However, that doesn't mean that he can't get involved the complex politics of the city's aristocracy.

* Morgan Detective Agency (w/ Michael Suttkus): The Morgan Detective Agency is set twelve years after the Reveal. Ashley Morgan (jr) is a private detective and bounty hunter with psychic powers. This, unfortunately, doesn't mean her life is a hot mess as she's also a failure at every career she's ever had. That doesn't mean she can't try to redeem herself by taking on the worst monsters of New Detroit.

I hope you'll check some of them out or other works by me like the Supervillainy Saga, *Agent G, Cthulhu Armageddon, Lucifer's Star,* and *Wraith Knight.*

Thanks!

ABOUT THE AUTHORS

C.T. Phipps is a lifelong student of horror, science fiction, and fantasy. An avid tabletop gamer, he discovered this passion led him to write and turned him into a lifelong geek. He is a regular blogger and also a reviewer for The Bookie Monster.

BIBLIOGRAPHY

The Rules of Supervillainy (Supervillainy Saga #1)
The Games of Supervillainy (Supervillainy Saga #2)
The Secrets of Supervillainy (Supervillainy Saga #3)
The Kingdom of Supervillany (Supervillainy Saga #4)
The Tournament of Supervillany (Supervillainy Saga #5)
The Future of Supervillainy (Supervillainy Saga #6)
I Was a Teenage Weredeer (The Bright Falls Mysteries, Book 1)
An American Weredeer in Michigan (The Bright Falls Mysteries, Book 2)
Esoterrorism (Red Room, Vol. 1)
Eldritch Ops (Red Room, Vol. 2)
Agent G: Infiltrator (Agent G, Vol. 1)
Agent G: Saboteur (Agent G, Vol. 2)
Agent G: Assassin (Agent G, Vol. 3)
Cthulhu Armageddon (Cthulhu Armageddon, Vol. 1)
The Tower of Zhaal (Cthulhu Armageddon, Vol. 2)
Lucifer's Star (Lucifer's Star, Vol. 1)
Lucifer's Nebula (Lucifer's Star, Vol. 2)
Straight Outta Fangton (Straight Outta Fangton, Vol. 1)
100 Miles and Vampin' (Straight Outta Fangton, Vol. 2)
Wraith Knight (Wraith Knight, Vol. 1)
Wraith Lord (Wraith Knight, Vol. 2)

Michael Suttkus, II, lives in Leesburg, Florida, with three cats, one of which actually likes him, and his family, with whom he fares better. When not working at a game store, he's playing games, reading science books, or otherwise being incredibly nerdy. Also writing! Because he has to feed cats whether they like him or not.

BIBLIOGRAPHY

I Was a Teenage Weredeer (The Bright Falls Mysteries #1)
An American Weredeer in Michigan (The Bright Falls Mysteries #2)
Lucifer's Star (Lucifer's Star #1)
Lucifer's Nebula (Lucifer's Star #2)

Curious about other Crossroad Press books?
Stop by our site:
http://store.crossroadpress.com
We offer quality writing
in digital, audio, and print formats.